FLAPJACK

FLAPJACK

Daniel Ganninger

Flapjack
ISBN: 1491249471
ISBN-13: 978-1491249475

This book is a work of fiction. Names, characters, places, and incidents either are products of the author's imagination or are used fictitiously. Any resemblance to actual persons, living or dead, events, or locales is entirely coincidental.

Printed in the United States of America

To Lisbeth

-Prologue-

The light from the street lamps illuminated the inside of the sedan as it moved slowly along the deserted city street. The vehicle followed the curves of the road until it arrived at a pair of stone pillars that began the perimeter of a university campus.

"Ready the supplies," a large, burly man barked from the front passenger seat of the black sedan.

Two men in the back seat followed the order silently, reaching for black bags at their feet.

"Let's get this done. No screw-ups and stay concealed. We don't need any unwanted visitors. You know the plan—in and out, that's it. We'll get further orders when we get inside."

"It's a little strange, don't you think, Sarge?" the driver of the vehicle asked Sergeant Walker.

"We just follow the orders, Turner. We're not getting paid to think."

Turner nodded and turned his gaze to the blackness outside the window.

"Gott, Parker, is everything ready?" Sergeant Walker inquired.

"Yes, sir," the pair answered in unison from the back seat.

Sergeant Walker opened his door and moved to the sidewalk as Gott and Parker scrambled out and followed close behind, single file. The Sergeant turned back to the awaiting vehicle and spoke quietly.

"Turner, meet us at the extraction point on my call. If we're not out in twenty minutes, you leave without us. Understand?"

"Yes, sir. Twenty minutes," Turner repeated. "It ain't like Kandahar, is it, Sarge."

"Nothing could be like that hellhole. Remember, twenty minutes, no more, no less," he ordered again.

Turner sped off up the street and left the three men alone on the sidewalk in the dark, between the round columns of light from the street lamps.

Sergeant Walker gave a wave of his hand and the men began a slow, crouched jog into a grove of trees just beyond the entry columns of the university.

The group moved silently and methodically through the trees, careful to avoid any lights from the nearby buildings. The Sergeant quickened their pace as they neared an open plaza and a group of well-lit structures.

It was 3:23 in the morning on a warm June night, and the campus laid mostly deserted. The team needed to move quickly to avoid the occasional campus police patrol, or students who may be traveling through the campus after a late-night summer study session.

The men made it safely across the plaza and closed in on a stone and glass five story building. They were only three minutes into the operation when they heard voices coming in their direction; a group of students returning to their dorms after a night of clubbing.

Walker held up his fist and stopped the other men in their tracks as the students passed by, unaware of the three men lurking in the shadows. As the party revelers disappeared in the distance, the team continued their movement to the building's edge and hid behind a large group of shrubbery.

"Gott, take up position here and keep us informed of any movement," the Sergeant ordered.

Gott handed Parker his bag who hiked it up on his shoulder.

"What you got in here, rocks?" Parker whispered to Gott as he heaved the bag farther onto his back.

Gott gave him a sly smile. "I wouldn't jostle that bag too much," he warned.

"Ready the radios," Sergeant Walker announced, ignoring the exchange between the two men.

Each man put in an earpiece and tested them for the proper sounds.

"Loud and clear," Gott announced. "Fifteen minutes and counting."

"No one in or out that front door," Walker ordered Gott, pointing at the building. "Let's go Parker, try to keep up," he barked.

The men moved to the side of the building and arrived at a fire exit door that stood on the windowless side of the structure. A lone light illuminated the door. Parker pulled a towel from the bag and climbed the stairway. He reached up, placed the towel around the light, and smashed it. The light went out and the shards of glass fell harmlessly into the towel. The door became black, and the men were hid in the darkness.

Parker placed the wrapped up towel back in his bag and pulled out a large pair of wire cutters. He methodically moved to a metal encased wire protector and carefully cut the wire, disabling the alarm to the door.

Sergeant Walker calmly checked his watch as Parker continued his work on the door, this time replacing the wire cutter with a crowbar. Parker placed the tool between the door and the metal casing and pulled, wrenching the door open after one effort.

The men pulled up black hoods from around their necks and opened the door, causing a stream of light to exit from the stairwell inside the building.

Sergeant Walker moved through the door and up the stairs as Parker followed close behind. The team continued until they reached the fifth floor. A fire door led into a hallway of the floor, but before entering the Sergeant keyed his radio once, giving Gott the sign they had entered the building.

Parker set to work again. He took out a snake-like tube attached to a small portable video screen and placed it between a crack in the door as he opened it. On the screen the hallway appeared deserted. He scanned both directions for any unwanted guests. When he was satisfied that the hall was empty, Parker gave the Sergeant a thumb-up sign.

Sergeant Walker wasted no time and moved into the hallway. He paused at each door until he located office door number 515. Sergeant Walker confirmed the number on the door to what he had written earlier on his wrist and the numbers matched. The Sergeant keyed his radio two times and received two audible beeps from Gott. All was clear. Sergeant Walker motioned Parker to the door.

The office door had a keyless lock and a card reader attached above the door knob. Parker pulled out a card that had a wire attached to a small box. He slid the card in the slot above the door knob and numbers began to fly across the screen on the box. After a few seconds the numbers stopped. He pulled the card out just as the tumblers clicked, and a small green light appeared on the door.

Sergeant Walker moved in first, with a flashlight at the ready, while Parker dragged the bags in the room. The Sergeant keyed his radio three times and checked his watch. It had been ten minutes since they had started the operation, and they only had ten minutes to finish.

"Let's see what we're supposed to do," he told Parker, who milled about behind him awaiting orders.

Sergeant Walker pulled out his cell phone, scrolled for the letters "WM", and pressed the button to connect to the programmed number.

"We're in. What are your orders?" the Sergeant asked.

"Find the two black boxes as planned. Retrieve both and retrieve any hard drives." The voice paused. "The other team hasn't been able to locate the professor, so I want you to torch the entire laboratory."

"Yes, sir," Sergeant Walker stated coldly.

"After completion, drive to the Wilmington airport. A flight will be waiting."

"Wilmington. Yes, sir," the Sergeant said again.

The line went dead and Walker put the phone back in his pocket.

"Clear out the hard drives and wire the area," Sergeant Walker ordered Parker. "I'm going to look for these black boxes."

Parker dropped the bags and pulled out a pair of pliers and a battery powered screwdriver. He used his flashlight to survey the room and counted four computers. Parker used the pliers to rip off the casing of the nearest computer and turned the machinery on its side to get to the hard drive. He quickly unscrewed the drive from the casing and tossed it in his bag. Parker repeated the process at the next computer without concern about subtlety or care.

Sergeant Walker used his light to look through the nearby desks in an attempt to find the black boxes. He had a small picture of what he was looking for, but the multitude of electronic equipment made it difficult to discover in the dark. As he neared the back of the room he noticed a small table against the wall with wires protruding from it. The wires were connected to a nearby oscilloscope and a laptop computer. Walker followed the lines to the tabletop, and there sat the two black boxes that matched his picture. He wasted no time in callously pulling the wires from the boxes that were slightly larger than a deck of playing cards. Sergeant Walker placed the boxes into his bag along with the laptop from the table.

Parker had finished his first job of removing the hard drives and began the more delicate task of placing the dangerous explosives around the room. He reached in the bag Gott had given him and took out detonator cord, an electronic timer, and a small quantity of Semtex; a general purpose, plastic explosive. It was malleable and the size of sticks of chewing gum. This is what Gott had warned him about. The explosive was essentially harmless in its present state, but that would soon change.

Parker began to place small pieces of the explosive around and under the various computers and tables that scattered the room. He spliced each with a piece of detonator cord and connected them to the electronic timer. The goal was to keep the explosion contained to the room, and the subsequent fire would be contained by the overhead sprinklers. The team didn't need to draw attention to themselves by blowing up most of the building.

Parker set the timer as Sergeant Walker waited impatiently behind him. They had four minutes remaining before Turner would leave. Parker nodded to Walker that he was satisfied everything was set-up correctly and the detonation wouldn't blow a hole in the side of the building.

Walker surveyed the room one more time, making sure they hadn't left anything behind. He keyed his radio three times and pulled out his phone to call Turner.

"We're ready," Walker informed the driver.

Turner didn't answer and began to move toward their extraction point.

Parker moved to the door and used the camera to check the hall again. It was still clear. The team moved out of the office and down the hall to the fire door exit where they descended the concrete stairs, back to their original entry point.

As the men rounded the last stairwell the fire door leading from the first floor suddenly opened. A security guard strolled through and met the men by accident. Panic crossed the guard's face as he gawked at the black clad men. Before the guard could react to the sight Sergeant Walker jumped toward him, grabbed him by the front of his shirt, and spun him around to face Parker.

Parker reacted and pulled out a handgun. But instead of shooting the guard, he struck him squarely on the head with the butt of the gun, knocking him unconscious onto the floor. Walker pulled the man under the stairway while Parker began to bind his hands and feet with electrical wire from the bag. Walker taped over the man's mouth and shoved him farther under the stairwell, out of view from someone entering the area.

One minute remained on the timer as the team ran out the door with their packs. They noticed the black sedan approaching up the street as they moved from the building. Gott appeared as they reached the vehicle.

Turner saw the men and slammed on the brakes. When he knew everyone was safely in the car he jammed the accelerator, leaving a screech from the tires as they left.

Sergeant Walker turned and peered through the back window. In the distance he noticed a dull orange glow and heard a faint thump from the fifth floor window as the explosives detonated, destroying the laboratory. He pulled the black mask off his head, revealing a sweaty face.

"Good work, men," Walker announced. He turned and faced forward as the car sped down the street. "I need to make a call that we've had a successful operation."

-Chapter 1-

The sound of whirling motors resonated outside my bedroom window, and I pulled my pillow hard over my head, attempting to make the sound go away. It was the first day of April, and a thoughtful lawn crew were doing their daily wake-up call at my luxury apartment home, as the management chose to call it.

I decided it would be best to go ahead and stumble out of bed. As I made my way to the bathroom, I ran my shoulder into my bedroom wall and tripped over clothes strewn on the floor. I missed the toilet, took a five minute, slightly warm shower, and shaved my face with a sub-standard razor. It was quite a way to start another day.

Before leaving the apartment, I took a quick gulp of some questionable orange juice that resided in my refrigerator, and off to work I went, ready for anything.

Possibly some excitement or drama awaited me this day, but so far it wasn't turning out that way. A crappy commute through crowded freeways and rude drivers confronted me as I went to my home away from home.

I worked at Tesla Technology Suppliers. It sat on a grassy knoll behind a gleaming ten story office building in an industrial park in northern San Diego, California. The company was named after the great inventor, Nikola Tesla, who demonstrated wireless communication in 1893 and was a pioneer in electromagnetism. But Tesla Technology was not as great as the inventor's name it used. Tesla himself might wonder why his name was placed on a sign where the "s" had slid off many months ago, and the "T" and "e" were obscured by a mutant tree that pushed up the pavement in front of the building. Instead, we were referred to as "la Technologies". Either we were from Mexico, given our location in southern California, or if we were lucky, from France. Neither of those spots helped business.

I was never sure what we really did. It had something to do with copper for electronics, or some such thing. I was an Account Executive, and unfortunately, the title didn't fit the job. I simply made sure we got paid for this copper stuff we were selling to someone to put into something. It could be sliced, eaten, or worn as a hat for all I cared. It didn't matter to me.

"You parked in the wrong spot again," I heard as I was greeted by Belinda, our sloth-like receptionist who peered at me over her thick glasses. "They're coming to pave that area today, you knew that," she told me scornfully.

"They can pave over my car today for all I care. I got an envelope in the mail that says I have parking privileges anywhere in the state. I could even park on someone, if I liked." I strode past her, not making eye contact.

"Uh-huh," she muttered, tapping away on her computer keyboard with her nicotine stained fingers.

I walked slowly to my "office", a six-foot by six-foot cube I had christened, "The Madman's Sanctuary".

A voice boomed from a neighboring cubicle as I sat down. "Did you know Elvis and Nixon had a private meeting where Elvis wanted to help with the war on drugs? He even got a complimentary badge as a member of the Drug Enforcement Agency."

"That's a fascinating tidbit of information," I replied flatly, fiddling with things on my desk.

This was a common occurrence between my cubicle neighbor and me. He always attempted to stump me with little known trivia early in the day. We used it to decide who would pay for lunch.

"Don't tell me you're not interested in the paradox and irony of that meeting," the voice snapped back.

"It is quite fascinating. But did you know Elvis also gave Nixon a Colt-45 and family photos to commemorate their meeting? Plus, Presley requested to be a Federal Agent-at-Large in the Bureau of Narcotics and Dangerous Drugs. He was concerned about the increase in drug use in the country."

"Yes, but why was that nutty?" the voice questioned.

"He had something like 5,000 pills prescribed in the months before he kicked off. I believe it was narcotics and amphetamines," I replied smugly, as I scoured the papers on my desk. "You gave me an easy one this morning, Galveston. Lunch is on you."

"So I'm a little off my game, so sue me," Galveston said dryly from behind his cardboard and metal partition, the sound of a clicking mouse coming from his desk. He was cheating, no less, and using the computer to facilitate his questions.

It had become a morning ritual with us—useless banter about useless facts of the world. We had both become obsessed with these history bits that few realized occurred and even fewer cared about. It told so much about the way we receive and disseminate information and how little everyone knows about true history, but we mainly used it to fight the urge to put our head between the cubicle walls and end it all. So that is rather melodramatic, but Galveston had become the one saving grace in this seventh dimension of hell we kindly referred to as, "la Technologies".

Dan Galveston was his full name, I think, as he only liked to be called by his last name. I always joked that he changed it to that after he threw a dart at the globe and managed to hit the Texas City of Galveston. He told me it was either that or La Marque, a city up the road from Galveston, but that one sounded fruity, and he didn't want to be called a dandy his whole life. I went ahead and believed him about his name, but not much else. Galveston was an enigma, only in the sense that he could change his persona in an instant to suit the situation he was in. He was a quick thinker, quick witted, and very smart. He was the one thing that challenged me in this rathole.

Galveston was officially called a Sales Representative—a title he hated. He would have preferred to be called a lackey; he felt it suited him better. Galveston and I had arrived at this place at similar times and under similar circumstances. We both had gone through major career changes. I from the world of academia and business, him from the real world, I surmised.

Galveston's voice came from behind the cubicle wall again. "I had a guy this morning tell me that he didn't receive his latest shipment, and boy, was he pissed. I told him, 'Look, Ed informed me that you didn't want that shipping until tomorrow.' Of course that was a complete pant load. I had pulled up Ed's name off their website. It ought to take him at least two hours just to figure out who the hell 'Ed' is, and why vice president Ed was making these decisions."

We commonly worked with companies that were too big for their own good, and like a government, they had complicated bureaucracies where little got done and one hand didn't know what the other hand was doing. Galveston was a master at this manipulation, and for good reason. We didn't work with the most competent of people, nor did we have a very competent structure in this place. Taking a few liberties when in a jam only made our jobs easier, plus it was good fun.

We were minor slackers, not major ones. We showed up for work and did our job every day; we just did it with a little more flare to keep it interesting.

"You should have said that we stopped shipment because we had gotten a call from the creditors saying they're going bankrupt, but nobody had the heart to say anything," I quipped.

"Nothing like giving the poor schlub a coronary first thing in the morning," Galveston fired back, holding a grunting laugh.

I made the decision to try a little work and perused my inbox for new items for the day. Check on two problems with a shipment, another customer didn't receive the right stuff, memo from our glorious leader with one, two, three misprints. Next was a letter from a customer about stopping future business with our company, and under it a handwritten note from Belinda about the paving of the parking lot today which I tossed into the trash—two points.

I clicked on my computer, an ancient machine about a step above an abacus. As it whirled to life I strolled over to Galveston's "Den of Sanctitude", as he referred to it, and peered over the wall.

He had sheets of paper strewn everywhere, his superior filing system. He called it A.M. and P.M.; the A.M. he would do in the morning, and the P.M. would get stuffed in the inbox of Hank in the next cubicle who was usually getting over a hangover for half the morning.

"Where's lunch today?" I asked. The orange juice I drank earlier had already lost its punch.

"I have a coupon for Rusty's Barbeque." He produced a ratty piece of paper, torn unevenly from side-to-side.

"Pencil me in," I replied as Galveston taped it to his calendar.

"Done, and today I'll buy the water."

The morning passed without incident. A few phone calls here, a bit of day dreaming, a trip to the bathroom, a drink at the water cooler, avoidance of our boss, and a return to my desk to see that my computer had almost made it halfway through booting up. I sat down and sighed heavily.

Galveston grunted from behind his blue cubical wall, obviously checking his stock picks in hopes of stumbling on the next great start-up or tech stock that would take all his worries away.

I wasted more time by watching Stan, our esteemed leader, crouched in his office as he saved the world from its many problems. Stan was a heavy set guy, to put it lightly. His dreams consisted only of the gin and tonic he would put down that evening. Stan was constantly hatching schemes to convince his wife that he couldn't come home on time. I didn't know what Stan was up to after work, and I didn't want to know. I needed to get a good night's sleep.

My morning productivity was of course, nonexistent, and when lunchtime rolled around Galveston and I made our escape past Belinda's sullen gaze of disapproval.

"Little early to be leaving for lunch, don't you think?" Belinda snapped, again peering over the flat plastic rim of her thick glasses in her most annoying way.

"Actually, we were just going out to vandalize your car," Galveston said as he strolled past her. "Would you like one scratch or two?"

"You really shouldn't provoke her," I said to him when we were out the door.

"Ah, she's non-provokable. She's like someone hired a gigantic rock and told it to get a personality."

Galveston opened his car door and popped my side. We slid in and drove to Rusty's, a slightly beat-up restaurant with greasy tables and an even greasier staff, but the best real barbeque in town. We got our food and sat down at the nearest table.

"I actually have something important to discuss with you today—for a change," Galveston started.

"If you're going to tell me this could change my life, I'll just walk back, thanks," I told him in my most disdainful tone.

"No, this is actually legitimate and serious. It's seriously legit. I got a call from an old acquaintance of mine. I thought about it last night, wrote up a couple things, and figured you might be interested. With or without you I'm going to try it." Galveston squinted his eyes and furrowed his brow, his best serious look yet. The hair on the back of my neck stood up.

"My first question then; is this legal, and how much will it cost me?" I asked with an air of suspicion.

"It's only slightly, just slightly, on the fringe of illegality, but only if you're looking at that sort of thing. I have it all worked out," Galveston answered quickly.

12

I felt as if he was going to tell me he had a plan to bilk little old ladies out of their bus fare or Social Security checks.

"I want to start an investigation service. Like a private eye but a little more secret. We would deal with things private investigators wouldn't touch," Galveston told me bluntly. "I'll explain why I want to get in this business and why I want you involved. I have it all planned out."

I didn't say anything and ate my sandwich slowly. My interest was piqued however, because when Galveston said he had worked something out, I believed him.

-Chapter 2-

We sat in the restaurant for an hour or so as Galveston told me his awkward business plan and why we needed to quit our jobs. I tried to remember the many joyous times I had at "la Technologies" and failed to find any. I was beginning to believe our lunchtime meeting could become my own personal kick in the pants.

Sometimes a person needs a defining moment to take them out of their comfort zone and plunge them into a sea of uncertainty. This could be my opportunity to take a risk. What did I have to lose, and what could be the risk? Unfortunately, at this particular moment, it felt like everything.

Galveston began by regaling me of his personal exploits in the previous year, his need to do something different with his life, his fine automobiles, of which he had none, and his extensive oversea activities, which he curiously didn't elaborate on. What brought him to this place, this moment of action? Everyone's life has a story, poised as a drama, a comedy, sometimes slapstick as mine usually felt, but as he talked he opened up about more than I bargained for, and more than I really wanted to hear.

"I think I have to explain some things to you, why I want to pursue my ideas. I'm just tired of giving up," Galveston said.

"What do you mean?" I inquired, tearing my napkin into tinier and tinier pieces.

"Well, I haven't been that honest with you. I'm not some 'fly by night salesman' or some 'big idea man'," he said using air quotes with his fingers. "Things happened that kind of forced me out of the life I knew."

"Like what? You ran with the wrong crowd or something?"

"Yeah, maybe. This business is supposed to be my new start."

"Oh my God," I thought as he said these words. Was he some sort of white collar criminal, someone in the witness protection program, or worse yet, a mobster? Had this guy started out as a woman? My mind raced as I pictured Galveston dressed in high heels and a bad dress with his chest hair popping out, saying, "Well, I think I'll be a dude."

"I don't even want to know. Please tell me you're not some long lost criminal," or a gal named Shirley, I thought.

"No, no. Let me tell you," he leaned back in his chair, half smiling.

He moved his plate aside, pulled out a picture from his wallet dated May 1999, and placed it in front of me.

"You probably thought I'd say I had a sex change," he laughed, smacking his hand on the table, not knowing he had read my mind.

"Yeah, no, nothing like that," I replied, shifting uneasily in my chair.

"This ought to help with evidence of who I was," he said, tapping the picture with his finger.

In the photo was Galveston in a dark blue suit and tie, shaking hands and smiling in front of a sign for the Central Intelligence Agency with the President of the United States.

"You were a spy?" I exclaimed loudly, holding the picture up.

"No, no, no," he said as he slapped the it back onto the table, looking around as he did. "The politically correct term is intelligence officer, and no, I wasn't one. Come on, calm down," he quieted his voice. "Let's use some discretion. I was officially a private special consultant for counter-intelligence. I wasn't employed directly by the government."

"This is all a little much for me to handle," I stammered, spilling soda down my chin.

"Just wait there Nancy, let me elaborate a little. If you think I'm a nuts and don't believe every word, then I promise I'll never bother you with this again."

"Well, I already think you're nuts, and you're already bothering me," I replied while he rolled his eyes.

He began by giving me a narrative, just like a flashback in a movie. If nothing else he was a good storyteller.

"Let me take you back to a time of innocence and..."

"Hold it," I said, stopping him mid-sentence of his rant. "Just get to the point, will ya?" I retorted.

He sighed, and a sly smile came across his face as he began to tell his story.

-Chapter 3-

Galveston began by explaining how he graduated from Rutgers University with a degree in political science.

"I was a below average student, probably near the bottom, if not fully at the bottom," he told me, though it seemed he was exaggerating.

After getting his act together, he managed to go to graduate school, somehow making it into the Elliott School of International Affairs at George Washington University. In the process he had racked up mounds of school and credit card debt. Saddled with bills and a newly printed diploma, he took a low-level position in the State Department, mainly just answering phones and pecking at a computer.

A friend had him apply to the State Department's Bureau of Diplomatic Security. It offered many of the challenges he had been searching for; foreign living, travel, and law enforcement without the pesky steps to get there. The Bureau of Diplomatic Security took him on a different life path, and ultimately a collision course with his future.

My mouth was agape at this point. This was fascinating, but what did he want with me and with this new business?

Galveston continued on a rapid pace. He explained how he spent many years bouncing from embassy to embassy worldwide before being assigned to Brussels, Belgium, where he participated in the security mission for the European Union. In ten years he had fostered connections with a variety of agencies; such as the National Security Agency, CIA and FBI.

"You don't say," was all I could mutter as I chewed on some ice from my empty glass, riveted by the facts he was laying out in front of me.

"I should have just stayed where I was. I had a great job, but for some reason I was looking for more, to make more of a difference," he told me, twirling a napkin in his hand. "A really dumb move on my part."

He resigned from the Bureau of Diplomatic Security after his ten year anniversary. The connections he had made then led him to the smoky world of the consultant and work as a private government contractor.

"I was doing okay and working out of London, but then I had to get out, and out of any government work. Of course a woman was involved and that's a whole other story in itself," he told me as the waitress eyed us intently, seeing if we were ever going to pay our check. "It was during this time that I made the biggest mistake. At the time it seemed great, but man, was I stupid," he said shaking his head. "It was at this point where my life really changed."

-Chapter 4-

During this "stupidity period", as Galveston so lovingly called it, an informal meeting popped up between him and a government liaison for a company called Black Bear Security.

Black Bear was a multinational company with ties to many governments and private organizations. It employed contractors that provided security, investigatory services, and covert operations. It also dabbled in corporate espionage. I assumed this was similar to how someone likes to dabble with golf on weekends.

Galveston had garnered quite a reputation as a master investigator and was eyed by the top brass for his uncanny ability to assess a situation and unravel pieces of an investigation. For that skill he was invited to join Black Bear as a security consultant and to use his connections in the FBI and CIA to increase the scope of Black Bear's work.

"Why did you join them?" I asked.

"Money mostly, and I got to stay in one place for a time; at least that's what I thought would happen. But things changed quickly. I was usually involved in preliminary items, not knowing the end result of my work," he stated flatly. "I powered through the ranks of a backwoods hobbit to become a mighty steed," he told me proudly.

These were his nonsensical words, and I wasn't sure how much more of that I could take. Essentially he rose through the ranks, bringing on more delicate assignments. Apparently it was at this point that things got complicated.

"I didn't know all the details, but I met a man named Wallace Murray once at a meeting in D.C., at Black Bear headquarters. Murray used to do black ops for the CIA. I think he only set up covert operations for the company, mostly domestic corporate espionage kind of things at first, you know, computer hacking and sabotage, fuzzy things that went unnoticed. I know he had mercenaries on the payroll, and some juiced up ex-special forces guys, the ones that had no conscience and took orders well. He chose the real winners and expected some nasty things out of them, if that's what it took. I think he may have been dropped on his head a few thousand times as a kid." Galveston paused to take a drink and to see if I was still following along.

I listened carefully as Galveston spun his tale. Surprisingly, I continued to be riveted to my seat, but I didn't have any idea of what was truly factual and what was embellishment. Galveston continued again, taking time only for a few small breaths as he now quickened his speech further.

"A weapon's company hired Black Bear to find out if they were dealing with illegal gun dealers, and they gave me the case. It was, unbeknownst to me, my last case. It dealt with large sums of money being transferred in and out of a Cayman Island's bank account. I eventually traced the money to a guy connected to some of the biggest arms dealers in Eastern Europe and the Middle East. The name was Wallace Murray." He stopped as if I understood the connection.

"I should have told the FBI, but I followed the rules. If you came across something or someone in an investigation that was related to Black Bear in some way then it must be reported to upper management. I filed a report to the Black Bear management and heard nothing. Days passed, then weeks, and still nothing. Then all hell broke loose. I got a call to bring in all my computer hardware because we had, quote, 'a serious matter to contend with'. That matter was me." He pointed his finger at himself and looked me straight in the eye. I could see by his tone and expression that even talking about it made him angry.

"I had my credentials taken away, my hard drives were destroyed, and an allegation of impropriety while on duty was thrown on my record. They accused me of using the Black Bear database for personal and financial gain. They had phone records, computer records, and multiple transfers into my bank account from all over the world. My credentials with the CIA and FBI were toast. My sole friendly contact at the FBI, David May, tried to find Wallace Murray, but found he didn't exist. All just a figment of my imagination, I guess. Just like that, all my work, gone."

"Well, what was the story with this Wallace Murray, or whoever he was?" I inquired.

"I'll guarantee you he was somehow involved in those arms deals and it's a pretty safe assumption Black Bear knew about it. I mean, Black Bear employees have some of the highest security clearances of a private corporation in the nation."

"Well, did you ever hear what happened?"

"No. All the Black Bear guys are paid too well to talk."

"What do you mean by that?"

"Let's just say that there is a certain understanding that if you talk, Black Bear will get to you, somehow, some way. It's like putting the fear of God into people who have no fear."

"Why haven't I ever heard about them getting into trouble before?"

"Well, one, Black Bear is huge, two they have their hands in a lot of pockets, way down deep, and three, they do a lot of non-controversial work to offset the nasty stuff. So now you know the story behind what put me here at our lovely company. I want out now, and I can't pass up the opportunity to get back in the game. It's work I want to do again, and I want you to join me in the insanity."

I absorbed all the information. Who was this guy? I wished I was just at home enjoying a stiff drink, watching a bad comedy on TV, and dreading the next day of work. Galveston noticed my consternation and reached for the bill.

"My treat," he said, smiling.

-Chapter 5-

Galveston and I said nothing as we walked back to the car. I opened my door and Galveston piped in over the roof of the car.

"So what do you think?"

"What do I think about what?" I inquired.

"Going into business together. I need a partner,"

"Why me?" I asked him seriously. "Why do you want me as a business partner?"

"I need someone strong in the financial aspects of a business, you know, the ability to actually run a business. I don't have a clue about that. I've done some research on you, Roger. I know you have a Doctorate in Economics. I know you worked at the International Monetary Fund and had your own consulting business." I grew quiet at the recital of my past.

"That was a lot of years ago," I said softly, "and if you learned all that, you probably know the rest of the story."

"I think I know enough that your story sounded a lot like mine. You were underappreciated and at the wrong place at the wrong time, that much is certain. Your business background is strong, and you know about international affairs. I want you to manage our finances and negotiate contracts. Plus you need a fresh start, instead of the goofy paper pushing you're doing now." He stopped and smiled. "Also, I need someone who doesn't have anything else going on."

"Oh, thanks. Does my life have that little meaning?"

"Right now it does. I mean, come on, I'm offering you low wages, unpredictable prospects, terrible hours, days of uncertainty, and a wish you had never come into contact with me. Who would pass that up?"

"Well, when you put it like that."

"Yes, and don't forget the travel. Piss poor hotel rooms, little sleep— that just sweetens the pot."

"How can I possibly say no?"

"I tell you what. If in one month you aren't satisfied, I'll give you all my savings. That will cover you for a month until you find another half-assed job, but who wants that stability? I don't want to leave this parking lot until I have a yes or no. The time is now," Galveston pressed me.

"You sound like a timeshare salesman."

I thought about it for a minute. I believed Galveston when he told me he was terrible at the financial aspect of running a business. I knew this already from our work at "la Technologies". He made me feel needed, and I could get whatever his idea for a business was off the ground, probably with one hand tied behind my back.

"I already have our first client lined up," he said smugly, and I took another moment to think about his proposal.

"An investigator," I thought. I had no clue what that entailed, but from his stories I believed he did. The thought of working longer at Tesla sent shivers down my spine. I could always get a job at the local McDonald's if it didn't work out.

"Oh, what the hell," I told him quickly. "How tough a business could it be? Alright, you've got one month, no longer. I'll see it through and if I'm not completely satisfied, you'll pay me. Deal?"

"Done," Galveston said rather gleefully.

I nodded. I couldn't believe what I had agreed to; an operation with no business plan, no real customers, and no product. But the stories had intrigued me, and Galveston's confidence overrode all my uncertainty. Still, I felt like a person who had just been sold an elixir from the traveling medicine man.

"Alright," Galveston said as he got in the car, rubbing his hands together. "Let's go quit our jobs."

Chapter 6

"I'll do the quitting for us. This is your first lesson on my side of the business. Always have an out. I have all the ammunition we'll need. Just let me do the talking and you wait here. Give me ten minutes."

I sat down on a brick wall outside our office, shaded by a poor excuse for a tree. Exactly ten minutes later Galveston returned with a manila folder in one hand and a box in the other.

"What's the story?" I inquired, skeptically.

"I simply put our conditions and terms of voluntary termination from the company on the table," he said.

"English, please," I replied.

He paused as if giving some great dumbed down version.

"I told him we are quitting, effective immediately, no questions asked. I then told Stan he had five minutes to get our checks or I was going to post the pictures of his carnal affair with Belinda on the internet, along with a friendly email to his wife explaining where her husband had been during those long, late hours of work," Galveston said smugly.

He pointed to a white envelope in his hand. "I said these would never see the light of day." He handed me the envelope. I nervously ripped it open and peered inside, expecting to see sickening and horrendous photos.

"Oh my God," I exclaimed, shaking it upside down. Nothing came out.

"You blackmailed him?" I said loudly, shoving the envelope back at him.

"Again, the voice. Didn't your mother ever tell you to use your inside voice? You have a lot to learn about discretion." He scolded me like a child and grabbed the envelope.

"I call it non-factual persuasion. Technically, yes, it is blackmail, but that's not the point. I stitched everything up in a short amount of time. You're not very observant, are you. Those two couldn't keep a secret if their life depended on it," he instructed.

"How did you know?"

"I didn't know 100 percent. Have you ever heard of Occam's Razor? In a nutshell, the simplest explanation to an observation is likely the correct explanation. How many bosses leave the office four or five times each morning to talk to the secretary, when they could just use the intercom? How many bosses lean over their secretary's desk, touch her arm, and help her with email? How stupid do you have to be to not figure out email after a two year tutorial? The simple explanation—they were having an affair."

"But to want Belinda? Even for Stan, that's pretty low," I replied in disgust.

"Don't ask me why or how, and please don't make me even conceive the two of them doing anything but slopping hogs after work. I don't know, but the signs were there; the little glances, the little laughs—and I saw both of their cars parked at the motel down the street," he laughed. "I kind of put it together." He handed me a piece of paper from the box sitting on the wall. "Cash it in good conscience. You have received lesson two in simple observation and part of lesson three in gentle persuasion." I reached for the paper slowly, still in a state of shock and now fully unemployed.

"I would hate to see your non-gentle persuasion," I said, realizing I had exited a terrible situation and entered into a terrifying unknown.

-Chapter 7-

I still did not know what my new job truly was or what business plan I would need to implement. For someone who viewed risk as an extremely predictable, well thought out plan, this all proved disconcerting. But the sense of excitement was definitely there, and it was tough to quell. I was moved forward by stories of clandestine meetings and international intrigue.

Our new business would be a kind of private eye firm, but since neither of us were licensed we couldn't call it that. Instead, we would operate in the same smoky arena of the consultant in which Galveston had been involved before.

Galveston would get the clients and do the investigations or consulting. I would handle the business side; the contracts, the expenses, and the bank account. Galveston also agreed to educate me as a junior consultant, slash, investigator.

During our meeting it became evident that while Galveston knew everything about investigating and sleuthing, he really knew nothing about business. He was shocked at what we needed to do to potentially make a profit, and the luster of the idea began to wear off. We had limited funds, but Galveston assured me we would have clients. They might not be clients as wonderful as we wanted, but they would be money paying clients nonetheless.

But I vastly underestimated my role in the business. Galveston wanted to involve me with the investigations immediately.

-Chapter 8-

Our first month of employment together would prove to be uneventful. No clandestine meetings or international intrigue. There wasn't even national intrigue, but I decided to stick with it despite depleting all of Galveston's savings.

We set up shop in Galveston's spacious one bedroom pad, complete with a 70's era couch, a slow computer, and a refrigerator filled with old mayonnaise, pickles, and milk from the Reagan administration. It was like two college roommates deciding to go into business together selling bellybutton lint, because not everyone had some.

We started with simple background checks, employment histories, and driving records. It helped keep us solvent and in business, but it wasn't breaking the bank.

Our first big job came from a contact at an insurance brokerage firm. Galveston had met this man through casual conversation about cars at a local tire store. He was a lead underwriter at the company and spoke of his frustration about possible insurance fraud. The underwriter was convinced that one of the claimants they had made payouts to was faking a worker's compensation injury, and due to a pending lawsuit was costing the insurance company hundreds of thousands of dollars. No one could prove this guy was faking, but they were convinced he was.

We'll call the guy Rick, because that was his name.

"I recommend driving at the guy with our car and then make him leap to safety, proving he was not injured," I told Galveston, regaling him with my best plan. This course of action didn't sit well with him, however.

"If the guy isn't faking and we pop him with our car, then what?" Galveston inquired. I still had a lot to learn about the investigation business.

Galveston approached the case much more deliberately. In two days Galveston had enough information to know when this guy blew his nose or flushed his toilet.

We sat in front of Rick's house for hours, just waiting to take a picture of him doing something out of line for his injuries. At one point Galveston became impatient and ordered me to knock on his door and run away. A seemingly simple plan, but one I was not willing to do.

"Why don't I just kick him in the jaw? He'd chase me then," I joked.

"Don't question, just do, lesson eighteen," Galveston snapped. Obviously he wasn't thrilled with my idea.

I must mention something about Galveston's rules, his "lessons in insanity" as I liked to call them. They rarely made sense. He would commonly throw out a random lesson number and follow it with some mundane advice. The scary part was, to him, these weren't random numbers. I had a frightening thought that he actually had these written down somewhere, or they were actually encased in his brain.

I would have written them down if I would have known that later they would prove useful. I also didn't realize that this seemingly simple operation was a test case for future operations. This was our pregame warm-up.

I decided to follow the order and gingerly stepped out of the car and made my way around it, crouching and looking both directions. I made my way across the street, stooped over, looking like the Hunchback of Notre Dame, doing a half step in each direction.

"What are you doing? Dodging gunfire?" Dan yelled. "Just go over there like a normal human being and knock on the door. That lurching walk doesn't look out of place at all," he said sarcastically.

I immediately stood up and composed myself. I ran over and knocked on the door of the house, as Galveston had instructed. I quickly looked both ways down the street and scurried back, jumped headfirst into the passenger seat of the car, and hunched down.

"You looked like a wounded horse," Galveston laughed, making bobbing motions with his head.

"You're sitting there yelling at me while I'm doing the grunt work. You're telling the whole world that we're up to something," I exclaimed.

"Look around. This is a working class neighborhood with a median age of 103. You could set off a nuclear bomb here and nobody would notice or care. Now just sit and wait." I sat in the seat looking straight ahead, feeling burned and embarrassed. I was a greenhorn, but what was this berating going to prove.

"I just want to see what he'll do. We could wait here all day, but this is quicker and has a little more pizzazz," Galveston threw his arms up and gave me the jazz hands.

Nobody came to the door after ten minutes of waiting, and Galveston was becoming even more impatient.

"Okay, do it again,"

"Are you serious? I'm not running over there again," I pleaded.

"Sure you are, and this time, yell that you're from the Department of Water and Power."

I tried to explain my case, but Galveston would have nothing of it until I reluctantly agree.

As I ran across the road another time, I crouched low, swinging my arms wildly as if avoiding bees and doing my best wounded horse on acid routine. I raced to the door, knocked hard and yelled, "Water and Power Company!" I then nervously turned the other direction, found the nearest pair of bushes, and jumped behind them, panting.

I noticed that Galveston had crept around the car, and before I realized what he was doing I heard a crash. Galveston had broken a pane of glass on the front of Rick's porch with a rock, and jumped out of sight behind the back of our car.

"Oh, there's our boy, here he comes, faster than I expected," I heard Galveston say loudly.

Rick came darting out the front door, down the steps, and hopped across the grass, looking for the culprit. He moved rather elegantly, like a cow dragging a bucket it got a hoof stuck in. He definitely wasn't a man in extreme pain. I sunk down in the dirt behind the bush as far as possible, hoping Rick wouldn't see me.

Rick huffed and puffed outside his house for five minutes, turning, bending, squatting; all the things he shouldn't have been able to do. Rick finally gave up and returned inside, obviously perturbed he didn't get to punch someone in the face.

"Run back over here, will ya?" Galveston tried to yell to me in a whisper.

"Okay, hold your horses," I yelped back at him. I moved from behind the house and began to move across the street.

"I think I see him coming," Galveston said, pointing at the door of the house.

I felt a rush of adrenaline and crouched low, like that would help conceal my position.

"Oh, sorry," Galveston said loudly, "I guess it was a mirage."

I stood up, peeved, with my hands on my hips and began to walk back.

"Okay, now you do need to hurry, I really do see him coming," Galveston said seriously.

I once again went into a strange run, looking both ways as I crossed the street, and flew into the passenger side door, breathing hard.

"Where is he?" I gasped.

"Oh, sorry about that. I've got to get my eyes checked. It was just a bird, a really large, fat, white bird," he laughed.

"Haven't you heard of the boy that cried wolf? The wolf ate him," I scolded.

"I'm sorry, it was just too easy. I apologize. I really needed to see how fast you were, or was it how gullible?" He laughed again and rubbed his chin in fake thought. "That went better than I thought," Galveston quipped as he put away the video recorder. He noticed the consternation on my face. "What are you worried about?"

"I'm worried that we could get arrested. This isn't what I signed up for."

I'm not sure which laws we had broken during this little operation, I'm sure there were many. I couldn't remember if it was against the law to impersonate a water and power man; I sure hoped not.

"Don't sweat it. That was good fun," Galveston said slowly, nodding his head.

I would get him back at some point, but right now I was glad it was mostly over. I had a sinking feeling we would be ramping it up a bit from this point on. The pre-game warm-up was over, now it was on to the big game. If only I had known what we were getting ourselves into.

-Chapter 9-

We returned to Galveston's humble abode, the headquarters of Icarus Investigatory Services, or as we called it, Icarus, or more simply, "Ick!". Galveston and I had come up with the name after a study of Greek mythology. Our business name was an ode to the mythological boy who flew too close to the sun with wings of wax. The wings melted, he tumbled to the earth, and went splat on the ground. Galveston told me this is probably how we will feel every day, flying too close to the sun.

The insurance company awarded us with a check in the mail along with a bonus I had stipulated in the contract for bringing the case in under our scheduled time. We had potentially saved the insurance company hundreds of thousands of dollars. They would have settled quickly due to the abysmal safety record of the construction company Rick worked for and a need for it just to go away. For our two days of work we received eight thousand dollars, and it was plenty of money to split fifty-fifty. I now officially liked my new job.

I was in, all in. The excitement was palpable now, and I had a new sense of purpose. I was bringing order to an otherwise chaotic world. Alright, that was a bit dramatic, but there definitely was an amount of fun and interest in my new endeavor that I found, well, gratifying.

During the rest of March and into May we picked up other cases, examined records, did interviews, and gathered contracts. I started to get the hang of things, even the lingo that was spewed out, all under the watchful eye and tutelage of Dan Galveston.

We had become a well-tuned unit, like Laurel and Hardy mixed with Starsky and Hutch. We received more and more job opportunities. Some successful, some not, and many times the company that hired us was wrong. Key contract negotiations allowed us to rack up sizable payments and stay, barely, in the black.

We proved ourselves to be better than other investigators by bringing our cases in under time. Regardless of how long it took we would only get paid one sum. No made up hours or crazy bills for a thirty dollar ham sandwich, or four hours of billing for paperwork. We convinced our clients that they were saving money with us over other investigators. We didn't have a real office, no other employees, and only a cheap fax machine, so our overhead was nonexistent. This allowed us to get our price below what anyone else was offering.

By June things were going well. Word of mouth spread and we put our feelers out for bigger fish to fry. We developed more scrupulous and unscrupulous measures, choosing to take a more creative approach to things. We would pose as everything from janitors to handymen to exterminators, with Galveston's mouth leading the way.

Galveston said believing you are who you say you are helped ease the pain of, technically, committing breaking and entering, or fraud. We had an almost cavalier approach to our exploits and on our next job, the biggest yet, we would have to pull out all the stops.

Chapter 10

On a small Mexican airfield across the border from Arizona, activity was increasing at a dirt airfield simply know as Elias North, about 30 miles south of Yuma, Arizona.

It was a dusty, dirty, and sparse place. Yucca plants and cacti dotted the landscape and a rough dirt road careened its way around rocks and through shallow ravines toward the field. Sitting under the blazing June summer sun were two off-road Jeeps parked under the limbs of a paltry mesquite tree. Five men with rifles on their shoulders were scattered about, dressed in green army fatigues. One man, known as Colonel Espinosa, fiddled with a satellite phone.

"Vamanos muchachos," he barked at the rest of the men. The men immediately jumped in their vehicles and bumped their way to the end of the dirt runway, which was rutted and soft, the product of poor upkeep and care.

The Colonel stood up in the Jeep and turned his gaze to the north. On the horizon, low over the terrain, a dot appeared and grew larger.

The outline of a twin engine Rockwell 690B Turbo Commander emerged and began its approach to the runway with its wings wavering in the wind. It was a light transport aircraft, capable of carrying heavy loads for its size, but on this day it was only carrying one piece of important cargo. It touched down, sending up a billowing cloud of dust that floated down the runway and settled over the waiting men.

The plane's door popped open and out stepped a neatly dressed man in a long sleeve shirt and pants with dark sunglasses. It was Sergeant Walker. He reached to his seat and pulled out a silver briefcase, larger than what a businessman would carry.

Walker began to walk toward the Colonel, but stopped midway and held out his hand. With his fingers he flashed a one, four, one and three. The Colonel punched the numbers into his satellite phone, put the phone to his ear, listened for a few seconds, and then waved to Sergeant Walker. Walker set the briefcase on the ground, turned, and got back in the plane.

The aircraft bounced back down the runway, past the on-looking men, and lifted off, spraying dust over them again. The sound was deafening as it climbed away from the dirt field, staying low to the terrain. The case stood alone at the side of the runway and Colonel Espinosa did not move, nor did his men. They just kept their eyes trained on the silver case. The plane faded from sight as he brought the phone back up to his ear.

"The case, it has arrived," he said in English into the phone.

"Good, you'll have your payment when I have confirmation of delivery. Your bonus will be at your hacienda awaiting your arrival," said the monotone voice on the other end.

"Excellent," the Colonel answered.

He motioned for his men to return to their Jeeps while he walked towards the far end of the runway. One of the vehicles pulled beside him and a soldier handed him a black duffel bag. The Colonel pulled out a radio, spoke in Spanish, and walked to pick up the silver case.

After a few minutes, another plane appeared into view and landed, just as the first. Colonel Espinosa walked to a Beechcraft King Air as the door to the aircraft popped open. He made his way inside carrying the duffel bag and the silver case as the departing Jeeps left the dirt runway.

The pilot skillfully maneuvered to the opposite end of the runway, turned around, and applied full power. The plane lifted slowly into the hot air and faded into the blue, cloudless sky. It would be a long journey for the Colonel to his final destination before he could return to his home in Mexico.

Chapter 11

The jobs since the Rick insurance scam had been much easier, or maybe it just seemed that way. Our next job was going to be our first big game.

This big break came from a strange late night call from, of all things, a toy company. It was a case that would push the boundaries of our Boy Scout behavior.

The company was called Playcom Educational Products, Inc. We were told it was a small upstart in Burbank, California that made interactive toys for kids; the learning ones that we all should have used when we were young to mold our minds into well-adjusted, intellectual people.

We managed to wrap our minds around the crux of the case which had to do with a project called *Happy People*. It was a slightly inane, or insane toy that brought the cultures of the world to the fingers of your child. Galveston and I thought of it as a steaming bowl of cultural stew. It consisted of music, geography, language, and bouncy little cherubs dancing across the screen in their country's native garb while calling out things in French, Spanish, even Dutch and Swahili. We didn't really understand the hubbub about such a product whose sole purpose seemed to give your child the wonderful experience of an acid trip. Apparently, it was a feat of magical engineering.

Playcom had a prototype and employed the help of a software development company called Genesis Solutions, Inc. to complete the software for the project. The COO of Playcom, Stanley Clostine, informed us that Genesis had been unable to finish the project for some unknown reason. Clostine found out through a few informants that Genesis had been secretly marketing the Playcom product to the heavy hitters of the youth toy market, especially Hasbro and Mattel, under a different name called Global Kids, codenamed *Adamanthea*. Both of the companies had shown an interest in purchasing the rights and design of the toy.

Playcom wanted us to go into Genesis, steal back the plans, and make sure they couldn't continue production. Genesis actually designed software for defense contractors, security companies, and the government. It wasn't in their mission plan to market kid's toys, but we figured they just saw the dollar signs from the potential of the product. We came to realize that the toy business was not so fluffy and cuddly. It's a billion dollar industry, sometimes more brutal than any other business sector. Elmo and SpongeBob Squarepants aren't usually hugging and shaking hands. Many times they pull out weapons and have a good, old-fashioned street fight. For us, however, it was going to be a big, fat payday.

Genesis would have the plans securely hidden away, and we needed to become much more creative to get them. We were going to need a little outside help.

-Chapter 12-

Galveston had a few contacts in the area of computer geekery, but there was only one person he felt could handle a job of this size with the discretion it would need. Galveston considered him a super geek, but only in the nicest of terms.

Alex Jubokowski had a resume a mile long. He was a former computer programmer with the National Security Agency, had designed software for missile defense systems for Northrup Grumman, written security software for giants Microsoft and Bank of America, and implemented tracking and distribution software for FedEx—just to name a few. He did this all before the tender age of thirty.

Boredom set in, however, and Alex set his sights on Las Vegas, that wholesome city in the desert. He developed an algorithm to predict the next sequence of numbers on slot machines; a hobby he started back in his days at MIT, and a once thought impossible task. He got caught of course, not using the algorithm, but trying to purchase a slot machine on the black market. Alex somehow escaped prosecution, but word had spread about his impropriety and his job prospects dried up. He was just the guy we were looking for.

Upon meeting Mr. Alex Jubokowski, my stereotypes got the best of me. I expected to meet a thirty-something, short, nerdy guy of Polish descent with little to no personality, wearing glasses and a pocket protector. Instead I met a tall twenty-something man of Indian descent wearing a black Pantera t-shirt, black leather jacket, misplaced earring, and riding a Kawasaki Ninja ZX-10R crotch rocket motorcycle. Along with that he had one hell of a gregarious personality. I liked him from the beginning, and I knew why Galveston had him in mind the whole time.

We met him at our palatial rolling estate, which disappointed him when he found out it was Galveston's apartment.

"Judo!" Galveston quipped, thrusting out his hand.

"You know I always hated that nickname," Alex responded.

"Yeah, whatever," Galveston smiled, slapping Jubokowski on the back, "Judo, Roger Marshall."

I offered my hand, "very nice to meet you. I've heard very little about you," I laughed.

"Nice to meet you too, Roger. I've heard absolutely nothing about you," he responded dryly.

"I'm glad I could be of such importance."

"How in the world did you let this guy talk you into anything he's involved in?" Jubokowski questioned, smiling and pointing at Galveston.

"Actually, I'm an escaped mental patient."

"You would have to be, wouldn't you? I tell ya, this guy has gotten me involved in more things than I care to say. Half-cracked schemes, touting of federal laws, you name it," Jubokowski explained. "More than once I thought I was insane."

"That's the way I feel every day with this guy," I retorted. I finally had someone who felt my pain.

"If you guys are done with your warm fuzzies, I'd say it's time to get down to business. We have a lot of work to do," Galveston said as we all walked up the steps to our glorious headquarters.

"Jubokowski?" I began. "Can I ask you how you got that name?" He looked me squarely in the eyes.

"Well you see, when a man and a woman…," he started, gesturing with his hands.

"I mean, it's an original name, not usual with someone of your, ah, appearance," I said cutting him off mid-sentence, "I think I know about the birds and the bees part. I'm curious to know your heritage."

"Why, because I look like I just got off the boat?"

"Well, yeah," I replied.

"Fair enough," he said shrugging his shoulders. "It's pretty simple. My Dad is a Polish Jew and my Mom is an Indian Hindu."

"That's quite a match."

"Yeah, it's hell on dates. I guess you can consider me a, ah, Hindjew," Jubokowski laughed.

"Oh that's good, and I guess you can't eat pork or beef," I responded.

Galveston turned his head as we walked in the front door.

"I'm sure there's a large Hindjew contingent in the U.S.," Galveston joked.

"You know, not as many as you would think. We're not a real strong demographic group," Alex replied.

I bet Alex had received this question a few times, and I liked him already. He would fit in well as part of our merry band of misfits.

"I can't believe all the fuss about a kid's toy," Alex started. "But hey, it's not for me to question. Dan, I got that information for you."

Alex pulled out a piece of paper from his back pocket. Galveston read over it quickly and placed it on the table in front of us.

"That's what I thought," he said, shaking his head.

"What is it?" I inquired.

Galveston looked over the paper again. "Genesis is one heavy hitter. They're going to be a tough egg to crack. Roger, remember rule 107, never, ever, underestimate your opponent."

"He's filling your head with those silly, nondescript rules, huh?" Alex said.

"Yeah, since I met him," I replied with a sigh.

"I hate to admit it, but they're good rules. I learned more in two months from this joker than my full term at the NSA," Alex said smiling. "You know, Gal," Alex continued with a wink, "these guys have serious computer security as well as physical security. It's going to be virtually impossible to get into the system from the outside. They have two or three layers of security before you can get to their internal servers, not to mention watchdog programs, high-level encryption—the works. The only real way is from the inside."

"You know, I've thought about that, and I have a plan."

"And how do you plan to pull this off?" I asked.

"Simple," he said, "We're going to find out who is in charge of the product, and he's going to give us the password to the plans."

-Chapter 13-

Dan laid out his plan, and Alex added the technical parts. I acted merely as a waterboy. My part had essentially been done. I had secured the finances and the contract rate if we succeeded. The rest was up to these two, ah, team members. The plan was actually ingenious and simple, as hard as it was for me to stomach saying that.

Clostine informed us that an executive named Dart McLeod was in charge of the *Adamanthea* project. Why anyone would name their kid Dart, I'll never know. Maybe he had a pointy head at birth, but nonetheless, that was his name.

We needed to get Dart's password, and the easiest way Alex could think of was through a simple process called keylogging. A program installed on the computer would record the keystrokes on the keyboard and send the information to us. The problem was Dart needed to install the program on his computer and then log into the internal server of Genesis. If we could accomplish that, we could then roll in, access the designs, and get rid of them. It was a vital step in our plan.

We solved this problem with a simple email message to Dart. The message was daftly written by Galveston with a keen eye on juicy morsels of information. It had to be believable enough that Dart would open the attachment we sent with it and not ask questions. It would be a lucky break for us, but knowing human nature we knew Dart would have to look.

We disguised the email as a consultant to Genesis named Charles Tanqueray and sent it late in the day. Hopefully Dart's knowledge of 19th century liquor distillers was poor, or he didn't like gin. Mr. Tanqueray was of course the namesake for Tanqueray gin and a man who came from three generations of clergymen. He didn't go the religious route, however, and began to distill gin in 1830, shipping it to the colonies of the British Empire where people began to develop a taste for Tanqueray and tonic. Despite this bit of historical information the email read:

To: Dart McLeod, Project Engineer
Subject: Sensitive and Confidential, Problems with *Adamanthea* Product

My team has identified and modified key design flaws in the original design of the *Adamanthea* prototype product that would have increased production costs dramatically and not allowed ample physical computing space for safe and effective operation of the product. We have made modifications to the product's internal design. The updated schematics have been included as an attachment to this email. These modifications will reduce production costs by 50 to 75 percent of the original estimates.

You are to immediately implement these new design changes into development by order of the Genesis CEO Frances Drake. This information is highly sensitive. Please review these plans in the attachment to this email ASAP. Thank you for your cooperation in this matter.

Sincerely,
Charles Tanqueray, Sinclair Consulting Associates

The email was so completely far from the truth that we were bordering on a Nigerian money email scam. We hoped we hadn't written too much fiction. If our calculations were correct, and they seldom were, Dart would open the attachment and unknowingly install the keylogger program while looking at a mess of useless computer schematics. Alex assured us it couldn't be picked up by any of the spyware or anti-virus programs Genesis was running.

We waited to see if Dart would take the bait and access his Genesis account after reading our email. This is where we would get his username and password into the Genesis system. If Galveston's knowledge of human behavior was correct, we would soon have our answer.

We began to panic as they hour stretched past 5:00 P.M. A full day could be lost, or suspicion could be raised if Dart didn't open the email attachment. It was time we didn't have to lose.

Finally we saw words cross the screen of Alex's computer as the keylogging program sent us Dart's keyboard inputs. We knew Dart had read the message and almost simultaneously opened the attachment placed in the email.

"Naughty, naughty. You should never open email attachments that are fishy," Alex said.

We now added another broken law to our books–computer fraud.

Dart accessed the email late enough in the day that he wouldn't be able confirm its authenticity until the next day. If he had accessed it only a few hours earlier and did some investigating, then we would have been sunk. Our timing couldn't have been better.

It was as if we had strings attached to Dart's arms and legs. He rapidly sent off a reply to our email saying there was nothing in the attachment and questioning our role in the product. He wasn't going to get a reply. We still needed Dart to want to check the authenticity of our fake schematics with the real plans. Again, our puppet didn't fail to disappoint.

Dart immediately logged into the Genesis system and meticulously keyed in his username and password for entry into the system. We all wrote the keystrokes down in unison, giddy at the find. He must have pulled up the plans for *Adamanthea* on his computer, looked them over, and been thoroughly confused. Now we had to get into Genesis that night.

Chapter 14

We rented a van for the night's stakeout operation; a nice, white Ford van, disguised with a big dent in the side. Galveston had bought a big magnetic sticky pad for the sides of the vehicle that read, "TS Services. You break it, we fix it", along with a fake number that would forward to our cell phone, just in case some snooping guards wanted to make a call.

Alex attached two small cameras on the dash and put tinting over the back rear door windows. Galveston loaded a few random tools, a pair of pliers, rope, wire, and a tool belt, along with three blue work shirts that read Dale, Joe, and Fred.

I was in charge of food and drinks. I loaded the van with a cooler full of caffeine and sandwiches, a coffee pot, and figured some trashy reading material wouldn't hurt. We were going to be in close quarters, for most likely, a large amount of time, and we had a long drive from San Diego to Los Angeles.

No stone was left unturned, and we didn't want any surprise guests. We put on our TS Services shirts as we made our way to our "target" (one of my new found vocabulary words). I was Fred, Alex was Dale, and Galveston was Joe.

We pulled up to Genesis about 2:00 A.M., the witching hour. We felt we were prepared for this portion of the operation since we practiced it at our stronghold nights before. I had rehearsed my part in front of the mirror and had even written out a few note cards just in case I forgot something.

Genesis was in a large five story building, brightly lit from the outside. A lone security guard sat at an oval desk watching an episode of Hogan's Heroes on a small portable TV.

The basic plan was this; Galveston would infiltrate the building, work his way to Dart's office, log in to his computer, and install a program that would allow us to get into the system later and download the *Adamanthea* file. Alex could then hack into the internal servers of Genesis and cause a block in the system after we got the file. In addition, he had written a nasty little virus that Galveston would install, effectively shutting the entire network down. It would take Genesis days to figure out what happened to the network. By that time we would be long gone. This is exactly how we hoped it would go down.

We had our bases covered, and Galveston was prepared for anything; security cameras, keyless entries, or motion detectors. Lucky for us, janitors don't make much money, and after paying off a Genesis janitor for a little information under the guise of a federal agent, we had been able to obtain the location of Dart's office.

Galveston planned to pose as a maintenance worker. He supplied himself with a large amount of keys and wore an excessively large tool belt.

I parked the van a few spaces down from the front door of Genesis and set up the cameras toward the entrance to the complex, just as Alex instructed. Galveston exited the van and made his way to the door, talking indiscriminately on his phone while looking and pointing; all part of the act. Alex sat in the back of the van in front of his laptop, ready to relay instructions to Galveston.

The cameras were up and running, and they gave me a clear view of the surrounding area. Galveston even had a small, discrete earpiece attached to his radio that allowed us to speak to him directly.

"Alright, Danny boy, all clear," I said with an air of importance. "You have a guard at a table at your 9 o'clock, 300 feet away from your position."

"I could really get into this," I thought, thinking back on the many spy movies I had seen on TV and in movies.

Galveston turned toward the van and made an "L" sign with his hand on his forehead along with a smile plastered on his face. I soon realized he had just called me a loser.

"You know it hurts my feelings when you do things like that," I said, keying the microphone.

He turned and gave me the cut sign to his throat.

Galveston walked to the door, jingling as he went. He got to the glass door of the building and rapped on it. The weary guard looked up, jolted from his seat, and walked to the door.

"Can I help you?" he said, reaching at his belt in his gray uniform.

"Hi. Yeah, I'm Joe Ghirardelli," Galveston started, an ode to the Ghirardelli chocolate company of San Francisco, one of his favorites. "I was just called. I'm the electrician you guys called a while ago. I have a work order for something on the second floor, looks like a wiring problem in offices 214 to 216. Sorry I'm just getting here, but we had an emergency at the Aon Center."

The guard opened the door and let him in.

"You know, I don't got nothin' about this. Follow me over and we'll check it out," he said, motioning to the desk.

Galveston walked inside and pulled his hat lower on his head, hiding his face while not looking up.

The guard was nice, pleasant, and helpful. This wasn't something out of the ordinary. Most maintenance calls took place at this time of the night. Galveston dropped his bags in front of the desk.

"Yeah, you might have to call my dispatch. I mean, I'm only about six hours late. I wonder if they thought we had already been out," he lied.

"Let me check. Hold on." The guard scanned a clipboard on the desk. "Yeah, I've got nothing here. What company are you from?"

Now we had done our homework on this one and knew that Genesis had its own Information Technology, or IT department. They were in charge of the networks and computer systems inside Genesis but subcontracted to a company called TS Services to deal with wiring issues in the walls.

"I'm here from TS Services. We've been here before. Are you sure there's nothing in your log? It was an emergency call. Something about a power flicker in the grid." This was completely false and made-up, but damn, it sounded good.

"No, nothing," the guard answered as he looked through papers on the desk.

"Here." Galveston handed him a fake work order. Alex had written a nice piece of fiction. It read:

2nd story, offices 214-216, no LAN line power, grid fluctuations and overvolt conditions. APU powering down. Grid A7-A8. Diagnose and correct ASAP. Emergency call and pricing.

"It's all Greek to me. Let me call my supervisor and find out what to do," the guard replied after reading the work order.

"Between you and me, I wish you wouldn't. I'm going to get in a heap of trouble if they find out I'm coming six hours late. My boss won't understand either. He'll chew my butt on taking so long on the Aon job. He'll probably dock my pay," Galveston pleaded, and confided to the guard's blue collar side. "I tell you what, just let me look, and if it's going to take too long you can call your supervisor to let them know we'll be upstairs for a while. These things are usually a quick fix; a loose connection, a reswitch, something like that. You can call my dispatch if you're still not sure."

"Yeah, let me do that first, just so I have some confirmation. What's the number?" the guard asked.

"Right there," Galveston said, pointing at the work order.

The guard dialed the number, and the phone rang in the van. Here was my time to shine.

"TS Services dispatch," I answered reading from my script.

"Ah, yeah, this is the security service at Genesis Software. I have a Joe here for some work?"

"Joe? Oh no, is he just getting there? Yeah, he was supposed to be there six hours ago. Tell him that he has two more jobs to do before six. He really needs to hurry. The Aon building needs him back quickly, they're still having problems. What's that work order number," I inquired, hamming it up. The guard read the number and I read the work order verbatim.

"If at all possible, could you get him in and out as soon as you can? I need him back on the road."

"Yeah, okay," the guard answered slowly.

"Just give us a call if there are any problems. Have a good night," I quickly said.

"Alright, you too." The guard hung up the phone and looked at Galveston. "You have two more jobs," he said smiling.

"You're kidding me. What a disastrous night," Galveston feigned frustration. "Do you think I can go up now?" he asked.

"Yeah, I guess I'll show you up. Let me call the other guard and tell him I'll be away from the desk for a second. This won't take long, right?"

"Not long at all," Galveston answered slyly, with a smirk on his face.

Galveston pushed one of the bags he brought under the front of the desk, out of sight of the guard. They made their way to the elevator and went to the second floor. The elevator opened up to a bank of cubicles and glassed offices looking to the outside. Galveston carefully timed how long it took to get to the second floor.

"I'll check each office. Then I'll check the network room. How about we start with 214," Galveston said.

"Yeah, okay. Let me open it up." The guard walked over to office 214, unlocked the door and flipped on the lights, illuminating a desk, work terminal with a keyboard, and a few chairs. There were no papers out and the office was neatly kept. Galveston walked in, set down his bag, and began looking through it.

"Ah, crap," he said, looking perturbed. Galveston pulled various items out of the bag, searching for something. "I left my other bag downstairs. Could you do me a huge favor and go down and grab it for me? I can go ahead and get started on this one."

"Ah, yeah, sure," the guard answered, obviously uncomfortable. "Where did you leave it?" he asked.

"At the desk, and I forgot I even brought it in. It has my voltmeter in there. I can go ahead and check the connections while I wait for you."

"Yeah, okay, I'll be right back."

"Great," said Galveston, heading for the computer monitor in the office.

The guard turned and left for the elevator. Galveston immediately assessed the situation. It was a workstation with a central processing unit, or CPU. This meant it was a standalone computer with its own hard drive instead of a terminal that was connected to a distant, host computer.

"Skipper to the Professor and Mary Anne," Galveston announced into a radio he pulled out of his bag.

Our earpieces in the van sprang to life and blared the words. Alex and I looked at each other.

"The Professor and Mary Anne?" I said to Alex, "I'm assuming I'm the Professor; you must be Mary Anne," and I motioned to him.

"Yeah, we're here. What's the story?" Alex asked.

"This must be Mary Anne," Galveston joked. "I've got a CPU."

"Thanks for that," Mary Anne, clearly offended, cleared his throat. "Alright, listen up. Windows NT?" Alex inquired.

"Yeah, I think," Galveston answered.

"Good. You should see a login icon for the system. Type in the username and password and then hit enter," Alex said, beginning the instruction.

"Hold please," Galveston answered. He then did precisely what Alex asked. Galveston carefully keyed in each letter of the username and password from the one Dart gave us.

"Okay, done." Galveston checked his watch; he had two minutes left before the guard should return.

"Next, plug in the flash drive to the USB port. The file, 'Annie Oakley' should pop up after you plug in the flash drive. Double click it, and it will load onto the computer," Alex told him.

"Okay, hold on."

Galveston again did as he was instructed. The "Annie Oakley" program started and he watched a status bar appear, apparently loading data into the computer system. He checked his watch again as the status bar proceeded toward 100%. Galveston now had thirty seconds until the guard returned.

"It's almost loaded," he said into the radio.

"Pull the flash drive out when it's done," Alex began again.

Just then, the elevator door opened, and the guard came out holding Galveston's bag and began walking down the hall. Galveston cleared the screen and knelt down, pulled the flash drive out of the port, and reached to drop it in his tool belt. Instead of dropping noiselessly in a pocket of the tool belt, it dropped onto the carpeted floor. The guard appeared at the door, and Galveston stepped stealthily on the flash drive, which was about the size of a cigarette lighter.

"Here's your bag," the guard said.

"Thanks for that. I think I already have the problem figured out." He scooted his foot toward the bag and then crouched down, pulling the bag toward him.

"Is that the network room?" he asked, pointing to a closed door by the elevator.

As the guard turned he quickly grabbed the drive and threw it in the bag.

"Uh, I don't know. Do you need to find it?" the guard inquired.

"No, I don't think so. Let me just check the other offices and if they look alright, I think we'll be done. The IT guys must have inadvertently fixed the problem," Galveston fibbed.

The pair moved to the other offices. Galveston entered each one and jiggled a few wires, pulled out a voltmeter, and checked the wiring, having no clue what he was doing.

"Yup, everything looks good. I think we're done. I don't see any problems." Galveston shrugged his shoulders and grabbed his bags.

The pair went back to the elevator and took it down to the lobby. As the door opened on the bottom floor another guard appeared.

"Damn it," Galveston thought, "it's time to pull a rabbit out of the hat."

"Hey," the first guard said, "we're all done up there."

"I didn't know we had any maintenance scheduled," said the second guard, whose identification tag read "Jeff".

"Yeah, me neither. That's why I'm six hours late," Galveston interjected, giving a quick laugh, "and there's nothing wrong," he added, taking hold of the conversation. "I tell you what. I'll just cancel out the work order. My bosses won't like me doing that, but I know you guys have to keep a record of who was here. Somebody won't be happy getting a bill for work that wasn't done, or needed," he lied. "If you give me the work order I'll call the IT guys tomorrow."

Galveston needed that work order to make sure there was no record of him being there, and to ensure a bit of safety. He hadn't counted on dealing with two guards, but that was par for the course. Guard Jeff looked thoughtful.

"I don't know. I don't care if they get charged, but if the work was supposed to be done we need a record of it," guard Jeff responded.

"Well to be honest with you, I want to cover my own ass too. I mean, I am six hours late. I was supposed to be here no later than eight and here I am at," Dan looked at his watch, "two-thirty in the morning." Galveston was pandering to the men to help a poor schlub out.

"I don't see a problem with that," the first guard answered.

"Yeah, it's okay, I guess," guard Jeff said, after thinking for a moment.

They gave Galveston the work order he brought with him and he asked for the IT department number just to make it look like he gave a crap.

"Thanks, fellas," Galveston said while he gathered all his things. He hiked his bags onto his shoulders. "I'd say it was fun, but at this point I still have a long night ahead." Galveston moved toward the front door and opened it. "Thanks again for the help." He gave a friendly wave and turned to leave.

Guard Jeff said loudly, "how's Mike doing over there?"

Without flinching Galveston turned, "Mike Fletcher? He's alright. Damn fool broke his leg falling off a ladder. He's in a cast up to his neck. You a friend of his?"

"Uh, no," guard Jeff stammered. "I meant another Mike."

"Who? Mike Jones? That's the only other Mike I know. I haven't been there very long though."

"No, you must not know him. Have a good night."

"You guys have a good night too. I hope you don't get too bored." Galveston gave another friendly wave and closed the door behind him. "Amateurs, but nice guys," he thought. He had played off of confusion and empathy to get the job done. Lesson 112, he told me later. Galveston walked to the van and got in the front seat.

"Professor, Mary Anne," he announced to us, "we're out of here."

-Chapter 15-

We quickly began the long drive back to our fortress of solitude in San Diego. Unfortunately, we still had a lot of work to do. Alex set up his computers in the office living room and began pecking on the keys as the clock passed 5 o'clock in the morning.

He managed to get into the Genesis system easily using the "Annie Oakley" virus. Alex weaved his way through a series of backdoors and open ports which allowed him to get into the internal workings of the system. It was an easy task with the intricate knowledge Alex had of security systems.

"Annie Oakley" masked our every move. We were just another computer, out of thousands, bouncing off their servers. Alex provided another source of security by masking our computer's address to various cities around the world; from Prague, to Amsterdam, to Seattle.

At this point we had been without sleep for over 24 hours, living off of coffee, highly caffeinated energy drinks, and items with large amounts of high fructose corn syrup.

The mean, little program we had installed on the Genesis computer system, the "Annie Oakley" virus, sprung to life and unraveled itself like a giant hydra monster. Galveston and I didn't understand how it all worked; we just knew it did work. We again took technology for granted, like so many others. We never asked Alex what his true snooping capabilities were and figured it was better to leave that alone.

We could now use Dart's internal username and password to access the more secure areas of the Genesis system which contained the *Adamanthea* plans.

Dart McLeod had two usernames and passwords. One was for a general login to the system, a simple one that consisted of *DMcLeod* and *Ferrari442*. Galveston joked this was obviously a little gift he planned to get for himself.

The internal username and password to the secure area would have been impossible to break without the keylogger and had a complex password. Alex typed it in slowly, careful not to make a mistake. It read, *Dart_McLeod_RD*, and the password was, *877x4vst*779j-31st5*.

"Well that would have been easy to crack," Alex said sarcastically as he finished typing the string of characters. Alex informed us that, "figuring out the string would have been like trying to pass a watermelon through a garden hose." The encryption of the password was accomplished by a 64 bit Blowfish cryptographic block cipher. This was the fancy way of saying tough security.

Alex quickly scrolled through the file folders he saw on his computer. This was highly sensitive stuff and consisted of defense contracts and plans. He finally located the *Adamanthea* file. It was large and would take time to move over. Alex began uploading another nasty little virus that would lay dormant for a while, avoiding detection by anti-virus software because technically it didn't exist.

It would tick down after a few hours and release its viral contents like a time release capsule, rendering all the files near it useless and trashed. It was a nasty little bug. We had nicknamed it "Grumpy", because damn, it had a serious attitude problem. Alex assured us that it would relegate itself only to the files in that area dealing with the *Adamanthea* project. The last thing we needed was every geek this side of the Mississippi descending on Genesis to "oh" and "ah" over this new threat. After "Grumpy's" viral belch, it would go dormant again.

This would help mask what we had done. I was secretly feeling sorry for the employees at Genesis that would have to clean this mess up. Somehow noting my trepidation, Galveston said quietly, "They'll survive. It's a huge company."

I knew all that, but it still hung over me. We were damaging work from behind a computer screen that had nothing to do with our case, just so we could end up making a few bucks.

I had come from a different world in which I stuck my head in the sand. In the world of academia, the worst people would do was publish or perish. Academics who released junk research on "Danish boys who eat waffles develop elevated blood sugar levels", published in the Journal of Breakfast Dietary Habits, was the worst I had to contend with. Guys and gals doing whatever it took to reach tenure, sit back, teach one class a year, and spend fifteen minutes a week in their office for students, while berating those same students for wasting their time. "I'm tenured, damn it!" they would exclaim.

Galveston by nature was much more cynical and suspecting. He was by all accounts, a realist, having been exposed to the real world of corporations, governments, and politics. I too had experienced that governmental bubble of political horse trading, but never truly realized what went on behind closed doors. I had been a policy developer and analyst, buffered from the dog-eat-dog world of those back room dealings.

Up close and personal was how Galveston operated, which often opened him up to the surly underbelly of the cutthroat, greedy people he came in contact with. I was being exposed to the same ugly element and quickly becoming jaded, slowly leaving the optimist in myself behind.

"I'm all done," yelled Alex, bolting me from my silent bit of retrospection.

He had already downloaded the file and waited for "Grumpy" to do its bit. We now had proof of our work. He deleted the original plan from the Genesis server and made some final checks that all the files we needed were copied. The virus would unravel at any second, and those files we had just downloaded onto our own hard drive would soon be useless on the Genesis server, and useless to anyone that tried to retrieve them.

It was almost over. I spied the couch blissfully, and planned to dream of beautiful women feeding me grapes like in so many Roman depictions. Alex and Galveston continued to look calmly, but nervously, at the screen. Galveston sat like a general finishing up a battle. He looked swollen around the eyes, like a puffer fish. I hallucinated that his head began to float from his body, a clear sign we hadn't had enough sleep. Galveston peered over Alex's shoulder, letting a yawn give way.

"There it is," Alex said, pointing to the file named *Adamanthea 39598253* on our computer hard drive.

"Can you open it?" Galveston asked.

"Yeah, no problem, but why?" Alex answered and questioned.

"I just want to see what we have, uh, borrowed."

Alex opened the file, revealing a window with large amounts of text followed by a page of design schematics.

"That's a lot of stuff. Go ahead and print them if you can," Galveston ordered, noticing something peculiar.

"You're the boss."

The printer whirled up and spit out twenty pages. Many of the first pages looking like gobbledygook; no inherent pattern or meaning of words. Galveston reached for a few of the fresh pages off the printer and looked at them inquisitively.

"Is this coded or something?" he asked, and then handed a few of the pages to Alex.

"I'm not sure. It looks like pieces of a data stream, probably a program that was made in-house by the Genesis engineers. If we had more time I could do some snooping, but I wouldn't recommend it," Alex said tapping on the computer screen.

"I agree with you, go ahead and shut her down." Galveston continued to study the pieces of paper. "You know, it almost looks like it could be a cipher, you know, code."

"It's called cryptology," I interjected.

"Thanks, Mr. Science. Here," he gave me a few of the sheets, "see what I mean? There seems to be a definite pattern of some sort."

"I see what you mean," I said studying the paper. "There is some sort of sequence going on here, but I can't figure it out. It's only in the first few pages too, and then it goes back to a bunch of crazy symbols."

Alex finished exiting out of the Genesis system, and he too set his sights on the papers, studying them closely. Then a smile crossed his face.

"You know what this is?" he asked as if we hadn't been asking the exact same question. "This is a good, old fashioned Trimethius Tableau. If I can remember correctly, it was invented around the Renaissance period. It was an expansion, more or less of the Caesar shift. It uses a matrix of every letter of the alphabet, twenty-six rows and columns and you read down each row to decipher or encrypt the code."

"You know I have no idea what you're talking about," Galveston chided him.

"To put it simply for you, it's an old cipher, an old way of writing secret code."

"So this is old?" I asked like a naïve school boy.

"No. It's just someone didn't want anybody to read this part of the file, but they also didn't want to make it too complicated that no one could figure it out. I haven't seen this since my training at the NSA. Why are you so interested in this anyways?" Alex asked.

"I'm more interested in the file name. It looks very familiar— *Adamanthea 39598253*. There is something about that file name, but I just can't remember." He slid back in his seat. "I need a stiff drink and a good nap," Galveston said as Alex began closing the files and exiting out a backdoor in the Genesis system.

I popped open some of our finest bubbly in response to his comment, a two liter bottle of generic cola, poured out three glasses, and added a generous portion of rum to each.

"Three cuba libres," I announced handing out the glasses like a pompous bartender, a job I had held in my younger days. "Cheers, gentlemen." I held my glass high, waiting for a ceremonial clink from my compatriots.

"I think I'm going to cry," Alex said dryly.

"I think I'm going to throw up," Galveston retorted.

We clashed our glasses together and downed our drinks like drunken alcoholics. Galveston put his glass down and wiped his mouth.

"I don't know about you two, but I smell like the stench of death. I'm going to shower, put on my jammies, and hit the hay. You guys can do whatever you want. We'll find out what damage we did tomorrow."

We said our respective goodnights even though it was eight o'clock in the morning, and retired to our respective hovels. Mine a one bedroom apartment next to a rundown strip mall, and Alex to his four bedroom home near the coast. Alex was doing better financially than what I had figured. It seems he was spending time with us out of boredom and a need for a new challenge.

Galveston stayed at our office, for it moonlighted as his home. He fought the urge and temptation to think about anything further. Instead he chose the better approach, get a good night sleep, finish up the job tomorrow, and then with a fresh mind, plot our next move. He closed the curtains, blocking the light, and with his curiosity at bay crawled wearily into bed.

It seemed the *Adamanthea* project was all wrapped up, but we would learn the file was just the tip of an iceberg.

-Chapter 16-

"Citation four-three-echo cleared to land two-eight right," the pilot of the Cessna Citation X business jet repeated to air traffic control as they bounced in the clear air.

He pulled the power back slightly and lined up the plane perfectly with the runway centerline, gently caressing the plane to the ground.

The pilots maneuvered the plane to the opposite end of the field and to the front of a large gray hangar. Two black Suburbans were parked near the hanger door, surrounded by neatly dressed men wearing sport coats. The cabin door of the plane swung open as the engines powered down, and stairs lowered to the ground. Colonel Espinosa bounded down them carrying the silver case. He was met by one of the men who had been standing in front of the waiting Suburban.

"Everything in place?" the man asked.

"Yes, and no problems. Everything was on schedule. I did what I was instructed," the Colonel answered and handed the man the case.

He looked it over carefully. A small green LED was lit on the case near the latch.

"It all looks good. No tampering and everything is clean. After verification of the contents we'll transfer payment to you," the man told the Colonel.

"Yes, of course. I'm looking forward to it."

"Here is your ticket. You're on the 10:15 to Mexico City. It will be up to you to make it back home from there. Please use anonymity. This isn't something we want going around," the man instructed the Colonel.

The man pulled out a small matchbook sized device and stuck it in an opening next to the green light. The small light changed to red as it was inserted.

"Good," the man announced dryly and without a smile. He motioned with his hand to another man at the Suburban who opened up a laptop on the hood of the SUV. After a few seconds the man waved back.

"Your funds have been transferred, and we have your bonus being delivered to your home as we speak."

"Good, good," the Colonel said while holding the airline ticket. "I won't ask you how you got it."

"That probably wouldn't be a smart idea," the man snapped back. "Make sure you're on that plane, and remember, speak of this to no one."

"Of course, of course. I shut my lips. Pleasure to do business with you," the Colonel said, but not before the man had already turned and walked away.

The Colonel watched as the man carried the case to the black Suburban, got in, and almost immediately sped away. Colonel Espinosa flashed a smile on his face, thought of his good luck, and made his way to the airline terminal for his journey home.

-Chapter 17-

Galveston called me at home the next morning, waking me from my wonderful slumber.

"Hey sleepy head, get over here, will ya?"

I peered at the time.

"What?" I said groggily, rubbing my eyes. "How about after twelve. I feel like I've been hit by a Mack truck."

"That's understandable. Get over here within the hour then. Alex is already on his way."

"Well thanks for taking my needs into account," I replied sarcastically.

"I did. I was going to tell you to get here immediately, so I figure I'm throwing you a bone," Galveston replied insensitively.

"You have a heart of gold you know."

"I know. See you in an hour and bring some food. Bye."

"Yeah, Yeah," I said grumpily.

I struggled up from my bed, ironing the kinks out of my body, and prepared myself in the bathroom. I was becoming excited as I readied myself. What was the story going to be, and what damage had we done?

I couldn't eat, but I obliged my partners and stopped off for donuts and coffee. I arrived at our so-called office a little after 9:30 A.M. I was never one for being punctual.

Alex and Galveston were bright eyed and bushy tailed. They were clearly as excited as me. But Galveston exhibited a bit of trepidation for all of us.

"So what's the story?" I asked hurriedly before I was even in the door.

"What did you bring? I hope it's some pigs in a blanket. I love those things," Galveston said grabbing the box from me. "Donuts? You just got donuts? Mindless calories," he mumbled, already with half a jelly-filled protruding from his mouth.

"I didn't know you were so concerned about your health before," I told him.

"I am now."

"Okay, you got your food. Now what's the story?" I pressed.

"First things first, what are we going to get paid?" Galveston inquired with glee.

I reached for a piece of scrap paper and leaned forward in my seat.

"Well, if all is successful and based on my estimates, we may get paid this amount."

I wrote on the piece of paper, folded it, and slid it to Galveston on top of the coffee table in front of him. He slowly unfolded it and nervously looked at the figure.

"Here, let me reattach your retinas," I said to him, noticing his surprise.

"Wow. That's a lot of zeros." The paper read $30,000. "Are you serious?" he asked me.

"Yep, that's about right. Of course the breakdown will be different based on the distribution," I told him.

We previously had agreed together that 40% would go directly back in the business, and 60% would be split evenly three ways, between each of us. The business got $12,000, and we each received $6,000, all for essentially one week of work.

I had managed some contractual magic. I had to apply stipulation after stipulation while forcing myself to be confident in our success. We came in under time, under budget, stayed concealed, and potentially saved Playcom millions of dollars. I leaned back in my chair.

"Not bad, is it?"

"Not bad? If you weren't a disgusting man, and it wouldn't give me the feeling of expelling my half-digested donut, I'd kiss you," Galveston retorted.

"Oh, that's lovely to hear. What do you think, Alex? Do you plan to stick around and see what other high jinks we can get ourselves into?"

"Why not? I think I'm going to kiss you no matter what," Alex responded, with a scary glint in his eye.

I felt a new sense of purpose, one of the great financier. I couldn't do the jobs of Alex and Galveston nearly as well, but they couldn't pull off my job. That's why I was here.

Playcom was willing to pay. The potential losses superseded the measly amount they would pay us. I played on this fact and it succeeded, along with stipulations of increased payment for coming in under time.

We all glowed over our new found bounty. Maybe we glowed too much.

"Did you figure out what that code was? Not that it matters now since we're going to get paid," I asked Galveston.

"Alright, alright," Galveston said exhaustively. "You better sit down."

I grabbed a donut and sat on the couch. Galveston smiled, revealing bits of jelly goo around his mouth.

"That file caught my attention," Galveston began.

"What do you mean?"

"Well, as Alex was pointing at it, I noticed the name and numbers and something just clicked. Where had I seen that before? And then, I remembered." He held up his finger as he took a sip of coffee.

"You know I worked for Black Bear security, right?" He asked us, as if we didn't know that information.

"Yes," I answered.

"Well, that file name was so peculiar. I learned during an investigation that Black Bear would name their black ops after Greek, Roman, or Egyptian mythological figures. Sometimes they would use team names corresponding to letters of the phonetic alphabet; Team Alpha, Bravo, Charlie. They used these in conjunction with the names of these gods. You know, like, Jupiter Bravo. After this it would be followed by a large group of numbers. I never knew what those numbers meant, but most likely they were some sort of code. I bet it made it easy for them to list their operations that were secretive in nature."

I twisted in my seat again, my ears perked up, and I scooted forward, anxious to hear more.

"So you think that Genesis is doing something with Black Bear?" I inquired.

"I don't know if they are, but this file name stood out. Every single time I saw these names I knew they were usually associated with something pretty bad, or pretty illegal. I looked up the name *Adamanthea*. She wasn't a Greek god, but a nymph who helped Zeus and hid him from his father, Cronus, who was going to swallow him or something nutty like that. The numbers following the name are exactly as I remembered them, but this time there was no phonetic alphabet. The god Black Bear chose explained the operation. It helped keep everyone on the same page, but a degree in Greek mythology may have been a prerequisite to figure out what operation you were involved in," Galveston stopped and caught his breath, already thinking two steps ahead. "You remember the story I told you about when I got let go from them, right?"

"Yeah," I answered.

"Well Osiris Echo was one of the things I came across when I did the research about arms dealers related to Black Bear. I never knew what that was then."

"Osiris was the lord of the dead in Egyptian culture, I believe," I piped in. "That's a morbid one, but it fits."

"Right, and all those arms were for rebels in Africa," Galveston continued.

"So what, you have an old vendetta to return? I mean, who cares. That was history. I don't understand. What do you plan to do with this?" I asked again.

"I don't know," he sighed, "it just seemed like a strange coincidence to run across something like this."

That would be the understatement of the year.

-Chapter 18-

As curious as it was, it had no bearing on our newly minted operation. Galveston seemed to let the matter fade and began to change focus, even before we had our payment in hand.

"You know, we need some new digs, a new place to call home. We can't continue to do business in this hole." Galveston already had his sights set on a new place.

"I agree," I added.

I was hoping we would start to move towards more legitimacy, maybe not continue with the current reckless behavior we now exhibited. No one in our merry band was licensed in the state as a private investigator. I hoped that we could rectify that and become slightly more legal.

I broached the subject with Galveston who agreed, but he was aloof about a timeline for such a thing to happen. It might just be something that I would need to do on my own.

During the next few days we took a little break. There were no new jobs that we knew of so we took advantage of the downtime and looked for a new office. Galveston found a nice little office in a business park between a medical supply company and a dog grooming business. Two businesses I'm sure we would frequent.

We immediately put down a payment and moved in a few desks, a file cabinet, and Alex wired it for internet access, allowing us a connection to the world. Expenses were kept low, but we decided we needed a new member, someone to man our extensive, one line phone system, and vast financial resources.

Alex had our perfect subject in mind. Galveston and I had only one stipulation; it must be a woman, and she must be of an acceptable nature. It was our polite way to say that we had grown tired of looking at each other's mugs day in and day out and preferred someone with hair longer than to their ears.

He had an old friend that he assured us would be just right. She was flexible, had another job, since we paid very poorly, and had smarts. Her name was Jane. She was an aspiring actress, a college graduate, and desperately needed a day job. She also had legs up to her ears, which made coming to work that much easier. It was appropriate that she was an actress since most of our business was just an act.

She agreed to start right away and fit right in quickly. She organized our files, manned the phones, and answered the two calls we would get per day, beautifully. Everything was going well. We had two new potential jobs. Easy ones that required more sitting research than legwork, and I began looking in on getting my private investigator license.

Almost a week had passed since the Genesis job, and unfortunately, according to the rubber band theory, that just couldn't last. The rubber band theory is this; things go well in life, everything just clicks along, opportunities rise and problems fall, the rubber band of life is stretched slowly. Unfortunately, just like a rubber band it can only stretch so far, and at some point it must return to its original position or it can break, causing everything to go back to the start. Our rubber band had been stretched to its limit. It didn't break, but on a Friday morning it returned to its original position and maybe even spun into a knot.

-Chapter 19-

I wearily looked at the clock as my phone rang; it was 7:15 A.M. The caller I.D. revealed the number I knew it was. I silently cursed the device and pushed the talk button.

"Yeah," I answered with eyes closed and mouth feeling as if some small rodent had decided to make a home there.

"Whew. You better get to the bathroom. I can smell your breath from here," Galveston said, much too cheerily for this ungodly time of the morning.

"You know I can't operate before noon. What the hell do you want?" I really couldn't function very well this early. My brain always felt like it was on a siesta.

"Hey, get up, get your dress on, and meet me for coffee." Galveston clearly ignored my plight. He was always too chipper in the morning.

"Can't it wait? I'll bring you some coffee if you just leave me alone. I will spit in it of course."

"Oh, that's lovely. Crawl yourself out of bed, spray some water on that bird's nest you call your hair, and get over here," he said.

Clearly the insults helped my motivation. I knew it was pointless to fight and I relented, pulling myself from bed. He would just keep calling until I gave in. He was persistent about such things.

"Alright, just don't call again. I'll see you at eight," I told him.

"Oh, and don't forget to bleach that mouth of yours," he said as I hung up on him, something he was used to by now.

I stumbled to the bathroom and examined my faux Mohawk bed head, slowly cleaned up, and got ready for an uneventful day. We met at a small coffee house a block down from our new office. Galveston was nice enough to let me buy.

We slowly finished up our coffee and decided it was time to get to the office, arriving at our new den of solitude around nine o'clock.

Jane was busily typing on her computer and reading a magazine at the same time. She looked stunning every day, and I always wondered what time she had to wake up to get looking like that. It was a nice thing to see early in the morning, and I had developed a little crush the first time I had laid my eyes on her.

She greeted us warmly, but more nervous than usual. As I pushed the thought back that she needed a morning hug, she motioned to Galveston.

"Dan, you have visitors. They insisted to meet with you, and one of them said he was an old friend of yours. I told them I didn't know when you would be here and would leave you a message, but they insisted on waiting. The one man said you would understand?" Clearly she was troubled and now definitely needed a hug and consoling by me.

"Hold it, cowboy," Galveston said instinctively, reaching his arm out straight across my chest, stopping me in my tracks. "I think she's doing okay." He could clearly read my body language and the sad puppy dog face I made. My face burst with embarrassment.

We stood back and peered through the door. Two men sat with their backs to us, both with black suits on.

"Do you recognize them?" I asked, continuing to look at Jane.

"No, I don't recognize the backs of their heads, and hey, focus."

Galveston snapped his fingers, jolting me from my dream. The ray of light I had created around Jane vanished. I had it worse than I thought.

I looked at Galveston, and he motioned with his hand to follow. I followed him into the office, fighting the urge to not look back at Jane. Now this was getting ridiculous.

"Hello gentlemen, what can I do…" Galveston stopped mid-sentence, the smile fell from his face, and he turned a shade of white I hadn't seen before. He now recognized the man that had stood up and turned toward us as we walked into the room.

"Dan Galveston. Long time no see." The man near the door stuck out his hand.

"David, how are you?" Galveston stammered and shook his hand. "David May, this is Dr. Roger Murphy, my business partner."

Galveston rarely used my full name and credentials. He usually would introduce me under some fake name just to watch me squirm, so this was definitely a different case.

My memory swirled to recognize the name. It sounded familiar, but I couldn't place it. Obviously he was an acquaintance of Galveston's, but I didn't know if he was a positive or negative one.

"Nice to meet you, Dr. Murphy," he said.

"You can call me Roger. I don't go by that title anymore, and nice to meet you too." We shook hands, and I noticed he was cleanly dressed in a pressed, black suit with a noticeable bulge in his suit jacket.

"I think I've mentioned Special Agent May to you, Roger. I don't know if you remember."

A memory came flooding back from months before. The blood left my face, and I turned bone white as I felt my heart rate increase. A pop-in by the FBI, friend or not, was definitely not good, especially after some of the stuff we had been pulling.

I nervously nodded my head that I did remember, but no words of confirmation came out of my mouth. Galveston's demeanor had returned, and he was now in full business mode.

Agent May introduced his companion; a wiry looking fellow that had no smile, wearing a suit that was too small. He offered us a steely gaze.

"Dan, Roger, this is Walter Ackers. He is with Atwater Security."

We both nodded in unison toward him and offered our hands for a handshake. Galveston moved to his desk and sat down.

"Gentlemen, have a seat." Galveston motioned to the pair. They sat down and I took up position in a chair next to Galveston's desk. "It's good to see you, David. It's been a long time. What, two or three years?"

"Yes, about that long. I see you've gotten back off the ground again. You know I always thought you got a raw deal, right?"

"Yeah, I know. So what brings you here?"

Galveston leaned back in his chair and put his hands behind his head, obviously having an idea why. I obviously had no clue, but edged to the end of my seat to find out. I remembered Galveston speaking highly of David May, and recalling that he had been a friend of his in the Bureau. I hoped this was just a social call to catch up on old times.

"Well, Dan, I just came to ask a few questions," May started while crossing his legs. "I'll just cut to the chase. I've received credible information that there was a break-in at a local software company. I was wondering if you would happen to have any knowledge of this. Have you heard about it, or heard anything about heavy hitters in the area hacking into computer systems?"

"You'll have to be more specific. We hear a lot of things. I guess I would need more information if I was to help you," Galveston answered coolly and without a hint of guilt.

"It was about a week ago; pretty simple, but sophisticated. We believe there were sensitive files hacked from a company called Genesis Software. Mr. Acker here thinks there is a connection with a maintenance man that came in the night before the break-in. The night security guards don't have a record of his work or a reason for him being there, except for what the maintenance worker said."

"It seems the security guards need a lot more training, or maybe they were never trained well enough in the first place," Galveston said again coolly.

He glanced at Mr. Acker, who now shifted uncomfortably in his seat and tightened his lips. May stifled a smile knowing Galveston was goading our new, found friend.

"So did you get a picture of this guy? I mean, the maintenance person."

"Not clearly they didn't. He seemed to know where the cameras were and had a hat pulled down low on his face. He did have a tattoo on his left forearm."

"Galveston has a tattoo?" I thought, never remembering that.

Galveston leaned forward onto his desk, nonchalantly showing his forearms. Mr. Acker peered over, seeing nothing. The skin on his arm was clear as a bell. Galveston was way ahead of them.

"So you have security guards letting people in that shouldn't be there, and a guy with a tattoo but no face. I'm not sure how you want me to help you with this, David."

"I let Mr. Acker know that I had a contact that may be able to help him. I heard you were back in business and that Alex was back in town."

Galveston held back a flinch. May knew all about Alex and his technological skills.

"I have one more bit of information. Actually, Mr. Acker did this work for me. He found out an employee's username and password was used to get it."

"You don't say." Galveston kept to the similar line, but knew this was not good information.

"So why don't you think this guy could steal these files?"

Mr. Acker chimed in at this point, itching to get in on the conversation.

"This particular employee was not in the building when it occurred," Acker started.

"He could have accessed it from his home or some remote source. You know that isn't hard to do," Galveston answered again.

"These were highly encrypted files and could only be accessed from inside the building. Plus at the time of the break-in he was engaged in some other, uh, activities."

At this, I edged even farther forward in my seat. What had our boy Dart been doing? Even Galveston raised an eyebrow.

May smiled. "At the time of the break-in he was engaging in an affair with the vice president's wife."

My mouth opened wide while Galveston's eyes almost popped from their sockets.

"He definitely had other things on his mind then," Galveston said dryly, looking at me.

"Exactly," May replied. "He confessed this to me when I interviewed him, and unfortunately, I confirmed this with a very surprised woman. So this guy couldn't have done those transfers from his computer. He clearly was involved in more pressing affairs."

"Pressing affairs? That's an understatement," Galveston said, suppressing a smile. "I still don't have any new leads for you though, but we could look into it. I tell you what, if Mr. Acker could talk to his higher-ups, and we find out some useful information, then maybe we could work out a payment system. You know I don't do anything for free, right, David?"

"Yeah, I know. I think we could work something out, but only for useful information."

Galveston put his finger to his chin as if calculating a new found solution. "I may have some information, but I can't disclose it in front of you, Mr. Acker—privacy reasons of course. If David finds it credible he'll fill you in. How does that sound?"

May paused. "I think that would be fine. Why don't you wait outside, Walter. We'll leave after I hear this," May said, turning to Ackers.

"Okay," Ackers answered, getting up to leave. "Nice to meet you Mr. Galveston, Dr. Murphy." He nodded to us both and headed for the front room, closing the door behind him.

I moved back in my chair. I felt like leaving too. At least I could join Mr. Acker in the front and stare at Jane for a while, but I was in this as much as Galveston was.

"I think we're ready to cut the crap, don't you, David?" Galveston stated.

"I think so," May answered seriously.

"So what information do you have that brought you here, and how the heck did it get to your desk."

"Well, I know all about Playcom, and I know they hired you. Your operation was very similar to the Multan Pharmaceuticals incident, wasn't it?"

"Yeah, well, you stick with what has worked in the past, right?"

I sat glued to my seat, listening to these two talk shop and not knowing one thing they were talking about.

"How in the world did you get involved in this?" Galveston asked again. "I didn't think anyone would trace it back to Playcom."

"One of those files you lifted from Genesis was a file named *Adamanthea*. I know all about that file."

Galveston lowered his head slightly as May continued to explain how he found us. "You see," May paused, "we hired you."

Galveston's head shot up. "We hired you?" he inquired. "Who's we?"

"The Bureau. We hired you to lift that file."

I sat stunned at the information, and Galveston appeared to have the same reaction.

"We've been tracking this file for a while now, and due to some recent events needed to find out what it was. Unfortunately, we didn't have the legal ability to do so," May stated slowly. "When I found out you were back in business it all came together. I figured you would be the right man for the job because there are only a few people in the country that could have lifted that file. It was a lucky break for us that you got Alex involved."

"I can't believe it," Galveston stammered. "We were working for the FBI. So Playcom is just a shell?"

"Completely made up," May said quickly. "Just a ruse."

"But why? What is so important about this *Adamanthea* file? Military? A congressman's indiscretion?"

May grew even more serious. "This information is highly classified, but I've gotten permission to disclose it to you. It is only known to me, the Special Agent in Charge, and the Director of the Bureau. When it came across my desk I knew you would be the right man for the job."

"Not to seem ungrateful, but why couldn't you guys handle this on your own. You have more resources and smarts than we do."

"Our hands are tied. Let's just say that certain things we need done are not under the scope of the FBI. It could raise some eyebrows if we tried, and we need this information. It's a matter of national security."

"Who are you after?"

"That's the biggest problem, we're not sure. We don't know anything about the file or what it means. We just know it has a connection to a sequence of events a few weeks ago. Let me fill you in on the background information we have." He opened up his portfolio and pulled out a manila folder as Galveston and I sat riveted to our seats.

"On June 2nd, there was a break-in at a lab at Dartmouth University. It was the lab of a Dr. Edward Sloan, a respected engineering and physics professor at the University. He specializes in energy generation and electrical conductivity studies, and he has a well-established lab. They were testing materials that improved electrical currents and how these materials could be used in all types of products at a micro or macro level. According to one of his students he wanted to improve power consumption of different products by using different materials. In the past few years his research changed, and he became obsessed with batteries of all kinds–from small disposables to the large storage batteries used in ships and planes." May paused for a second, scanning his notes.

"He started devoting more time to what he called, 'building a better battery'. Now none of this is out of the ordinary, but on June

2nd, the lab, as I said, was broken into and destroyed. All his files went missing, computer hard drives were stolen, and all his equipment was eradicated. No one saw or heard anything except for a security guard who got attacked by men in black. Dr. Sloan was out of town, supposedly in Memphis at an electrical engineering convention. But when he was contacted, no one was able to find him. He never checked in at the conference, but was on the plane to Memphis. We haven't been able to find him since. His home was also broken into and ransacked."

We stared at May as he continued his synopsis, still trying to conceive how we got involved in this.

"This is where Genesis comes into the picture. A few days after the break-in we got an anonymous tip that a software engineer at Genesis named Marcus O'Leary hacked into the Dartmouth servers and removed a few secure files that belonged to Dr. Sloan. We managed to get O'Leary to confess that he stole the file and placed it at Genesis under the name of *Adamanthea*. This was all he knew, and he didn't know who gave the order. We haven't had any additional leads since then; no Dr. Sloan, no DNA at the crime scene, no traceable devices, no witnesses, nothing. A complete dead end all the way around."

"So what was he working on that was so important?" Galveston interrupted.

"Dr. Sloan, per our investigation, has developed, of all things, a highly efficient, super battery. We don't know all the particulars about it, of course, but after interviewing a number of Dr. Sloan's graduate students we began to get an idea of what he had invented. It appears that Dr. Sloan developed a battery that works in parallel, like stories of a building. One layer supplies and resupplies the previous layer increasing the efficiency by seventy-five percent, and decreasing the size by anywhere from fifty to seventy-five percent of a conventional battery."

Galveston and I looked at each other and shrugged our shoulders, not knowing what the hell May was actually talking about. We had a feeling he didn't really know either as evidenced by his constant reading and searching of the papers he had placed across his lap.

"The students said he had been testing it on a variety of electronic devices and had been able to increase the battery life from hours to days and weeks. O'Leary explained that the *Adamanthea* program could be for a computer control that would modulate the output of the battery to increase the efficiency even more. He said Dr. Sloan even had a plan in his schematics to be able to mass produce the tiny battery."

I looked at Galveston, his mouth was slightly open and his eyes were wide. I didn't understand the implications of such a potential breakthrough, and looked between Galveston and May for guidance. Clearly they were impressed and understood. A battery, that was it? Who cares about some stupid battery that allows me to yack on my cell phone longer before I had to do something as tough as plugging it in to recharge.

"What's the big deal? So he made a better battery. It seems rather silly," I openly said to both of them.

Immediately May and Galveston looked at me.

"Are you kidding?" Galveston said grinning. "Don't you understand the implications of such a thing? I mean, if this guy has come up with this battery, and it works, plus it can be mass produced; it could revolutionize the world. Think about what batteries are in. Cell phones, cars, smoke detectors, ships, planes, computers. You could have an electric car or hybrid that could get six hundred miles to the gallon. Ships could run on batteries. If the size is as small as David is saying, you could put these in everything. It would be the greatest invention of the 21st century. It would slash oil demand and cut energy costs drastically. This might be one of the scariest breakthroughs imaginable," Galveston explained to me.

May chimed in, taking Galveston's lead. "It is also our belief this battery is what instigated these events over the past few weeks; the break-in to Dr. Sloan's lab, his disappearance, and the emergence of this *Adamanthea* file. Governments or businesses would do anything for this technology, or not do anything and destroy it. Do you think that Saudi Arabia would be pleased to know that oil consumption would be shattered? A government or business could make billions of dollars on such technology. The uses could be endless. It is our belief that someone is thinking the same way, and they are doing whatever it takes to get their hands on this technology."

I sat dumbfounded. The implications of this technology started to sink in; a complete removal of dependence on foreign oil, clean air, complete economical advancement for developing countries with no drawbacks. These would all be positive things that could occur. But I also pondered the negative effects; a massive loss of jobs, decreased income for nations dependent on energy production, and the trickle effects on all other areas of business and commerce. The Canadians, for example, are our biggest supplier of foreign oil, and something like this would put them out of business. There were also the political implications. I was still an economist, businessman, and political scientist at heart, and I had a definite cause for concern on how other nations would respond. There could be dangers of increased tension, conflict, and war as nations tried to protect their interests.

I saw their point and was embarrassed for not having seen it sooner. The ramifications could be devastating. I saw why May and the FBI had tiptoed around it. The furor this battery could create would be extraordinary.

Galveston regained his faculties. "Now I know you're not giving us this information out of the kindness of your heart. What's the catch?"

"Well, there is another reason I made sure I hired you, not just because we couldn't get that file on our own," May began. "Genesis is not an independent company. They are a subsidiary of a much larger organization." May paused and cleared his throat before continuing. "They're owned by Black Bear Security."

"You don't say," Galveston said, not changing his demeanor, but realizing why we were hired in the first place. "So what now? We did the job you wanted, I don't have any vendettas."

"Maybe not, but the government needs your help; I need your help. We want you to work for us in locating the batteries and Dr. Sloan, by any means necessary."

Galveston let out a guffaw. "I don't think so."

"Let me put it another way. You have to work for us." May said the words clearly and with force. He meant business and from his new tone I could tell he wasn't interested in taking "no" for an answer. Galveston picked up on his demeanor, too.

"So let me get this straight, and correct me if I'm wrong, but you want us to find somebody doing something wrong, and oh, I don't know, do whatever it takes. Such as things like wiretapping, hacking, breaking and entering."

"Now, on the record, I never said such things, but we simply want private supportive investigatory services to independently research items in our investigation that we currently cannot allocate the manpower toward."

"Wow, very well said. That was crystal clear, wasn't it, Roger?"

"Crystal," I answered.

"As you know, the information I have about your company and your latest job proves to be highly illegal."

"But you guys hired us!" Galveston exclaimed.

"You'll have to prove that. Did you ever talk to an agent? I know you didn't. I can easily make this go away. I'll make sure Mr. Acker doesn't ask any more questions, and I'll assure you there won't be a connection between you and Genesis. It's a federal matter now. In exchange for helping the Bureau, you'll be helping yourselves. I don't think I can put it anymore succinctly. I mean, I've got you with breaking and entering, computer fraud, and a host of other federal crimes."

The anxiety welled up in me and I started to become dizzy, but Galveston remained calm. He knew something I didn't.

"I guess you're telling us we have no choice but to cooperate. You'll tie up the loose ends?" Galveston asked.

"Of course."

"So the choice seems to be this; possible jail time, or the potential for getting killed," Galveston said reluctantly.

"I think I'll take my chances on choice two, if you don't mind," I interjected quickly. Galveston nodded his head in agreement.

"I don't want to have to put the screws to you on this. As crazy as it may sound, I still consider you a friend first," May said to Galveston.

"You sure have a funny way of showing it."

"My hands are tied on this and the powers from above are very interested in getting this wrapped up legitimately, or illegitimately as the case may be. Let's do this; I'll talk to Mr. Ackers and then be right back to discuss all the details."

"What are you going to tell him?" I asked.

"I'll let him this has become a government investigation, and his services will no longer be needed. He wants this done as much as you two because his job is on the line. End of story. Why don't you discuss it and I'll be back."

"You're still going to pay us, right?" Galveston threw out the question as May got up from his chair.

"You'll get your money," May told him, "and we'll make sure you're taken care of if you get this job done."

"I'm not sure I like the sound of that."

May smiled as he left the office, motioning for Ackers to follow him outside. My heart palpitations subsided, but were replaced with rage.

"I know what you're thinking and what you're going to say," Galveston started. "If you want out, I won't stop you. I'll even give Alex the same option. I'll tell David that everything will fall on me if we have to take a hit. I'm sorry I got you involved in this."

"I'm a big boy," I said, my rage subsiding. I couldn't leave him to handle this on his own. "I knew what I was getting into, but I should have spoken up. I don't think this was the excitement I was looking for. I mean, can't we just go legit. My blood pressure is up, and I think I'm losing my hair. This is just too much."

"I understand," Galveston said quietly. "I'll respect whatever decision you make."

May entered the office again and sat down. "It's been handled. Mr. Ackers is very relieved. I'll call the CEO of Genesis and let him know about our investigation."

"Where do you want us to start?" Galveston asked, getting right down to business.

"We need you to look into a lead we have. Dr. Sloan has a daughter from a first marriage. We believe he had been corresponding with her, and she was the last contact he made before his disappearance."

"You want us to talk to her?"

"Yeah, but there's a slight problem with that." He gave a look of consternation. "She just happens to be in a, ah, witness protection program."

"You guys can figure that out. What's the problem?" Galveston asked.

May thought to himself before answering. "We have a political problem with that. You see, she's not under the protection of the Justice Department."

"What? That's ridiculous. You're the FBI, you can do anything you want if it's federally related, right?" Galveston asked.

"Not exactly." May dodged the questions like a politician. "She's a British citizen, and we don't know where she is."

"Hold it, hold it." Galveston became clearly exasperated with the roundabout question and answer session. "She's in a witness protection program in Great Britain? Is that what you're getting at? Deal off, nope, no way. This deal is off. I know where you're going with this," Galveston exclaimed, getting up from his chair. He began waving his arms like a madman.

"Dan, calm down," May tried to console him.

"What is it, why is that so bad?" I stuttered, thoroughly confused. Had I slept through a portion of the conversation?

"So this is the other reason why you're here. Nope, not going to do it," Galveston turned his back to May, shaking his head.

"Look, you'll just have to chalk it up to a crazy coincidence."

"I'll say," Galveston cried, continuing to shake his head. "When were you going to fill me in on this tidbit of information?"

"It's been a few years. I thought you might be over it. I guess you do hold your grudges," May told him.

"Hell yes I do. What that woman put me through."

A woman, somehow a woman was involved, and by the way it sounded it was a woman Galveston had some history with. I smiled at the thought.

"What's the story there?" I asked excitedly, hoping for a juicy bit of gossip.

"You see," May started turning toward me.

"Don't you tell him anything," Galveston yelped, but May continued.

"Galveston's ex-fiancé happens to be an assistant to the Chief of SIS, and a former field agent in counter-espionage."

None of this information was known to me, and not that Galveston's history mattered so much, but I had no idea what these two were talking about. I found out the SIS is the Secret Intelligence Service of the United Kingdom and the equivalent of the CIA. It is often referred to as MI6 and made famous by none other than James Bond. At least I knew who we were dealing with.

"Galveston and his friend had what you could call a tumultuous relationship when he was stationed in London a few years back," May said continuing his history lesson. "She cut out on him, and he didn't hear from her again. Eventually she told him she had been called back to field service and that she couldn't handle a long distance relationship."

"She asked for a transfer and ran away like a frightened little girl," Galveston added, fuming. "That's all he needs to know, don't tell him anymore."

"No, that's okay, please, do tell," I goaded so May would spill more juice.

"The point is you have a contact in the SIS, good or bad. Elizabeth could potentially find Dr. Sloan's daughter, Margaret. It would take us weeks to get the clearance to find her in a witness protection program, and its weeks we don't have."

Galveston continued to sit in his chair, and after taking some deep breaths stood up to stretch, not saying a word.

"That little vein on his neck is about to spurt blood. He'll tell me in due time," I said and pointed towards Galveston's tomato red face. "Maybe we should get down to the business at hand."

-Chapter 20-

History proves that giant leaps in technology are not generally accepted by society, but over time society tends to adjust to such innovations. It is usually all a knee-jerk reaction, however. How could a lone professor develop such a revolutionary idea for a battery and did it even work? On the other hand, there are many advances found by accident or by one person.

For example take Vaseline, or petroleum jelly to be more exact. In 1859, a chemist named Robert Chenebrough was interested in petroleum products. He noticed oil workers applying a dark, thick substance on cuts, burns, and abrasions to heal their wounds. This seemingly useless substance collected on the pump rods of oil wells, obstructing the workings of the rig. Chenebrough collected this "rod wax", as it was called, and returned to Brooklyn, New York from the Pennsylvanian oil fields. He spent years perfecting the "rod wax" into a colorless, odorless gel that he called Vaseline, a combination of the German word for water and the Greek word for oil. He had created petroleum jelly which today is used in a variety of ways; from rubbing on a chicken's comb to protect it from frostbite, to healing wounds and protecting skin. So it wasn't too outlandish to entertain the thought that Dr. Sloan could have invented this amazing device.

With all that said and thought, we had some serious decisions to make on how much we would get involved. First, I needed to decide if I was going to stay employed with Galveston any further. Maybe I'd return to teaching and a comfortable office. I could pump out a few papers which would only be read by a handful of people and live out my life in a state of utter mediocrity. Or I could turn the other way and jump into a semi-fictional world, with an unknown future, and variable levels of lawfulness and security.

May sat looking at Galveston, awaiting a response to his offer of working with the FBI.

"What do you think?" May asked, shuffling his papers back into the manila folder. "If you agree to work with us, I need you to leave immediately, contact Dr. Sloan's daughter, and let me know what you find."

Galveston leaned back in his chair as his horror subsided over the possible reconnection with his ex-love. "Would that be it?"

"That would be it. I figured you would want to know what Black Bear was up to. I'll give you time to think, but I need to know by the end of the day. The Bureau will be your funding source. I've arranged for money to be placed into your bank account to cover your costs. If you're successful we'll reward you handsomely. Your first payment could be in your account by day's end."

"Well, that's nice to know the government wants my help so badly," Galveston said looking at me.

"Just tell me by the end of the day. Only contact me at my personal number, nowhere else." May slid a number on a piece of paper to Galveston and then got up and started for the door. "You know the importance of this. Please don't force me to do something I'll regret."

With that shattering statement, May left the room, leaving us alone.

"You have no choice, do you?" I asked Galveston from my seat.

"No," he sighed. "He'll do whatever it takes to get me involved. He's sitting on too much information about me, and the stakes are too high for him to let us slide by."

"It's either take this deal, or spend time and money hiring a lawyer," I told him.

We sat for what seemed like hours, contemplating the information, but it had only been a few minutes.

"Well, I'm in if you're wondering," I said meekly. "I mean, what else do I have going on. I actually knew what I was getting into."

"You really don't have to. This is going to be tough, and it won't stop," Galveston warned me. "They'll want us to keep going."

"If nothing else, at least I'll get to meet someone who's actually fallen for you."

"Don't remind me. I think I'll go ahead and make the call."

I stood up, my knees feeling weak, and noticed that I was quietly excited.

"I think we're going to London," I said loudly, smacking my hands together. "I think Jane needs to go with us."

-Chapter 21-

The two black Suburbans bounced across the potholed roads as the city began to fade away, and the scenery began to change to a thick, forested jungle. The silver case from Colonel Espinosa sat next to a man in the back seat of the second vehicle.

The group finally arrived at their destination; a nondescript road that led into the jungle. They followed the curvy dirt road until a white gleaming building appeared ahead in the distance. The vehicles screeched to a stop in front of the building, and the men got out and dusted themselves off after the long, dirty drive. They were met at the front door by an aging gentleman with a white beard and white hair who stood sweating under the hot summer sun. The man with the silver case walked toward him, wiping the sweat from his brow.

"Is everything in place?" the man from the Suburban asked.

"Yes, yes," the older man stammered in English, with a heavy accent. "We have all the equipment in place. Is that it?" he asked, pointing to the case.

"Yes," the other man answered. "I want to watch how everything is set up, Dr. Patelo."

"Yes, Mr. Murray, of course. Please, let's go in," Patelo said nervously, and motioned for Murray to follow him through the steel door of the building.

Murray turned to his driver, "Secure the area and take up position on the road until you're called."

Two men got out, holding Heckler and Koch MP5 submachine guns and took up positions outside the front door, methodically checking their weapons.

Patelo looked more nervous and opened the door, gazing back at the man with the silver case.

"They're just here for a little extra insurance. I hope you'll keep this between us," Murray assured him.

Patelo nodded his head as they entered the building, leaving the two gunmen outside to bake in the excessive heat.

It was a metal building but air conditioned inside. The cool air fogged up Murray's sunglasses and he took them off and wiped the moisture from the lenses with his shirt sleeve, revealing dark eyes and a stony face.

The building was open inside and a few workers moved about, oblivious to the arrival of the men.

"Dr. Patelo, we have the clean room ready," said a squatty, slightly obese, balding man, wearing a white lab coat.

Dr. Patelo motioned for Murray to follow, and proceeded to the back of the building where a large, iron door stood. Dr. Patelo punched in a long set of code on a keypad next to the door, and placed his hand on a pad underneath the keypad. A red light over the door turned to green, and after a few audible beeps, the door clicked open and they both walked inside the dimly lit enclosure.

"As you can see, we have met all of your requirements and specifications," Dr. Patelo said pointing to the door. "Only Dr. Morales and myself have the key entry and finger ID."

Neither man spoke as they proceeded down stairs to a basement. They stopped at the bottom where it opened up to a large, brightly lit, white room, with four people moving about inside. They were fully covered in white coveralls from head to toe, with only their eyes exposed.

"This is our clean room and a sterile environment. I must ask you to be decontaminated if you would like to bring the case in."

Murray washed his hands and stood in a stall where jets of air blew over him and the case, while a vacuum sucked the air out of the stall.

"We can't take any chances with contamination. A micron of dust or foreign matter can have harmful effects on even the toughest circuits."

The men entered a small glass enclosure as the door closed behind them. A loud, sucking sound occurred as the pair felt a pressure change in the air.

After a few seconds the glass door opened to the main clean room, and the workers inside stopped and watched the pair come in.

"Put the case in that enclosure and we'll decontaminate," Dr. Patelo instructed Murray.

A worker positioned himself in front of a wall mounted box. Murray put the case through an opening, punched in a code on the case, and opened the latches. He pushed the case toward the worker who opened the lid and revealed the contents inside.

Everyone crowded around the window to the box, gawking at what was located there—two black, rectangular boxes, each the size of a deck of playing cards, secured and surrounded by black foam. The worker carefully took each one out and opened the black boxes separately, revealing a small, gray, metal square with a circuit board on top. The other box revealed an even smaller gray square attached to a mess of wires and a small LCD screen. Dr. Patelo strained to see through the glass past the other onlookers.

"Good, good. We are okay to remove them. Carefully take them out and place them on the table," he said to the worker.

One by one, the worker removed the items from the enclosure and placed them on a stainless steel table in the middle of the room, and was surrounded by a bank of laptop computers. Dr. Patelo moved to the table and looked at them closely.

"If you are satisfied, I will have the guard accompany you back out. We have a lot of work to do," Dr. Patelo said, turning to face Murray.

"I'm satisfied. We need these to be up to production capacity. I'll be back with my men in two days. I expect, and hope, you will be ready," Murray said, almost threateningly.

"Yes, yes. We will be ready and will report our results," the doctor said clearly.

"Good. We don't like to be disappointed."

Murray moved back to the airlock and began to remove his coveralls. Turning back to Dr. Patelo he said, "Remember, I'm not to be contacted for any reason. We'll see you in 48 hours." Murray disappeared up the stairs, leaving the workers in the room alone. Dr. Patelo sighed stressfully.

"You all know what to do. Let's get started. We have a long night ahead," Dr. Patelo instructed the workers.

Like a fire from a starting gun the workers began a flurry of activity, poring over the newly acquired objects.

Chapter 22

"Jane should go with us," I pleaded to Galveston.

"What for? If I don't know why," he answered, smiling.

"It's not like that," I said, squishing my face. "I think we need her around if we need to convince your ex-fiancé to help us. I mean, if she isn't ready to see you like you're not ready to see her, then we may need a woman's touch," I added, thinking quickly on my feet.

"You actually may have a point," he answered, supposedly seeing my point.

"Yeah, I'd hate to get there and not get to talk because she's still ticked at you. Sometimes a woman can just sense what another woman is going through."

Galveston thought for a second. "Okay, go tell her. It doesn't hurt for her to come," he said rather smugly.

I ran out of the room to tell Jane the news of our trip, proud in the fact that I had pulled one over on Galveston. I wouldn't allow myself to admit it, but I really wanted Jane to go for a variety of reasons, and very few of them business related. I had used my skill of negotiation to convince Galveston that Jane was an integral cog in our massive machine. Jane, of course, was ecstatic at the news and raced home to pack for the trip.

May had deposited the money he promised. I stared at it for a minute and hoped it would be enough to cover our activities. We were $20,000 richer, but I knew that amount wouldn't go far in today's economy. I would have to watch the money closely for us to come out a bit ahead.

We found ourselves jetting to London from San Diego via New York City the next day. Galveston was quiet the entire flight while I talked to Jane. I hung on her every word. "So what do you want to do with your life? Do you like pets? Do you have a boyfriend?" It was all the standard, small talk stuff.

Alex stayed behind at the office to man the phones and to make sure no one repossessed our new office furniture. He was working on finding our contact, Galveston's former love, and her possible whereabouts in the city of London.

We managed to leave within a day of acquiring our new mission, and I was amazed Galveston had agreed to this course of action.

We arrived at Heathrow airport early on a Thursday morning with a severe bout of jetlag. We decided to stay in one of the many extremely overpriced, tiny hotel rooms dotting the city of London. Being the gentlemen we were we got Jane her own room, adjacent to ours. Galveston and I, on the other hand, had to share a bed that was so small our feet hung off the end. It was a moment we both agreed to never talk about.

We began some much needed sleep to improve our faculties after the rigorous journey, but we minimized the time to just a few hours.

I awoke after an uncomfortable nap on our lumpy mattress and checked to see if any messages from Alex had arrived on our laptop about Elizabeth's address.

She was a public figure now and would be easy to find, or so we hoped. The problem was Galveston had no motivation to find her. He began making excuses why he shouldn't see her. He convinced Jane to be Elizabeth's first contact.

It was up to Galveston to make the big sell to find Dr. Sloan's daughter. We weren't even sure Elizabeth would have any pull in finding her, or why she would want to. I hoped guilt over dumping Galveston would set in, causing her to help us.

Alex eventually got us the information we had been waiting for. Elizabeth rarely worked from her office, preferring to work from her home. She lived in the Cheswick area of west London; an affluent, upscale enclave of upper class flats, restaurants, and hotels. She now spent most of her time doing research for the SIS instead of the clandestine work she had done in previous years.

We rented a car from our central London hotel, no small task or expense in London, and left around seven that night. Galveston was in charge of negotiating the London streets in our rental car. It proved to be much more difficult than back home, even with his previous knowledge from living and driving in England.

The lovely London scenery passed us by, and we enjoyed it as we traveled through the strange land. We left central London through Waterloo and over the Thames River. We drove past St. James Park, Belgravia, and Hammersmith, before arriving in Cheswick. We managed to find Elizabeth's flat without a problem. It occurred to me that a courtesy call to her would have been polite, but Galveston scoffed at the idea when I brought it up.

A plan had unfolded on the way to Elizabeth's home. Jane was going to go to the door, ask to see Elizabeth, and then let her know who was there to for her. On the drive Galveston had sat silent, but now as we sat in front of her flat, he seemed to have a moment of revelation.

"I'll go," he stated. "She's from my past and I'll face it. I won't like it, but I'll do it."

Jane and I nodded and said nothing, until we saw he had mustered the courage to open the door.

"Stay strong," I said half-jokingly.

He gave me a sigh, slowly got out of the car, and moped his way to the door. I noticed he had on his best pair of fancy slacks and Italian hand-made loafers.

He composed himself and checked his hair in the door window as he pushed the buzzer. Jane and I pushed our noses against the side glass of the car, like rubberneckers looking at the scene of an accident, or in this case, pending disaster.

"This could be a train wreck, or like watching a bad love story," I said to Jane, but neither of us could turn away.

Galveston stepped back from the door as it slowly opened and a beautiful brunette appeared, dressed in a short black dress and no shoes. Her face told the initial story–a look of utter surprise. A few quick, unknown words were exchanged between the two as Elizabeth held her look of shock and surprise, her hand now covering her mouth. She then did what none of us would have anticipated. She flung out her arms and wrapped Galveston in a big bear hug, tears rolling from her eyes.

Jane and I looked at each other with our mouths agape. She released him after a minute and motioned for him to come inside.

Galveston turned to us and raised his arms in an, "I don't know" pose, and followed her inside.

"Maybe it's some random woman who's just lonely," I said to Jane.

"I've heard the British are really nice," she replied. We sat staring at the door, and I tapped the glass.

"I think our friend has found a new lady. Let's get some fresh air. This may take a while."

Jane and I got out of the car and waited by the curb on a bench as the cars passed by on the street. I started in again on the small talk with Jane. We discussed the weather, spots we would like to see in London, and the English reputation for substandard dental work which we hadn't seen.

The night was cool and overcast, with a hint of rain, the seemingly most common of meteorological events in London. I offered my coat in a gentlemanly manner, she accepted, and I sat shivering in the cool breeze. Did we have a connection here? I watched her lips move seductively. I think she was talking about what she wanted to eat later, but I hardly knew. If I leaned over and kissed her, would she smack me or accept?

We were sitting under a lamp on a street in London, what better situation could exist for a chance at romance. "Just do it, you wuss," I thought. Now or never. I began to lean towards her and lightly grabbed her bare elbow under the coat I had laid over her shoulders. She stopped talking and looked at me, her eyes radiated in the light, her face soft and beautiful. She gave a small smile and moved toward me. I leaned in farther and closed my eyes, my face close to hers, waiting for the soft touch of her lips.

Wham! The door behind us slammed shut, and we were shocked out of our romantic stupor.

"Hey!" A voice boomed behind us. Jane looked back as I put my face in my hands.

"Hey, we're all set," Galveston yelled, loud enough to wake the dead. He came bounding down the steps toward us. "What are you two doing sitting there? Why aren't you in the car?" he continued on loudly.

"We weren't sure how long you would be," Jane answered.

"We thought you'd be a little longer," I said disgustedly. "You jerk," I thought, staring straight ahead.

"What happened?" Jane asked. "And why did she look so glad to see you?" We were expecting a little more shock, but Galveston looked guilty.

"I kind of left out something about Elizabeth. You see, she kind of thought I was missing and presumed dead." He said this as if it was no big deal.

"She thought you were dead?" I exclaimed turning to face him.

"Well, yeah. I was upset after she left, and I regret it. But you know, I didn't think I would see her again. I had a friend of mine send her a letter that I was missing and presumed dead during a diplomatic mission to South America," he said dismissively. "She was happy to see me alive. I did it when I was angry."

"How could you do that to someone?" I waved my arms at him.

"Take it easy. I smoothed it out. I told her I lived with a tribe of native Indians in the Amazon who rescued me before I was able to make it back to the U.S."

"Yes, that sounds realistic. That is really low. You didn't happen to tell her you lied to her, did you?"

"It never came up. I mean, come on, I got us another meeting with her to talk about our situation. She'll help us now."

I was shocked at Galveston's complete lack of caring about another person's feelings. I got up from the bench and pulled Jane up.

"Come on Jane. Let's go back to the hotel," I said, as we began walking back to the car.

"Wait, what's the problem?" Galveston said holding up his hands, standing on the sidewalk.

"You can find your own way back, but not with us," I yelled at him. "We'll see you when you figure out that what you did wasn't right. Now give me the keys."

Galveston stood with a look of disbelief and slowly handed me the keys. He plopped down on the bench we had been sitting on and watched us drive away into the darkness.

He sat quietly underneath the streetlamp with his elbows on his knees. Galveston sat there for ten minutes and finally got up and went back up the steps to Elizabeth's flat. He rang the bell and waited for her to arrive at the door.

She opened up the door, again surprised at who was standing in front of her. Galveston looked at her seriously.

"Can I come back in? I think I better tell you something."

-Chapter 23-

Dr. Patelo leaned over the table, his back beginning to strain because of the long hours of work. He peered through a small magnifying scope, illuminating a network of circuits on a television monitor next to him. A digital clock clicked down the time on the wall, revealing the time left before Murray would return. Fortunately they were ahead of schedule, but the sense of urgency continued to be evident.

He handled a highly sensitive voltmeter, placing the probes methodically from circuit to circuit and recording the values.

"Fantastic," he muttered to himself. "So simple. So elegant."

It was as if he was looking at a piece of fine art, noting the intricacies of the paint strokes on the canvas.

"Marco, bring over the plates."

A short man appeared behind him carrying two small, metal plates.

"Attach the clips to plate one." Marco followed the instruction carefully; attaching an alligator clip to the edge of one of the plates. Dr. Patelo took the other clip and attached it to a circuit on the board which ran to a small LED light. As soon as he attached it the light sprung to life.

"Excellent. That's the output point. Amazing." He looked at the monitor and stood up, extending his back in a stretch. "Print out the schematics. I need to make a call." Dr. Patelo left the table and picked up a nearby satellite cell phone. He pulled out a piece of paper from his pocket and dialed the number on it.

"It's Dr. Patelo, we have finished and have the schematics."

"Good. Are you sure it's in working order?" The voice on the other end was low, but he recognized it as Murray.

"Yes," Doctor Patelo answered nervously. "It's ready for the pickup."

"And you found no peculiarities in the design?" Murray asked.

"No, none." It was a strange question, Patelo thought. Was he supposed to have found problems? They told him it was a full working prototype. Dr. Patelo was only in charge of the reverse engineering of the device, not working out problems. In addition he was employed to develop and design a way to begin a crude production line to manufacture the device. Finding problems in the design was something he had no time for. It worked, and that to him was all that mattered. He wasn't getting paid to make it better.

"Send us the schematics now. When we have received them one of my men will retrieve the case within the hour. Have all your people leave immediately. Dr. Morales is awaiting your plans. You are to leave alone and not on the bus with the others. Do you understand?"

"Uh, yes. I understand, and I will send the plans now."

"Good work, doctor. Everyone can go. Thank you for your work," Murray responded, hanging up on Dr. Patelo

The words were unsettling, and Patelo could sense something ominous in Murray's voice. He never had trusted him, but when this opportunity had come along he couldn't pass it up. The money was more in two days than he could have made in six months of work on his own. He might now be able to pursue the life he had always dreamed of and work on his own interests instead of the interests of others.

Patelo was the only one, besides Dr. Morales, that knew the true nature of what they were working on, but his growing unease was rising over the whole operation. Something was not right, and he felt these men would not be pleased with disappointment, whoever they were.

The workers from the lab left quickly at Dr. Patelo's urging, and in an instant they were gone, leaving him alone in the clean room. He walked over to a computer and punched in an email address, but then curiously he stopped and grew scared. Who did these men work for? Had he been so blinded by money that it didn't occur to him that these plans could be used for unscrupulous means?

"I need a bargaining chip," he thought. Maybe it was time to alert the authorities, or better yet, the media. The options swirled in his head. For the time being some slight changes in the plans would have to do.

He quickly opened up the schematics on the computer screen and looked them over carefully. Dr. Patelo decided one change would be enough to cause a glitch, but not impair the design completely. He used the cursor on the design program to simply move one circuit's connection to another transistor, alternating the circuits. They showed up on the schematic as simple lines connecting one electrical area to another. This would effectively allow the device to work, but with a problem. It would burn out that particular circuit if the voltage became too high.

It would take time for someone to run through the schematics and pinpoint the problem, but it could easily be done. He needed to develop another problem quickly. He decided on removing the last piece of the puzzle he had found, the electrical output circuit, the piece that allowed power to flow from the device. It wouldn't make the device inoperable, but it would prove much more difficult to figure out, causing the power output to be half of what it should be. Plus it would give him the option of having the fix, quickly and easily.

Dr. Patelo walked over to the case and removed the two devices. Using needle nose pliers he removed the output circuit carefully and rerouted the circuits. It was a move anyone with electrical knowledge could perform, but to figure out what he had done would prove much more difficult. He placed one of the small circuit connectors in his pocket and crushed the other. A vital piece of the original design sat safely in his pocket.

This was his power play, his bargaining chip if things went bad. Originally it was supposed to be a cut and dry job, but when men with guns began to show up, his feelings had changed. He began to think about what he had gotten himself into. He went back to the computer, saved the schematic design, and sent it over a secure connection to his contact. A "transmission successful" message appeared as he finished the upload of the file.

After finishing he logged on to his bank account and watched the screen for a few minutes, until finally he saw what he wanted to see—a jump in his account balance by $50,000. He smiled as he soaked in the number.

Outside, the workers from the facility were boarding a rundown bus. They piled in and exchanged pleasantries, not fully aware of what they had been working on. After the bus was full and the facility was empty the bus fired up and drove off down the dusty road, leaving Dr. Patelo behind, alone. A lone, white car was all that was left in the front of the facility.

Back down in the lab Dr. Patelo hurriedly readied the case; the feeling of unease continuing to gnaw at him. His conscience began to weigh on him, but he had his security and felt it in his coat pocket. What was this going to be used for, and what part had he played?

A loud knock came from the door behind him, and a man in all black was standing at the glass door, pointing at the case. Dr. Patelo grabbed the silver case after closing it, walked through the airlock, and handed the case to the man. The man took the case without speaking and disappeared back up the stairs.

Dr. Patelo switched off the lights after a few minutes, darkening the equipment inside and walked up the stairs. The place was deserted and ghostly, not a soul about.

"I need a smoke," he thought to himself. He walked through the building and switched off the lights. He swung open the front door and tried to adjust his eyes to the inky darkness.

Dr. Patelo had gone two straight days with little to no sleep and was ready to return home. After closing the door he reached in his coat pocket and pulled out a hard pack of cigarettes. He fumbled one out of the carton and lit it, puffing the smoke into his lungs. He checked his pocket again and felt the circuit between his fingers.

Suddenly the cigarette dropped out of his mouth to the ground, and a split second later a stifled bang let out, shattering the silence. His body shuttered and slowly crumpled to the ground. His hand fell from his pocket, and his lifeless eyes stared toward the starry night sky. Blood began to pool around the back of his head.

The night sky was then filled with an earth shattering blow. Subsequent flashes of fiery red threw fingers of extreme heat out from the building as it erupted in a cataclysmic explosion. The explosion punched smoke into the sky, leaving behind only a mass of burning, twisted steel and aluminum. The deafening roar awakened sleeping birds from their nesting spots in the surrounding forest, causing them to escape from the inferno and the spot where the white building once stood.

Chapter 24

I awoke early the next morning in our cramped London hotel room. I had walked Jane to her door the previous night and only received a hug, but I was spinning even after that. It seems we at least made a connection. Galveston had never returned to the room that night, and like a nervous wife I called the front desk for messages. No one had called.

I stood with a toothbrush dangling from my mouth as the hotel door swung open and Galveston strolled in, primped and fresh.

"Where have you been?" I muttered with toothpaste foam covering my mouth.

"Nowhere, Mom," Galveston replied as he sat on the bed and kicked off his shoes.

"Why didn't you come back here?" I asked him like a nervous spouse.

"Well, you kind of told me I couldn't, so I took that as I shouldn't." He pushed himself back on the bed and clicked on the TV. A newscaster was spilling out the news. "I love the British media, they have so much more spunk than those weenies back home." He pushed the pillow behind his head, getting comfortable.

"What's the deal? You've already created a mess, now what?"

"Relax. You would be happy to know I have smoothed everything out."

I took this as yet another fib and felt my anger rising.

"How have things smoothed out? We don't have time for you to play these head games with your little friend. What, did you decide to call her and tell her you had a terminal disease?"

"You know, that isn't a bad idea, but no, I didn't tell her that."

"So you talked to her again?"

"If it makes you happy, yes, through most of the night and into the morning. I spent the night with her."

"You slept with her?" I exclaimed loudly, shocked and rather impressed.

"Technically, no, but I slept beside her in another room on the couch. It was too late and she let me stay." He pulled his gaze away from the TV and looked at me. "Look, I told her everything, and all of it the truth. I apologized, and I got out how much it hurt when she left. It was not a proud moment for me." He turned back to the TV. "I told her why we were here, what we needed, and why I needed her help. There is one problem though."

"And what would that be?" I asked.

"I think I've fallen for her again. I'm still crazy about her. She's great. Funny, smart, and that body, oh, that body," he said, continuing to watch the TV. "We're meeting with her this afternoon. She thinks she can get the information we need by then."

"Wait, wait. You've fallen for her? How could you fall for her in one night?"

"It all came flooding back. She's got this crazy stranglehold on me. No one has come close since. I know it's crazy to hear coming from such a rock solid guy like myself, but man, that body– oh, that body."

"Enough about her body. I'm sure it's lovely."

"Oh, you don't understand. She can do this thing with her legs and..." Galveston started.

"Okay, that's quite enough," I stopped him while he laughed at me. "Now what about this meeting?"

"These are terrible." He was now trying to eat stale French fries, or chips as they're called in England, sitting on the bedside table. He scrunched his face as he did.

"Hey, focus. The meeting?"

"Four o'clock, London time. We'll meet her in a coffee shop by her office. I think she's into me. This time it will be different."

"I have to get some air." I walked to the door and began to go out.

"Hey!" Galveston yelled at me. "You and Jane can go with us. We'll double date."

I muttered under my breath, left the room, and closed the door behind me. The problem was I forgot my pants, and I was now standing in the hall in only my boxer shorts. I walked back in and the pants came hurling toward me.

"Thanks," was all I could grumble.

I was relieved, not about my pants, but that Galveston had redeemed himself. I couldn't show that I was actually proud of him. That was rule 182.

The rest of the day we parted ways. Galveston holed himself up in the hotel room watching quirky, poorly understood British comedies. I followed Jane like a lapdog, checking the sights. We stopped by Piccadilly Square, Big Ben, and the British National Museum. The whole time I hung on her every word. The business we were supposed to be engaged in floated to the back of my mind. Instead, I thought of nothing more than this lovely lady.

We arrived back at our hotel around three o'clock. I left Jane at her door and found Galveston sprawled on the bed with food cartons scattered about and a bag of sweets balanced on his chest wearing nothing but his underwear.

"This is a sight I hope I can forget. I think I've burned my retinas."

"Hey, you know you're seeing nothing but an Adonis of manhood." He stuffed more food in his mouth. "Good day with Jane?"

"Yes. Very good. Very, very good."

"You know you're her boss. There's no fraternizing in our company."

"Well then, I quit." I set myself on a chair by the bed and noticed a plump man on TV making a joke that only an interpreter would understand. We wasted away the next half an hour in our room until our big meeting with Elizabeth.

The hope was that Elizabeth could get to Dr. Sloan's daughter, Margaret. We were running out of time, and we needed to be out of London quickly.

We met Elizabeth in a small coffee shop near the SIS headquarters at Vauxhall Cross while Jane excused herself to do some important shopping.

Galveston was correct in his description of Elizabeth. She did have a fantastic body and was very sharp. Years of training and work in MI6 had paid off. She was obviously good at what she did and understood the importance of what we were doing.

Elizabeth spoke with an eloquent English accent. She could talk about cleaning gunk out of her ears and still make it sound elegant. After the necessary introductions were made, Elizabeth, almost immediately, went into her quick report.

"Margaret has the assumed name of Gabriel Smit. She lives alone near the town of Tadley in the county of Hampshire. She is divorced, no children, and works at a local flower shop." Galveston looked dreamily at Elizabeth, so I assumed I would have to take the lead on questioning her.

"Why is she in hiding?" I questioned seriously, while Galveston only smiled and sighed.

"I'm not sure, something about her ex-husband's ties to the Russian mafia. Great Britain doesn't have a formal, central government controlled program like the United States. Witness protection in the UK is controlled by the regional police forces so any information is difficult to obtain."

"When was the last time she saw her father?" I asked.

"It's been at least five years. There is a report that she went against the wishes of the police and had a secret phone location where she would speak to him."

I looked at Galveston who continued to be in a stupor. I snapped my fingers in front of his face, snapping him from his euphoria. A smile crossed Elizabeth's face.

"It appears you gentlemen have impeccable timing. I learned that she fears for her safety. If someone else is trying to get to her it will only take a good government contact to find out where she is, just as you have done with me. I'll take you to her, but we have to be truthful with her. Tell her all you know and the danger her father is in."

"I agree," I said, peering at Galveston with a judging stare.

"What?" he said loudly. "Uh, yeah, me too."

Elizabeth smiled again. "Well gentlemen, let's get started."

Chapter 25

We drove outside the city limits of London to Tadley, a quaint, picturesque area of the country with rolling green hills and neatly arranged cottages. I secretly wished I could live in a location like this–possibly with Jane.

Margaret Sloan's house was off the main thoroughfare and down a small, winding dirt road. A small cottage came into our view, decorated with an array of flowers and planters, along with a small vegetable garden on the side of the house. A bike was parked in the front, outside of a white fence. The place was like something out of a Jane Austen novel.

Elizabeth reached into the glove box of the car and pulled out a Sig Saur 9 mm handgun and hid it in her coat. This was indeed turning exciting. Elizabeth offered another handgun to Galveston, which he accepted, using his pants pocket as a holster. I was offered no such protection, but I wanted no part of these devices.

Elizabeth knocked on the door, and it opened slightly. She pushed the bottom of the door with her foot, revealing what was once a neatly arranged cottage. Elizabeth paused and looked back at Galveston. He was already in a crouched position with his gun pulled out and resting on his thigh.

"Margaret? Margaret, this is the police," Elizabeth called out loudly, "from the magistrate. We need to talk to you." She awaited a response and upon hearing no answer began to enter through the door.

Galveston motioned for me to get behind him. Obviously something was amiss. I attempted to follow, but he and Elizabeth had already disappeared through the door. I hurried through and could now see in the house. It was a mess. Tables were overturned, books and papers were everywhere, a smashed TV laid on the floor, and the walls were curiously pitted with large holes.

Elizabeth and Galveston both sensed the urgency of the situation and had their guns up in a shooting stance, quietly scanning the room. I watched Galveston as a tense look crossed his face, and I cowered behind him.

Elizabeth began to slowly move through the room and into the hall, softly saying Margaret's name and the words, "orange leopard". This was the safe word to alert Margaret that we were friendly.

We moved farther through the house. Each room was a mess and shattered objects littered the floor. Elizabeth continued to methodically check all corners, nooks, and crannies. She motioned for Galveston to check the small kitchen as I stayed in the main living area near the front door, unsure of what to do.

Things had taken a bad turn from what I could tell. I heard Elizabeth down the hall saying Margaret's name again followed by the words "orange leopard".

"That's a funny word," I said to myself out loud. "Orange leopard. Come here orange leopard. I'll take an orange leopard," I nervously joked to myself, playing as if I wanted a drink with that name.

All of a sudden, I heard three knocks from behind a wall, near a wood fireplace. I yelled to Galveston and Elizabeth who responded quickly, racing toward me. We all gathered near the fireplace, trying to determine where the knocks came from.

"Margaret? Orange leopard, Margaret," Elizabeth said to the wall.

I stifled an insensitive chuckle because it was rather odd to be saying these words to the wall. I was startled, however, when an almost invisible portion of the wooden wall began to move and slid up like magic, revealing a small hole, about four feet square.

We immediately heard someone repeating back the words "orange leopard" in a shallow, breathless voice. A hand came jutting out of the hole in the wall.

"Margaret," Elizabeth said as she reached for the hand.

A head began to appear followed by the torso of a woman in her forties. She inched her way out of the hole and was covered in dust. She was clearly distraught and kept repeating the safe words until her body was entirely on the ground. Elizabeth pulled her up and hugged her while Galveston left to continue his examination of the home.

Elizabeth pushed back the hair from over Margaret's eyes. She had never met the woman before, but held her as if she was a mother holding a child.

"Margaret, are you okay?"

"I, I think so. It was so quick. I barely had time," she stammered.

"What happened?" Elizabeth asked soothingly, rubbing her back.

"I, I've been in there since yesterday. I wasn't sure if they were coming back. I didn't have my phone and the electricity was cut. I, I..." She continued to stammer, having difficulty getting out the words.

Elizabeth moved her over to the couch as I cleared a path. Galveston continued to be on edge and went out the front door to check the outside again.

"Margaret, who was here?" Elizabeth asked softly while holding her hand.

"I don't know. I got home from the shop and made dinner. The power went out and I tried the phone, but it was dead. It was then that I saw headlights out front. I panicked and crawled into the safe room. There were loud bangs and footsteps, and they just began tearing things apart. They were ramming holes in the wall and making so much noise, but no one spoke. I thought for sure they would find me."

"They weren't subtle," I added, putting my fist in one of the holes in the wall.

"Roger, please get her some water from the tap," Elizabeth instructed me.

I rushed over to the kitchen and filled up a large glass with water and offered it to her. She gulped it as Galveston came back into the room.

"The outside is clear. I found some tire tracks. Looks like two large vehicles, probably a couple of SUVs." He holstered his gun in his pocket and kept his eyes trained on the windows.

"I need to make a call. Just stay with her, Roger."

Elizabeth immediately began to dial her phone.

"How you doin'?" I asked grabbing her, as if I didn't know.

"Okay I guess, now. You two are American. Why are you here?"

"We'll get to that in time," I told her, "right now just relax. We'll make sure you're safe." I wasn't sure if we really could make her safe, but figured that was what she needed to hear.

Elizabeth returned from her call.

"They'll have you evacuated within the hour," she said.

Margaret looked worn out. She had been through so much.

Galveston walked slowly around the room, his hand poised over the gun in his pocket. He looked toward Elizabeth. "This wasn't done by the mafia. This was done by a professional, organized team."

"I know," Elizabeth answered. "I think you boys better ask your questions." She turned and looked the shaken woman in her eyes. "Margaret, you need to do something for me. These men were never here, just me, okay? You'll understand why." She said this seriously and without flinching.

Galveston picked up the lead. "Margaret, your father is missing, and that's why we're here. We're currently helping the FBI locate him, but they wanted us to find you first. We have information that he sent you something, something that may help us in finding him."

"I don't know what you're talking about. I haven't talked to my father in years."

Elizabeth cut in. "We know you have a number you've been using to contact him and that's alright, but we must know what he sent you."

Margaret sighed. "Yes, he did send something a week ago, and I haven't heard from him since." She unzipped the couch cushion and pulled out about five pages of paper. "He said to keep it hidden, so I did. I didn't know what to make of it at the time."

"Can I see it?" Galveston asked.

Margaret handed over the papers. The first page was a message and the rest were complicated drawings of a design none of us understood. Galveston perused the first page and read it to himself.

My dearest Margaret,

I am glad you are safe and well. I wish I could be there to see you. I'm sending you something very prized to me and my research. I ask you to keep it very safe and hidden. Things have been happening here in the last week which have made me nervous. I'm not sure, but I think someone has been following me and been in my home. Strange people have been asking about my research. I'm close to realizing a dream, an item that could change how we consume energy as human beings. I plan to release my findings at a conference in Memphis in two days. Once it is out I should be safe. I am sending you the original design. I know you can keep it safe. I'll contact you after Memphis to let you know how it went or you can call me. I think the Memphis area code is 272. I'll talk more about it later. I can't wait to see the Memphis Parkland. I love you and I will talk to you soon.

Love, Dad

Galveston handed the letter to me and I passed it to Elizabeth. We looked it over carefully.

"He hasn't sent anything else?" Galveston wondered aloud, looking at the pages of drawings.

"No, that was it. What happened to him? What was he working on?" The worry was clearly etched on her face.

"He went missing before the Memphis conference, and his lab has been destroyed. We're not sure by whom. We believe your father has somehow developed a battery that is so revolutionary that it would probably be the greatest invention of the 21st century." Her mouth went open after Galveston said these words.

"But he's just a materials engineer," she mumbled.

"Well, he may be an engineer that has stumbled on the way to bring energy independence to the world."

The words clearly struck her hard, and she seemed to understand the implications. She was smart and knew what lengths people or governments would go for such a device.

"We're running out of time," Elizabeth said looking at her watch.

"Margaret, we need to take these with us and analyze them," Galveston told her.

"I guess, but how will I know about my father?"

"Elizabeth will keep you informed. The first thing is your safety. Let us do the rest." Galveston said this forcefully, noting the time again.

"Yes, yes, anything to find my father safe. Promise me that."

"I promise," but it was a promise Galveston wasn't sure he could keep.

"You two need to go. Go out the back and head up the road about a kilometer. I'll flash my lights when I'm nearing you. Now go," Elizabeth instructed, pushing us toward the door. "Margaret, these men were never here, for your father's sake."

"Alright," she answered, still in a state of shock at the continually stressful situation.

Galveston and I took the pages and raced out the back door to a wooded area behind the house. We followed the road away from the cottage, keeping out of sight behind the tree line.

"Exactly how far is a kilometer?" I asked him as we raced behind the trees.

"Good question. I know it's less than a mile. I guess we'll keep moving until we can't breathe anymore—which should be about another twenty feet," he responded, already gasping for air.

We noticed a stream of car headlights moving down the road at a high rate of speed as we continued behind the tree line. We stopped and watched them race past, staying concealed all the while behind the thick branches. We had made it out just in time.

-Chapter 26-

Elizabeth picked us up on the edge of the road after thirty minutes of waiting in an area of itchy brush. Elizabeth arranged for Margaret to be moved to a safe house on the outskirts of London. We hoped Margaret would understand the explicit need to keep our visit quiet because we needed to quickly get out of the country.

I was silent during the drive back to our hotel and the expansive city lights of London. I digested what we had just encountered while Galveston and Elizabeth chattered incessantly the entire way. Elizabeth had tasted the thrill of the hunt again—and clearly liked it.

Galveston and I woke early the next morning. I had slept in my clothes, falling asleep as soon as my head hit the pillow. We had a morning flight back to San Diego via New York City, and I was in charge of informing Jane of our plans. I went to her door and knocked softly, still in my clothes from the previous day. She answered wearing nothing but a huge, terry cloth robe that covered every inch of her body.

"Rough night?" she asked, noticing my previously used attire.

"You don't want to know," I answered, still half-asleep.

I informed her of our itinerary and our flight plans. She too was half-asleep with her eyes half-closed and looking lovely as ever. We were a weary crew, at least Jane and me. Galveston proceeded to jump off the walls, however, as hyper as a six-year-old. Obviously he must have had a good night.

We gathered our belongings and took a shuttle to Heathrow. I purposefully didn't ask questions; I didn't even want to contemplate the next step. I was already too tired.

There hadn't been a mention of Elizabeth since we had awakened. I applauded Galveston's fortitude, until I saw him standing at the gate with a tall brunette. It was Elizabeth, and she had a small overnight bag filled with guns and daggers and nunchucks, I'm sure.

She had spoken directly to the Chief of MI6 the night before and received a special clearance to work this case. I realized I would now be fielding many more love questions and body comments from Galveston. I was not relishing that part.

Elizabeth and Galveston were both working their cell phones before the flight. Elizabeth was trying to ascertain who Margaret's unwelcome visitors were while Galveston spoke to Alex back in San Diego. I was sure Alex was sunning himself on his large backyard patio near the beach.

On the flight Galveston and I were debriefed–my first. Jane sat next to me, oblivious to our discussions, watching and listening on headphones to a bad, in-flight, teeny bopper movie.

"I've always wanted to be debriefed," I said to Galveston.

"I was already debriefed last night," Galveston said, smirking.

"Oh, that's just sick," I replied reaching for an in-flight magazine—and the barf bag.

I was used to his sophomoric humor, but I prayed he was kidding and tried to avoid the visual. Elizabeth slid us a few papers from her seat, not hearing our witty repertoire.

"I have the information on our infiltrators," she said in her eloquent British accent. "Our agent in Intel tracked the airports, train stations, and car rentals in the surrounding area around the time of the break-in. A line worker at South Hampton airfield loaded a Dessault Falcon jet at about 9:40 P.M. yesterday evening with nine men. The plane was to arrive in Paris at Charles De Gaulle Airport. Apparently the plane diverted to the Canary Islands before taking off again for Paris. I'm still waiting on the customs information from the Canaries. The plane is registered to a private contractor, Le Ciel Aviation, out of Paris."

Galveston and I were beginning to nod off from this wealth of information, but Elizabeth continued.

"The company that hired the plane is out of Belgium, called Montenegro Exploration Limited. That's it, that's all I have."

I continued to nod off, but Galveston looked odd and stared straight ahead, with surprise on his face.

"What was that name again? The ones who hired them?" he asked Elizabeth.

Elizabeth ran her hand down the paper. "Montenegro Exploration Limited. Why? We checked them out. It's a North Sea oil exploration company."

Galveston shook his head in disbelief.

"What?" Elizabeth stared at him.

"It's a front, it doesn't exist."

"What do you mean it doesn't exist? And a front for what?"

"It's a front for Black Bear Security."

Elizabeth's eyes grew cold and even the hairs on my neck began to shiver.

"For Black Bear?" she asked.

"The same Black Bear you worked for?" I inquired.

"No, a different Black Bear," Galveston replied bitingly. "Yes, the same Black Bear. It's the front company for their European covert operations. Black Bear Security has front organizations to hide their more unscrupulous activities. It's actually a real company that's involved in oil exploration, but they use its freedom of movement and funds to run covert operations in Europe, Africa, and the Middle East. What better way to move people and supplies around the world than looking for oil," Galveston explained to Elizabeth and me.

"But why the Canaries?" Elizabeth asked.

"I'm sure they offloaded there and took another flight or a boat, who knows, but we're dealing with mercenaries here, from Black Bear."

We all sat dumbfounded at the earth shattering news. How could a private organization have such a sophisticated system?

Galveston continued. "This confirms they're behind Dr. Sloan's disappearance. If that's the case, we're in for a heap of trouble. Alex said the design we sent was completely plausible. The battery could easily be developed from those drawings. It seems they will go to any lengths to get those plans."

"But why did they leave so soon?" I asked.

"I don't know, but guys like this don't leave until they meet their objective. Someone sent them to find those plans or Margaret. I think we need to make a little stop in Memphis," Galveston told us.

"What could we possibly find in Memphis?" I asked.

"That's where we'll find Dr. Sloan."

Chapter 27

Elizabeth and I didn't press the issue for the rest of the flight, and instead got some well deserved sleep. Galveston stayed awake and busily scribbled notes. He would let us know why he thought Dr. Sloan was still in Memphis in due time.

Jane had finished her movie, and I informed her of our diversion when we arrived in New York. Despite her protest she would return to San Diego alone and check-in with Alex the following day at our office.

We got off the plane at Kennedy International in New York and caught the earliest flight to Memphis. I decided to accompany Jane to her connecting flight to San Diego and walked her slowly to the gate. We found a few empty chairs away from the crowds and began to talk about life and our visit to London.

"Thanks for letting me go with you two. It was, uh, interesting," she started.

"Yeah, I know, about as interesting as watching paint dry," I retorted.

"Well, I didn't have anything else going on. Just wait until you see my time card." We both laughed. She had made this trip truly special for me, even if I didn't get to spend as much time with her as I wanted.

"Take a break when you get back. I'm sure Alex is out surfing or breaking into a bank's computer for fun."

"Yeah, I'll check on him," she replied. "You know, I wanted to talk to you about what almost happened the other night." Her words were cut off by the announcement for her flight.

"Yeah. Me too." I didn't know what else to say. We were able to talk like best friends, albeit with a high amount of sexual tension thrown in. Our connection was just comfortable and comforting.

"I better get on before they leave without me." She stood up and I followed. "I had a great time—if you can believe it. I hope you guys find what you're looking for. I'll see you in a few days?" she asked hopefully.

"If all goes well sooner than that. I had a great time too. Have a safe flight." I always hated this salutation. Like a passenger has any bearing on how a flight goes. Are they able to crawl in the cockpit to help the pilots out or something?

She reached out and gave me a long hug. I smelled her hair and felt her body pressed against mine in a long embrace. I considered it to be a piece of heaven.

"Bye, Roger, see you soon." She walked away and turned back, giving me a slight wave of her hand. I garnered the strength to wave back.

I watched her get a place in line and she checked her ticket, ready to hand it over to the gate agent. But then she whirled around and headed back to me, a serious look in her eyes.

"Did you forget something?" I had barely gotten the words out of my mouth when she planted a warm, long kiss on my lips while holding me tightly. My head swirled as she slowly pulled back and looked into my eyes.

"I'll see you soon," she said softly, and turned back to get on the plane.

I stood smiling, my body energized, but my legs felt like two gigantic pieces of licorice. I didn't dare move from that spot and watched her disappear down the jetway, giving me one last minute wave. I stood in the same position for what seemed like hours, reliving the moment in my mind with a goofy grin plastered on my face. Suddenly I felt a slap on my back from Galveston that returned me to reality.

"You got Jane off okay?" he asked.

"I'll say," I replied, still gawking at the jetway.

"Huh?" He said, looking confused. "Hey, we got a flight. The four o'clock to Memphis. Hello. Hellooo," he said waving a hand in front of my face. I didn't dare tell him what had happened. I didn't feel like getting a ribbing for the next few days.

"Yeah, I heard you. Four o'clock to Memphis, right." I broke out of my trance and followed him over to Elizabeth. She had set up camp in a chair overlooking the tarmac.

"So I know you guys are wondering why we're going to Memphis," Galveston said to Elizabeth and me, practically reading my mind.

"I was certainly wondering why," I said.

"There was something odd in Dr. Sloan's message to his daughter, and I don't think she picked up on it." He began to pull out the papers with the messages. "This is the problem I'm having. Why would an organization like Black Bear spend the money, the time, or the risk to break into Margaret's house? Why go to all the trouble if they've kidnapped Dr. Sloan?"

"Maybe he's refusing to talk to them," I interjected.

"No, they would get him to talk. We're not dealing with people that believe in waiting. These guys play hardball. They would stop at nothing to get the information."

Elizabeth pecked away at her laptop. "What if they have Dr. Sloan and he can't reproduce the battery without these plans? It is a complex device."

"But it really isn't that complex." Galveston said to her. "Alex said he could put it together with the right supplies in under four hours. I think the facts are this: they don't have the final plans, they don't have Dr. Sloan, and I think they knew Margaret had the final design."

"Then why Memphis? How do we know that he didn't just drive off somewhere when he got off the plane? Maybe he went home." I threw out all the possibilities I could think of.

"I believe he's in Memphis from the message he sent to Margaret." Galveston showed us the message and ran his finger down the page until he found the sentence he wanted. "This line, 'I can't wait to see the Memphis Parkland'. I don't think it's a typo. I think he was trying to tell her where he would be. Elizabeth, do a search on the Memphis Parkland."

Elizabeth began typing in the words on her laptop. "Memphis parks and recreation, Parkland Hotel, parks in Memphis," she read aloud.

"That's it. The Parkland Hotel. Open that one."

"Parkland Hotel, downtown Memphis, yes, there it is," Elizabeth announced.

"Now check what the area code for Memphis is," Galveston instructed.

Elizabeth searched for the answer. "901," she replied after finding it.

Galveston ran his finger over the paper again and began reading aloud. "'Or you can call me, I think the Memphis area code is 272'. I think that's where Dr. Sloan is at. The Parkland Hotel, room 272, Memphis."

I sat amazed. I couldn't believe it could be that easy.

"I think you may have something here. It still seems like a long shot, but plausible," Elizabeth said proudly.

"Why don't we call him then, see if he's there. It would save us time," I asked, thinking the sooner I got back to San Diego and Jane, the better.

"No way," Galveston sneered, "that's all we need; he gets spooked and then we have to find him all over again. We need to be in that hotel and at his door, that's the only way. I don't know why he would wait it out, but I have a feeling he doesn't know who he's dealing with. And I don't know how long he might stay there."

We had our plan, but calling it a long shot was an understatement. Surely Galveston wasn't this smart.

Chapter 28

We arrived in Memphis, having passed the time on the plane trading those tiny liquor bottles between us.

We traveled Interstate 240 to the city center and found the Parkland Hotel, a large glass tower with a large interior atrium. I wouldn't have minded being there for a few weeks either–preferably with Jane.

The elevator took us to the second floor as Galveston and Elizabeth plotted intricate ways to get Dr. Sloan to answer the door. They tossed out ideas such as stealing uniforms and posing as the housekeeping staff, posing as the Memphis police, or making the fire alarms go off. I proposed an even zanier idea. They would stay out of sight, and I would knock on the door.

"It might just work," Galveston conceded.

We didn't know what we would tell Dr. Sloan, if indeed he was there.

Luckily the halls were empty as we stepped off the elevator, and we followed the placards to room 272. I motioned for Galveston and Elizabeth to stop and then walked to the door and knocked.

I heard rustling inside followed by the unlocking of the door. It cracked opened and there stood a short, balding man with a gray beard, wearing glasses.

"Can I help you?" he asked nervously, but politely. I hadn't even thought of finding out what Dr. Sloan looked like, but this man sure looked like a professor and similar to the older men I had spent loathing the last year of my academic career.

"Hello, sir. Are you Dr. Sloan from Dartmouth University?" He appeared uneasy at the question, but a covert specialist he was not.

"Why, yes. I'm Dr. Sloan."

"Nice to meet you, sir. I know your daughter, Margaret. My colleagues and I just came from seeing her yesterday, and she gave us this."

I handed him the message he had sent her.

He looked at it quickly, and I could tell he was not pleased. He began to inch his feet backward with one hand still on the door.

"How did you get this?" he demanded angrily holding up the piece of paper, his eyes burning from behind his glasses.

I was taken aback from his reaction, figuring he would have been grateful for the information. I decided to choose my words wisely, but couldn't find any.

"Who are you and why won't you people leave me alone?" he demanded.

I turned around, wondering if there were others standing behind me.

"You people? Uh, Dr. Sloan, we have been looking for you."

That was obviously the statement the good doctor had not wanted to hear because he began to slam the door. Luckily, Galveston was standing out of sight, and as the door began to close he jumped in front and stopped its closure by jamming his foot against the door jamb. In a flash Galveston kicked the door open with his foot, Chuck Norris style, as Dr. Sloan raced into the bathroom.

"That went rather well, I think," Galveston said, turning to me.

"Yes, very smoothly," I answered.

"Dr. Sloan, we're working for the FBI, but we aren't federal agents. We work privately. They hired us to find you. We know about what you've invented, and we're here to protect you. We've already made Margaret safe, and she wanted us to make sure you were safe." There was no reply to this statement. "We need to know who is after you. Someone already tried to hurt Margaret, and we stopped them. We don't want the same to happen to you. If you come out, I promise we'll get her on the phone to talk to you directly."

Elizabeth pulled out a folded envelope of paper and began to dial on her cell phone.

"Just give him this," she said to Galveston. He looked at it and slid it under the door.

Moments passed until we heard the ripping of paper as the doctor opened the envelope. Elizabeth had thought ahead for such a moment. It was a letter from Margaret, and it explained who we were and why he needed to help us. The door slowly opened, and Dr. Sloan crept out with tears in his eyes.

"She's not hurt, right?" he asked distraughtly.

"No, she's fine, just a little shaken. They took her to a safer place," Galveston answered.

Dr. Sloan went to the bed, sat at the edge, and wiped his eyes with his hand.

"She's all I've got, and I never get to see her. I can't believe I've gotten her involved in this."

Elizabeth brought the phone over.

"Here she is. She's doing well." She handed him the phone and he reached for it, shaking.

"Margaret?" he asked sheepishly, and immediately he showed signs of relief when she answered.

We moved to the other side of the room like a herd of cattle, giving him some room to talk. The room was large and unusually immaculate; unexpectedly tidy for someone living out of a hotel room and suitcase. The only thing out of place was an array of electronic equipment, and a small black box that sat on a corner table.

As he continued his conversation we quietly discussed our next move of getting him out quickly. We needed him safe until we had some answers. At least the professor had checked into the hotel under an assumed name. It was a smart move for someone without experience in such matters. Dr. Sloan finished on the phone and gave it back to Elizabeth.

"I'm sorry. I'm just afraid of what to believe," he said.

"It's understandable. I'm just glad you didn't try to club us or something," Galveston joked, lightening the mood.

"A few more minutes and I would have. Margaret explained how you all put her at ease, and I thank you. Now what the heck is going on?"

"We were hoping you could tell us," I said.

"First, I'm impressed you found me from my message. I was hoping Margaret would figure it out and call me, but I guess its best that she didn't."

"Yeah, that's true. We're just glad we got to you first," Galveston told him.

"Do you know who is after me?"

"We have a good idea who it is, and they're not trying to find you to give you an award. They definitely want what you have."

The words seemed to put Dr. Sloan at ease. He knew now that his instinct was right and things weren't as they appeared. His fight or flight response was correct, and his choice of flight was the most appropriate of decisions.

"What tipped you off to a problem?" Galveston asked as he sat down across from the professor.

"As you probably know from my message, I had strange men making inquiries into my work."

"How could anyone have found out what you were working on?" I asked.

"It must have been about a year ago. I was approached by a group of specialists that were interested in the current research I was doing. I was developing and testing materials that could reduce the ionization potential between a distinct subset of materials. Thereby increasing the capacitance and reducing the electrical loss while keeping the amplitude and resistance at a level that would provide a normalization of electron flow through the medium in which it was tested."

Dr. Sloan had just entered his professor mode, and our eyes and brains began to glaze over.

"Uh, yeah. You know doc, uh, we're not that bright. How 'bout in English?" Galveston retorted.

"Oh, sorry. I was researching how I could make an electrical circuit very efficient without reducing the electrical output or degrade the current."

"Thanks, and you were looking at different materials?" Galveston inquired

"Yes, mostly the standard ones you've probably heard of; nickel, cadmium, lithium, zinc, copper, along with some synthetic insulators. I was basically looking for a combination that could be used in industrial applications, like electric transmission lines. I was able to come up with a mix that reduced the loss of electricity during transmission by almost twenty percent; a huge number in today's world."

"And why is that important?" I asked stupidly.

"Well, when you have an electrical current that flows from a power plant, about seven percent of the electrical current is lost out of the power lines. If those lines carrying the electricity were made more efficient they could transmit the same amount of electricity a farther distance. This would result in a decreased loss of electricity, a significant reduction of corona discharge, and the elimination of a transformer at the output point to step down the voltage. Basically, we could send more energy with less effort. This means less cost and need to produce as much energy."

I felt as if I had just finished a college level physics class. What it had to do with our present problem, I had no idea, but I felt I was a slightly smarter person because of it. Galveston seemed to understand it all and forged ahead with his line of questioning.

"But who were these people in this group?" he asked, rather astonished.

"Oh, they were just other researchers, mostly in the private sector. They heard me give a talk about it at a conference in Chicago about the future of energy production. They wanted to look at how my applications could be used in their work."

"And you agreed?"

"Of course. I'm just a researcher. Most academics never get to see their work used in real world applications. I was ecstatic."

"Then you were able to help then?"

"To a point. Unfortunately the costs were too high. I mean, the materials I'm talking about would probably take decades and millions to implement into the energy grid, or even longer. They knew this too."

"What was the group called?"

"It was called the Energy Conservation Consortium, but the company that wanted to fund my research was Global Energy Enterprise."

Galveston looked at Elizabeth who was already writing down the names.

"Had you heard of this group before?"

"Yes, many times, and I was glad to be associated with them. They are a non-profit company that tries to bring energy solutions to third world, second world, and underdeveloped countries, with no political expectations or reward. I was honored to be working with them."

"So you basically did what you could for them, but it sounds like it didn't work out."

"Well, yes, but it did help their body of knowledge. The consortium is a think tank on how to bring energy to people who really need it and possibly change lives."

"And they have had successes?" Galveston continued his questioning.

"Oh yes, many. They've set up power plant operations in Africa and South America, as well as some rural areas here. It's not on a large scale, but it has created far reaching changes in these areas. They focus on renewable sources since those aren't influenced from outsiders, and they're quicker to build. They have implemented solar, wind, hydro, even geothermal in a few locations."

"Interesting." Galveston stroked his chin as Elizabeth scribbled on her notepad. "Now when did the battery come into play?"

"I felt badly that I wasn't able to help the consortium's cause further, but they got my intellectual juices flowing. I thought, if not on a large scale why not a small scale. There are many others smarter than me looking at the same thing, some for their entire careers. I figured what better thing to try developing than a highly efficient battery. If it didn't succeed I could, at least, share my failures in the hopes of helping another researcher. I wish I would have failed completely, though."

"Why is that?"

"As you can see I've been living as a recluse in a hotel for the past few weeks."

Galveston recoiled from the biting report and understood his point.

"How did it come to this then?" He asked.

"I took my work from the transmission lines and decided to incorporate the materials into a battery. I started to work on the problem and by a stroke of luck one night I used a new mix of materials. I put together a rather rudimentary battery with the circuits I had already developed. I set up a crude experiment to establish a baseline to work with. I hooked my cell phone up to the battery, and I left for the night. I came back the next day and my phone was still fully charged. I was shocked so I left it for another day, then another. Two weeks passed before it finally ran out. I went through all the numbers and made a cleaner version. I got even better results each time, until after the tenth revision I came up with that." He pointed to the table and the black box.

"So you kind of stumbled on it?" Galveston asked, surprised.

"Not just stumbled, I fell over it; and over it again. I decided to let the consortium know my results, but not before I had a full working prototype. That was my goal. I wanted them to be able to take it to Global Energy in full working order. I thought that would be my contribution."

"And you took it to them?"

"Yes, after I felt I had most of the bugs worked out. They were as shocked as I was, but many were scared over the implications of such a device. I agreed to show the rough plans to the head of Global Energy."

"Who is the head of Global Energy?"

"I don't know. I never met him. I know he's a private businessman, and it was his money that had started the organization."

We looked at each other, thinking of the same thing. This could be our man, the root cause of all this chaos, and the man that may have started the ball rolling.

"Then what happened?" Galveston asked.

"I was told he had heard about it and agreed it was revolutionary. He wanted to back it and develop the technology immediately, but Global Energy wanted exclusive rights to it. I balked at the idea. I became uncomfortable with any company wanting it to themselves. Instead I planned to present it at the energy conference here in Memphis. That was last week, and as you see, I didn't make it to my lecture."

"But what made you not go?"

"I got a call in my office from Dr. Richard Blout, a physics professor at Brown. He was one of the founders of the consortium. He warned me that something was wrong. People were asking questions about the device and its capabilities, along with who had developed it. Dr. Blout wasn't comfortable with the actions of Global Energy and feared for my safety and the future of the battery. He encouraged me to go public as soon as possible. I decided to take an earlier flight to Memphis to get myself set up for the conference."

Unbeknownst to the doctor, the earlier flight, by a stroke of good fortune, or dumb luck, allowed him to avoid the same men who would later blow up his lab.

"When I got to Memphis I checked my phone. I had twelve or so messages, many from members of the consortium, all telling me my lab had been destroyed. This was when I decided to send Margaret the message and the only copy of the battery's final plan. I had to lie because I really didn't know what was going on."

"Did you have the design on those computers in your lab?" Galveston continued to question.

"Nope, nothing. The preliminary designs were on a secure server at Dartmouth, the final one was sent to Margaret, and a copy is right here." He pointed to his head indicating it was in his brain.

We each processed the information. There were so many more questions, but we didn't have time for the answers. Every minute we stayed put us closer to danger we weren't prepared to deal with. All of a sudden we heard a loud rap on the door.

Chapter 29

Galveston sprung to his feet. We had left Elizabeth's heavy armory back in London because airport security didn't look kindly on those sorts of things. He positioned himself close to the door and reached into the closet, grabbing the closest thing he could find—the foldable metal tray with straps that you set luggage on.

Three long raps on the door occurred again. Elizabeth instinctively grabbed Dr. Sloan and pushed him into the bathroom. Galveston held up the tray, reached for the door handle, and quickly swung the door open.

"Ahh!" came a scream from the hallway.

It was the maid, just trying to make up the room. We had given her a slight heart attack.

"Oh, sorry," Galveston said, still holding up the luggage rack. "Uh, we just need some fresh towels."

The maid nervously reached to her cart and handed them over.

"Thanks," Galveston replied, throwing the rack back into the closet as the maid retreated for the next room.

"I think we're a little on edge, don't you?" Galveston remarked, closing the door.

"I'll say," I said, sitting back down on the bed. "You know, we might have wanted to just look through the peephole."

"Now you tell me."

Dr. Sloan came out of the bathroom. "I think I would like to leave," he said.

"I'll go along with that. I'd rather not repeat that performance. Why don't you gather your things. I'll call down and get you checked out. Elizabeth will drive you out of here, and if it's alright with you, to San Diego. She'll keep you safe until we can get a handle on this. It's time we let our FBI contact know what's going on."

I wasn't sure how good an idea this was allowing someone who's used to driving on the wrong side of the street to drive cross country. But Galveston assured me it was the best move. Elizabeth knew how to move someone secretly through much worse circumstances than we ever could have imagined.

116

Dr. Sloan gathered up his suitcase and laptop as Elizabeth left to bring the car to the front of the hotel. I noticed him pick up the black box that sat on the table.

"So that's the battery?" I asked him as he put it in his bag.

"That's it, the cause of all the trouble. A full working prototype, minus the software needed to run it properly," the doctor announced.

"Was that the only one you made?"

"No, I have two other prototypes, versions eight and nine, each one better than the other. They're both close to the one I have but lack many of the capabilities. Those were in my lab, however."

Interesting, I thought. That might prove useful later, and I decided to keep it to myself for the time being. Galveston had enough to think about now.

After Dr. Sloan packed we hurried him out the door and went down to the hotel lobby. We produced a collective sigh of relief as we watched Dr. Sloan leave with Elizabeth. We went the opposite direction and travelled to the Memphis airport.

Our plane arrived at LAX well after midnight, and we walked to the pickup area. Elizabeth had left a message that they were safely in Dallas and would make the final push for San Diego tomorrow.

Jane had been nice enough to pick us up at the airport and drove us back to San Diego. She looked healthy, beautiful, and rested. I hated to think what I looked or smelled like, but she gave me a long hug anyway.

"I'll call David and have him meet us face to face tomorrow at our office. He'll be shocked at who we've found," Galveston told us.

We arrived back at the office after 2:00 A.M. Galveston said his goodbyes and told me to meet him tomorrow at 10:00 A.M. He left Jane and me at the office alone.

"Would you like me to follow you home?" I asked, truly worried about her safety after such a long, late night drive, and not about the possibility of seeing the inside of her home.

"Oh, you don't have to, but thanks. How about I call you when I get home?"

"That would be great. Oh, and Jane, would you like to go to dinner sometime?

"How about tomorrow night? I would really like that."

My heart fluttered like a school boy. I had gotten a first date.

"Great. I'll talk to you in a little while. Thanks again for coming to get us."

"Not a problem. I was actually looking forward to seeing you."

I tried not to show how excited I was at the statement.

We said our goodbyes, and Jane gave me a departing hug before we made way to our respective homes.

I slept well that night, after Jane's call of course.

-Chapter 30-

I rolled into the office a little before ten o'clock the next day. Galveston was already there and looking unusually tired. We had been going for two days straight, with no end in sight.

Galveston had talked to May the night before, and he had agreed to meet us at the office this morning. Alex had been working all night, poring over the design plans and gathering information about Black Bear. He did this between cocktails, of course.

May arrived promptly at ten, alone. He was calm, cool, and collected, but I noted a little apprehension, that he knew something we didn't. Galveston guided him into the back office and I followed, closing the door behind me.

Without wasting time May began moving into his line of questioning. "How did the London trip go? Were you able to find Margaret Sloan?"

"Yes, after cajoling Elizabeth we were able to find her. Margaret gave us the plans to the battery her father had sent," Galveston told him.

"You did? Excellent. Where is it?"

"We have it in a safe place, but we ran into a problem."

"A problem? What kind of problem?" May's excitement grew.

"Black Bear made it there before us. Luckily we found Margaret and the plans before they did. They tore up the place, and they were definitely in a hurry."

"You guys did a good job and the government appreciates it. Your work is done. We'll handle it from here."

"That's it?" Galveston asked.

"Do you want something else? We had a deal and you completed it. The Bureau doesn't need you further."

"Are you sure? There isn't something else? I mean, there isn't a certain professor that you would like us to find in return for a new business proposition?"

"What have you done, Galveston?" May questioned.

"You must have known I wouldn't have stopped. We've taken things into our own hands."

"Oh, God," May replied flatly. "What do you want?"

"Just a new job–with pay, of course."

May thought for a second. I was not a good judge of character, but I could tell May knew Galveston would want a piece of the action. A smile crossed his face as he realized his manipulation was working.

"We may need your help with some other things," May told us, saying more with his demeanor than with his words. "We need to find the professor, that's the first step."

"Way ahead of you, David," Galveston said proudly. "We found Dr. Sloan, and we have him safe."

I figured May would turn his look to anger or shock. Instead it turned into a state of glee.

"You found him and he's safe? That is great news. Where is he now?"

"Not so fast. First, why don't you fill us in on everything you know."

"Fair enough." May sat back in his chair. "I don't know what Dr. Sloan has told you, but we have a suspicion that the head of a non-profit company called Global Energy was interested in Dr. Sloan's battery. We narrowed it down to one person. You may have heard of him. His name is Weston Chase."

Galveston shrugged his shoulders, but I perked up. I had heard of him and interjected my thoughts into the conversation.

"Yeah, he's a self-made millionaire," I said.

"Try billionaire. Chase used to run a company called Data Stream. It was one of the businesses that revolutionized the way credit card and ATM transactions were completed; probably fifteen years ago. Chase has become more of a recluse in the business world in the last few years. He changed to a sort of philanthropist. About a year ago he started the Chase Foundation. That's when he formed a non-profit company called Global Energy Enterprise."

We sat glued to our seat as May continued. "We've known of some strange dealings going on in this company—Global Energy. We found out they had been contracting out to a security company for things they were doing overseas. My inside contact told me Chase was becoming increasingly concerned about security. Global Energy does projects that other organizations won't touch in some pretty dangerous, unstable areas; physically and politically. My contact was concerned that Chase was using questionable ways to deal with security. He felt they were losing sight of the overall mission of the Enterprise, and there may be some illegal activity going on."

"Who is this contact?" I asked.

"Dr. Richard Blout, a member of the Board of Advisors. He has been suspicious of Chase's motives behind being involved in Global Energy."

"Richard Blout? That's the man who warned Dr. Sloan about people asking questions before he went to Memphis," I told May.

"It was Dr. Sloan's battery that got Richard suspicious. He said Chase became very interested in it."

"So let me get this straight. You guys got information that some illegal things may be going on in these other countries, and this security company may be using Global Energy as a front?" Galveston asked.

"Pretty much," May answered slowly.

"Who is the security company, if I don't already know."

"Black Bear, of course," May answered nonchalantly.

The statement sunk in and Galveston knew his hunch had been right. The pieces were correct.

"It all fits, David. I recognized the *Adamanthea* file at Genesis. It is very similar to how Black Bear names their covert operations. It has the same structure as I remembered, except it was missing the team name designation. The numbers that followed the name are still a mystery. It's definitely Black Bear coding."

"I agree. Black Bear is involved," May replied. "That is why we needed to see what was in *Adamanthea* file. From what we've seen it looks like plans for a production line."

"Dr. Sloan has three prototypes, and they have two of the inferior versions. They must have somehow figured out that the prototypes weren't the final version and then found out, as you guys had, that Sloan sent the finished plans to his daughter," Galveston surmised.

"It may have bought us some valuable time that they didn't get the plans. I'm sure they have a contingency for finishing the battery without it. Probably to find Dr. Sloan at any cost."

"What do you think Chase is up too, and for that matter, why would Black Bear be involved?" I asked, curious at his thoughts.

"You know, I don't have a clue. Even though I've been able to get more information about Chase, he still holds his cards close to his chest. At least we have Dr. Sloan now and the plans he sent his daughter."

"Can't you just get a warrant to check out Black Bear or Global Energy?" I asked, figuring it was as easy as shown on T.V.'s "Law and Order", or "CSI".

"No way, no real proof. We can't just barge in there. Plus a judge would never approve a warrant based on the conjecture and speculation we have. He'd laugh us out of his office. That's why I needed to employ your help."

"I'd say we were grateful, but then I'd be lying," Galveston said, laughing. "So, do you want to hire us again? You know we can do things that you guys aren't allowed to do."

May peered at us thoughtfully. His job would be on the line with this decision. If things went bad he would be out a career, but if he didn't, and went charging with the full force of the FBI, then all the players would scurry to their holes.

"I don't know. It's awfully risky. How do you feel about this, Roger?"

I was shocked at getting an opinion in the matter, and thought about it for a few seconds. I could be done with this whole operation; free and clear with a few extra bucks in my pocket. But then I thought of Margaret and Dr. Sloan and our encounter together. This was a moment where I could walk away and no one would think differently of me. Or I could take the challenge and stop an injustice in progress.

"I'm crazy for thinking this, but I agree with Galveston. We're already in this too deep, and I'm afraid Dr. Sloan is in grave danger. I think it is now our responsibility, so I'm in."

May took another second to think it over. He had many options to think about, and he knew we were right. The Bureau would have a much better chance at success with people that wouldn't have their hands tied.

"We do need your help. We'll give you an extra payment, I'll make sure of it," May said.

"Excellent. Roger will write up the proposal. I'm sure you'll be able to deliver."

"I don't think it will be a problem. Let me get the go-ahead from the top. They are extremely interested in this, but I'll keep your names out of it. They wouldn't want to know anyway, in case something goes bad."

"I think we have a deal then," Galveston announced and plastered a smile on his face. He had made it back into the game.

-Chapter 31-

We all decided to take a bathroom and water break before we continued. The timeline was swirling in my head, and the primaries in our little play were varied. Right now it was difficult to keep it straight, mainly because we didn't have a clue what Black Bear, Chase, or Global Energy were really after. We gathered again in the office after our bladders had been relieved, and Galveston wasted no time getting back to business.

He showed a renewed sense of energy. This would indeed call on all his skills, and I would need to step it up and contribute any way I could. It should have been a five or six person job, but all we had were each other. Only Galveston and I would be in the field. I was still unsure of Elizabeth's ultimate role in our little drama.

"What if Chase isn't involved in this? What if it's only Black Bear?" Galveston asked May.

"I've had similar thoughts. Blout said Chase has made many inquiries about finding Dr. Sloan. Chase even contacted the Bureau in Boston about the professor's disappearance and had pushed them to act as quickly as possible. He even offered to hire private investigators. I've had no indication that Chase even realizes Black Bear is involved or what they are up to. He has told Dr. Blout that he wants Dr. Sloan back safe so he can release his discovery to the scientific community."

"It doesn't sound like he's involved," I interjected.

"No, but it does sound like Black Bear may have found out about this invention and decided to pursue it themselves. That makes much more sense. Who in the organization is pulling the strings, and how did they keep it a secret?"

"That's a good question. Dr. Sloan should be here today, maybe he has a thought. I'm planning on having him stay with Alex at his home. Alex has plenty of room and a nasty little security system," Galveston informed May.

"I would like to talk to Dr. Sloan."

"Agreed," Galveston replied, but he knew he needed to protect his friend May, and his job. The less information he knew right now the better.

"Keep me informed. I'm going to call you tomorrow after I look into all the members of the Board at Global Energy and Black Bear. Someone is not playing by the rules."

May rose from the chair, an indication our meeting was adjourned.

"Thanks, David." Galveston said, as May left the room.

Just then, the phone rang. It was Alex.

"Hey, I think you guys better get over here. I've been doing some peeking into the Black Bear system, and I think you need to see this."

"What is it?" Galveston inquired.

"I think you better just get over here. You're not going to believe this."

-Chapter 32-

Alex didn't allow us any more questions. I was sure he wanted to bask in the glow of what he had found, or maybe he just couldn't explain it over the phone.

We raced to Alex's house which sat on a cliff overlooking the Pacific Ocean and had an infinity pool in the backyard. Alex was not hurting for money.

We parked in the circular driveway and let ourselves in.

"Alex," Galveston called out.

"I'm back here," a voice called from the recesses of the home.

We walked down a long, brightly lit hallway, and entered a large room with a bank of windows that brought in the ocean view. The rest of the room was scattered with computers of every shape and size, and a multitude of other equipment littered the walls. A tacky, velvet Elvis hung over the spot where Alex sat, engrossed at the images on a large, 27-inch monitor.

"Good Lord man, do you think you have enough stuff?" Galveston joked.

"You should see my garage. Come here, look at this."

On the screen was a jumble of messages and characters. Alex had hacked into the email servers at Black Bear—no easy task.

Large companies saved everything, and Black Bear was no different. He had searched through all the messages and came up with two that matched the timeline we knew of. The two messages were encrypted, so he ran it through his decryption software so we could read the words. It was not completely understandable, but the subject could be deciphered.

The first message was at the time of the break-in to Dr. Sloan's lab. It was a cell phone message sent to an internal account. It read:

Items 2 acquired. Will transport now. Target not found. Area neutralized clear. Transfer 0900 CMH.

The second message was more of the same language, and a reply to the first message.

787VR arrival. Col Espinosa at 77M at 1700. Payment ready. Return immediate. 27982 to 254010018 at 1340. Items intact.

Then the last line made our blood run cold.

Acquire target after delivery and eliminate.

"Hold it, there's one more reply," Alex told us. This one was much more explicit.

Big Green was not located and is missing. If found, eliminate.

"*Big Green*? Who is that?"

I looked at Galveston, and we shrugged our shoulders together. I thought about the words in the sentence for a second. Dr. Sloan was the only item missing and not located. But where had I heard the words *Big Green* before? It then hit me from out of nowhere.

"*Big Green*. That's considered the nickname of Dartmouth. I did a lecture there once and thought it was funny the University didn't have a mascot, except for an unofficial one called Keggy the Keg." I was amazed at my revelation.

"That makes sense for it to mean Dr. Sloan, but it definitely isn't good that they want him eliminated. They do mean business, don't they," Galveston said, and I nodded in agreement. "Alex, good work. Can you print those out for us and see if you can locate something on this Col Espinosa name."

Galveston wrote the name down and pondered its meaning. "Col Espinosa?" he questioned. "What could that mean?" He continued to look at the words and then suddenly slapped the table. "He's a Colonel I bet. Alex, try Colonel Espinosa. Now, let's see if we can figure out the rest of the messages."

We spread the printouts on the desk next to Alex and put on our thinking caps, which were now tattered and soiled. We would see whose cap was largest.

Galveston read through the messages again.

"Okay, we know the timeframe from what Dr. Sloan and David told us, and we know when the messages were sent. Let's see here—*Two items acquired.* That has to be the prototypes Dr. Sloan was talking about. The *target* is either Dr. Sloan or the fully functional prototype, if they know it even exists. I would say it means Dr. Sloan since we now know he's *Big Green.* *Area neutralized*? I don't think I even want to know about that one." He stopped for a second before I interrupted.

"The break-in. I bet you they were talking about the break-in at Dr. Sloan's Dartmouth lab that night," I said proudly.

"Sounds good, we'll go with that. Now this one—*Transfer 0900 CHM.* That looks like the time they were going to move it, 9:00 A.M. Dr. Sloan was already on the early flight to Memphis by then. It looks like he just missed them."

Galveston thought about the words further. I was unable to give him any help and had no idea what the letters on the page meant.

"Alex, look up KCHM under airport identifiers for the country."

All U.S. airports are identified with a four letter code. Most of us knew them as three letters—LAX, BOS, ATL. But in the U.S. they are always proceeded with a "K", in the Caribbean it is a "T", and in Canada a "C".

Alex began pecking away at the keys.

"Looks like KCHM is Port Columbus International, in Ohio," Alex answered.

"So they were transferring the items to the airport at 9:00 A.M. They wouldn't have been able to drive it to Ohio from New Hampshire in time. They must have flown. Alex, look up *N787VR* on the FAA Airplane Registry site."

"Okay, hold on."

We waited for our answer.

"It's a Rockwell Turbo Commander registered to Quantum Aviation out of Newport News, Virginia. It shows that it's been pulled out of service and put up for scrap."

"Okay, the plot thickens," Galveston announced gleefully. "Where were they going? Now look up *77M*, Alex,."

"Okay, hold on." Alex quickly pecked at the keys again. "Looks like it could be Billings, Montana; Hespeira, Switzerland; or somewhere in Mexico."

"The one in Mexico, dirt field?" Galveston asked.

"Yeah, how did you know? It's right across the border, near Arizona."

"There are a lot of small dirt fields in that area, and there probably aren't too many Espinosas in Switzerland. Plus the Turbo Commander has been the plane of choice for many an unscrupulous activity. You know, drug running, et cetera. It carries heavy loads, is fast, and it's good at flying close to the ground. They probably stopped at one of the dirt fields on the Arizona border before they flew it into Mexico. I would bet someone put this tail number on it so it couldn't be traced and then flew it over the border. Roger, write this down—Flightplan for 787 Victor Romeo."

"Alright." I fumbled around looking for a pen, and when I found one I wrote the words down on a piece of paper.

"Hey, don't write on that," Alex exclaimed.

"Why not?" I asked.

"That's my order for lunch," he said, trying to grab the paper away.

Galveston ignored us and summarized his findings.

"They took it to this field in Mexico and met this Espinosa fellow at 1:40 P.M. The rest of the message is self-explanatory. They would pay *Espinosa* and return immediately. The next message is a little more difficult. Okay Alex, check the registry for *27982*."

"I'm not getting anything for that one," Alex stated, dejectedly, not finding an airplane registered with that number.

"That's okay, let's keep going. We'll get back to that one later. We may not even need it," Galveston assured him.

Galveston continued on to the next portion of the message. "Now what does this mean, *254010018*?"

We scratched our heads in unison, and Galveston moved over Alex's shoulder, still trying to figure out the previous numbers. I sat staring at the numbers, hoping to contribute in some way.

Was it an internal code that only Black Bear would know about, a combination, or time? It could be anything. I studied it closely and looked at it in the context of the message. *27982 to*

254010018 at 1340. We knew the first group of numbers had to be an airplane, most likely, and the last group was the time. The message said *to.* Could it be a place? Maybe a code of where they were going? Then it hit me like a brick. I flashed back to my hiking days and my lessons in orienteering.

"Alex, do you have a globe or a map?" The pair didn't turn from their work, but Alex managed an answer.

"Yeah, I keep a globe in my kitchen. I like to look at it in the morning over breakfast." I didn't get the sarcasm until Galveston stifled a laugh.

"A map or atlas? Anything?" Still they didn't pry from their work. Alex pointed to a nearby bookcase.

"I think there's an old National Geographic atlas there. Do you think this is really the time for a geography lesson?"

I ignored the comment and began searching through the bookcase until I found the atlas. It was about ten years old and still had the names of countries that were long since removed or renamed.

I began flipping through it until I got to the America's page. I ran my fingers down the page and then across, stopping at a point on the map.

Alex and Galveston were now arguing about where to look next. I walked over and plopped the Atlas in front of them, right on the top of Alex's keyboard. They both gave me a startled look.

"What the…" Galveston started, but I interrupted immediately.

"Right here. That's where they went," I said proudly, pointing to the spot on the map. A look of confusion crossed both their faces. "I mean, this is the general area. I'll bet you'll find an airport there."

"What are you talking about?" Galveston tried to say again.

"Those numbers," I began, running my fingers across the page, "they're lines of latitude and longitude. *Twenty-five* degrees, *forty* minutes north, *one hundred* degrees, *eighteen* minutes west."

They sat dumbfounded, more surprised by my success then by the information.

"They went here." I again pointed to the page. "Monterrey, Mexico."

Galveston, realizing my coup, slapped me on the back. "Well done, Roger! I knew you had it in you. Alex?"

"I'm already on it," and he was, bringing up a map of the area. "Monterrey International Airport."

I stepped back and basked in the glory. We had the general direction of where they took the devices, but there was much more to know.

"Alex, keep looking for this Espinosa character, we need to know about him. I just hope he wasn't the target. Roger, that was fantastic!"

I stood proudly. I had helped with one piece of the puzzle, but where did Galveston get all this aviation knowledge?

"Come on Roger, it's time to take a break. Let's see what Alex has to drink."

I followed Galveston to the kitchen, and we eagerly peered into the refrigerator. It was organized by food type and use, all neatly arranged.

"Is there something Alex needs to tell us? This is the weirdest fridge I've ever seen," Galveston said, as he stuck his face in. "Look at this; camembert cheese, a tin of caviar? Who does he think he is, Julia Child? Who eats this crap; and Perrier? Who still drinks this?" he said, holding up the beverage.

I looked in the door. All the jars were label side out, and were of an imported variety. I held up one of them; a jar of black currant jelly from France.

"He sure is some sort of dandy," I retorted to Galveston, who held back a laugh while sniffing the cheese.

"I think he might have a touch of OCD thrown in. I just want a beer." Galveston sifted past the exotic fruit section until he came out with an imported Chimay Belgian beer in a huge, fancy bottle. "This will do, I'll split it with you."

I nodded my head and then searched for some glasses, which I also found neatly arranged. We enjoyed our half of a beer while Alex continued his search.

"Ahhh, nectar of the gods," Galveston said, smacking his lips.

We pounded the rest of the beer from our glasses just before Alex let out a yelp. He had found something, and we raced back to the room.

"When you said Mexico, I searched a database of Mexican military officers," he started as we arrived in the room. "Colonel Alfonso Espinosa, member of the Mexican Armed Forces stationed in Monterrey, and head of an artillery brigade."

"Mexico has an artillery brigade?" I asked seriously.

"Yeah, they use those air guns that fire T-shirts at sports events," Galveston quipped.

Alex continued his search, and ignored our witty banter.

"I found a message about him in the Black Bear database. It looks like they hired him for a security detail."

The message was hastily written, but was detailed. It simply said Espinosa would provide security for the handoff. Colonel Espinosa also requested a certain piece of antiquity as additional payment along with his monetary payment.

"That's strange, why would he want an antiquity?" I asked. Galveston was wondering the same.

"I don't know, maybe he's independently wealthy, and there's no corruption in Mexico." He said this last statement sarcastically. Everyone knew Mexican government officials enjoyed being bribed.

"It doesn't sound like they gave the prototypes to him, but I wonder how much he knows. They could have stopped there and handed the prototypes off. We need to check this out."

"And how do you propose we do this?" I asked.

"Well, he should be easy enough to find since he's in the military," Galveston stated before Alex joined in.

"You know, I have a Spanish speaking friend named Manuel. He owes me a favor. I introduced him to his wife, and then I helped him get a divorce. I think he still lives in La Paz. I'll talk to him, and maybe you two can meet him wherever Espinosa is. He can be your official translator. The two of you don't need to be traipsing around Mexico alone anyway."

"That sounds like a good idea." Galveston said as I stood by thinking that it was a terrible idea. I didn't want to go to Mexico.

"How much can we pay?"

"You decide, Alex. Whatever will get him to Monterrey."

"Will do," Alex replied.

"Wake me up when you have an answer. I'm taking a nap." Galveston went into the living room and threw himself on the couch.

I decided I would take a siesta by the pool since we were in a Mexican induced mood.

An hour passed before Alex woke us and had us gather back in his office for another debriefing.

"I have answers for you, and they're not good. Manuel will meet you in Monterrey, and he'll do it for $1,000. I've already arranged him a flight and a hotel. The problem is, Colonel Espinosa was in the base infirmary, and they've just transferred him to a Monterrey hospital. They don't know what's wrong with him."

Galveston rubbed his eyes. "Yeah, that isn't good news, but we have to see him. At least he can't run out on us."

Galveston's brain was working because I could see the little veins popping on his forehead and the hamster running the wheel in his head. Either that, or he was having a stroke. I almost hoped for the latter.

His eyes got wide. "I've got a great plan."

"Uh-oh," I said softly.

"Looks like we're going to Mexico! We leave tonight," and he held up his hand in a number one pose.

"Can't we leave in the morning," I implored immediately.

"What the hell for?" He questioned back.

"Because," I started, "I have a date."

Chapter 33

The board room was immaculate. A majestic, mahogany table filled the center of the room, and the walls were covered with deep, oak paneling. Large vases filled with various flowers dotted the corners of the room as the light poured in through floor to ceiling windows.

There were two men in the room; a few papers strewn in front of them. They sat at one end of the large table and were both clothed in finely tailored custom suits and sat in large, leather back chairs. The environment was relaxed, but serious.

"How we doin' on this thing?" The larger man asked, peering over horn rimmed glasses.

"We're on schedule. The *Adamanthea* plan has been completed and the manufacturing process is ready. It's going to take a little more time because we don't have the final plans, but we have men working on that. How about the legislation?" The smaller man scribbled some notes on a pad.

"Those pods won't know what hit them. We have to have public pressure for this to pass and higher oil prices will help. I can get the bill out of committee. That will make your business procedure much easier."

"That's what we'll need."

"Everyone will be forced to vote for it, if not it would be political suicide. We've worded it well, and it should pass easily as a rider to another bill. What about our little problem?"

"We've taken care of a few links in the chain, but we've lost Dr. Sloan."

"You've got to get a hold of that guy. What about his family?"

"Nothing," the smaller man answered.

"Keep your ear to the ground. We need to make sure he won't talk until we can make an announcement about this product. I don't want that little bastard to ruin this whole thing. You better take care of him."

"We're working on discrediting him. I want you to assure me that if we go to these lengths, you'll get that legislation through."

"You just worry about your end. I brought you guys into this, and I can take you out. In D.C. terms it's deny, deny, deny."

There was obviously a power struggle between these two, with egos out of control.

The larger man continued. "If you do what you say, you'll be a very rich man."

"I'm a little concerned about Weston Chase."

"I'll take care of him. That stupid bastard Chase doesn't know what's going on in this room. I hope you guys can keep quiet if we have problems."

"I'm sure we can, but the more we do, the more questions arise. I don't want Chase to suddenly change his mind."

"Fair enough, but if it comes down to it, I'll hope you'll perform."

"We'll do what it takes to keep things quiet."

"I guess we don't have any more to discuss then, do we?" the larger man said sarcastically, and began arranging his papers. A knock came from the door. "Come in," he said.

"Sorry, sir, but you have a call from Washington. They said it was urgent."

"Yes, Susie. I'll take it. Oh, and get that envelope for Mr. Placer, hun."

"Yes, sir," she answered, and left the room.

The larger man got up from the table and leaned over Mr. Placer.

"Find that Dr. Sloan and make sure he's quiet and out of the picture, immediately." Placer didn't answer him and looked straight ahead. "Hey Susie, get me a cup of coffee, will you girl?"

The larger man left the room, leaving Placer alone. He placed the papers in his briefcase and got up.

"Thank you Senator, you asshole," he mumbled.

Chapter 34

Galveston agreed to my request. If he had not, I might have injured him in some way. He had sensed my pending insanity and gave in. We would leave for Mexico in the morning.

I left Alex's home and returned to my own as Galveston stayed behind and formulated our impending plan; the next step of our unending quest.

The information we were getting now was massive. We had movements of Black Bear, financial transactions, and messages, all from the ingenious and utterly frightening touch of our resident computer geek.

I got home and readied myself for my date. Galveston had given me only one piece of advice—fake an injury and garner sympathy, rule 108. I decided to completely disregard his advice since his history with the opposite sex was not all that stellar.

Elizabeth had arrived with Dr. Sloan, safe and sound. She put him up in a downtown San Diego hotel and instructed him to stay put.

Elizabeth arrived at Alex's house just as Galveston was finishing up a talk with David May. Galveston's seemed to flutter when he saw Elizabeth. He bounded over but stopped short so as not to look too eager.

"I'm glad you're safe," he said, giving her a hug, as if he had any worries over her capabilities. "Everything good?" he asked.

"Lovely, just tired. I'll never get used to American driving."

"Yeah, we drive on the correct side of the road, and we do the speed limit, for the most part," he joked, alluding to the stereotype that the English were rather aggressive drivers.

"Quite," she answered, "may I have a drink?"

"Certainly, I have a lot to tell you."

Galveston left and got her one of the Perrier he had derided before. He then filled her in on all the new information.

About this time I met Jane at her house. She looked beautiful, decked out in casual wear, her hair up in a pony tail. We exchanged small talk at her place before we started off to the restaurant.

Not two minutes into our date my phone began to ring. I looked at it and it was Galveston. I pushed the ignore button. "Not tonight, buddy boy," I thought. Whatever it was could wait until morning. I didn't have the heart to turn it off completely, and instead I set it to vibrate. If it got bad enough I would talk to him.

Jane and I talked like old friends. The conversation was easy and fun and flowed from one topic to another. I had never felt so comfortable before, and she had such an air of ease. She seemed genuinely interested in what I had to say, which I found shocking, for some reason.

Back at the house, the information train steamed on. Alex and Galveston busily searched the web with information May had given them about the Board of Global Energy, while Elizabeth snoozed on the couch.

"None of these guys have the power to pull off something like this. They're either academic types, or the head of some foundation," Galveston told Alex.

It was true they were striking out. None of the Board members would've been able to coordinate all the pieces; until they got to the last name, Senator Edward Eastman, the newest member of the Board. He was the only politico and the only one with power, but would his biography support the motivation?

As Alex pulled it up, indeed it did. He was a staunch environmentalist and socialist leaning senior Senator from Connecticut. He wasn't that terribly well known, or well-loved, but he had an enormity of power in the Senate. He was the Chairman of the Senate Committee on Energy and Natural Resources, and a member of the Senate Finance Subcommittee on International Trade, Customs, and Global Competitiveness. He was also a career politician, serving most of his adult life as a moderate economist and was courted and lobbied heavily by trial attorneys. He sat on two boards, both non-profits; the Global Energy Consortium and Center for Democratic Initiatives. He had been investigated five times by the Senate over the course of his career, and twice by the General Accounting Office because of fundraising infractions.

Eastman was known in Washington as a hard-nosed Senator who would often berate junior members to vote his way on sponsored bills. He hadn't introduced a meaningful piece of legislation in his career, but managed to sneak through some pork barrel projects to his state. He was married with two children, both adults, and had accusations, more than a few times, of marital infidelity. A news report they found described him as being very engaging, polite, and very manipulative, with a hot temper and a firebrand style of politics. He was often absent from votes but managed to easily win every six years due to an aggressive political team. Eastman was no saint, but what politician is? Out of all the names, he stood out like a sore thumb.

Eastman's environmental stands were radical. He saw nothing wrong with eco-terrorism and was staunchly against oil exploration. He was a strong advocate against "Global Warming", or what it was now so lovingly referred to as "climate change". He was also an opponent of anything related to consumerism. Ironically, even with these beliefs, he often flew in a private Gulfstream V jet, had an 8,800 square foot house, a beach house in Myrtle Beach, South Carolina, and an upscale townhouse in the swank Washington D.C. enclave of Georgetown.

"This guy doesn't practice what he preaches," Galveston said aloud. "Look at this one." He pointed to a link on the screen. Alex brought it up and the pair read it over. "He has heavily invested in 'green' companies. This guy is one big walking conflict of interest. I would say he has some motivation on being involved in all of this," Galveston said, referring to our current situation.

"I agree. This reads like a rap sheet," Alex acknowledged.

"I guess he's well-liked, though. This editorial says, 'Senator Eastman has the panache to console a mother and baby that everything will be alright while stealing the mother's purse and the baby's pacifier, all at the same time.' I would say that seems to sum him up in a nutshell." They continued to pore over the wealth of information from the internet. "That reminds me," Galveston said, grabbing his cell phone, "I have to make another anonymous call."

The phone began to vibrate in my pocket just as I was eating my swanky pork chop. I let it continue until it stopped. A few minutes later it went off again; and then again after that. Jane, sensing my distraction, stopped eating her pasta primavera.

"You might as well get that. You know he won't quit calling."

"Yeah, I know." Just then it gave another annoying vibration. "I'll be back in a second." I walked to the outside of the restaurant. "What!" I yelled in the phone.

"How's it going hot stuff? Made it to first base yet?" Galveston's voice boomed over the phone.

138

"No, but my phone has. What could be so important that it couldn't wait until morning?"

"I just wanted to tell you to meet me at the airport in the morning at eight o'clock. We're taking a flight out of Montgomery Field."

"Eight? Isn't that a little early?"

"No. Just be there."

"Can I go now?"

"Oh, just one more thing. I think we found our mole."

"Mole? What do you mean?"

"Possibly our guy behind this thing, a Senator Edward Eastman."

"A Senator? A U.S. Senator?" I asked naively.

"No, a Roman Senator," Galveston answered sarcastically. "Yes, a U.S. Senator. Pretty dirty guy. We don't have a definitive link, but we're working on that. The other Board members just don't add up. I'll fill you in tomorrow."

"That's mighty nice of you."

"Oh, and another thing. Did you fake an injury yet? Make sure you do it in front of her house."

"I'll take that into consideration," I replied incredulously.

"Have a good time, sunshine."

"Yeah, thanks," I said, and hung up the phone. I made my way back to Jane.

"What did he want?" she asked.

"Nothing important, of course. We're meeting at the airport tomorrow. We're going to Mexico for a day or so. The rest of his conversation was filled with yapping." She smiled brightly, and we were finally able to finish our dinner in peace for once during the night.

We spent the rest of our date strolling in the moonlight along the wharf. I took her back to her place, and we exchanged pleasantries at the door, gave each other a nice kiss, and said our goodbyes.

"Would you like to come in for a while?" she asked me softly.

"I better get going. I have to meet Dan early."

"I understand."

"I had a great time," I said, giving her a long hug.

"Me too," she said.

I turned and started to return to my parked car, and then sensed my folly. I thought quickly and immediately grabbed my leg.

"Ouch, my hamstring. It's acting up again," I said hamming it up.

"Are you okay?"

"Oh, just an old football injury," I joked. I had never played a day of organized football in my life. "Can I come up and get a drink of water? That usually clears it up."

Jane smiled, obviously seeing through my ploy.

"Sure, follow me."

-Chapter 35-

I arrived late to Montgomery Field, an airport north of downtown San Diego, disheveled and tired. Galveston was already waiting for me in the parking lot.

"So how'd it go, stud?" he asked right away.

"Fine, fine," I said, getting my bag out of the back of my car.

"Looks like you could have used a little more freshening up."

"No, I'm good. Ready to go."

"Yeah, I bet," Galveston said, smiling. "A friend of mine is going to fly us. Come on."

We went to the security gate where Galveston punched in a code. We walked across the tarmac to an awaiting Cessna 400 Corvalis aircraft.

"Where's your friend?" I inquired.

"I don't know. He said he would be here. I'll get the plane ready for him. Put your stuff in the back and get in the passenger side."

I placed my things in the cargo hold and stuffed myself in the passenger right seat. Galveston climbed in the pilot's seat and looked over the controls.

"Pretty complicated, huh?" he said to me.

"Yeah, I'll say. Lots of knobs and buttons."

"Ah, it can't be that hard. You know, we can't wait for him forever. I bet we can get it going for him." Galveston started pushing buttons and moving knobs. "That looks about right, I bet."

"Don't mess with that," I shrieked, clutching my seat.

"He told me he keeps the key under the seat." Galveston reached down and pulled out a key.

"Hey, what are you doing? Put that down!"

"Relax. Let's see what this sucker does." He put the key in the ignition, moved some knobs, and turned the key, starting the engine. "Wow, just like when I play that game on my computer." I was petrified as I looked out the front at the spinning propeller blade. "You better get your headphones on, it's going to be loud," he yelled.

I nervously stuck the headset on my head and reached for my seatbelt, following Galveston's lead.

"Okay, that's good," I yelled back, "turn it off! That's enough playing around." Galveston was clearly amused.

"Ah, let's just move it a bit." He pushed the throttle forward, and we began moving toward the taxiway. "I just hope this thing has brakes," he exclaimed through the intercom.

The plane jerked to a stop, right before the taxiway leading to the runway. "Whew. I thought I'd never figure that out," Galveston said to me. I was not amused.

"Just shut it off, before we get into trouble."

Galveston was now laughing hard and could barely keep his headphones on. He composed himself and keyed his microphone.

"Montgomery Ground, Cessna two-zero-one-victor-tango with romeo, taxi IFR." The radio chattered with instruction.

"Cessna two-zero-one-victor-tango, Montgomery Ground, taxi to Runway two-eight right via taxiway Alpha and Hotel. Hold in the run-up area for a release time."

Galveston read back the instructions verbatim and was still stifling laughter while he taxied the single engine airplane toward the runway.

"When were you going to tell me you could fly?" I questioned.

"I was hoping you wouldn't figure it out until we were in the air."

"How long did you have this planned?"

"About five minutes before you got here. I had already got our instrument clearance and thought I would have a little fun with you," he said as he negotiated the plane down the taxiway.

"Well, I hope you enjoyed yourself."

"Are you kidding? It was great! I'll never forget your white knuckles on the dash. That was priceless."

Galveston changed to the tower frequency and got a takeoff clearance almost immediately.

Galveston pushed the throttle forward, and we lifted off into the air. We made a turn to the south before being transferred to SoCal Approach, the air traffic control for the area. We would pass over San Diego, the border and Tijuana, and then turn to the southeast to track our way to Monterrey, Mexico. It was a clear day, and we cruised at 11,000 feet. I finally began to relax more and more as the flight progressed, somehow trusting Galveston's flying skills as we travelled farther south toward the Mexican interior.

I watched as the ground changed from the city of San Diego to the roughness and chaotic outline of the city of Tijuana. Eventually, all I saw was light brown ground dotted with scrub brush, winding dirt roads that crisscrossed in every direction, and alternating terrain that changed from mountainous to sprawling desert. I silently ruminated over the cost of this little sojourn. I was privately peeved Galveston didn't consult me, but this sure was an easy way to travel.

We caught some mountain turbulence as we crossed over the Sierra Juárez Mountains and left the Baja California peninsula behind.

Monterrey is situated in the interior of the country near the east coast of central Mexico, about 1,100 miles from San Diego, and 400 miles north of Mexico City.

The Corvalis is a fast airplane and travels at a maximum speed of 235 knots, which allowed Galveston to calculate a flight time of four and a half hours. I quit looking out the windows too often and pushed the thought back that if the plane went down there was nothing around but desert.

During the en route phase of our flight, Galveston briefed me on the newest member of this little fiasco, Senator Edward Eastman. After he was finished, I used the remainder of our time to broach the subject of the cost of this flight.

"When are you planning to let me know how much you spent on this little journey? You know you're not supposed to try to make any financial decisions."

"My friend said we could use his plane for free. He owes me a favor. We just have to pay for fuel."

"That's some favor."

"Well there is a catch. We have to help his kid sell all of his candy for his baseball fundraiser."

"And how much candy would that be?" I asked.

"Oh, about twenty cases. See, aren't you proud? I figure we'll get Alex to buy them all. We'll just tell him they're fine French chocolates."

"From now on though, tell me about all the expenses."

"Yes, Dad," Galveston said sarcastically.

Galveston had worked out a good deal, and it didn't mean schlepping bags through security with all the other cattle.

The rest of the flight was uneventful, and we were afforded a nice tailwind from the west that sped our progress. We flew over Monterrey about 2:00 P.M. Central Time.

Galveston set the plane down gently while fighting a nasty crosswind blowing over the runway. As we taxied to a tie down spot we were met by a Mexican customs agent who was nice enough to rifle through our bags. We tied down, prayed the plane would be in the same place when we got back, and made our way to the front of the airplane terminal. A short, skinny, young man approached us.

"Hola, Senors'. Are you names Dan Galveston and Roger Murphy?" He said in broken English.

"That's us," Galveston answered. "You Manuel?"

"Si, Senor, that is me," and Manuel pointed to himself.

"Excellent. You know where we're going?"

"Jes, I know where the Colonel Espinosa is. Here I have a car."

Manuel led us to a rental; an old Volkswagen Beetle, slightly destroyed. Manuel drove us through the streets as he used the horn religiously and cursed the other drivers. He must have not been a day over 22 or 23.

"So how do you know Alex?" I asked.

"He stay at the villas where I work. I help him many times. He got me a promotion and now I have nine people work under me." He pulled both hands off the wheel to show us the number on his fingers. "He is big help to me."

"That guy sure gets around," I told Galveston.

"I think he spent a good amount of time in Mexico. You know, when he had to lay low," Galveston informed me.

We arrived at our destination, Universidad Autónoma de Nuevo León Hospital, a large, white stone building on the campus of a university. Manuel parallel parked the Volkswagen skillfully between two other non-descript cars on the street, making sure to tap the bumpers of the other cars with his own as he angled in.

"We here," he announced proudly.

Galveston then explained to Manuel why we were in Monterrey and laid out our plan.

"Were you able to find out his condition?" Galveston asked.

"Jes, the Colonel is in very bad shape. He in the main medical ward."

Galveston had thought out the plan carefully. He picked up his bag and set it on his lap. He then pulled two white lab coats from the bag and a stethoscope, placing it in one of the coat pockets. Next, he produced two cards from the bag; one for me, and the other one for himself. On it was my driver's license picture, a picture he knew I was not fond of. On the I.D. I had a cheesy, pencil thin mustache. I didn't remembered growing one, ever, but upon further inspection I could see it was added in. "Dr. Joseph Rogers, Epidemiologist, Centers for Disease Control and Prevention, Atlanta, Georgia", it read.

"So I'm a medical doctor now?"

"Yeah," Galveston answered, "you've been promoted."

"Let me see yours." Galveston handed back his I.D. and it read, "Dr. David Hammerstein, Epidemiologist, Centers for Disease Control and Prevention, Atlanta, Georgia". I studied it over and noticed something different about the picture. I held it up to Galveston's face and saw that he had a new chin and nose.

"I see you went with a musical theme," I said, tapping his name on the card.

"Very observant," he replied. It was an ode to the great musical producing team of Rogers and Hammerstein.

Galveston handed me a coat and instructed me to put it on. It was itchy, and in ninety degree heat, uncomfortable.

"Manuel, you're just our translator, that's it, okay?" Galveston told him.

"Jes, sir," he answered.

"Roger?"

"Yes," I answered, trying to get my arms in the sleeves of the white jacket.

"Memorize your new name. I'll do most of the talking, but I want you to talk to the Colonel. We need to know what information he has, where he went, and what he was doing there. I don't care how much you have to lie, or 'fib', if that makes you feel better. I'm going to try to keep the doctors and nurses occupied, if I can."

"I don't know, it sounds awfully risky."

"Nah, it will be fine. Just get him to talk."

"And how do I do that?" I asked nervously.

"I don't know. Just do the best you can, but stay in character. Don't lose sight of that." Manuel now looked nervous. I bet he wished he would have asked for more money. "Okay, we're all clear, right?"

Galveston slid his coat on and handed me a folder with a few papers inside. He had another folder for himself. We got out of the car and straightened our coats.

Manuel followed behind as we walked to the hospital doors and went inside. There was a crowd of people in the main lobby, some sitting in wheelchairs and others talking loudly in Spanish. My heart raced as we approached the receptionist who was busy looking at a Mexican newspaper.

"Manuel, ask where we can find Colonel Espinosa and his doctor."

Manuel moved to the front of the desk and spoke in quick, succinct Spanish. The receptionist continued to look at the paper in front of her, stopping just long enough to peruse a patient list. She nonchalantly answered him and pointed to a bank of elevators behind her.

"He in medical ward two, third floor, intensive care unit," Manuel told us.

We moved toward the elevators before she stopped us, handing out three visitor tags. I was already beginning to sweat in my white coat, the air as stifling inside as out. We took the elevator to the third floor.

"Okay, its showtime," Galveston said as he smoothed out his coat and checked his glasses, as if he were entering the stage for a performance.

The doors opened, and we stepped into the second world's answer to medical care. I was shocked and surprised that it resembled the hospitals in the States. This particular hospital was one of the best in Mexico.

There was a large room with beds laid out in succession to the right. Nurses milled about while family members crouched near the beds, talking with patients. Manuel pointed to the left, and we followed him through a pair of double doors that led to a nurse's station and some private rooms along the wall. A nurse sitting at the station looked up as we approached and did a double take. It probably wasn't often they had two gringo doctors here.

"Manuel, tell her we are from the U.S. We're doctors from the Centers for Disease Control, and we would like to speak to Colonel Espinosa's doctor."

Manuel followed the command and conversed with the nurse. She got up and went to a nearby phone, made a call, and spoke to Manuel again, in Spanish of course.

"He's on his way up," I told Galveston.

"How do you know that?" he inquired.

"I speak a little Spanish," I said meekly.

Actually, I used to speak fluent Spanish, but right now I was rusty and out of practice. I had minored in it in college, and used it during my years dealing with South American and Mexican investors. I didn't mean to let it slip though; I didn't want to have the burden of all the communication.

"You were holding out on me," Galveston smiled deviously, reveling in the new information. Manuel continued to talk to the attractive nurse. "What's he saying to her now?"

"I think he's trying to pick her up."

Manuel turned to us and said, "the doctor, he coming," and returned to the nurse, smiling as he talked.

We both surveyed the area as Manuel continued his pursuit. The intensive care unit was laid out in an "L" shape with windows allowing a view of each room. The equipment was slightly antiquated, but the staff was attentive, moving silently in and out of the rooms, tending to their patients. I admired the work of the nurses who didn't seem concerned about their environment. I had expected much worse and was surprised that the hospital, overall, was clean and in good working order.

"Can I help you gentlemen," a voice from behind us said in excellent English, with only a slight Mexican accent.

"Yes sir, hello," Galveston said after turning toward him.

He was a slightly overweight man in his forties, his white coat open in front and a polo shirt underneath. He had the sleeves of the coat rolled up, and it was too small for his large frame.

"My name is Dr. Hammerstein and this is Dr. Rogers. We're sorry to come unannounced, but it was important that we be here personally. We've come from the Centers for Disease Control in Atlanta." Galveston handed over his I.D., and I nervously fumbled mine from my pocket. I wiped the sweat from my palms as he examined them both.

"The CDC? I'm Dr. Garcia. I haven't heard about a visit. What brings you to Monterrey?"

Galveston stayed calm and cool.

"Again I apologize for the intrusion, but we're tracking a couple of cases that have originated from visits to the U.S., particularly in the Phoenix, Arizona area. We have some information that," Galveston looked at the papers on his clipboard, "an Alfonso Espinosa visited a clinic there about four months ago. We've had some other cases that we managed to hunt down similar to his at that time. We are concerned it may be a mutated strain of tuberculosis." Galveston had obviously done some homework before our visit, because after he mentioned tuberculosis the doctor's eyes leapt and his eyebrows rose.

"Tuberculosis? Mr. Espinosa doesn't present with the symptoms of tuberculosis."

"Neither did our other cases. That's why we're here. We're trying to isolate the strain, but unfortunately our other cases have expired. May we have a look at his medical record? We would like to call our office within the hour."

The doctor was caught off guard from the information. Tuberculosis was highly infective, and the Colonel wasn't in isolation. I looked over at Manuel, still working on the nurse, oblivious to our meeting.

Galveston continued with his fictional discussion. "If you and I could look over the records while Dr. Rogers interviews the patient, it would be greatly appreciated."

"Yes, I think that can be arranged, of course. Please, follow me." I stood rigid while Galveston followed the doctor to the medical charts.

"Uh, Dr. Rogers, you can begin the interview." Galveston motioned for me to head in the other direction.

"Uh, yes. Where is Mr. Espinosa's room?" I asked.

"Room three," Dr. Garcia answered, not looking up from the chart, "and the gown, gloves, and mask are in that cart." He pointed to a wheeled cart next to a wall.

I walked over and opened each drawer, revealing a variety of medical devices. I had no clue of their uses.

I found the gown, gloves, and masks in the bottom drawer. I pulled out a disposable gown first and attempted to put it on backward before realizing my gaff. The gloves went on no better as I attempted to thrust my fingers in the latex. I put the mask on and secured it to my face. I thought I would pass out from the garb, but took a deep breath and headed into the room. A fan attached to the wall blew air about the room, and Colonel Espinosa lay in the bed, his head slightly elevated. He was connected to a multitude of lines and tubes. He had oxygen pumping in his nose through a nasal cannula, and a pair of IV's pumped a clear liquid into his veins. He stared up at the ceiling, his breathing labored and heavy. I moved to the side of his bed as the surrounding monitors beeped incessantly.

"Colonel Espinosa?" I questioned.

He turned his eyes toward me but didn't move his head. The mask was tight on my face and stifling, muffling my words. There would be no way to speak my version of Spanish with such a thing on so I peeled it from my face and put it under my chin.

"Hola, Colonel Espinosa," I spoke in my most clear and succinct Spanish. "Me llamo," oh, God, I had forgotten my fake name and reached for my I.D. I then stopped, thinking that may be a little obvious. A musical duo; Hall and Oats, Sonny and Cher? And then it finally occurred to me. "Me llamo Dr. Rogers," I said proudly. "Vivo en America. Veng aqui con otra Doctor, porque tenemos preguntas sobre tu salud. Necessito habler con su esta bien?" I told him I was with another doctor to find out why he was sick, and I needed to ask him some questions.

Espinosa blinked and stared at me blankly before clearing his throat. He answered softly, his lips dry and cracked.

"Yes, that okay," he responded in almost perfect English.

"Thank God," I thought, "he speaks some English."

"Good Colonel." I took a deep breath and staged the question in my head.

"These might be personal and in no way will I repeat them to anyone. Did you receive something in the last few weeks on a dirt airfield in northern Mexico?"

His eyes grew wide, and it appeared he was trying to move but couldn't. He blinked a few more times, his breathing quickened.

"It's very important for me to know Colonel. Your life may depend on it."

He stared at me intently.

"Yes," he answered softly.

"What did you receive, Colonel—money?"

"No," he replied, and I realized I needed to ask more open ended questions or I would be here all day.

"What did you receive, Colonel?" I asked again. He again hesitated and shifted his eyes away, but then decided to answer.

"A case," he said slowly.

"Do you know what was in the case?" I pressed.

"No. I only transported it." He seemed to garner more strength, but didn't take his statement any further. I decided to play a little more hardball.

"Colonel, we have information that these men you worked for are trying to kill you. They've said it in a message. Now it's time to be straight and honest with me. If you don't, you could die. Now where did you take the case?"

He looked at me horrified, the words, I could tell, were now beginning to sink in. He sighed heavily and his breathing quickened.

"I flew from the field in northern Mexico here to Monterrey to change planes to a jet. I transported the case onto the plane." He drew a large breath from the nasal cannula. "The plane flew to Sao Carlos, Brazil where I handed it off to a group waiting at the airport. I then flew from there to Rio and then on to Mexico City. I drove back to Monterrey."

"So you weren't sick that entire time?" I asked, checking my watch for time.

"No, not until I got home, here in Monterrey."

"What did you get for doing this Colonel?" He again thought before he answered.

"Money, and..." He stopped short of telling me more, obviously afraid of my response to the rest of the answer.

"What else, Colonel," I again pressed the question. He hesitated again before answering.

"A statue, they delivered me a statue that was waiting for me at my home."

"A statue? Of what?"

"The Aztec god Tonatiuh. A small statue bought from an archeologist on the black market."

"Then when did you get sick?" I asked, confused at his answer.

"When I touched the statue. I immediately felt sick when I touched the statue. It is a cursed statue."

The response was unexpected, and at the time made no sense. He was this sick from touching a statue?

"You asked for this statue?"

"Yes, for my collection."

"And who were these men?" He was beginning to grow weary from the questioning, and I knew I didn't have much time.

"I don't know. I really don't know," he said, and began to close his eyes. I knew I might only be able to get a few more answers to my questions out of him.

"Where is the statue now?"

"At my home," his eyes now fully closed.

"Who got you to do this Colonel?" I lightly shook his hand. He waited, and I was unsure if he even heard my question. "Colonel, who got you involved in this?" I asked again. One eye opened slowly.

"Patelo, Ernesto Patelo, my friend."

His eyes closed fully again, and I tried to arouse him with a few shakes of his hand. He didn't respond, but luckily was still breathing. I knew I had pushed him hard, but they were questions we needed answered. I knew my time was up, and I began to walk to the door while taking off the gown and gloves. I then heard a whisper from behind me.

"My desk, in my desk," and the Colonel's voice went silent.

"I've killed him," I thought, but noticed that the heart rate monitors still showed active beating of his heart. I quickly scribbled down all that he had told me on the papers Galveston had given me, paying close attention to circle the name of Ernesto Patelo.

Chapter 36

I stood at the door of the hospital room trying to process what happened when suddenly an alarm sounded from a monitor at Espinosa's bed. Almost instantly a nurse blew past me, yanked the nasal cannula off his face, and replaced it with a mask. I stepped back as Dr. Garcia and Galveston came rushing in.

"He's in shock," Dr. Garcia yelled, looking at the monitors, and immediately gave the nurse orders. They stabilized his erratic heartbeat quickly, and the Colonel's breathing normalized after a few minutes.

"What are we working against?" the doctor asked us.

Galveston and I looked at each other, dumbfounded by the question. I thought for a second, and it occurred to me what was happening to the man in the bed.

"He doesn't have a strain of tuberculosis," I said. Galveston's face turned white, thinking I was going to blow our cover. "He's been poisoned."

The doctor was shocked. "Poisoned? What kind, and how do you know that's the cause?"

"Something at his home poisoned him. We need to go there and find it." I figured this would be a good line for our escape, plus we needed to find out what was in that desk. The Colonel probably had not been truthful with them about when he got sick, most likely to cover his impropriety. Galveston was confused but went with the story I had started.

"Yes, that's a good idea. Where can we get his address? This may be our only chance to save his life."

"Get it from the nurse. Hurry, I don't know how long he will hang on."

The doctor went back to looking at the monitors. Galveston and I quickly turned and left the room before any more questions could be asked.

We paused at the nurses' station to retrieve our translator.

"Come on, lover boy," Galveston said, grabbing Manuel by the shirt collar, pulling him away from his conversation.

"I call you," I heard Manuel say as we dragged him backwards. "Oh, I was so close."

"You didn't have a chance," Galveston retorted.

We went back through the double doors toward the elevators but detoured down the stairs next to them.

"What's the hurry?" Manuel yelped.

"Ask him," Galveston said, pointing toward me.

"You need to drive us, Manuel. I hope you know Monterrey," I said to our new colleague, but realized we had forgotten something. "Ah crap, Dan, we forgot to get the address."

"I'll be back," Galveston shouted, already leaping back up the stairs, skipping one at a time as he went. He left Manuel and me standing in the stairwell.

"So, do you know the Monterrey streets?" I asked him.

"Pretty good. I had a senorita here. She had a brother. He don't like me. I got to know some of the streets well while he chase me."

"I hope so. We need to get to this guy's house, quick. Go get the car and meet us in front. We'll be down in a second."

Manuel nodded his head and raced down the stairs, disappearing beyond the adjacent stairwell. Just then I looked up. Galveston was already returning with a piece of paper in his hand.

"I got it, let's go." He waved the piece of paper and raced past me down the stairs.

By the time I caught up he was already out in front of the building and making his way to our VW chariot. Galveston handed the sheet of paper to Manuel, and I was relegated to the cramped back seat—again. Manuel revved the engine and tore off from the hospital down a twisting street.

It was obvious after twenty minutes of aimless driving that Manuel had no idea where he was going because we wound up back in front of the hospital. Consequently, we forced him to stop at a service station and purchase an actual map, instead of relying on the distorted map in his head. We drove for another half an hour winding and curving our way through the narrow streets of the city dodging pedestrians and other cars.

We finally arrived at the outskirts of the city and a neighborhood of expansive, and expensive, gated homes.

"227, that's the one," Galveston announced, pointing at a rusted gate bordered by two stone pillars. He jumped out and tried to open the gate to the driveway, but it was locked. We would have to make our way on foot.

Manuel pulled the car off the road and cut the engine. It sputtered to a stop. I extracted myself from the back seat and met Manuel and Galveston at the gate; the pair already plotting how they would get in. Manuel was the smallest of the three of us and was put in charge of opening the gate. He nervously pulled a stick of Canel's chewing gum from his pocket and began to chew it incessantly, surveying his duty.

Galveston put his hands together, and Manuel stepped on top of them with one foot, flung himself to the top of the pillar that stood on one side of the gate, and grunted as he pulled himself over the fence. He tried in vain to open the gate, but was unable. Galveston proposed for me to be next. He would wait at the car while we found what we needed.

The gate was too high for one person to scamper over without something or someone to push from. I repeated what Manuel had done, but with less grace, as Galveston pushed me to the top. I heaved my overly heavy body to the other side of the fence while Manuel attempted to soften my fall. I dusted myself off after I got on the other side.

"Alright, Manuel, let's go."

We gave Galveston a wave and moved up the short dirt road to a surprisingly modest two story house, decorated in front with a small grove of palm trees.

I ran to the front door hoping it was open, but unfortunately it was locked. Manuel made his way to the side of the house and yelled when he found an unlocked window. I arrived to find him struggling to get the window open.

With a little teamwork we were able to force the window open and began to crawl inside; listening carefully for a bark or growl from some unwanted creature.

I decided to go in first since I heard and saw nothing. I grunted as I pulled myself through the tiny opening, the sweat accumulating rapidly on my face.

I found myself in a small bedroom decorated with bright vibrant colors and a mixture of Mexican and South American art. Manuel appeared behind me almost instantly, due to the product of youthful exuberance.

"You check the house to the right, and I'll go left. We're looking for any statues or an office, but don't touch anything." I barked the orders, and Manuel jumped at the command.

As I made my way to the left I entered a hallway, and then a large, open foyer. Each room I passed was dotted with art and trinkets; one man's obsession with times of old.

In the foyer I spotted the front door and a myriad of statues on pedestals. They all looked the same to me, but one stood out from the rest. It glistened in the sunlight streaming from the windows and an overhead skylight high in the ceiling. The statue was smaller than the others and looked older; more weathered.

I got close to it and examined it under the available light. The pedestal it sat on was high, and it didn't quite sit right. This had to be the statue of the Aztec god Tonatiuh, or so I hoped. I was no Aztec aficionado. There was a liquid on it, almost the consistency of syrup, and had a faint odor of what I could only describe as "foul". Small bubbles were present on certain portions of it.

I learned later that Tonatiuh was the fifth and final sun god of the final era of the Aztecs. He demanded human sacrifice, or he would refuse to move through the sky. It was ironic that in this present day he might have another victim of sacrifice.

"Manuel, come in here." Manuel hurriedly appeared and peered over my shoulder.

"That don't look right," he said in a low voice.

"I agree. Is this the Aztec god Tonatiuh?" He shrugged his shoulders and reached to touch it, and I grabbed his hand quickly. "Ah, I wouldn't do that, unless you want to end up like Espinosa." Manuel dropped his arms to his side.

"It stinky," he said holding his nose. "It smell like fish rotting in bucket of water." As much as I appreciated his visual, my mind was busy plotting how we were going to get it out of there.

"Go look for a case or something. I'm going to try to find a stick. We'll push it over and into whatever you can find."

"Jou the boss."

Manuel disappeared again. I also left the room in search of a stick. I still needed to find the office, and quickly did as I rounded a corner from the foyer.

The office was filled with more artifacts and artwork. It was wood paneled and in the middle of the room sat the desk Espinosa had mumbled about. The desk was wooden and neatly arranged with a lamp on top. I moved around it to find that there was only one drawer, and I opened it. There were stacks of opened and unopened envelopes, and a stack of loose papers. I tried to look through all the papers, but there were too many, and I couldn't make out anything of significance at that moment.

I decided I didn't have time to try to delve through the entire stack and hoped what we needed was contained within the top bundle. I could always mail it back to the Colonel later, after I invaded his privacy. I stuck the pile of papers under my arm and made sure I hadn't missed anything. On the desk I noticed there was a beautiful, brass letter opener with a bone handle. "This would do nicely as a stick," I thought.

Upon leaving the room I glanced at the pictures on the wall. They were filled with many of the Colonel, posing in his military garb with other soldiers. There was also a Certificate of Merit from the Grupo Aeromóvil de Fuerzas Especiales, or GAFE, the Mexican Army's Special Forces Corps. I didn't even know they had such a thing. Other pictures were of Espinosa posing with big game fish when he was in a healthier state; a large smile on his face.

I returned to the front foyer with papers crammed in one hand and the letter opener in the other. Manuel had returned before me, carrying a lovely pink, designer suitcase.

"That color suits you," I joked, walking toward him.

"It was all I could find. It was in the back of the closet, next to a big gun locker. I won't mind."

I put the papers on the ground and moved toward the pedestal. I instructed Manuel to open the case and put it in front of the statue. I would then use the letter opener to push it in. Manuel opened the case, and a pair of shoes fell out as he held the lid. I poked the back of the statue with the letter opener, and it began to jostle from its perch. As I pushed it farther, a curious thing happened. A whining sound emanated from the base. Before pushing it more, I peeked under the statue and saw it was sitting on a small button. We had an Indiana Jones situation here. It seemed to be attached to an alarm, but an alarm that would send who? I decided I didn't really want to find out and stopped my push.

"Manuel, just scoop it up with the suitcase. I'll hold this button with the letter opener."

Manuel clumsily kept the case open, and when I motioned I was ready he shoved the case around it. It plopped in the case with a thud, while I put pressure on the button. Manuel immediately closed the case leaving me holding the button down. I could see the liquid had left a nice ring on the pedestal from where it had slid off the statue.

"Do you see anything I can put on the button?" I asked him.

He looked around hurriedly, smacking his gum more.

"The shoe, give me a shoe—and your gum."

Manuel grabbed one of the shoes from the floor and the gum from his mouth. He handed them both to me.

"Put it right on top."

Manuel carefully placed the gum and shoe on the top of the letter opener's tip.

"I think that's got it," I told him and slowly moved the opener from the button. It precariously held in position.

"I don't know if that will hold it for very long," I started, but Manuel didn't hear me. He was heading for the window we came in.

I grabbed the papers off the floor, and by the time I made my way to the window, Manuel had tumbled out of it and was already dusting himself off in the yard.

As I went back outside the window we heard a loud screeching sound and the clang of heaving metal. I turned to see a metal panel close from above the window. The screeching got much louder and became deafening.

Manuel raced from the yard to the front gate, and I followed closely on his heels, startled from the sound. All the windows of the house had closed up with metal shutters, trapping any would be intruders inside; which could have been us. Galveston waited eagerly at the gate.

"What happened?" he yelled over the whining blare of the alarm.

"Push it through the bars," I yelled at Manuel.

He began to shove the pink suitcase through the bars, but it got stuck halfway. Galveston pulled hard on the handle, and effectively ripped it off due to the force. I ran up behind and gave the case a swift kick, sending it skidding across the dirt road.

"Well that was effective," Galveston managed to quip as I gave Manuel a boost over the fence, and he in turn helped me scale back over.

We didn't waste any time with explanations. Galveston picked up the case and threw it in the car as we jumped in. Manuel ground the gears as he floored our lovely escape vehicle away from the house. As the dust settled behind us we steadily calmed ourselves and began to relax.

"What happened back there?" Galveston asked, eyeing the road.

"He had some sort of alarm installed. We could have been trapped inside," I said excitedly.

"Yeah, you were lucky. I noticed something strange about that house."

"I'm glad you tried to warn us," I said, agitated by his words.

Manuel was sweating nervously. I was surprisingly calm, having become used to our antics. I settled myself into the back seat and scattered the various envelopes and papers beside me.

"What did you find in there?" Galveston asked, as he too wiped the sweat from his brow.

I stared at the papers. "I'm not sure. We got the statue. Clearly there is something sticky on it that I'm assuming shouldn't be there. I'm betting that is what poisoned Espinosa."

I began to go through a few of the papers, mostly financial items of no importance, until I came across an envelope addressed to Colonel Espinosa dated just about two weeks ago. It had a postmark from Sao Paulo, Brazil. I did my best to translate the Spanish writing and was just about to ask Manuel for help, but I thought otherwise since he was driving.

It was a rough translation, but I was able to determine the general theme and managed to decipher the following from the letter.

Dear Alfonso,
Thank you for the contact. I have moved into the new apartment in the city and the move from Rio was easy. I will be unable to contact you directly since I don't know where the facility is yet. I met with the man you told me about. I am excited that this opportunity will allow me to further my

own research. The secrecy behind this project has me worried. I am wondering if I am getting in over my head. I'm not sure I trust these men. When I am done I will meet you in Monterrey. I have received the preliminaries of the project and have begun working on it as we had discussed. It won't be the same as when we worked together during Special Ops. I will send you my new address in Sao Paulo.

Ernesto

I searched through the other letters and saw nothing more from Ernesto Patelo. At the bottom of the stack of papers was a neatly folded piece of paper. I opened it and read the contents. It was Espinosa's itinerary for what would be his fateful encounter with the silver case.

Flight one arrives 13:30 77M, agent will exit and leave case on ground. Do not touch or attempt to open or contract terminated. Confirm with predetermined satellite phone number last four digits. Plane one will depart immediately. Flight two depart 13:55 to Monterrey Intl. Change planes. Flight three depart 15:20. Arrive at Sao Carlos. Flight to Rio and Mexico City will be arranged on arrival.

It appeared as highly organized and professional, with little room open for error. But why go to the trouble of doing this? Why not just fly it directly to Brazil?

I posed my questions to Galveston and filled him in on the letter and the itinerary. I handed over the papers for him to look at as I continued to try to unravel the many pieces of the puzzle

"Look how hard it has been for us to trace their pattern. Would we have been able to figure out what they were up to by anything other than luck?" Galveston surmised openly as we reentered the city.

I didn't really understand at first what he meant by the statement, but then I got it. Galveston was trying to think like they were. "What procedures would cover their tracks and allow the least chance of being traced by any government or private organization," I thought, putting myself in the operatives' minds. It would have been easier and faster to just get on an airline and fly the device to Brazil; what we hoped was the ultimate destination. But that could be traced easily, and the FBI could unravel it in a few days. The more stops they did, the more muddled the trail, but they were dealing with intermediaries that didn't have the same alliance to them as their own agents. That had been our stroke of luck.

"They were trying to stop the trail with this Espinosa guy," Galveston explained. "They shouldn't have flown from the U.S. They should have just driven it across the border and flew it out of Mexico."

"His friend's name is Patelo, and the Colonel said this is who got him involved. From the letter it appears it was the other way around. The Colonel got Patelo involved—but why?" I asked Galveston.

"That's the million dollar question, my friend," Galveston replied.

"It appears he now lives in Sao Paulo and moved from Rio de Janeiro, probably just a month ago. And then we have this poisoning thing. Why try to kill Colonel Espinosa?"

"I can think of many reasons. We have some good leads now." Galveston turned to me from the front seat. "We have a lot of thinking to do, and we have to ask the Colonel some more questions. First, who is this Patelo, second, what does he do, and third, now that I think about it, who got the Colonel involved?" Galveston again wiped the sweat from his forehead with his shirt sleeve. "I know one thing though; our answers appear to lay in Brazil."

-Chapter 37-

"Manuel, stop at that store, I need to make a call. I can't use my cell phone here," Galveston said, pointing to a small grocery store with a TelMex payphone out front.

Manuel pulled into the parking lot where the small grocery store sat, surrounded by a bevy of food stalls. Galveston got out and went to the nearby payphone. He used a calling card and feverishly punched in a bunch of numbers on the phone before dialing the number to the hospital.

I stayed in the back of the car and tried to tear my legs off the vinyl seat to readjust myself. I observed people scurrying to and fro, unaware of the curious Americans that held such dire information about the future use of energy. This was why we were here, I thought. These are the people Dr. Sloan's invention could help, maybe making life a little more simple. But we were fighting a multi-headed hydra, a monster of tremendous proportions, fueled by greed and power, unsure of how many heads the monster had. We could make a difference and stop their quest. We had to be smarter, and now, much more careful.

Galveston came into view out the front of the windshield and entered the passenger side of the car. He slumped down in the seat and sighed, leaving the door open.

"Well, it's not good news. The Colonel is dead; cardiac arrest and respiratory failure."

"Oh, no," I gasped. "We're too late."

"No, we never had a chance. We're just lucky we got to him when we did."

Manuel just stared at us, noticeably shocked at our complacency over the Colonel's demise. Galveston sighed again.

"Yeah, we had no chance. Black Bear wanted him dead, and they wouldn't have allowed anything for him to be cured."

"Are we going to take the statue to the doctor?" I asked.

"No, I think we need to take it and get it analyzed by May. Maybe he can figure out where the statue and the poison came from."

I didn't relish the idea of flying with the thing that just killed a man, but I understood his point and the importance of getting it analyzed. It was the only material evidence we had on who was doing this. It was becoming more clear that the trail really did point to Black Bear, but the nagging question still remained of who was ultimately behind it.

I looked at Manuel, forgetting our new teammate was not abreast of our plan. His face was pale, and he seemed to scoot his back more firmly to the seat and the door, as if waiting for a chance to escape. Galveston noted his unease.

"Manuel, why don't you go get yourself a drink; you look a little shaken." Manuel slunk away from the car as Galveston and I discussed our next set of moves.

What was Black Bear planning? Clearly they would go to any lengths to accomplish their objective, but the bigger question still lingered like a smelly fish, why? Why would a company jeopardize their standing in the international business arena, as well as open themselves up to potential and complete self destruction? Galveston looked to me for answers, as I was the supposed "expert" in all economic things.

I had mulled these questions over before, and I managed to come up with the main driving forces of this unscrupulous activity. Money and power. Men and companies had been driven by these two things through history, dating back to the East India Trading Company in the 1700's, and to Enron and WorldCom of the late 20th century. They were all fueled by the insatiable need for more money and power, until they imploded. But they all had another motivation that was more subtle—fear. That was the motivation I found more intriguing.

What was Black Bear afraid of? If a company is profitable and confident in their business, why take unnecessary risk? This is what I needed to explore. I had an idea that Black Bear wasn't a robust titan as it seemed, but similar to a frightened teenager who didn't want to get caught after taking Dad's car out for a night of partying. Galveston enjoyed my analogy and understood what I was saying. It became apparent we had to get back to San Diego, and fast. We had a lot of work to do, and we were still vulnerable due to that tiny file at Genesis. It would only be a matter of time before Black Bear made the link, and we turned from the hunter to the hunted.

Chapter 38

Manuel joined us in the car again, a little more relaxed. He drove back through the city and to the Monterrey airport. There was no use going back to the hospital now; it would have only opened us up to questions we could not answer.

We got out of the car and carefully pulled out the pink suitcase. Galveston placed it in his bag and covered it with clothing, effectively contaminating all his belongings. We didn't need to have gone this far only to have a customs agent find a very questionable Aztec statue. This wouldn't have sat well with the Mexican authorities.

Luckily, our plane still sat in the same place. The area around the private airplanes was poorly guarded, and I tossed the bag over the airport fence near our aircraft, out of view behind a few used oil drums. It wasn't the most brilliant of plans, but we had to take this course of action instead of taking the chance someone would find it through a customs search.

We said our goodbyes to Manuel, and Galveston shoved a wad of cash in his hand before we left him at the car. He waved gingerly at us before squealing out of the parking area. It almost appeared he was glad to get rid of us. Galveston went through the air terminal first, and I followed behind him as I did my best not to look guilty.

Galveston was able to retrieve the bag discretely as I distracted the ground personnel that milled about around the plane. He placed it far back in the aircraft, well out of sight behind an aft cargo wall.

We were soon in the air bouncing our way back to San Diego, attempting to race the dwindling light. Galveston engaged the autopilot at our cruise altitude and relaxed in his seat.

"I need a beer," he said through his microphone, his voice cracking over the loud prop noise.

"I agree," I responded, amazed at the amount of dials and glass laid out in front of me. I never asked where Galveston had learned to fly, but right now I was just too tired to care.

There was so much I didn't really know about Galveston, some of it I probably didn't ever want to know. But he really didn't know much about me neither. He probably didn't care to know I liked collecting stamps and enjoyed good coffee. Not too interesting for a guy who could fly airplanes and dated English spies.

Our flight proved to be uneventful, and the deep blue of the Pacific came into view as we made our way up the Baja coast over the border and into California.

"How much did you give Manuel before we left?" I asked as San Diego Lindbergh International appeared off our right wingtip. It was a welcome sign that we were closing in on Montgomery airport.

"A thousand bucks," he answered nonchalantly.

"A thousand dollars, in cash?" I exclaimed. "How much cash did you bring?"

Galveston did the arithmetic in his head.

"Let's see, I've got about two thousand left so..." He continued to do the math.

"Three thousand? You were carrying around three thousand dollars, in cash, in Mexico?" I became exasperated.

"Yeah. It was safe. I was carrying it in my underwear."

I flashed to Manuel. The poor kid was carrying around a load of money that had spent a day residing around Galveston's crotch. I felt myself beginning to do a simulated dry heave at the thought.

Galveston banked the plane carefully and lined up for runway two-eight right. I had made it back from Mexico in one piece at the hands of a man who felt it was okay to hold large amounts of cash in his undergarments. Galveston carefully taxied back to the parking spot we had left that morning, shut the airplane down, and secured it. He was visibly exhausted.

We called Alex, who admitted he was sunning himself by his pool. He told us he heard from Elizabeth. She was finding it increasingly difficult to keep Dr. Sloan under wraps. He was becoming impatient and frustrated over the progress.

"I think Alex needs to start pulling more weight," Galveston said wearily.

"What do you mean?" I asked.

"I think he needs to take in a boarder; a sixty-year old boarder with a pot belly who has extensive knowledge of electrical engineering."

I thought about it a second and figured it could be humorous.

"I agree," I added, "they have a lot in common."

"We'll spring this on him when we see him," Galveston said while putting up his charts. I nodded again and smiled in agreement.

Galveston and I tied the plane down and parted ways. It was a little before eight o'clock, and we decided the best course of action was to go home and catch up on some much needed rest and relaxation. We planned to get together in the morning at Alex's house to work our way through the new information.

I called Jane on my way home and was relieved to hear her voice chipper and upbeat. Galveston took charge of the pink suitcase and planned to deliver it to May for analysis the next morning.

I had a stiff drink as soon as I arrived home to try to help me to sleep, but the scenarios kept playing themselves out in my head. What was Black Bear planning? What were they doing in Brazil? What was the Senator's connection? And who was this Patelo character? The bigger question continued to linger and appear in my head. What was Black Bear afraid of? These questions would have to wait until morning.

Chapter 39

I awoke with a start as my alarm blared out the latest top forty radio hits followed by some nincompoop who spoke in his best DJ voice. The sounds wrenched me to a sitting position. I punched the clock to silence the clatter and waddled to the bathroom. I felt like I'd been struck by a Mack truck. My legs and back hurt, and my rear wasn't feeling much better. After what seemed like hours I managed to awake from my stupor and drove quickly to Alex's humble abode.

Galveston beat me there and was already waiting inside. Alex was in a truly disgruntled mood; Galveston must have already told him of his new roomy. I was disappointed I had missed his reaction. It must have been great.

I tried to get myself settled, but before I could, Galveston reached hyper mode, like a kid who had just eaten too much sugar.

"Alright, Alex, now that we're here, I need info on an Ernesto Patelo. He's an acquaintance of Colonel Espinosa."

Alex began typing dejectedly, probably still thinking about how he was going to entertain Dr. Sloan.

I positioned myself at an adjacent computer and began to surf the web, anything to pass the time while Alex did his work. Something caught my eye almost immediately. I don't know why, but it seemed to stand out. The news article read, " Rebels Destroy Nigerian Oil Outpost". I clicked the link and read through the article.

Lagos (Reuters) – A major explosion was reported at two of the main

export oil terminals of Nigeria's Bonny crude oil loading platform

early Thursday morning. The explosion completely destroyed the two

offloading output terminals for oil produced from the Niger delta

region. The fire continued to burn throughout the afternoon as fire

crews tried to control the blaze. "Oil production has been ceased indefinitely until security concerns are addressed," a spokesman for

Royal Dutch Shell said, a principal operator of tankers in the area.

The Nigerian government has blamed extremist rebels for the explosions and has plans to move troops into the area. No group has

claimed responsibility for the attack. The Niger Delta produces an

estimated 2.3 million barrels a day according to U.S. government

sources and has seen drastic cuts in production of up to 450,000

barrels per day due to recent conflicts with militant groups. The price

of oil rose today on the news of further cuts in oil production in the

region, which threatens to disrupt global energy capacity demands.

I sat staring at the article. "Could there be a connection here," I thought. Nah, they wouldn't go to these lengths; they wouldn't dare. On the other hand, they did poison someone using an Aztec statue, broke into a woman's house in England, and already tried to kidnap an esteemed professor.

I then thought over the connection logically. The gears in my brain moved exceedingly slow, the rust and cobwebs from the previous night were causing the neurons not to fire. I gave myself a quick slap in the face, and the sound reverberated around the room. Alex and Galveston stared at me pitifully, as if I had lost my mind. I gave my face another good smack and told myself to think. Yeah, that did it, I was clear and my face now hurt. I felt like a fool, but I was awake. Just as the slap on my face got the attention of Alex and Galveston, these explosions would get everyone's attention.

I resolved that it came down to a simple case of cause and effect, supply and demand. Actually eloquent, I had to admit, as I read the article again. They cause an explosion and cut off the supply of much needed oil to a hungry global economy. The effect would be increased demand, and a nasty little rebel group would get the blame. I just knew it had to be Black Bear behind this explosion.

They were intentionally trying to drive up the price of oil, and they were doing it the most quick and effective way they knew how by blowing the hell out of a major oil producer's infrastructure. But again the question returned for the millionth time—why? I had to find this out, now.

Galveston and Alex were so enthralled with searching for Dr. Patelo that they hardly knew I was in the room. At this point I was only speculating that Black Bear was involved in these explosions, because I had no proof. I looked up Black Bear on the financial pages. It gave all the information on the company. Black Bear had made 237 million in revenue the last quarter, with a healthy earnings report. It was hardly proof of a company struggling for a profit. The stock price was holding relatively steady at twenty-three dollars a share. Visibly not a sign a company is doing poorly. Black Bear also had announced some new government contracts that would pad their bottom line in the coming years.

I searched through the old news items. Most of the news was about the company acquiring new contracts and the ebb and flow of the company's stock price. But one item stood out.

About six months ago, Black Bear agreed to provide security services to Global Energy Enterprises in their overseas operations. It explained that Global Energy Enterprise was a non-profit company that supplied energy solutions for developing countries. This was the organization that Weston Chase had started, and the one Dr. Sloan had told us about. As I read further the story quoted a speech from Black Bear CEO, Timothy Placer. It read:

> We have established a grant to Global Energy Enterprises for their continued good work in developing green energy alternatives for areas of the world in need of these services. In addition to this grant, Black Bear Global Security will supply all the services for this great organization to safely implement all of their alternative energies, such
> as solar, wind, and clean fuels. In response to the growing need for all people to have access to alternative forms of energy, and in cooperation with the government of Brazil, we will start up our newest endeavor, Ecomax Clean Energy. This may seem strange given that our primary business is

security services, but we feel this will significantly diversify our position in the world marketplace.

With our know-how in security services we will be able to ensure that new breakthroughs in energy technology will be accessible by all who are in need.

It tugged on the heartstrings. These great bastions of American capitalism wanted to help all the lonely, desolate peoples of the world. I continued to read the transcript, transfixed to the words.

Ecomax will research and develop alternate forms of energy, and we have already begun to employ the best and brightest from the scientific community. We have also begun the research and development of a cleaner burning hydrocarbon fuel and the development of more effective battery technology.

The transcript ended, and the story behind it summarized the feelings of investors.

Response on Wall Street was mixed with the stock closing lower on the news. Investors seem cool to the idea of a security company entering the volatile and uncertain world of alternative energy solutions from the ground up.

I was stunned. They really were doing this, and I had to admit that it was a brilliant plan, if not devious, with the insider information we knew. But if I had been an investor at this time I would have run for the exits. A company that had no experience in energy beginning a start-up, from scratch? Not something I would put my money into. There were still answers I needed, however, and further questions to form.

Just then I heard a clamor from across the room.

"We found him," Galveston yelled, and I spun my chair toward him. "Here he is—Ernesto Patelo." He pointed to the screen in an act of satisfaction.

"Let me guess," I started, "he works for a company in Brazil," I scratched my head to let the tension build, "and I bet it's called Ecomax." I let the words sink in and watched Galveston's and Alex's expressions fade from excitement to amazement. They stuttered in unison at my Yuri Geller like powers.

"How did you...what...how?" Galveston stammered.

"I did a little research of my own. I think we need to have a little pow-wow."

Chapter 40

I relayed all the news I had gathered; the explosion, the Black Bear bottom line, their help with Global Energy Enterprise, and the start-up of Ecomax in Brazil. They sat transfixed, and I held their attention with every word I said.

"I think I follow, but I'm still confused," Galveston said as I finished with my information. "Break your theory down— in a nutshell."

"You and your nutshells. Okay, I'll try to dumb it down for you," I said, joking of course. "Maybe I'll start from the beginning. That ought to help us see the timeline better. Black Bear offers to provide security for Global Energy in the bad, rough parts of the world so they can implement whatever; it doesn't really matter."

"Who got them to do that?" Galveston interrupted.

"I don't know, but Black Bear gave Global Energy a grant, and they became a prized child and a buddy. Global Energy knows what Dr. Sloan is working on, and as a cover Black Bear starts Ecomax, strategically placing it out of prying eyes in the U.S. They put the company in Brazil where Ecomax would be out of sight from U.S. regulations and investment law, all under the guise of helping the world, the environment, etcetera. Black Bear steals two of the battery prototypes right as Dr. Sloan leaves for Memphis. But the two they steal aren't the final version." I was in the zone, one thought coming after another, like the joy in finishing the last pieces of a jigsaw puzzle. "Black Bear flies the prototypes to the airfield in northern Mexico, and with Colonel Espinosa's help, they're exchanged to another plane. They're then flown to Brazil where Espinosa hands them over and returns to Mexico. The one man that is aware of this hand-off is poisoned and now dead."

"Colonel Espinosa?" Alex jutted in.

"Exactly," I answered coolly, enjoying my new found respect. "They manage to silence him. The trail was supposed to go cold right there."

I looked at Galveston and Alex to make sure they were following me. They both stared intently, waiting for the next sequence of events.

"Now this is where it gets messy," I warned them. "Black Bear sends a team to England to retrieve the final plans. They probably had the same information as the Feds. Somehow they knew the prototypes weren't the final version. The trip to England was an effort to get the final design while Genesis developed software for a production line."

"Black Bear must be confident they can produce it," Galveston added.

"I think it went to Ecomax to be developed, but without the final plans they would have to reverse engineer the battery to set it up for production, costing valuable time. Stay with me here. Nobody would be interested—yet," I said, with dramatic effect. "To accomplish this feat they blow up a major oil export center. The explosion is blamed on terrorism, the markets respond with supply fear, and oil prices rise drastically. Black Bear plans to capitalize on the high oil prices with the release of the battery, making a lot of people very, very rich."

Alex and Galveston sat stunned and nodded in acknowledgement at what was, in theory, a simple plan, but amazingly difficult due to its many steps. They began to pepper me with questions like I was an esteemed professor. I don't know about the esteemed part, but I did consider myself an expert in economics and finance.

"What do you think they'll do next?" Galveston asked inquisitively.

"Actually, I'm bothered by this one explosion. It's not really enough to cause a long-term drop in oil supply. I think they're going to strike again," I said.

"Another explosion? Do you think in the U.S.?" Alex asked.

"I don't think so. Too easy to investigate. I think they'll go after another major export area. Probably in an area where we don't have good relations. This would ensure that the U.S. won't be able to investigate." I leaned back in my chair. "I'm confused about two questions, though. One, what is the catalyst for them to do this, and two, what is the truth behind Black Bear's bottom line? I think that's an area we need to figure out. I would bet Black Bear isn't doing as well as their financial and accounting reports show."

"I agree," said Galveston. "I think there's some 'cooking of the books' going on. Alex, look into that. Find out any information you can on Black Bear. Contracts, law suits, liquidity issues, anything that sounds like they're not doing as well as they say they are. Roger, who do you guess may have started this?"

I thought hard for a second, trying to formulate an intelligent answer.

"You know," I began, "for Black Bear to pull this off they're going to need help. Chase could have started it, but why? He has no reason, that I can see, and I don't think Black Bear acted alone. They would need assistance, probably in the form of government help. They need a strong motivator to investors, higher oil prices won't be enough. It would have to come in the form of government intervention."

Galveston raised his eyebrows at my statement. A light bulb seemed to appear over his head, and I knew what he was thinking.

"The government, huh. How would they help?" he asked.

"Well, if the U.S. government eased restrictions on foreign investment, or offered incentives for investors in 'green' technologies, that would do it. Investors would pour money into such things, but that would be a big 'if'," I answered as Galveston looked thoughtfully at me.

"A Senator could do such a thing, right?" he asked.

"Yeah, I guess." I knew where he was going with this.

Galveston flipped through some papers on his desk and muttered to himself.

"A Senator, that's it. Right here."

He handed me a paper with the list of the Board of Directors of Global Energy Enterprise and pointed to a name. Second from the bottom was a name that we were familiar with—Senator Edward Eastman.

He moved to the computer I was using and began typing before I could say more. It did seem farfetched. A U.S. Senator? I guess stranger things have happened.

Alex and Galveston continued to frantically research from our technological information center. I decided to get something to drink in the kitchen as they did their work. I hadn't even asked about Ernesto Patelo. We would know his fate soon enough.

Before arriving in the kitchen I heard a knock on the door and went to answer it. It was Elizabeth with Dr. Sloan, and I welcomed them in. Dr. Sloan looked overly tired, the product of living out of a suitcase for the past week. Elizabeth guided him to where Alex and Galveston were working. I heard chatter as they exchanged pleasantries, and I returned to the kitchen to find a drink.

As I reached for a glass in the cupboard I heard another knock on the front door.

"Now what," I thought. I moved to the door and looked through the peephole. It was May, alone, waiting at the door.

I yelled to Galveston, "May's here!"

I heard a clamor of footsteps and noise coming from the back room. Galveston immediately appeared in the foyer in response to my yell.

"Dr. Sloan isn't here," Galveston told me as we met at the door. "I think we need to keep him under wraps until we figure this thing out. The less David knows right now about his whereabouts the better."

I wasn't sure what he was getting at. I assumed that keeping Dr. Sloan's whereabouts secret would stop the Bureau's temptation of trying to use him.

Galveston swung open the door. "David!" he exclaimed. "Have I got a prize for you."

May was taken aback by the exuberance.

"I'm a little hesitant to take it off your hands, but I have the lab waiting to take a look at it," May responded flatly.

Galveston moved to the closet door nearby, opened it, and on the floor sat his black bag with the pink suitcase inside.

"I wouldn't open it if I were you," he warned May. "And you can keep my clothes. I don't think I want them back." Galveston cautiously handed the black bag to May. "Let me know what you find. We have a lot of things working right now."

"Good, you'll fill me in when you're ready, right?" May asked.

"Of course," Galveston replied.

"And what about Sloan. Where is he, and is he safe? We would really like to talk to him," May inquired, as Galveston had expected.

"He's safe and in a hotel. I'd rather you wait until we get more information, as a favor to me. He's just too hot right now. I'll tell you this; everything he has told us we have told you. Deal?"

"Alright, deal. We're devoting much of our time to the leads you've already given us."

"There's more to come, that's for sure. This thing is big, David, real big. I don't know if you boys know how far this thing goes."

"We're beginning to get that feeling. It's going to be a mess."

"I figured you knew. I'll call you soon," Galveston said while he seemingly pushed May back through the door and gave a wave goodbye.

"Oh, by the way, Galveston, be careful. We're dealing with professionals."

"Now you tell me," Galveston laughed. "Talk to you soon, David."

Galveston closed the door and turned to me. "I don't want to tell May anything until we know the whole story and can protect ourselves. He'd have the Bureau in here in a second if he knew what we knew."

I understood his reluctance. The last thing we needed were Federal agents scouring over everything we had worked so hard to find. We still had to look out for ourselves first. Our livelihood and safety had to take first priority over everything else, as callous as that may sound.

Galveston and I walked back to Alex's office.

"You can come out Dr. Sloan," Galveston yelled. Dr. Sloan emerged from a closet in the room, appearing more disheveled than ever. "Sorry, Dr. Sloan, we just have to be cautious," Galveston said to him.

"I understand, but I'm getting tired of hiding," he replied. We all felt his pain.

"Dr. Sloan, this is your new buddy, Alex. This is his house, and what is his is yours." Galveston answered for Alex who sat staring at the computer screen. He simply waved his arm over his head in an act of defiance.

"I appreciate all you've done. It's good to get out of a hotel for a while," Sloan answered.

"Yeah, put your feet up, relax, and make yourself at home. We'll get some fresh clothes for you. Alex has a huge closet," Galveston said, ribbing Alex, as he in turn flashed Galveston a dirty look. "Alex, could you find the good doctor something to eat? I'm sure he's famished."

Alex grunted and moped his way toward the kitchen.

"Follow me, Professor," he said dejectedly.

"You're really putting the screws to him," I said.

"Ah, he's okay. He's getting too tan. This will help keep his mind off of sitting by the pool and sipping his fruity drinks," Galveston replied, smiling. "Boy-oh-boy, Elizabeth, do we have a story for you." Galveston grabbed Elizabeth's hand and squeezed it, obviously glad to see her.

He gave her a short synopsis of our travels, what we had figured out so far, and our theory about Black Bear's next steps. Elizabeth was shocked, and intrigued, at the scope.

"I feel I must get the Agency involved. These things are also of importance to my government," she told him. Galveston was hesitant, but Elizabeth had resources at her disposal that were endless.

"Maybe if you can find out what the real story is in Nigeria. We'll never get it from the news wires. We're still going on a hunch on that one," Galveston requested.

"Let me make a call." She pulled out her phone and went onto the patio.

"Did you find out anymore about Black Bear or the Senator?" I asked him after Elizabeth left the room. I had to snap my fingers at him in the process to get him to listen.

"Uh, yeah, yeah," he said breaking away from his stare at Elizabeth. "From what we found it looks like Black Bear isn't doing as great as they appeared, just as you suggested." He pointed to a page on the computer, and I scanned it quickly.

Black Bear had lost two lucrative security contracts in the Middle East in the previous year. They had also lost a trio of lawsuits. Two were from foreign governments, and one was from a private company. One case was settled for an undisclosed amount, and the other case was settled for 14 million dollars, payable over five years. The private company's lawsuit payment was still pending. This company was seeking damages of 80 million dollars due to accusations of a hostile takeover, records tampering, and lost revenue. It seemed Black Bear had a history of unscrupulous activities. Black Bear was being hammered by lawsuits. I figured in the amount of two recent contracts losses, and based on my best estimation, the numbers were clearly in the red. Black Bear also tried to expand into other areas of business that didn't relate to their own. When I checked on the other companies they had acquired I found that those companies were doing terribly.

Black Bear had engaged in a classic case of expansion when the money was rolling in, and to fund their expansion dreams incurred a large amount of debt. Now they didn't have the money to cover the costs of doing business. The companies they had acquired were just a money drain. Nobody wanted to buy them. A security company shouldn't be trying to run an iron ore production facility in Russia, for example. Black Bear had their hands in so many companies that it was difficult to track. Most were foreign, which was attributing to Black Bear's demise. In order to stay solvent there had to be some creative accounting going on.

In each quarter Black Bear showed a significant revenue growth, but it didn't add up to what was really occurring. Why hadn't Wall Street caught on to this? Most likely Black Bear was doing a credible job of cooking the books, moving money between one entity to another each quarter, making it seem as if they were making money. But that couldn't last for long. They were being driven by fear; the fear of going out of business, the fear of losing investors millions of dollars, and fear that the Securities and Exchange Commission could investigate them when the balance sheets didn't add up.

At this point they needed a huge infusion of money, and fast, to stay viable and solvent, because they were hemorrhaging money at every turn. They didn't have the assets to cover their losses and soon they would be out of money completely and bankrupt, or worse, sold off in pieces. According to my rough calculations this would occur by year's end. I showed Galveston my numbers.

"Yeah, they're in a world of hurt. They don't have the money to cover their expenses, and they can't borrow more because their credit is topped off," I told him.

It was also a classic case of corporate panic. Business had been booming then it went flat, and to compensate they spent more money. But instead of gaining they ended up losing more and more profit. The executives were panicking and picturing the loss of their mansions, sports cars, and power.

"Wait until you hear about our Senator friend," Galveston told me.

"I'm sure it's a glowing report. He helps all the sick children and works in a soup kitchen, doesn't he."

"Yeah, and he steals welfare checks, and gets kickbacks for supplying the soup. He's a nasty little guy. You wouldn't know it from the crap he spews. I read some of his comments, and I felt like I had to take a shower afterwards."

"Great, another hypocritical politician," I responded with disdain.

"Seems Senator Eastman likes the ladies too. I find it hard to believe they like him back. This is what we found." Galveston scrolled through another screen on the computer. "Eastman touts himself as an ardent environmentalist. The problem is he's invested in so many 'green' companies and has shamelessly shaped public policy for them. He's power hungry, no doubt about it. As you know, he's a career politician. He's the Chairman of the Senate Energy Committee, and he sits on the board for Global Energy. This ties him to Weston Chase," Galveston reported.

"He sure is one, big, walking conflict of interest," I added.

"Yeah, and here's the scary connection. He used to be a high ranking member on the Senate Armed Services Committee but was pushed off due to 'political pressure'. Possibly because of a midnight tryst. While on this committee he lobbied hard for an ease on restrictions of private security agencies involved in government contracts. It is widely known that Black Bear was one of his primary political contributors, and they benefitted heavily from his work. It's rumored he got a stake in the company under the table. Nobody can prove it, though. Eastman currently shows no obvious stake in the company."

I interrupted him. "But there are ways around that; offshore accounting, dummy investment companies, hedge funds. These are all ways to hide an investment."

"Exactly," Galveston answered. "There's one more very interesting tidbit of information that Alex found by chance. In a meeting of the Energy Committee, Eastman introduced the plans for a bill that would virtually eliminate import taxes on investments in alternative energy. This would allow companies to purchase their products with little to no import tariff."

I interrupted again. "This would allow companies to cut the prices of their products, thereby out-competing U.S. companies.

This would encourage investment with foreign companies that sold alternative energy solutions. More importantly, alternative energy products would sell for a quarter of what they would from U.S. companies. But I can also see the detractor's side. If this legislation passed it would harm the U.S. companies. They would have to compete with a foreign company on a level field. Now, let's say the oil demand was there, and everyone is hurting due to higher energy prices. Here comes a product on the market that is good and reduces energy demand—the super battery. Companies would be scrambling to buy this product. They now can get it at a reduced price because it can be offered by a foreign company at the same price as a U.S. company. Maybe this foreign company is, oh, I don't know, Ecomax. The interest in such an incredible product would be tremendous."

"That to me is a smoking gun," Galveston said, and I agreed.

Imported products are usually more expensive than the same products produced in the U.S. That's why imported beer from Holland is more pricey than good 'ole Budweiser, and the same reason why Budweiser would be more expensive in Holland (though I doubt they drink the stuff there). If that same Dutch beer was produced here it would almost be the same price. There are some exceptions; like plastic toys or TV's produced in China, Taiwan, or Mexico. They can compete with U.S. companies due to their inexpensive labor costs and poor economic conditions. We were referring to highly intricate and complicated energy supply systems costing hundreds of thousands to millions of dollars. U.S. companies would quickly be outdone by their foreign counterparts without the import tariff.

The Senator's plan would make the cost of a Belgian wind turbine the same as one produced in Colorado, and it dealt only with alternative energy, nothing else. The Colorado wind turbine company would have to lower their prices to compete, drastically damaging their bottom line.

Black Bear appeared to be creating the demand for oil and rising energy prices, while hiding in the background waiting for people to panic. Then, low and behold, a magnificent product will become available to all those gas seeking, energy guzzling Americans. They would be able to import the product for the same price as if it were made in the States, erasing the risk of the prying eyes of pesky government agencies and regulators. It would also fuel investors who would throw their money at this new glorious company called Ecomax, in the hopes of reaping the benefits and profits. Ecomax would be rich, Black Bear's stock price would soar and trade at a premium, and Senator Eastman and the execs at Black Bear would walk away with millions, if not billions of dollars, with no one the wiser. That is as long as they could get rid of Dr. Sloan. With Colonel Espinosa out of the way, Dr. Sloan was the only one who could pose a threat.

But they hadn't counted on a couple of ex-"la Technologies" employees getting in the way. They hadn't succeeded in this part of their plan, and we were going to make sure they never did.

"If this is all true, you know they're not going to stop. They're going to be desperate, and you know what that means, right?" I wasn't sure I knew what he meant. "They're going to eliminate, and I mean eliminate, anyone who knows about this. That means us, Dr. Sloan, Margaret, Elizabeth, Alex, everybody. They're going to hunt for Dr. Sloan and when they find him, which they will eventually, they'll find us," he said very seriously.

"Then what do we do?" I asked, searching for an answer. He stared at me, the anger growing in his eyes. "We strike at them first."

Chapter 41

I was shocked at his statement. I wasn't a mercenary like those at Black Bear. I had only fired a gun twice in my life. My world had been numbers and thoughts, not bullets and guns.

"This is getting out of hand—way out of hand," I said, stating the obvious.

"I'm not saying we're going in like Dirty Harry, but what do rich people fear more than anything else?" Galveston asked, his anger subsiding.

I thought for an answer. "I don't know. Not being able to find a cheap lawn guy?"

"True, but no. What rich people fear most is being poor," Galveston said bluntly. "That's what we're going to do. We're going to make them poor and relieve them of their pressure and burden."

"Why that's mighty nice of you, but you don't think they're going to let you waltz in and take their money, do you?" I inquired.

"Well, you're going to help me figure out how we're going to do this. You're the money man remember?"

"Yeah, don't remind me. I'd like to tender my resignation," I joked.

"So soon? Nah, you want to see how this thing turns out. This ought to be fun."

"Yeah, fun," I answered.

Elizabeth returned from outside, timing her entrance perfectly.

"I've contacted the agent in charge of our western Africa operations. They have no intel on a rebel uprising. He informed me of twelve dead total, thirty-two wounded. The remains of two men were found, shot multiple times in the chest," she told us.

"Who do your people think did it?" Galveston asked.

"They're unsure. Appears to be a military operation, but they are unsure of who. Those bastards blew the entire facility." Her English accent made all the words appear eloquent, but you could hear the anger in them.

"I better fill you in on what we've discovered. I think you'll want to call your people again," Galveston told her.

"I'll let you two talk. I still haven't gotten my drink. Plus I want to see how annoyed Alex is," I said walking out of the room. I was curious to see how Alex was getting along with his new suitemate.

I expected him to have Dr. Sloan shoved in a closet somewhere, or worse, in a headlock. Alex didn't like his freedom being impeded on by some outsider. He was barely able to handle the ribbing we gave him about his food and drink selections. I walked into the kitchen and stumbled on what could best be described as a reuniting of a long-lost father and son.

"Try this. It's fantastic. From the south of Spain. Kind of earthy, with a hint of currant berry, right?" Alex was pouring a glass of wine for Dr. Sloan, and he in return squished it in his mouth while swirling the wine glass in his hand.

"Ah, truly excellent. Yes, it holds its flavor in the back of my mouth. Is it an '82?" Dr. Sloan asked.

"No, it's an '84 Select," Alex said proudly, smiling widely. "Tell me more about your theory on electromagnetic passive circuits. I still have questions," Alex hurriedly asked, awaiting a response on bated breath from Dr. Sloan. Dr. Sloan swallowed and examined the glass.

"Let me start from my initial discovery..." Dr. Sloan started, and then stopped after seeing me enter the room. "Hello, Roger," he said, smiling.

"Hello, Dr. Sloan," I answered.

"Edward and I are discussing some of his early engineering theories. I can't believe you and Galveston didn't bring him earlier." Alex looked over at Dr. Sloan. "I told them to bring you over here earlier, Edward," Alex said scolding Galveston and me.

I think I was going to be sick. An industrial vacuum couldn't suck up harder than Alex at the moment.

"I just want a drink of water, tap water," I said moving past the two sommeliers. As I had my glass in hand, Galveston and Elizabeth burst into the room.

"We've got an idea," Galveston said boldly to everyone in the room.

I was determined to continue my quest for a lousy drink of water. I was thirsty and had been interrupted by May's arrival, our information gathering, and Alex's and Dr. Sloan's love fest. I just wanted a drink, and damned if I wasn't going to get one.

"Roger, pay attention and listen up. Elizabeth and I have a plan." He shot me a glance while I almost broke the glass between my fingers.

I set it down and sighed.

"What?" I exclaimed.

"We've been talking," he continued, holding everyone's attention for the earth shattering news, "and we're getting married." No one was amused. "Okay, Okay. We've been talking, and we're going to Brazil."

He stood with a silly grin on his face, awaiting a reaction from all of us. Everyone stared back like a herd of cows.

"Oh, crap," I said out loud in response. "That's it? That's your plan?"

"Well, there's more to it than that," he answered me. "Don't worry. I'll fill in the details later."

"Oh, that's great," I shot back briefly. "Now can't I just get a stupid drink of water?"

-Chapter 42-

Senator Eastman sat in his high-back, leather chair with his arms folded, awaiting his turn to speak on new business. This was a day he had been waiting for. He had planned and scraped together all of his political favors for this opportunity. A fellow Senator from Wisconsin finished his statement and gave up the remainder of his time to the Senator from New Hampshire.

Eastman motioned for his aide to hand him a blue binder. The timing couldn't have been better. The dramatic event that occurred a day earlier in Nigeria would only help bolster his argument, a fortunate turn of events for his piece of legislation.

In the blue binder was his grand plan to force change and alter the nation's energy policy. It contained many elements, but he planned to only introduce the first fragment of it. He figured the rest could wait until a later date. The Senator cleared his throat and took a small sip of water from a glass in front of him.

"Thank you, Senator," Eastman announced. "Gentlemen, the events in Nigeria have exposed the flaws in our energy policy and our reliance on foreign sources of oil, and as a nation, our reliance on fossil fuels. It is events like these that refute the argument that we can survive on more domestic drilling. We have the alternatives available, but not here at home. We must embrace the technological advances that those abroad have accomplished and implemented. By using them as a guide, we too can reach energy independence and will never again have to be held hostage to terrorists. That is why I propose to fast track my piece of legislation that would ease the United States' ability to use alternative forms of energy developed by our neighbors and allies, and allow the American people to take charge of their energy future." He paused and took another sip of water. "I am asking the members of the committee to fast track Senate Bill 174, the 'Foreign Alternative Energy Deregulation Act'. It is time we act to ensure our nation's energy future, and this bill will allow that to happen. I'll now give back the remainder of my time."

The Senator sat back in his chair. The case had been made and he was going to enjoy them scurrying around. "Idiots," he thought, "if they only knew."

His fellow Senators immediately balked at the idea. "We would just become dependent on other foreign governments", "the revenue lost would be absurd for such a plan", "American businesses would be crushed"; they were all valid arguments and not unexpected rebuttals to such a plan.

Eastman had heard all the arguments before, and it was playing out just as he had planned.

The Senator never expected agreement. He knew his bill never had a chance of even making it out of the committee. If by some miracle it did, it wouldn't make it past the Senate to go to the House, not yet at least. He sat back and smiled, handing his blue binder back to his aide. If they only knew how soon they would change their minds and how they would have no choice. He knew that when his bill didn't pass and a new, revolutionary product came on the market these same politicians would be screaming for this piece of legislation. People would pay almost anything for this new product. It wouldn't save them any money, but it would give them a façade, a fragile peace of mind.

Government revenue has to come from somewhere; fuel taxes, oil taxes, import taxes, corporate taxes. But all those tax revenues would fade or disappear to acquire alternative energy like the Senator was proposing. All that lost revenue would have to be made up somewhere. Tax hungry politicians would just have to be creative to get it back. He knew all about the creative ways to do this.

Eastman didn't really believe it would help the environment. The implementation would be too long, the costs too high, and the resources too great to be a viable full scale alternative, but the illusion would be present. That was what he was banking on, literally. The costs and revenue produced by this new industry would be grand, and all his fellow fat cats would be lining up at the Senate door with new, glorious tax proposals to get their own governmental piece of the pie. He didn't care. He would have his check cashed long before that ever happened. In the process he would get to help shape America in a new vision—his vision. He would change how the entire world consumed energy and in the process yield an even greater amount of power.

No, he never expected this piece to pass out of this committee, but the energy plan he had in his blue binder would ultimately make it—eventually. When nations would be clamoring for this new revolutionary device he would say, "I told you so." He could become the one man in the history books that led the United States into its new energy future. It was all based on the plan set out in his blue binder. The money he would pocket didn't hurt matters neither. "Yes," he thought, watching his fellow Senators. "Keep it up. Either way, I win."

-Chapter 43-

"We're on schedule." A voice from the speaker phone reverberated around the room

"Good, but I wasn't pleased to hear that your men engaged some targets during the last operation," the man on the other end said from his office in a house overlooking the waters of the Caribbean.

"It was necessary," the voice said, "just collateral damage. I never said this would be clean. You pay me to get the job done, not pussyfoot around," the voice shot back forcefully.

"Remember who signs your check, Mr. Murray," the man warned. "What's the status on *Project Atlantic*?"

"The teams are in place. I'll expect my third payment in my Cayman account promptly," Murray said.

"As always. Have you located the professor?"

"Not yet, but we will. We've traced a credit card transaction to a San Diego hotel gift shop. We believe he has help, but we're not sure who. I have a team going there now."

"And the FBI?" The man asked.

"Suspicious, just as you predicted."

"Good, we don't want them exposed too quickly. Be quiet about your operations there. Remember you're not operating in a foreign country. People tend to ask more questions in the States."

"We'll handle it. The professor will be contained."

"Very good, Mr. Murray. Discretion please. We're too close now for a screw-up. Contact me when you get the problem taken care of," the man said, ending the call.

The man peered over the landscape out to the sea from his palatial, seaside mansion, content that everything was going according to plan.

-Chapter 44-

Timothy Placer peered out the fourth floor window of his executive office at Black Bear corporate headquarters in Washington D.C. when his intercom crackled to life.

"Mr. Placer, you have a call from Dr. Morales at Ecomax," his executive assistant said.

"Thank you, Sally, put him through." He punched the speaker button on the phone. "Dr. Morales, I'm glad you've finally called. What is the status on production? I've been waiting all morning." There was a long pause. "Dr. Morales?" Placer pressed.

"Uh, yes, sir?" Dr. Morales said.

"What's the status?" Placer asked again, louder and more slowly.

"I'm afraid we have a problem, sir," Morales answered hesitantly.

"Well, what is it man?" Placer said, growing angry.

"We aren't going to make the deadline, sir. The product," he paused, "the product doesn't work."

"What do you mean it doesn't work?" Placer exclaimed.

"It's not correct. The production line is ready, but the design, there is something wrong with the battery. We need to talk to Dr. Patelo. He could get it straightened out, but we can't reach him," Morales said excitedly.

"Can't reach him?"

"He hasn't returned from the engineering facility. I even went to the facility myself, and it was abandoned."

"I don't like the sound of that. I hope Dr. Patelo hasn't tried to dupe us. Had you been there before?"

"No, but Dr. Patelo and I were the only ones with access to the facility. What are you getting at?" Dr. Morales asked, confused.

"I hope Dr. Patelo hasn't decided to take the plans and give us a non-working set. Those plans are worth a lot of money."

"I can't imagine him doing such a thing. It's not like him to do that. He's only interested in the research."

"Maybe that's what you think, but maybe he had alternate plans," Placer said, exasperated at the turn of events. "We are on a fixed timeline and every day we miss is costing us money. You're going to have to fix it yourself. How much time do you need?"

"Three days, I hope. I'll need to familiarize myself with the design and try to isolate the problem. I was only supposed to be in charge of getting the production line ready. I don't know if I can do this in such a short time," Morales said, weary of the prospect of finding a needle in a haystack.

"You brought in Patelo, so now it's your job. Just get it done, I don't care how. We can't lose any more time. Three days is all you get or everyone is out of a job," Placer threatened and knew he was also referring to himself. "I need to make a call."

"Yes, sir, we'll get right on it," Morales said and hung up.

Placer was angry. He didn't like problems, especially now at such a critical juncture. He grew angrier knowing that Dr. Patelo might have absconded with the correct plans to their newly procured product and hadn't held up his end of the bargain. It would have infuriated him even more if he knew that the location of the engineering facility Morales went to was not the one where Patelo had been. Instead, Patelo had been at a facility located over a hundred miles away, deep in the jungle.

Placer keyed his intercom. "Sally, get me Murray on a secure line."

"Yes, sir," she answered back. A few minutes passed until Sally had the call placed. "Mr. Murray on the secure line for you, sir." Placer picked up the phone this time.

"Murray?"

"Yes, sir?" Murray answered over the secure line that allowed them to talk freely without fear of being eavesdropped on.

"What is going on?" Placer questioned.

"I'm not sure what you mean, sir," he responded calmly.

"I've just got off the phone with Morales at Ecomax. The plans don't work and the device is inoperable. Morales can't locate Patelo to fix it. I'm afraid he has sabotaged the battery and run off with the plans. What do you know of this?"

"The battery doesn't work?" he said trying to control the excitement in his voice, more surprised that the device didn't work then of Patelo's disappearance.

"Morales says it doesn't and the plans are false. He even tried to find Patelo at the engineering facility, but he wasn't there. This wasn't supposed to happen."

Murray calmed himself before speaking. "We picked up the devices as planned and delivered them to Ecomax. My men observed him leave with his technicians."

"Well, he must have left with the plans too. You need to find him, and fast. Morales is going to try to locate the problem, but we only have a few days. This thing was supposed to be in production by now. You know we have to get this done before the next earnings report. I can't keep the security regulators off our back forever."

"I understand, sir. We'll find him," Murray said, knowing full well where Patelo was, and in what condition.

"Good. We can't afford any more mistakes."

"Yes, sir, we're on it," Murray responded and clicked out of the secure line.

Placer hung up the phone slowly. "Now what," he thought. The regulators would be all over Black Bear during the next earnings report. He knew they couldn't falsify their accounting records anymore, they had pushed it too far already. He felt the growing desperation in his gut. He didn't want to go to jail and lose his lifestyle in the process. They had to succeed, but now the production would be a full week behind schedule. Everything would now be cut much closer and the danger of losing the company became more prevalent. He keyed the intercom once again.

"Sally, get me the Senator, and tell his staff it's urgent." Placer reached for a bottle of antacids from the top drawer of his desk. It was going to be a stressful few days.

Murray, on the other hand, was more surprised than angry. He had seen the results of Dr. Patelo's tests. He knew he had received the batteries in working order and believed the design had been correct after Dr. Patelo's reverse engineering. Now he knew that one of the prototypes was flawed, and the one he kept to himself was also inoperable. Patelo had managed to change the plans and sabotage the battery. He didn't know why, but figured Patelo tried to steal the device for himself.

Murray would have been infuriated to know that Dr. Patelo had intentionally removed a prime circuit to the battery and changed the design plan before he was callously gunned down by Murray's men. All the events were due to Patelo's mistrust of Murray. The circuit that laid in Dr. Patelo's pocket would cause headaches for the man. Murray now had to find the inventor, Dr. Sloan, to make this device work, and he planned to use all his resources to find him. It occurred to Murray that someone was helping Dr. Sloan. "Big mistake," he thought, because the net was beginning to tighten around the professor.

Murray keyed in a number to his phone but hesitated before making the call. Their timeline and carefully laid plan was now in jeopardy. He had been relieved to know that Placer didn't know any more information, especially that Murray had kept one of the prototypes. Luckily, Murray had no idea Dr. Sloan had the last, fully workable battery.

No matter. They could continue their initial plan, and Black Bear would be exposed in due time. They just had to be patient and wait for the moves to unfold. Unfortunately for Black Bear, they would be the victim this time. Murray pushed to dial the number on his phone and a voice answered on the other end.

"Mr. Chase," Murray started, "we have a little problem."

-Chapter 45-

"What do they wear in Brazil?" I asked Galveston as we pilfered Alex's refrigerator.

"Oh, I don't know, clothes maybe?" Galveston answered sarcastically. "But not many clothes as I've seen from pictures."

"When do you want to leave?" I said, chomping on some sort of foreign cheese.

"How about the day after tomorrow. I think we need a little time to get our act together."

Elizabeth had decided to return to the hotel and get some work done. She convinced her superiors there was a political interest for Great Britain to be involved in this affair.

This device would affect the entire world and trickle down to all other nations. It wasn't our goal to keep this invention from the people of the world, but allowing Black Bear to control all of its aspects, patent it, or trademark it, would mean Black Bear would have all the power and essentially hold the world hostage for its use.

Alex and Sloan had retired to Alex's den, where Alex was showing him all of his latest gadgetry. He finally had someone to corner that showed interest in the things we didn't understand.

I planned to see Jane before I went home. I had missed her smiling face and was eager to talk to her.

Galveston wasn't going home either and made a side trip to see Elizabeth at her hotel. Galveston had offered for her to stay with him, but she had declined saying she would never get any work done. In his mind that was an excellent sign.

Right now we could relax, but tomorrow things would quickly become serious.

The next morning arrived abruptly. I was awakened by a ringing phone. I ignored the first ring and turned over, placing my pillow over my head to muffle the noise. The phone stopped and almost immediately began ringing again. I threw my pillow off my head and peered at my clock; 7:40 A.M. I grunted in frustration and reached over for the phone.

"Hello," I answered groggily.

"Roger?" It was Galveston, and he yelled my name in the phone as his voice crackled with static. "Roger!" he yelled again.

"What!" I yelled back.

"You need to get out of your house, now!" Galveston said frantically.

"What are you talking about?" I asked.

"Just listen to me. They found us, Roger. Get out of your house now."

"What? What do you mean?"

"Get out of your house," he said with frustration due to my lack of understanding. "Meet me at the corner of Cedar and Columbia near the airport. Get your bag together. You have five minutes. You're in danger. They've broken into the office, and they know where we live."

At these last words I sat bolt upright. The seriousness in his voice enticed me to act quickly.

"I'm on my way now," I told him.

I hung up the phone and jumped from bed, threw on a pair of shorts, and reached for my bag from Mexico, which fortunately was still packed and ready to go. I ran out my door, barely keeping my feet underneath me, and almost did a face plant on the sidewalk.

I calmed myself and remembered what Galveston had taught me. I began to scan the area while I walked, looking for anything suspicious, and quick-stepped my way to the driver's side door of my car. I nervously fumbled with my keys and finally opened the door. I started the engine and as it roared to life I noticed the gas gauge just a hint above the empty mark. In all the excitement of the last few days I had neglected one basic human need—gas.

I screeched out of my parking spot and plotted the way in my head on how to get to Galveston. How did they find us so quickly and did Galveston warn everyone? "Oh my God," I thought, "what about Jane?"

-Chapter 46-

I pulled my cell phone from my pocket and called Galveston, who answered quickly.

"Dan," I said eagerly. "Jane? Did you talk to Jane?"

"I couldn't get her on the phone. I'll keep trying."

"I'm going over there," I said hurriedly.

"No, get here first. Then we'll go together. It's too dangerous."

"I've got to go now. I can't wait."

Before Galveston could talk me out of it, I hung up and swung the car around in the middle of the road, heading directly to Jane's house.

I raced through the streets, beating the red lights and rolling through stop signs. The needle on the gas gauge crept slowly toward empty and suddenly the low fuel light popped on. I wished I would have read my car manual at some point to know how much fuel I had left, but it was too late for that. I managed to limp my way to Jane's house and parked down the street, out of sight of her front door.

I got out of my car, ran to the side of her condo building, and peered around the corner. There were cars parked along the street, and I moved from the corner of the building to the edges of the cars, hiding behind each of them. As I reached the last car, I looked ahead for any signs of life, and anyone bad lying in wait. I didn't find anyone or anything suspicious, other than myself.

I ran up to Jane's front door, knocked hard, and rang the bell. I peeked inside the door window and saw no movement. I then tried the door, and it opened as I rotated the knob. I pushed slowly on the door until it was fully open and walked inside after checking behind me for any unwanted guests. My heart rate quickened, and I began to breathe heavily as sweat began to develop on my face.

The apartment was intact and undisturbed. I prayed that no one had made it here before me. I began to give a yell to Jane but thought better of it. Instead I crept through the living room.

It was a large condo with two floors, and right then it was quiet. I walked into the kitchen and found nothing. I walked back to the stairs near the front door and started up slowly. With every step a loud squeak reverberated throughout the condo, like I was compressing an enraged mouse as my weight went into each rung. I had nothing to defend myself expect fists, and I clenched them tight until my knuckles went white. I got to the top of the stairs, knelt down, and craned my head around the corner, level with the floor, checking for feet in the hall that led to Jane's bedroom.

I heard rustling and water running from the bedroom. I got up off the steps and slowly walked to the bedroom door, which was open, and peered inside. The bed was unmade and clothes were sitting on top. I walked into the bedroom and to the bathroom door. It was slightly ajar.

"Jane?" I whispered softly. No response. My heart quickened further. I didn't want to look behind that door, but I gathered the courage and moved close to it. I carefully pushed it with my foot until it swung open.

"Ahhhhh!" A scream echoed from the bathroom, and the door swung violently toward me, smacking me in the face and sending me reeling back on my butt. I grabbed my face from the sting of pain. I looked through my watering eyes and saw a blurry Jane standing over me holding a hair dryer above her head while she was covered by nothing but a towel.

"Roger?" she said breathlessly. "What are you doing? You scared me to death." I was only able to grunt until I began to get my faculties back

"I'm just making sure you're alright," I gasped.

"I saw your body in the door crack. I didn't know it was you," she said, exasperated.

"I'm sorry. I just had to make sure you're okay. That door didn't taste too good, though," I said, continuing to hold my face.

She knelt down and grabbed my arm. "Here, let me help you up." She pulled me to a standing position, and I saw that her hair was wet after finishing a shower. One leg was still covered with shaving cream.

"I wish I had been a few minutes earlier," I managed to joke.

"I bet," she said, "you would have had quite a surprise. Now, why are you here?"

I remembered my primary purpose on coming over and managed to steer my brain in the right direction.

"I need to get you out of here—right now."

I reached for her clothes on the bed and handed them to her. She threw the hair dryer on the bed and reluctantly took the clothes from me.

"I don't understand," she asked with a look of surprise.

"I'll explain it all in the car, but for now, just get dressed. We don't have time. We have to get out of here." She noticed the angst in my voice and began to move more quickly. "I'll be right back," I said motioning for her to go even quicker, "and grab whatever else you need. I don't know when you'll be able to come back. Oh, and grab your passport." Jane shot me a confused look.

I left the room and began back down the stairs as Jane's voice trailed off in the distance.

"Where are you going?" she asked.

"Hurry," I managed to yell back to her as I raced down the stairs to the front door.

I glanced out the front window of the door, and luckily nothing suspicious was going on outside. I locked the deadbolt, slid the door chain on, and then went to the kitchen. I grabbed a wooden chair, returned to the front door, and crammed the back of the chair under the door knob, making sure it was good and tight. We wouldn't be going out that way. I then scurried back up the stairs.

Jane had managed to get her one unshaven leg toweled off and was mostly dressed. She threw some clothes in a bag and put some bathroom items on top. As she exited the bathroom, I entered it and searched around. I frantically looked for anything we could use as a weapon, in case we needed it. All I found was a can of hairspray and a nail file. I didn't know what I would do with them, but at least it was something.

"You having a bad hair day?" Jane asked, pointing at the hair spray.

"Yeah," I answered, "I didn't get to do my regular primping this morning. You ready?"

"I guess. I don't know what for, though."

"C'mon." I gently grabbed her arm and led her out of the room like a puppy on a leash, not letting her grab any more items.

We rambled down the stairs, and her eyes grew large as she saw the front door and the makeshift security system I had put in place.

"Who are you expecting?" she asked excitedly.

"You do ask a lot of questions. I'll tell you in the car," I said, now dragging her by the arm.

We walked through the kitchen and to the back patio door. I slid it open and walked outside to a small enclosure bordered by a small, wooden fence. I callously turned over a potted plant, dumping the contents on the ground, and used the pot as a step stool. Jane watched from the door to the patio, shocked at my treatment of her plant.

"I just planted that," she said.

It was then that my blood turned cold. I heard movement outside the front door. Jane spun around, looking toward the front door. Before she could say a word, I reached for her and pulled her out of the kitchen onto the patio, then grabbed her bag and threw it over the fence. It landed with a thud on the other side.

I noticed a dark outline of a man through the window of the front door. "Damn it," I thought, "they found her." I quickly motioned for Jane to go over the fence and then whispered the command to her. She stepped on the pot, pulled herself over the fence, and dropped to the other side.

I pulled off the top of the hairspray and threw the cap on the ground. I tossed the can over the fence, put the file in my pocket, and followed Jane's steps on the pot. I pulled myself up and over the fence clumsily. "I'm getting tired of fences," I thought as I dropped next to Jane who attempted to slow my descent.

I picked up the hairspray and grabbed Jane's arm again. We raced across the open courtyard between the buildings as I pushed Jane in front of me, her bag flopping off her shoulder as she ran.

"Get to that corner building. My car is just up the street," I told her from behind. She was scared and was only able to muster an "Uh-huh."

I heard a loud crashing sound from behind me. They had just broken into her front door. Jane was now a good four steps in front of me, and neither of us looked back. We stayed focused on the corner of the building. Jane made it around the corner and disappeared as I followed. Just as I was about to round it and out of sight, I felt a massive tug at the back of my shirt which choked my throat and sent me backward until I fell. I grunted as I skidded on the grass and looked up to see a large man standing over me, his eyes big and angry, with his teeth clenched.

"Where do you think you're going, pal?" he said angrily.

He began to reach down to pull me up by my shirt when I realized what I had in my right hand. As he leaned in closer, I clenched my body, drew up my right hand towards his face, and pushed the button on the can I was holding, sending a stream of hairspray directly into the eyes of the marauder. I held the button steady, showering his face with the spray, causing his eyes and face to immediately sting and burn from the chemicals. He gave out a loud yell and let go of my shirt, instinctively covering his eyes with both hands trying to rub out the burn, which only made things worse for him. He stumbled backward, continuing to grunt and yell.

I pushed myself up off the ground and stood even with the man, who continued to be unable to see. Without thinking, and with adrenaline pumping through my body in its fight or flight status, I picked up my foot and kicked at the lateral portion of the intruder's left knee, contacting it with the full sole of my shoe. I sent him crumpling to the ground in agonizing pain, now with one hand on his eyes and the other on his knee.

I didn't wait around to examine the extent of my Chuck Norris like strike, and instead raced around the buildings edge, out of sight. Jane was waiting near the street and was relieved when she saw me.

"I heard yelling," she said, breathless.

"I just had to kick some guy's ass," I said, in my most macho of voices, clearly scared out of my wits.

I again grabbed Jane's arm. We were close now, and I could see my car in the distance. We knelt down and crab walked ahead quickly, hiding ourselves from view between the adjacent cars lining the street.

Jane moved to the passenger door and got in, slumping down, out of sight. I got in the driver's side and noticed the car the men must have arrived in was empty and double parked in front of Jane's condo.

I didn't know how many of them there were, but we had to drive past them—there was no other way out. An idea flashed in my head as I started up the car and gunned the engine.

I approached the intruder's car and still saw no sign of anyone. I hoped my weak karate skills had slowed down at least one of the men. As I got parallel to their vehicle, I decided to implement my idea.

I brought the car to a screeching halt and jumped out the door, not noticing the horror on Jane's face at my actions. I reached for the nail file in my pocket, and using my shirt as a grip I jammed the file into the front tire of the other car as hard as I could. I plunged the file again and again, putting my weight behind it, until a small stream of air plunged out the sidewall of the tire, prematurely deflating it. I pulled out the file, hurried back in the car, and pressed hard on the gas pedal, sending us screaming down the street.

"Just a little insurance," I told Jane as I heaved for air. Jane just looked dumbstruck as she continued to crouch low in her seat.

I looked in my rearview mirror and saw two men moving toward the car, one moving fluidly, the other moving with a noticeable limp. The car began toward us, but then stopped, began to fade, and then disappeared in the rearview mirror as I made our first turn.

"Ha!" I yelled, slapping the steering wheel.

Jane continued to stay crouched. "Roger, what the hell is going on?"

I made another turn and increased my speed. "Well, Jane, it seems we've run into a little problem."

-Chapter 47-

We continued to race through the streets, and I slowed slightly when I felt we had distanced ourselves from the intruders. I filled Jane in on our problem, and how she was involved—not by choice. She was not amused and fought the urge to break down in tears in front of me. I grabbed her hand in mine.

"I promise," I started, "everything will be okay."

She relaxed slightly, but I could tell she was shaken, and rightfully so. I would be too when the adrenaline rush wore off.

In all the excitement, however, I had forgotten about that pesky low fuel light. I wished I could have done the Flintstone's trick and stick my feet out the bottom of the car to keep it propelling forward, but no such luck, my ankles weren't big enough. The engine sputtered, and we came to a rolling stop, three blocks away from where we were to meet Galveston. We were out of gas. Not a good thing to happen when there were slimeballs after you. We would have to make the rest of the distance on foot.

"Out of gas, aren't we?" Jane asked dryly.

I looked at her meekly. "Yeah, how did you know?"

"You were only looking at the gas gauge every ten seconds."

"I was hoping I could will it into rising. I guess my telepathic powers aren't what I thought they were."

She was not amused by my joke, and for good reason. I dragged her from her home, wet and cold, her front door was now ruined, I destroyed her nail file, used up her hairspray, and more importantly, put her life in danger. Now I was making this poor woman schlep down the city streets because I forgot to gas the car, while her home now stood wide open and exposed.

"Let me take your bag. Galveston should be waiting for us up the way," I offered. She looked at me with a look only a woman scorned could produce.

"I can carry my own bag, thank you very much," she replied. She was sticking it to me in only the way a woman can, making me feel like a scolded child; small and guilty.

I grabbed my own bag, sighed, and followed behind her silently, waiting for her to reel around and let me have it. She was a few steps ahead and going in the wrong direction.

"Uh, Jane," I said softly. "This way," and I pointed in the opposite direction.

She muttered and shook the hair from her face. She again quickly moved in front of me, but not before shooting me a piercing look of disdain. I lowered my head and followed like a frightened puppy.

The sun had popped out from the overcast sky as we lumbered toward the meeting place with our bags slung over our shoulders. We walked for half an hour, having been farther away than I thought. This didn't help my position with Jane. She would get over it in due time, I reasoned, especially when she understood the scope of what we were involved in. I was surprised at how bad I felt for getting her involved in this mess. I cared more for her than I had ever thought, and the guilt I felt proved it.

My cell phone gave a ring. It was Galveston, obviously wondering where we were. I didn't have the energy to tell him what had happened. We would have enough time for that later.

We walked through the last intersection when I caught a glimpse of Galveston, waiting impatiently next to his car. He ran toward us when he caught sight of us laboring with our bags.

"Finally," he exclaimed insensitively, grabbing Jane's bag from her. "I'm glad you're okay, Jane. What happened?" he asked.

"Please, don't ask," I implored.

Jane didn't speak. She was still quite upset and pushed past Galveston, continuing to walk toward his car. Galveston stopped and looked at me.

"Who pissed in her Wheaties?" he asked, smiling and pointing at Jane.

"Oh, I'm sure I had a hand in that. Unfortunately, I think you did too," I said with a tired voice.

"Great. Well, whatever I can do to help, I guess," he said, sensing my pain.

We followed her to the car where she was already sitting in the front seat, staring straight ahead.

"Oh, boy, this will be a fun drive," Galveston said as I got in back and he entered the driver's side.

He started up the engine and began the drive to our unknown destination.

"I hope you have enough gas to get to wherever we're going," Jane quipped.

"Enough gas?" Galveston laughed. "Of course. I'm not a moron," he joked. I rolled my eyes as Jane shot me a quick look, and luckily, a small smile. "Okay gang, here's the deal," Galveston said, interrupting our exchange of looks while he negotiated the city streets. "It seems we've been found, as you both know by now. I happened to go by the office early this morning and found it had been broken into. They pilfered everything; files, computers, everything. It was a mess."

"Damn," I said from the backseat.

"Yeah, our whole operation has been outed. David is already trying to reach his contact at Global Energy, Dr. Blout, the head of the Global Energy Consortium. He wants him safe. David is very worried about Blout now. He wants to put him under federal watch but hasn't been able to locate him."

"That's not good. I hope May finds him," I said.

"Me too. I'm not sure if they know we have Dr. Sloan. I don't know how they would, but we can't underestimate them. Rule 107, Roger, never underestimate your opponent."

"Yeah, I'll be sure to write that in my notes," I snapped back. Jane just gave us both a confusing look.

"Jane, I've arranged for you to take a little trip. Anywhere you want, just think of it as a perk of the job, a little paid vacation," Galveston told her.

"A vacation? Where, like the Caribbean?" she asked.

"If you want. We just have to get you out of San Diego until things die down." Galveston paused. "That's a poor choice of words. Until things settle down. Roger and I need to take a little trip to Brazil."

"Brazil?" she exclaimed, "why Brazil?"

"Long story. We just need to get you out of here and safe," Galveston told her.

I leaned towards Galveston from the back seat. "I think she should go with us. I want to keep an eye on her," I whispered.

"No way, too dangerous," he answered, looking straight ahead.

"I insist. She needs to go with us."

"I don't think so. It's too much. She's not involved in this."

Jane interrupted us. "I'm involved now," she said directly. "I want to go with you guys. People just broke into my house to do

God knows what. If it is truly my decision then I want to go," she said forcefully, and we were both taken aback.

Galveston sat silently for a moment and then answered reluctantly. "Okay, if that's what you really want."

"And you two are going to pay me for all my time," she said directly again.

Galveston smiled, admiring her aggressiveness. "Whatever you say, Jane. You're the boss."

I sat back in my seat, relieved that I would be able to keep an eye on Jane, but hoping we hadn't got her involved in something we couldn't control. Galveston drove to San Diego Lindbergh International Airport.

"Oh, by the way," Galveston said to me quietly, leaning back out of earshot of Jane. "May told me what killed Colonel Espinosa."

"Really? What was it?" I asked eagerly.

"Curare, a poison. It's often used by South American tribes and dipped on the tips of arrows to go after prey. It causes asphyxiation due to paralysis of the respiratory and skeletal muscles. It's slow acting and causes paralysis."

"Just a touch did that?" I questioned.

"Not exactly. It has to be injected or go through a wound."

"Then how did he get poisoned?"

"May said there were tiny barbs all over the statue, almost like fish hooks. That's why it was so shiny when you saw it. All the poison was hanging on those barbs. When Espinosa touched it he must have gotten tiny cuts on his hands and fingers and absorbed the poison into his body."

"You don't say," I said shocked. "I can't believe it."

"Pretty scary stuff. He could have received an antidote, but he never stood a chance."

I was amazed at how ingenious these people were with their methods.

"We've got to get these guys, Roger."

"I agree. Whatever it takes," I responded quietly.

"You know, I can still hear you two. I'm only sitting in the next seat," Jane said, giving us a look of contempt.

"Sorry, Jane," Galveston said meekly, "we thought you were hard of hearing."

Jane stifled a smile. "Well, just tell me what is going on from now on. I think I deserve that," she scolded.

"Yes, ma'am," Galveston and I said in unison, with our heads lowered like two admonished children.

Galveston peeked at me in the rearview mirror and flashed a smile. Jane was stronger and tougher than he thought. She would fit in nicely to our merry brood.

"Well, boys and girls, we're going to Brazil," Galveston told us as we made the turn to the airport, upon which he filled us in on our itinerary.

We were flying from San Diego to Houston, then on to Rio de Janeiro before grabbing a connection to Sao Paulo.

But what about the safety of the rest of our team?

-Chapter 48-

We drove into the long-term parking lot, picked up our bags, and walked to the terminal. Galveston seemed to notice my thoughts about everyone's safety.

"I've called Alex and Dr. Sloan. They made it out okay. They are driving to his villa in Mexico. I hope the intruders don't touch Alex's things. He has a tendency to keep a nasty, little security system set up at his house. He really doesn't like strangers," Galveston said to Jane and me.

"What is he, a drug smuggler? Who has a villa?" I inquired.

"That's what he told me. He seemed to enjoy throwing the word around."

"And what about Elizabeth?"

"She got an earlier flight to Brazil. I think she's going to contact an operative there who has all the tools we need." Galveston stopped at the crosswalk, waiting for the cars to pass by. "So, what happened at Jane's?" he asked me, this time truly out of earshot of Jane. I formulated my answer and left out the whole gas situation.

"Let's just say I kicked some ass," I said, trying to be macho but failing miserably. "I got caught by one of their guys, sprayed him with hairspray, and karate kicked him in the knee."

"Wow! You are a bad ass. Hairspray, huh?"

"Yeah, he didn't stand a chance," I said smugly, noticing his mocking tone.

There was still an hour before the flight, and it proved to be a nice reprieve from the craziness of the day. I sat down next to Galveston who sat staring at the airplanes outside.

"We're on the final stretch, I hope," he said, looking straight ahead. "May wasn't at all thrilled with us going to Brazil. To be honest with you, Roger, I don't have any idea what we're going to do."

I looked at him. "So you don't have a plan for us? That doesn't leave me very reassured."

"I'll figure it out on the plane. Don't you worry, I'll come up with something, but right now I've got nothing."

I didn't have an idea either but tried to be supportive. "Well, I say we find this Dr. Patelo and what role he plays. We know Ecomax is where they're planning to make the battery, and like you said, we need to strike at them first."

He looked toward me. "You're right. I did say that. I'll figure it out," he said confidently, and turned ahead again.

Galveston stayed wide awake on our trip to Houston as Jane and I fell asleep. He looked at us while we dreamed of puppy dogs and lollipops and pulled a pad of paper from his bag. Like a mathematician discovering a new proof, he began to write furiously on the paper. His eyes grew wide as the gears began to turn, and he figured out our plan.

-Chapter 49-

Murray pulled up a barstool at McCauley's Bar & Grill in central Chicago. He had been in the city for a few days since returning from Brazil. He ordered a Dewar's straight up from the bartender and sipped it slowly, watching the flat screen television on the wall as he occasionally checked his watch. It was just after 5:00 P.M., and the after work crowd was beginning to shuffle in for a post-workday drink.

Murray wasn't there for pleasure, or to meet friends after a long day, he was there for business. After downing the drink, he ordered another and found a table in the back corner of the establishment, away from the clatter of the bar. He checked his watch again and looked toward the front door, awaiting the arrival of his contact at 5:15 P.M.

The front door of the restaurant opened, and a large man strolled in followed by another large man, neatly dressed in a tailored suit and tie. The man in front was dressed in a sport coat over a polo shirt and saw Murray at the table, but didn't approach him. Instead the first man sat down at the end of the bar and ordered a club soda. The man with the suit passed him and upon seeing Murray, walked toward him.

"Right on time," Murray said to him without moving from his seat. The other man said nothing and pulled out a chair opposite to him. "What's this about? You know we shouldn't be seen together." The man he was talking to in the suit was none other than Weston Chase.

"It was important, and I can't trust phones right now," Chase told him.

"I understand. Shall we get to business then?" Murray inquired.

"Of course," Chase said seriously. "I need some extra insurance. That's what this is about. I got your report on what the team found in California. What is the current status there?"

"The team is in the process of finding all the contacts. We have the addresses of all of them, and we're trying to gather what they know," Murray told him, but left out the bit of information that they lost two contacts so far—a man and a woman. "We have all the information on these consultants that infiltrated Genesis. It seems they know about the device, but we don't know what they're doing with the information. The FBI is involved with them, but I don't know to what extent. We also haven't found Dr. Sloan, yet, but we will. It seems like you have a mole in your organization."

"I know. Dr. Blout has been talking too much. You know about May?" Chase asked.

"Yes, the FBI agent. Is that correct?"

"That's correct. Blout has been meeting with him and giving him information about me and the organization. I think he has become a problem," Chase said flatly.

"A problem, huh? And what do you recommend we do about this?"

"I think you know. He's a dangerous connection. He's been giving information about the board members of Global Energy and Black Bear's connection. He knows all about Sloan. I want you to take care of this quietly."

"I see. You know this will require an additional payment. This wasn't part of the regular agreement and will be much more public," Murray told him.

"I know. We can discredit Sloan, but we need Blout silenced. He's beginning to clamor to the board about Sloan's disappearance. When the device comes out he'll be able to connect the dots; I don't want that. Plus we need to give the Feds a dead end."

"How do you want it done?" Murray asked.

"An accident, something that can't be traced of course, and as quiet as possible," Chase answered. "You'll get an upfront payment of twenty thousand with a payment of forty thousand on completion."

"Agreed. I have a special person that can do that, but I need an additional twenty thousand."

"I can do that. So we have a deal?" Chase asked.

"Yes, we have a deal. It will be done by tomorrow. Blout will be out of the way as per your order." Murray said this without feeling, even though a man's life was in the balance.

"Tie up the loose ends in California. We need to get back on the timeline. Where is the device?"

"It's in development now. The prototype we have is much better than the one at Ecomax. It will be ready when the time arises, but we need Dr. Sloan to fill in the holes," Murray told him.

"And what about *Project Atlantic*?" Chase inquired.

"Still scheduled and everything is in place," Murray answered quickly.

"Good. We can't talk again in person."

"I understand," Murray said, nodding. "Not again. When I see payment in my Cayman account we'll start the operation."

Chase nodded in agreement and got up from the table. He didn't exchange pleasantries with Murray and left the restaurant, followed by the man that had been sitting at the bar. Murray went back to sipping his drink.

He reached in his pocket and pulled out a small, black, digital voice recorder and pressed the stop button. If this all went south, he didn't plan to be the one left holding the bag.

Chapter 50

"Here, turn here," the man said from the passenger seat of the vehicle. He flipped through papers on his lap. "Have you heard from team two?" he asked a man sitting in the back of the SUV.

"Not yet, sir," he said, looking at his mobile phone.

"Try to contact them, and when you do, give them this address. This is the man I'm concerned with now." He handed the man in the back of the vehicle a single piece of paper. "This man is former NSA. We're lucky we found his address at that office. Call control and see if they can get any more information about this Alex Jubokowski."

The man in the back took the piece of paper and dialed the phone, talking quietly while the vehicle drove slowly through a residential area filled with massive McMansions and curving hills.

The man in front consulted a handheld GPS unit. "Okay, stop here." He pointed to a curb in front of a semicircular drive. He rolled down his window, put his arm out, and made a circular motion with his finger to another SUV following close behind. "Ready the weapons. We take anyone alive for questioning—but no escapes," he said coldly.

The vehicle bumped into the driveway and intentionally stopped in front of a pair of garage doors, eliminating any possible escape route. The men in the first vehicle got out slowly and deliberately, careful to scan the area for witnesses to their intrusion. The men from the second vehicle moved quickly, and without speaking, fanned out around the house. They each pulled black sock masks down over their faces as they went, hiding their identities. They were careful to conceal their weapons as they moved, but luckily for them, the property was secluded from the adjacent houses.

The man from the front car, the obvious leader of the operation, walked slowly to the front door while the driver carried a large metal tube— a battering ram.

"Police, open up," he yelled, and motioned for the driver. The driver strolled to the door with the battering ram.

He gave a wave with his hand and stepped aside from the door. The husky driver threw the ram back and with one mighty hit shattered the door from its deadbolt, flinging it open in a splintering shower of wood. Immediately a whining sound came from the house as the men streamed in.

From around the back of the house came a shattering of glass. A fog began to emanate inside the house from strategically placed smoke grenades, which added to the confusion.

"Get that alarm under control," the leader told one of the men, who pulled out a tool bag and went to work on the alarm control panel just inside the house.

After a few seconds of working on the panel the loud sound stopped. The men moved silently from room to room while the leader coolly strolled behind them.

"All clear," he heard through his earpiece. "All clear in the rear," he heard from another team member.

The fog began to lift, and he began to see the other men emerge from different parts of the house.

"Back rooms, closets, attic, all clear, sir," a masked man said to him.

"Shit," he muttered and keyed his microphone. "Tear it apart," he said casually.

The men moved in unison away from him, turning things over in the room, and began to look through drawers and cabinets with a blatant disrespect for any neatness.

"Sir, we found a computer room," he heard through his earpiece again.

He walked over the newly broken glass and overturned furniture. The men went into Alex's office, the computer room, where they met up with two other men. The remaining two men stood guard by the front door as part of the group's carefully choreographed routine.

The computers stood just as Alex had left them, but now they were turned off.

"We're running out of time," the leader told the team's electronics expert. "Figure out what he's got here."

The electronics man pulled out more equipment, readying himself for what he would find. He turned on the computers and the screens popped to life. The man plugged in a laptop to one of the ports on the computer.

"That was easy," he announced proudly. "This guy doesn't even have password protection or encryption; an amateur move for an NSA guy. I should have his entire hard drive copied in five minutes. It's big, though."

"Just do it," the leader demanded, looking at his watch.

The other men milled about the room, examining the various artifacts Alex had accumulated over the years during his days of questionable activity. The laptop whirled to life, pulling off the information from Alex's computer—or so they thought. The electronics man continued to look at the screen until it suddenly froze, stopping mid-download.

"It stopped. Ahh," he grunted, "what's the problem?"

The other men turned around. He knelt down to the laptop and about that time heard a click. The screens of the computers went black. The men looked at the screens as a message popped up on the monitors.

"We know who you are", it read, "and you've been bad, bad boys". The men stared at the screen in complete shock and surprise. The words disappeared, and in its place a large picture of a hand appeared with the middle finger extended in the universal sign of goodwill.

Before the men could even react to the events, there was a sizzling sound and the monitors went black again. A crack of sound exploded in the room and electrical energy was sent rushing through all the equipment, followed by tiny electrical sparks of flashing light. The laptop sizzled under the new electrical load.

The electronics expert tried to react by pulling the plug on the laptop, but it was already too late. It had been fried by an intense electrical surge which melted the circuit board. Then, almost simultaneously, there was a whirling sound which came from the ceiling. The men looked up to find the sound but couldn't localize it. All of a sudden there was a tremendous pop and a purple liquid exploded in the room covering everything, including the men who stood shocked at the sight of the fluid coming from the ceiling. Smoke trails began to fill the room from the explosion, and the purple liquid began to find its way into every nook and cranny of the men and their equipment, coating them in a magnificent, deep, dark purple. As they tried to remove the liquid from their faces and realize what had happened, another alarm sounded, even louder than the first.

"What the..." was all the leader could muster before being drowned out by the screaming alarm. "Everybody out!" he yelled.

The electronics expert grabbed the useless laptop and slipped his way out of the room, following the other men. They raced to the front door and met the guards halfway. The guards stared in disbelief as the purple people looking like some sort of mythical monster headed toward them. The purple men pushed past them and out the front door, conveniently leaving colored footprints.

"What the hell happened?" one of the unaffected members exclaimed.

"Shut up and get in the truck," the leader said forcefully, attempting to wipe the liquid from his hands and face. The place was covered in the now familiar liquid, staining everything in its path.

Alex had acquired the proprietary liquid months before as part of his own personal security system. It was the same dye banks used in many money bundles that were being stored or transported. It was designed to explode if anyone tried to steal the money, turning it all into useless currency, and in turn making the thief an easy target for the police. In this case it had stained the intruders and dyed their skin, making it virtually impossible to clean off until it disappeared naturally. These men wouldn't dare travel in public anytime soon. It would take at least three days to wear off, regardless of how much scrubbing and showering they did. In addition, it stained their rental vehicles, which opened them up to being easily located if someone knew what to look for.

Alex had effectively put them out of business for the time being. The police were already on their way to respond to his backup alarm, and they would be surprised at the sight. The men clamored into the vehicles and quickly drove away. As each man pulled off their soaked masks, they revealed purple masked faces where the skin had been exposed. They looked like raccoons that had been caught rummaging through trashcans.

The leader immediately dialed his phone. "How am I going to explain this," he thought.

"We have a problem," was all he could say as he spoke into the phone.

-Chapter 51-

I awoke as the plane touched down in Houston and peered over at Galveston, who was still busily writing on his pad of paper. We taxied to the gate, debarked, and walked to our connecting flight.

Galveston bought a newspaper to pass the time. He handed it off to me to read while he ate, to see if there was any new information about the explosions in Africa.

I hadn't even gotten the newspaper open when I saw a new disturbing headline: *Explosions Rock Venezuelan Oil Platforms*. I hurriedly skimmed the article. Black Bear had done just what we predicted, but the speed at which they did it was the shocker. I read it further.

It seemed that the rhetoric was increasing from the anti-American Venezuelan government. They were blaming the explosions on anti-government rebels supported by no one other than the United States.

The explosions damaged two different offshore oil platforms, sending hundreds of thousands of barrels of oil spewing into the Atlantic Ocean.

"Black Bear obviously doesn't care about the environment, nor does the great Senator Eastman," I thought.

I pushed the paper toward Galveston and pointed at the headline, not saying a word. He continued to slowly chew on a muffin he had.

"Damn," he said with muffin still in his mouth. "Just like you said. They didn't waste any time, did they?"

"No," I answered. "I didn't think they would do it in Venezuela, but I guess it makes sense."

"How is that?" Galveston asked.

"The Venezuelan government doesn't particularly care for us. This ought to ramp up the oil prices worldwide quickly, especially for the U.S. I'm going to find a TV and see what they're saying about it."

I left Galveston and walked to one of the overhead televisions tuned to CNN. I strained to hear the commentators over the noise in the terminal.

The oil prices were rising on the news of the explosions. Oil output would be decreased worldwide due to the explosions in Africa, and now Venezuela. In addition, a blanket of fear would cover everyone's mind about the rising prices, causing companies and people to reevaluate how they did business. There were even calls for dipping into the United States' strategic oil reserves.

I thought of what the Senator was doing this whole time. He was probably sitting comfortably in his Senate office, watching the news unfold on his TV, waiting for his chance to release his new lifesaving legislation.

I walked back to Galveston, who had finished his snack and was poring over the news story as the announcement came on for the next leg of our flight. It was on to Rio, and I was still curious about Galveston's plan. It better be good.

Chapter 52

Before takeoff Galveston showed me a phone text message from Alex. It read: "Made it okay, call if you need us. Hope you're comfortable."

"Look at the picture he sent with it," Galveston said, pointing at the phone. Up flashed a picture of Alex and Dr. Sloan, each with a goofy grin on their faces as they held up large margarita glasses.

"Jerk," I said.

"I'm going to tell him they need to be in Rio tomorrow, just to tick him off," Galveston said, laughing.

"Beautiful," I added.

Jane found her seat next to us, and she patted me on the knee as she sat down. I had been fully forgiven for my gasoline gaffe. Galveston pulled out his papers and moved through them, scribbling notes.

I decided to focus on Jane again since we were now on more amicable terms. I was excited to have some "make believe" alone time with her. Jane reached her arm under mine and put her head on my shoulder. We both fell asleep in a glorious, comfortable slumber.

I slept hard until I felt a poke at my ribs. Galveston was watching an extremely bad in-flight movie while drinking a soda. He was jabbing me with his finger while he watched and drank.

"What are you doing?" I asked groggily, with one eye open.

"Oh, you're awake," he said, faking surprise. "Well, since you're awake, let me fill you in on what we're going to do."

"Okay," I said, wiping my eyes. I gently moved Jane's head to the window. "Let me hear it," I said to Galveston flatly.

"Good. Okay, here's the plan," he spoke quietly, almost covertly. "When we finally make it to Sao Paulo we'll find Ecomax and hopefully locate Dr. Patelo. Depending on what we find, we infiltrate the facility, sabotage the production, and then get out."

I waited for more. "You're kidding, right?"

"No, that's about it."

"So in all this time, that is what you've come up with? What the hell were you writing over there for so long?"

"Oh, this," he said, holding up his papers. "Sudoku. This crap is addictive."

"Sudoku?" I questioned. "A game? You've been doing a game this whole time?"

"No, this is no game, it's a mental exercise."

I could only roll my eyes. "What in the world would this grand plan accomplish?" I inquired.

"If they can't release the product, then they can't keep going with their plan."

"Right," I answered.

"So if they don't have one that works, then they're sunk."

"True," I said, "but that's not the point. Just the idea could be enough to get things rolling."

"Well, what's your plan?" Galveston asked.

I thought a second and then a minute. It was obvious he needed my help to come up with a more coherent plan. "I think we need to manipulate the market, or in this case, the potential market for the battery."

"Go on," he prodded.

"The way I see it, Black Bear or Ecomax releases a battery that is good, but doesn't have near the capability of Dr. Sloan's battery. If we could somehow manipulate the timing of the battery's introduction into the market with an alternative that is better, then demand for their so-called 'invention' would be non-existent."

"I see," Galveston nodded his head slowly and shuffled his papers. "We could break Black Bear, Ecomax, and the Senator, all at once. I see where you're going. I've got it, I've got a plan," he said holding up a finger.

"Do tell," I said shifting in my seat.

"Just as you said before, there needs to be an alternative, and our alternative will be the guy we've had the whole time—Dr. Sloan."

I gave Galveston a confused look. "You lost me," I told him.

"Dr. Sloan has the final prototype version. We do just what I said before. We get into Ecomax. I know we can do this because we have Elizabeth and the resources of MI6 on our side. There are agents on the ground in Sao Paulo already, and one of those agents has a contact at Ecomax. She said she can get us in, but that's it. They can't risk anymore than that. Our first step is to sabotage their operation. Dr. Sloan can educate us on the best way to do this. The second part is even more out of the box. Dr. Sloan doesn't know it yet, but he's going to get to do his long awaited Memphis presentation about his invention. He's going to do it as the President of our new technology company." Galveston hung the words out so I could absorb them. A tiny flicker lit in my brain. I understood where he was going with this.

"We beat them to the punch then," I answered.

"Exactly. We put the fear in them and watch them squirm," Galveston said confidently. "After that, we expose them for the entire world to see."

The plan was daring, stupid, and had so many variables that must be met that it was bound to work. We had made it this far, so why not? We would release Dr. Sloan's prototype before Ecomax and Black Bear could release their prototype. But they would have a huge problem. They would have a product that didn't work as well as ours. By our thinking, Senator Eastman would be pushing his legislation a few days before or after Ecomax's big announcement, but it would turn out to be useless because we would be first to the table. We would be located in sunny Southern California U.S.A., and not in some foreign country.

"You know a lot of things have to fall into place for this to work," I said with much apprehension.

"I know," Galveston answered. "It looks virtually impossible on paper, but so has everything else we've done." Galveston reached beneath the seat in front of him and pulled out an envelope. He pointed to the address on the front. "We have to find Dr. Patelo, find out what he knows, and tell him about Espinosa." We didn't know that would be impossible.

-Chapter 53-

Chase sat at the long table surrounded by other men and women of his elite set. He slowly chewed his beef Carpaccio that sat on top of a bed of arugula, and sipped on a glass of '61 Chateau La Mission Haut Brion Pessac Leognan Bordeaux—a three thousand dollar bottle of wine.

There was a good reason for this little event; show the investors that things were on track, and their returns would be sizable. He would have to lie about it, but this didn't faze him in the least.

Just as he finished his dinner and got a refill on his glass of wine, his phone vibrated. He excused himself quietly from the table and got up, walked to a nearby room, and answered it.

"Yes,"

"The operation is complete and clean." It was Murray on the other end.

"Good. Move to the next target and complete it. Only call me again when it's complete."

"Agreed." Murray answered, and quickly hung up.

Chase didn't care for Murray, but he was an unsavory essential for the plan to come to fruition. He didn't immediately return to the table, and instead made another call.

"Yes?" The husky voice answered on the other end.

"I'm glad I caught you," Chase said into the phone.

"Yes, what is it?" the voice asked dryly.

"We're on track. Our other little problem has been taken care of, and *Project Atlantic* was successful, as you probably well know. When is the announcement?"

"Three days. I've been assured of that. I noticed how your boys went about it. I hope they are covering their asses."

"Yes, they are, and they're closing in on the last contact. Murray's association with us is complete. Everything has been done as quietly as possible, as promised."

"I wouldn't call some of it quiet," the voice grumbled. "I don't want to be caught with my pants down."

"Probably wouldn't be the first time," Chase shot back.

"Watch it, Chase. I could have your ass in a sling, and I could still come out smelling like roses." The words had definitely hit a raw nerve.

"We're both in this, you know that," Chase said to the voice on the other end.

"I'm ready. In four days I'll get the FBI involved, and the whole thing will be blown. We better be ready."

"Of course, everything is in place. We can't be stopped now. Goodbye." Chase hung up the phone and returned to the table where the other patrons were finishing their desserts. He didn't sit down and rang his glass instead.

"Ladies and gentlemen, let me inform you of our progress."

-Chapter 54-

The plane landed in Rio de Janeiro, Brazil, after an eleven hour flight from Houston. It had been a long journey, but Galveston immediately began working the phone upon our arrival. He first contacted Elizabeth and then realized he had three messages from David May.

As he listened to the messages, I noticed his face change. Something was amiss. He put his phone away, and his eyes appeared sunken. Dr. Blout—Dr. Sloan's friend and May's contact at Global Energy—was dead. Supposedly the death occurred from an auto collision, but May didn't think it was just an accident. Black Bear was going after everyone that knew about the battery.

"These bastards aren't going to get away with it. We're going to find everybody involved, and the Feds better beat us to them," Galveston said angrily and with passion; he meant every word.

I felt his anger. These men were playing with people's lives for money and creating havoc in their wake. None of it sat well with the Boy Scout in me, if I had been one. I felt we did have a purpose, well beyond covering our butts or even making money for the business. Since our altercation at Jane's house, it had become personal. Now the killing of a colleague's friend, Dr. Blout, only angered me more.

"What else did May have to say?" I asked Galveston, who was finally beginning to calm down.

"Chase may be a prime player. He had been pressing Dr. Blout about the location of Dr. Sloan. May is going to a press conference where he will be able to interview Chase."

"Interesting," I responded, not knowing what else to say at the moment. We would just have to wait to find out if May could establish a connection.

We decided to put the information behind us for the time being and focus on the mission. Galveston and I would fly out the next morning to meet Elizabeth in Sao Paulo. We convinced Jane to stay behind at the hotel to await our return.

The conspiracy theories and paranoia ran amuck in my head that night at the hotel. Then it struck me—what did we really know about Weston Chase's motivation? He seemed concerned about Dr.

Sloan's disappearance and seemed to have a big stake in the production of the battery. He was a businessman, and once a businessman, always a businessman. Of all the conspiracy theories I thought up in the dark, this was the one that bothered me the most. He had the connection with Global Energy, the Alternative Energy Consortium, even Black Bear. I waited as long as I could before speaking up in the darkness of the room.

"Hey," I said softly. "Galveston?" All I heard was heavy, sleepful breathing.

I reached down in the dark and felt around for my shoe, and upon finding it, flung it toward the side of his bed. I heard him grunt as it missed the side of the bed and hit him in the head.

"Galveston? You awake?" I said again.

"Uh, yeah, what the hell? What is it?" he replied, rubbing his head.

"What do you know about Weston Chase?" I asked.

"What? Weston Chase? It's two thirty in the morning, go back to sleep," he mumbled.

"What do you know about him?" I inquired again.

"Same as you; rich guy, has lots of toys, a businessman," he said sleepily.

"But what do you really know about him?"

I heard the bed move and then his bedside light flipped on, causing us to squint at each other.

"What's on your mind?" he asked.

"I don't know. I've just been thinking that we don't know much about him. We've never really looked into his connection with this whole thing. What's in it for him?"

"Why does he have to be in it for something?" he queried.

"All his types are in it for something. He's a corporate raider, a businessman at heart. How did he know Dr. Sloan went missing so quickly?"

Galveston sat up in his bed. "You think he's involved in this thing more than we've been told?"

"I don't know, but he has connections to most of the players in this fiasco. It just doesn't make sense. Does he know we found Dr. Sloan? Did David tell Dr. Blout that we found Dr. Sloan?"

"No, I don't think so. David told Blout the Feds hadn't located him."

"I don't know why Chase would be so interested in Sloan. I just figured he wanted to make sure the battery would be in the hands of Global Energy, like they had agreed." Galveston looked at me, and a worried look popped on his face. "I just can't picture a guy like that not having an alternate plan for this thing," I said.

"I agree with you. It is sort of weird." He reached for his phone. "I have an idea that will help answer this question." Galveston dialed the phone and waited for the other end to pick up.

"Hello? What is it Galveston?" May said groggily on the other end.

"David, sorry to wake you. I know it's late, but we need you to do something when you talk to Chase, and it's going to be strange. I need you to tell Chase that Dr. Sloan was found dead in San Diego."

"What? But why?" May asked, still half-asleep.

"Tell him he was found last night, shot to death. Tell him the prototype wasn't found in his hotel room. Don't tell him anything else. Can you do that for us?" Galveston asked.

"Uh, yeah, I guess. It's kind of strange, but I'll do it. Where're you going with this?"

"We have some suspicions about Chase. Get back to me as soon as you know something."

"Alright, I'll call you tomorrow. Goodbye," May replied.

"Bye, David, sleep tight." Galveston set his phone down. "We'll see how much Chase wants this battery." Galveston slumped on the edge of the bed. "You and your night thinking, just go to sleep. I can't think anymore."

"Alright," I said putting my head back on the pillow.

But we wouldn't be getting much sleep. The thoughts continued to race through both our heads. What was Weston Chase really out to do?

Chapter 55

Our wake-up call was at 6:00 A.M. I needed some coffee, but not before I snuck in a wake-up kiss and goodbye kiss to Jane in her room. I gave her a wad of money to use as she liked because we weren't sure when we would be back.

We were the only thing standing in the way of the mercenaries' success, and we must be the ones to succeed. I parceled it into good and evil, right and wrong, and the just versus injustice. I felt better, stronger, and more courageous, with increased confidence and vigor. Maybe my kiss from Jane this morning had something to do with that.

"You ready?" Galveston said to me from behind. I turned around with steely eyes with a coffee cup in my hand.

"You bet, let's go."

"Well aren't you an eager beaver," he joked.

The flight from Sao Paulo went without incident—no emergencies, and thankfully, no pesky passport problems. We approached the sprawling and congested city of Sao Paulo and landed safely on the ground.

Sao Paulo is the hub of commerce and finance in Brazil and boasts a population of 21 million people. It is an extremely congested city with a developed metropolitan center and vast suburbs of slums. It has also been known for its extraordinary crime rate and dangerous areas, but this had waned in the previous years. The difference in the socioeconomic status of the people was evident, but they had a decidedly content air about them.

A young boy approached us on the concrete sidewalk outside the air terminal and motioned that he wanted money to carry our bags. He was dressed in dirty, shabby clothes, and spoke only in Portuguese. I reached for some money to give him, but Galveston stopped me and politely shooed the boy away. I looked at him in horror.

"Sorry about that, but if you start flashing money we'll have twenty kids around us in seconds. That's not the attention we need right now," Galveston explained.

I understood his point. We already stood out like a sore thumb, and the last thing we needed was a scene in a public place.

Galveston began scanning the area and noticed a sultry lady standing next to a car with tinted windows. It was Elizabeth dressed in a black dress, a large, flowing hat, and sunglasses. Galveston nodded his head to her, and we walked to the car.

We weaved our way across the street with our bags, dodging the heavy traffic coming from both directions. Galveston ungraciously took the front seat as I grabbed the back.

"Morning, love," he said to Elizabeth in a mock English accent and kissed her on the cheek.

I hadn't noticed that the boy outside the terminal had followed us across the road and was standing at the back of our car. As Galveston and Elizabeth were exchanging pleasantries and swooning over each other, I rolled down the window and motioned for the boy to come to the car. He came up to the window, and I pushed a few dollars in his hand before we began to drive away. I peered back as we left and saw a smile cross his face as he turned and ran back across the road. At least I may have made someone happy in this city, if only for a short time.

As we made it to the center of the city things began to change and well-developed areas with shops and quaint apartment buildings began to emerge. Elizabeth focused skillfully on the road, never taking her eyes off the clutter of traffic weaving its way around us.

"Where are we headed?" I asked toward the front of the car.

"We're going to Dr. Patelo's home. Elizabeth found out where he lives," Galveston said, facing forward. "It should be close."

We pulled up in front of a large high-rise, brightly decorated from the outside. It was an upscale building with a beautiful glass exterior and noticeably one of the newer buildings in this part of town.

Galveston decided to check if Patelo was home and left Elizabeth and I steaming in the car from the hot summer sun. He returned after thirty minutes.

"He hasn't been home in a while, but I did find this," Galveston said as he got back in the car.

"You broke in, didn't you?" I stated seriously.

"Of course," Galveston said, smiling daftly. "That's a no-brainer. Check this out and see what you can find." Galveston handed me a neatly bound notebook. "It has his entire timeline. I even saw pictures of him and Espinosa in his apartment."

I flipped the notebook open and read back through his writings. He had entries for mundane items he was working on and a to-do list of things to accomplish. Then an interesting entry struck my eye that he wrote about a month ago. It read:

Contacted by Jorge Morales of Ecomax about a new research opportunity in an energy transfer system.

I pulled out a pen, ripped out a piece of paper from the journal, and wrote the name down. I flipped the notebook to the next page.

Dr. Morales gave me the information about research conducted in Sao Paulo. Received design parameters. He wants prototype during week period at end of month. Needs personal staff of fifteen and project will be tightly controlled.

I flipped the page again and read on.

Talked to Morales today and received contract for work with Ecomax. If successfully completed will receive grant money of $1.5 million toward my current research projects as well as $100,000 personal compensation. Project is very secretive due to corporate espionage concerns. Morales asked me to get in touch with my contacts in Mexico. They need security to transport design. Called Alfonso who agreed to do the work.

I then read the next day's entry.

First payment received for staff. Project named Adamanthea, and the work location will be Summit Hill.

I again wrote down the pertinent information and flipped the page again. The next entry was strange, and the last one entered into the journal. It was a full two weeks later.

Summit Hill no longer the location, now going to Santa Rosa.

No personal items allowed, and Morales no longer my contact. Work to begin tomorrow.

I recalled the date from the letter we had from Colonel Espinosa and it fit perfectly with Patelo's timeline. What and where was Summit Hill and Santa Rosa? I pushed the journal and my handwritten notes to Galveston, but as I was handing them to him I noticed some scribbled words on a few of the back, mostly blank, pages. I could barely make out the words, but they seemed to be quickly written. They were directions to somewhere. I read through them carefully and near the bottom I saw words that read:

Turn left at Evangelista de Souza station.

"I think we have where he went," I told Galveston excitedly. Lucky for us, Dr. Patelo was a man of excruciating detail.

"I'll call Alex and have him check it out," Galveston said to me, already dialing his phone. He began to talk to Alex who plugged in the directions I had found.

"It's a dead end, just a railway station, nothing else. It's surrounded by jungle," Galveston said to me.

I skimmed the journal again. "There had to be more details," I thought to myself. On the last page of the journal, scribbled at the bottom of the page was 23 55 48.13, and 46 38 27.08.

"Have Alex find exactly where these coordinates are," I said showing him the numbers. He gave me a confused look and then realized these were the same type of numbers we had seen before.

Galveston read off the coordinates as Alex plugged them into his computer. "It's way outside of Sao Paulo, south of the city, and in the jungle. There is nothing around for miles, except for this train depot. He's going to send the directions," Galveston stated, continuing to hold the phone to his ear. "Get back to me on those other things as quick as you can," he said to Alex before hanging up.

"I think you just found where they took the device, Roger. We need to check it out."

I smiled at our good fortune, but I had a queasy feeling that we would find something unsettling.

Chapter 56

A ring came from Galveston's phone. Alex was forwarding the directions to the location at Evangelista de Souza.

Galveston had turn-by-turn instructions and began to read them out to Elizabeth as she raced to the outskirts of the city. We proceeded from one road to another until nothing but jungle surrounded us on either side.

We drove for hours until we arrived at the Evangelista de Souza railway station. It was a dilapidated building that saw little traffic either by road or rail and was nestled on flat land between the jungle. Just beyond the station we found our last turn.

Barely showing through the dense brush was a small road peeking out. Elizabeth swung the car onto the road. These were old logging roads that hadn't been used for years, but this was a newly graded dirt road.

We slowed our progress and began lurching and bumping along the winding road. We traveled up one hill to another and then back to the valley floor.

We drove through more jungle until the canopy opened up to the sky, and the trees disappeared from the side of the road as our destination came into view. I gasped at the sight. It looked as if a bomb had been dropped on the area, flattening everything around it. A twisted, burnt metal shell sat alone on the open land, and a burned-out car lay beside it. Everything was blackened, and as we got closer we could tell this was not normal destruction. Galveston's and Elizabeth's mouths were agape as we arrived.

"Oh, my God," Galveston muttered under his breath.

We got out of the car and walked to the edge of the burned-out building. The steel frame structure precariously stood erect, but leaned awkwardly. Elizabeth immediately dialed her phone and waited by the car, as Galveston and I walked to where the building once stood. We didn't say a word to each other as we examined the wreckage. I had no idea what I was looking at, but Galveston did.

"This was no ordinary explosion," he said to me, peering in the hole that was left by the blast. "It's much too uniform in shape and is spread out equally. Notice the charring on those steel struts. It was concentrated from the inside out. Either they had one nasty accident or this was intentionally set."

I noticed the pattern he indicated. The remaining steel had black encased on the inner portions and was deformed, causing the structure to fall in on itself from one concentrated, violent blast.

"There was a basement, too," he said, pointing to the middle of the building as he walked into the interior.

Debris filled a hole where a basement would have been, and I noticed stairs descending into the lower level. Everything was destroyed beyond recognition, but one thing was noticeably missing—bodies. Galveston had already noticed the same thing.

"No people," he said softly, almost relieved. "Even with an explosion like this we would see some bodies, unless they were all in the basement."

I shuddered at the thought.

We gingerly stepped back to the perimeter. The area was still very dangerous, and a misstep could send hanging metal crashing around us, or more importantly, on top of us. I walked over to the burned-out wreckage of the car ravaged by fire, now just a shell. As I closed in on it, I noticed an object that was different than the surrounding debris, and it laid well away from the building. As I moved closer, my throat began to close up and horror crossed my face. It was the charred remains of a person. I tried to yell out, but couldn't. It appeared to be a man, badly burnt from head to toe but whose features appeared clearly at least on one side. It was then that I got my first odor of a poorly decomposing body. I immediately began to heave, and I doubled over onto the ground. I pulled myself back from the body and put my shirt up to my face to try to stifle the smell.

"Roger!" Galveston yelled, seeing me on the ground.

He raced over as I waved a hand. He came up to me and noticed what I had already found, turning his head from the sight. Elizabeth heard the commotion and came over. She saw the body and helped me back away from the stench.

Galveston moved to the body with his shirt over his nose and mouth, and he began to look it over methodically. The body laid near the car, crumpled over, but away from the building. The blackened skin revealed where the man had gotten the brunt of the blast. He probably had been thrown toward the car, killing him instantly—or so we thought. The blackened areas preserved the features on one side of his face, but the rest was badly decomposed under the hot and humid conditions of the jungle, prime catalysts for quick decomposition.

Galveston peered over the body, moving it slightly with his foot. The body had a coat on at one time. It was mostly missing now, with the charred side burnt into the man's body. I managed to sit on the ground far enough away to not smell the odor, or get the full sight of the body, as Elizabeth stroked my head to calm my shattered nerves.

Galveston turned toward us. "This man's been shot in the head. He has a single gunshot wound."

I mustered some strength, held my shirt over my nose and mouth, and walked to the body as Elizabeth followed.

"Right here." He pointed at the skull and the entry of the fatal bullet.

A small round hole about the size of a penny was clearly visible. I managed to look at the face and studied the remaining features. Suddenly, a realization hit me like a brick, and I turned and raced to the car.

"Roger? You okay?" Galveston yelled at me, expecting me to stop and vomit. I grabbed my notebook from the car and returned to the body. "Roger? You alright?" Galveston asked, concerned.

I pulled out a picture from my notebook and held it close to the face of the lifeless man's remaining features, while I continued to hold my shirt to my face. I looked up at Elizabeth and Galveston.

"I think we just found Dr. Patelo."

-Chapter 57-

Galveston stared at me with a horrid look plastered on his face.

"It can't be," he stammered but realized the truth in my statement when he saw the picture.

I too felt his horror. We had traveled thousands of miles in the last few days to arrive at this; a wretched, disfigured, shell of a man. Elizabeth excused herself to call the Brazilian authorities. It was now a homicide. Galveston turned to me while I moved the dirt below my feet.

"Why do you suppose they killed him? I mean, if a guy is in charge of getting the battery to the production line, why would they go ahead and kill him? Why not just keep him happy and move him to Ecomax?" Galveston inquired aloud.

I shrugged my shoulders trying to figure out the mad reasoning.

"Obviously they wanted the evidence gone," I said, pointing to the obliterated building.

"I think they just want anyone who knows what this device is capable of to be out of the way, and permanently." Galveston knelt down next to the body again and began to check the severely charred pockets of the man's clothing.

I stared in disbelief. "What are you doing?" I exclaimed.

"Look," he said, "I'm not coming this far without making sure we've checked everything."

"But this isn't respectful."

"Respectful or not, I'm sure he would want us to nail these suckers." He continued to check the pant pockets and then the coat pockets, grimacing and holding his breath as he did. "Hello," he announced as he reached into the frayed and blackened front pocket of the formerly white lab coat.

Galveston pulled out an interestingly shaped circuit board with a small metal loop at the end, about the size of a large postage stamp. It had been partially melted at one end. He handed it to me as if I could decipher what it was. It had, from my best recollection of circuits, a few resistors and two small rectangular connectors. The board itself had a number and two small letters inscribed on it. It appeared to read 5MS.

"My team will be here in twenty minutes, and I've contacted the local authorities. I would suggest that we leave here quickly," Elizabeth said after using her satellite phone.

"I tend to agree with you, love. Let us make haste," Galveston replied smartly in his faux British accent.

"Does she ever find that annoying when you do that?" I whispered to Galveston.

"Nah, she finds it endearing," he said, but I happened to notice Elizabeth rolling her eyes as we moved hastily back to the car.

"What now, love?" she queried, and smiled at Galveston as she started the car.

"To Ecomax, of course. I think they're going to find that their operation has hit a snag."

Chapter 58

We bounced back down the dirt road we had previously traveled, spraying dust behind us as we went. The humidity had been steadily rising, and we now began to stream sweat, even with the air conditioner running full blast.

"Hey, Roger, send those pictures of the circuit to Alex." Galveston then informed Elizabeth of what we had found.

I fumbled the circuit board from my pocket, set it on the seat next to me, and snapped some close pictures with Galveston's phone. I sent it to Alex with the message: *Does Dr. Sloan know what this is.*

We continued on the dusty road until we were back to the main thoroughfare. A small, makeshift sign pointed to Sao Paulo, and we began the long trip to the bustling city.

A beep resonated from the phone. A message was waiting from Alex. It read:

> *It's an output circuit from the battery prototype, it regulates the voltage output from the battery itself. It is one of five circuit boards in the battery's housing.*

I looked at the message and typed back: *How does he know this?* A beep came back almost immediately.

> *The 5MS on the board is his. It's the series of the circuit board, plus his daughter's initials. Margaret Sloan, area five.*

"Well, that's convenient," I muttered to myself.

"What did Alex say about what you two found," Elizabeth said, looking in the rearview mirror.

I handed the phone back to Galveston, and he read the messages aloud to Elizabeth. Another beep came from the phone, and Galveston recited the text.

"Dr. Sloan used these abbreviations on the two of the three prototypes he made. This is one of those. It is an important piece and without it the battery does not work to its full capacity." He looked up from the phone. "That's interesting. Maybe Dr. Patelo knew what he had and kept this part out as a little security."

"That didn't work out for him, though," I announced.

"Nope, but Patelo gave us the break we were hoping for since he didn't include it with the prototype. Ecomax will have to try to solve the problem."

"What are you saying?" I asked stupidly.

"We need to find this Dr. Morales." He leaned back in his seat with an air of confidence covering his face.

"We're what?" I exclaimed from the back seat.

"You heard me. We've just been promoted to battery experts, and we need to find out what Dr. Morales knows. I think he'll need to be convinced to help us."

Elizabeth's contacts had already been working on finding him, and before we made it back to Sao Paulo we had an answer on the location of Dr. Morales.

We crossed into the outskirts of the city and drove toward a residential high-rise near a well-developed shopping district.

A call to Dr. Morales's apartment confirmed he was indeed in the building. Elizabeth would wait outside, out of view, until we signaled with a call. She would pick us up, and together we would drive off into the sunset. My stomach ached and my heart raced as we prepared, and I noticed that for once, Galveston was on edge too.

Galveston took a small bag out of his backpack and pulled from it what looked like fuzzy lint, dark in color. I realized what he had.

"You must be kidding, not a disguise again," I said, looking skeptically at the furry strip.

"We need a bit of concealment for the cameras, if there are any. See, I'm going to wear a beard." He pulled out another fuzzy object that looked like a ferret and began to stick it on his face.

"You look like someone's creepy uncle, or a homeless man. It suits you," I joked.

"Yeah, yeah. Now put yours on. I gave you the mustache." I reluctantly took it and stuck it with adhesive to my upper lip. "Wow, you look like some guy from the seventies. That looks terrible."

I looked in the side mirror of the truck. It appeared I had a hair follicular problem, and the color didn't even match my own.

"This looks horrendous. I look like I should be picking someone up at the disco."

"It's just to throw Morales off. You'll be fine," Galveston assured me.

"If you say so," I replied.

Elizabeth positioned the car on the side of the building out of view from the main door. We waited for someone to enter or exit the building to allow access inside.

A woman with a small dog finally appeared inside the door and struggled to get it open. Galveston had already jumped from the car and raced next to entrance, out of view from the older woman. I scrambled to follow, nervously fiddling with my itchy mustache the entire way.

As the door cracked, Galveston pulled it open for the woman. "Let me help you there," he said in English.

The woman smiled and said something back in Portuguese as she pulled the small dog by the leash onto the sidewalk.

Galveston motioned for me to follow. "I'm staying with Dr. Morales until Friday," he said loudly, in case the woman knew English or knew Morales. She didn't bat an eye as we intruded into the building.

Elizabeth's contacts had given us the number of Morales's apartment and a picture of the man. We opted to race up the flight of stairs instead of taking the elevator. Unbeknownst to us, there were Black Bear guards staying in an apartment close to Morales. They had installed cameras in the elevator and front door, and we had unknowingly evaded them.

Morales was on the sixth floor, and after panting up the stairs we rounded a corner and came upon his door. Galveston pulled out a small bag from his back pocket and produced a lock pick, a skill I didn't know he had. He quickly worked on the lock until the tumblers clicked, and the door opened.

Galveston and I moved slowly inside while a television spewed out music. A clinking of glasses came from the kitchen area, and as we moved toward the sound the back of Morales came into view.

"Morales," Galveston said quietly.

The small, portly man spun around quickly and dropped the glass he was holding, causing it to shatter on the ground. He had reading glasses on the end of his nose and raised his head at

Galveston's voice. He was noticeably surprised at the unannounced visit.

"Who are you?" Morales said in shock.

"No, you need to listen to us." Galveston walked closely to Morales and stopped in a menacing stance.

"Alright, I'm listening."

Galveston pulled out my notepad and the notes I had taken. "We know about your project and who you're working for."

Morales stood stunned. "What do you want?"

We could tell he was growing nervous, and I noticed him reach for a phone on his countertop. Galveston sprung into action and grabbed his hand before it reached the receiver.

"That wouldn't be a good idea, Doctor," Galveston said seriously, squeezing his hand with force.

Morales's face turned ashen and he leaned back, shocked at the two strange men that stood before him; one with a shaggy beard, and the other with a cheesy mustache.

"I think we should just tell him," I told Galveston.

"You're right," Galveston conceded. "Dr. Morales, we are contractors working for a government."

"You're not going to kill me, are you?" Morales asked, scared out of his wits.

"We don't do that sort of thing, but we do need to ask you a few questions—and we don't like untruthful answers," Galveston said in an aggressive tone.

Galveston ran with the Doctor's fear and could tell that Morales wasn't a threat. He was just a scientist caught up in something he didn't understand, but fear was a good motivator to tell the truth. Galveston wouldn't hurt a fly, but if pushed he could play the aggressor.

"Do you know Dr. Patelo?" Galveston asked Morales.

"Yes," he started nervously.

"Just relax, Doctor. We aren't going to hurt you. You just need to know the truth of what you're working on." Morales breathed a little slower, but was still tense.

"Dr. Patelo is a friend and colleague of mine. I enlisted his help in engineering this battery, but I haven't heard from him for a week. I checked his lab, and he wasn't there."

"The lab? You've seen it?" Galveston inquired.

"Yes, of course. I help set it up. It is just down the street in the old Summit Hill cannery."

"Who set up the lab?"

"Wallace Murray. He's the one who set up the operation here. He is a project engineer, I think," Morales said nonchalantly.

Galveston's eyes narrowed. He knew this name well from his days at Black Bear. I had to access the recesses of my mind, back to our original meeting to get the connection of who the man was.

Murray was the head of covert operations for Black Bear Security, and the man that most likely orchestrated the explosions in Africa and Venezuela. His men were the people Jane and I encountered in San Diego, and he had probably ordered Espinosa and Patelo to be killed. This was all circumstantial, but it was easy to connect the dots.

Galveston tried to compose himself, but I could tell his anger was growing. I decided I needed to take over the questions until Galveston could lower his blood pressure.

"Dr. Morales, did you know there's another lab in Evangelista de Souza?" I asked him.

"What? No. I know it's an area south of here, fairly uninhabited."

"Well, Doctor, we have some information that Dr. Patelo was working there, instead of at Summit Hill," I said, trying to break the news to him slowly about his friend.

"Really? I knew nothing of that, I swear. Why?"

I pulled some pages from Dr. Patelo's journal out of my pocket and gave them to him. He read them over slowly and looked up at me.

"Where is he, and why can't I reach him?" he asked.

"I'm afraid he's been shot and is dead. We were able to positively I.D. him from pictures. The building he was working in was completely destroyed by an explosion."

"No, it can't be Ernesto. He was supposed to be down the street, and then he was going to join me."

I gave him time to absorb the bad news. He was clearly distraught.

"I'm afraid it is, sir. You're working for very bad men and the product you're working on is part of it. It was stolen from a Dr.

Sloan, over a month ago from his lab at Dartmouth. Do you know a Colonel Espinosa?"

"Yes, Yes," he stammered. "I know Alfonso from a fishing trip with Ernesto. Ernesto got him a job in security with Ecomax. His job was to guard the battery out of the United States. I was told that was where it had been developed, but they didn't want to produce it there because of cost."

"I'm afraid the Colonel has been killed also, poisoned in Mexico. We were able to speak to him directly. That is how we got Dr. Patelo's name," I stated.

"I can't believe it. Am I next? What are they trying to do?" Before I could answer him, Galveston began to speak again.

"I think you need the whole story and what we have. I think you will change your mind after we tell you what we think Black Bear is going to do."

"Okay, okay. I just can't believe it," Morales stammered again.

Galveston set out all we had found. He didn't leave anything out. They sat for over twenty minutes, discussing all the layers of what we had discovered. Morales, with each passing minute, grew more and more shocked, and that shock soon turned to anger. Galveston had met his goal, Morales was with us now, and luckily, he was a very ethical man. Like us, he wanted justice for all the harm these men had wrought.

"What do you want me to do?" Morales asked after hearing all the information.

"We need you to make sure the battery appears completed," Galveston told him.

"But I can't figure out the problem. I've been working on it for almost two days straight without a break. I still can't iron out the problems. I told Placer I would have it ready for production in three days. There is no way I can make it work. That's why I needed Dr. Patelo."

"Don't worry about that Dr. Morales. I have the correct plans here, straight from Dr. Sloan. It won't produce a very efficient battery, but it will get it working." Galveston gave Morales a flash drive with the information on it. "Tell Placer that everything is on schedule. We still have more rats to flush out."

"You must get these men and bring them to justice for what they have done to Ernesto and Alfonso, promise me that," Morales pleaded.

"We'll do it Doctor, don't you worry," Galveston assured him.

"And why do you have on that horrible mustache and beard?" Morales questioned.

Galveston looked at me without a response. The jig was up. I decided I could scratch my mustache now.

The phone suddenly rang in the kitchen.

"It's the Black Bear guards checking up on me. We need to get you two out of here." Morales wasn't supposed to pick it up, it was an indication that they would be checking on him in minutes.

"What do you propose?" I asked him.

"The service entrance down the hall," Morales said emphatically.

"You're the boss. Let's get out of here," Galveston replied.

Morales took the lead and opened up his front door. The hallway was clear, and we began a quick walk toward the end and down the stairs that led to the service entrance at the rear of the building.

"All clear," he announced. "I'll do just what you told me. Please let me know what you two accomplish. I'll do everything I can here, for Ernesto's sake. Now go."

"Thank you, Doctor. We'll keep in touch, I promise," Galveston assured him.

We waved to the doctor as we jetted down the stairs. Luckily, it was just as Morales had described. The area was empty at the service door, and we raced out of the building.

"Can I check my drawers now?" I asked Galveston jokingly, trying to make the best of a bad situation.

Galveston managed a smile. "Mine might need to be checked too."

Elizabeth was waiting for us with the car's engine running. We jumped in and sped away.

"I take it that it was successful," she said.

"I hope so," Galveston said handing my notepad back to me. "I think it's time we got the hell out of Sao Paulo," he announced as we settled in for the drive to the airport. I assumed we were heading back to Rio before connecting with a flight home.

My bubble burst when Galveston instructed, "we need to get to Washington D.C., Black Bear headquarters, as quickly as possible."

"We what?" I exclaimed, not terribly excited about a new change of venue.

"We need to talk to Placer and put the fear of God in him. I have a feeling he isn't acting alone, and we need to find out who else is involved."

"Won't that just scare him away?" I asked.

"That's a chance we have to take. This thing is just too big for him to act alone, and with Murray involved, everything has changed. We need the earliest flight out of Sao Paulo to D.C."

"Uh, did you forget something?" I pressed him.

"No, I don't think so. What did we forget?" he asked me.

"Uh, our fellow employee, Jane, she's still in Rio."

"Oh, yeah. I'd appreciate you not telling that I forgot all about her."

"I'm sure she expects that by now," I quipped.

Galveston was now in full steam ahead mode. Washington D.C. was next, and hopefully it would bring us some closure. But for right now, all I wanted was some sleep.

-Chapter 59-

We made it to the airport safely and managed to get on the next available flight to Rio de Janeiro. Elizabeth would accompany us on the trip.

We rested on the flight from Sao Paulo to Rio, and upon arriving took the shuttle to the hotel where we had previously stayed. I immediately bid the two of them a good night and raced to Jane's room. I knocked on her door, and as she opened it her face lit up. She threw her arms around me and kissed me on the lips.

"I'm so glad you're safe," she told me excitedly as I hugged her. "How did it go?" she asked.

"Boy, do I have some stories for you," I said sighing. She led me into her room and closed the door.

The next morning we took the earliest flight out of Rio. Our only option was to fly back to Sao Paulo to get a non-stop flight to Miami. From there we could connect to Washington Dulles.

Galveston called Alex, informed him of our plan, and asked him to locate where Placer would be. May was meeting with Chase this morning at a conference in Chicago and was planning to give him the false information about Dr. Sloan's demise.

"So you didn't come back to the room last night. Would you like to kiss and tell?" Galveston asked as we settled in our seats. He attempted to goad me into revealing some juicy details, but I held firm.

"We had a lovely night talking and enjoying each other's company," I managed to say with a smile.

He jabbed me in the ribs with his elbow.

"I bet, you old dog."

If anything, this final stand would be a doozie, and I prepared myself mentally for the challenge. All Galveston would tell me was that I would know everything after our unscheduled meeting with Timothy Placer, the CEO of Black Bear.

"We have one or two days," he muttered to himself.

We eventually touched down in Miami. After a short layover we would be off to Dulles, and Washington D.C.

Galveston waited anxiously for May's call. He was probably questioning Chase as we spoke, and Galveston had a lot to tell him.

-Chapter 60-

May arrived at the downtown Chicago Marriott at around 2:00 P.M. to question Weston Chase. He would need to choose his questions carefully so as not scare the fish away.

Chase was attending an alternative energy conference and was one of the speakers from Global Energy Enterprise. Obviously this was a fitting meeting given the events that were currently happening in the world.

May entered discreetly through the service entrance to the large ballroom. He found a seat at the back of the room and surveyed the area. The room was mostly filled with egghead types and members of think tanks, with a scattering of businessmen with an interest in this information. May pulled out a notebook and got comfortable in a chair.

A man in a blue suit was just finishing up his talk. A smattering of blue and green graphs illuminated the screen behind him as he used a laser pointer to point out pertinent items. The man finished up his talk, and after the attendees gave a polite bit of applause, the moderator came up to the podium.

The moderator gave Chase a rousing introduction filled with accolades and well-wishes about all the wonderful work he had done in establishing his organization. The man, May recognized, was Weston Chase.

May looked around him and found an unused program sitting on a nearby seat. Chase's lecture was called, "Business Models in a Capitalist System to Increase Utilization of Alternative Energy Solutions". "Quite a mouthful," May thought.

Chase thanked the moderator, pulled some note cards from his suit coat, and placed some reading glasses on his face.

"Thank you again for those kind words, Mr. Franklin. If only everyone felt that way about me," Chase started, garnering a laugh from the audience. "These are trying times in the global energy market. World events continue to dictate how we, as a country, use our energy resources. Based on this dependence I realized the importance of starting an organization that was independent of political thinking and focused mainly on utilization of cost-effective energy solutions in developing countries. Lessons learned in those countries could be applied here at home."

242

May's eyes were already beginning to glaze over. He had heard this line before, just a lot of words with very little action, but he managed to stay focused on what Chase was saying.

"We live in a changing world and our business models must reflect this. During this lecture I hope to give everyone a sense of what it entails to survive and thrive in the energy sector. It goes beyond having good ideas and intentions. To survive in energy implementation and be effective we need a model that is productive, and even more so, profitable. Without profitability, we can't establish the need for these services. To change thinking and progress, we have to give the consumer, large and small, something they will need," Chase said.

May scribbled some notes on his pad. It was an interesting idea, and he agreed. If people wanted it they would buy it, it would become popular, and conventional thinking would change. In May's mind, Chase could have stopped there.

Chase continued his lecture. "Global Energy Solutions researches, develops, and produces alternative forms of energy in a cost-effective manner. We are a leader in energy production and work for public policy changes. We have already begun research and development on a new, revolutionary product that will change how everyone uses energy. Let's just say that it will be as simple as the cell phone battery in your phone."

May sat up at this news. Chase was giving overtones about Dr. Sloan's battery. He couldn't believe what he was hearing. Chase was telling how he was going to make money from Dr. Sloan's invention. No one in the room flinched, but May knew too much about the case not to notice what had been said. Chase was priming the pump for this group to expect a new, revolutionary battery.

May listened silently to the rest of the discussion. Chase proposed that in order for people to embrace a new technology certain restrictions imposed by the government must be lifted, and a product that was cost-effective needed to be developed.

"People would only be motivated to change for something that would positively affect their life," May thought. The dreams about saving the environment or cleaning the air only went so far with the average person. After forty minutes, Chase finished up his lecture and began to field questions.

May contemplated the content of the lecture. To truly embrace these new alternative energy sources so desired by the members in the room required complete regulation and mandates by the government, forcing people to change.

The thought hit May like a brick, and he scribbled a name on his notepad—Senator Eastman. The Senator, he knew from information Galveston had given him, was from the camp that dreamed of more government regulation on everything; fuel standards, environmental controls, paying for the miles you drove, and higher taxes on businesses and individuals if they didn't comply with the energy mandates set by the federal government. Most were such unpopular ideas that they never found footing, but now everything was different. The explosions in Africa and South America, the rising cost of energy worldwide, and the scare of "climate change" would force people to reevaluate their energy consumption.

Chase answered the last of the questions from the group, and the moderator took the stage again thanking him for his words. Chase walked off the stage and stood alone off to the side, a look of confidence on his face. A large, burly man approached Chase, spoke to him, and then backed away as Chase exchanged words with the moderator. May got up, straightened his sport coat, and walked directly toward Chase.

"Mr. Chase," May said coming up behind him.

Chase turned around, but not before May felt a hand on his shoulder.

"No more questions. Mr. Chase needs to leave the hotel," the large man said to May as Chase looked on

"I don't think so," May said to the large man as he politely showed him his badge. The man slowly took his hand off May's shoulder.

"It's okay, Campbell, bring the car around," Chase told the man.

Campbell complied and left the room, leaving Chase and May alone.

"Mr. Chase, Special Agent David May," he said, showing Chase his badge. "I just need to ask you a few questions."

Chase didn't flinch or even act surprised. "Of course, what can I do for you?"

"I just need to ask you about Dr. Blout. We are doing a follow-up on his accident because we've had some inquiry about foul play. You knew Dr. Blout well?"

Again, Chase didn't show emotion at the question. "Yes, good friends. It's just tragic what happened."

"I agree. Was there anyone who Dr. Blout had an altercation with?"

"No, never. Why? Do you have some information about him? What a terrible accident he had."

"We're just doing some questioning of people he knew. He was the head of the Consortium?"

"Yes, he helped me start the company. He was a good man and was doing some excellent research. I hope you don't think there was more to his accident than what was in the paper."

"No, not really," May lied. "We're actually trying to get some background on another case, another man you know, a Dr. Edward Sloan."

"Yes, Dr. Sloan, is he safe? He disappeared a few weeks ago and we've been trying to find out what happened."

"I'm afraid not. He was found dead in San Diego, shot at close range."

"Oh, no," Chase exclaimed. "Do you know who did it?"

"No, that's why I'm here, to see if there is any connection to him and Dr. Blout."

"That's just terrible. What kind of people would do such a thing," Chase said.

"I don't know, but were looking into it." May thought for a second and abruptly stopped his questioning. "If you or your people have any other information, it would be greatly appreciated by the Bureau," May said, noting Chase's demeanor.

"Yes, of course."

"You can reach me at this number," May told him, handing him a business card.

"Thank you, Agent May. I'll let you know if we come up with anything," Chase told him.

"Have a good day, sir."

May turned and made his way to the exit. He had more questions he had intended to ask but stopped short. Chase was cool and calm and showed little emotion to the news. May's years of experience told him Chase knew much more than he was telling, and he decided not to press further. May was afraid of frightening Chase away. He was just too polished and knew what to say—and not to say. May knew Chase was holding out information.

May dialed his phone as he got in the hotel lobby.

"Get Dr. Blout's car out of the impound lot and do a full investigative search for peculiarities—and use discretion," he said into the phone.

May realized Galveston had been right about Chase. He needed to find out more information about this new suspect but needed Chase to think he was off the hook. May still had no hard evidence of Chase's involvement and was beginning to get heat about the investigation from his superiors. Something bigger than he imagined was brewing, and May didn't have much time to figure it out.

Chapter 61

We arrived in Washington D.C. at Dulles International about 10:30 P.M. It had been an extremely long and draining day, but we weren't done yet.

Galveston read his messages. He had a text from May that said to call as soon as possible. Galveston had been waiting for this news—we all had. I was very interested in what role Chase played in all this and what May thought about their meeting.

"David, got your message, how did it go?" Galveston asked him without further pleasantries.

"It was interesting, very interesting," May started. "I think our Mr. Chase is involved, probably more than we think. I told him about Dr. Sloan, and he was pretty cool about it, really no emotion. I didn't press him further. I just got the feeling he was silently relieved. I don't trust him. I have a team examining Dr. Blout's car for any peculiarities and checking into all of Chase's latest moves. We'll see what we find," May explained. "Are you already back in San Diego?" he asked.

"Not exactly, David," Galveston said slowly. "We took a little detour."

"A little detour? What exactly does that mean?" May questioned.

"We're in D.C."

"D.C.? I don't even want to ask, but I know I have to. What happened in Brazil that made you stop in D.C.? How much am I not going to like this?"

"Oh, you won't like any of it, but it may be the break you've needed."

"Go on," May pressed.

Galveston proceeded to tell May about our exploits in Brazil. The same as he had to Dr. Morales just the previous day. May listened intently, silently shocked at the new wealth of the information, and horrified at the way we went about it. Galveston finished up but left the last bit of juicy information until the end.

"Guess who's behind this entire operation," he asked like a quiz show host.

"I don't have any idea at this point. Who?" May asked, exasperated at our situation.

"None other than Wallace Murray," Galveston said dramatically.

"You don't say."

"He planned the demise of our Colonel Espinosa, Patelo, the explosions, all of it—I bet."

"And do you have any hard proof of this?"

"Of course not. How good do you think we are? That's why we're here in D.C., to talk to Placer, Timothy Placer, the CEO of Black Bear."

"You're not going to talk to Placer, no way, no how. Let my men handle it from here. You guys have already broken enough international and federal laws under my watch. Let us handle it from here," May ordered.

"Uh, oh, David, you're breaking up, I can't...you...what..." Galveston mumbled, using shushing sounds between the words to simulate a breakup of his phone's signal.

"Alright, alright. That's enough. What do you need?" May asked, giving in to Galveston's childish ploy.

"We need some leverage with Placer. Can we use a promise of some federal leniency to get him to talk?"

"You know I can't authorize that, come on," May said, growing impatient.

"Uh, Oh, I'm losing you again, what...did...," Galveston pulled the stunt again.

"Okay, just be quiet. How old are you, six?" May managed to joke.

"I know you want us to find this out," Galveston pleaded.

May thought about the offer. This would be a big risk on his part. If anything went wrong, his career would be over, but he trusted Galveston. May wrestled with the decision. In any other case it would be strictly off-limits to question a potential suspect, but in this case things were different. He was already receiving considerable pressure to stop the investigation even as close as they were to resolving it. The case could be over if it got to his superiors that he was opening up another portion of the case and questioning a CEO without a shred of evidence. Either way, he was in a bind. He needed answers quickly, and he wanted them now.

May sighed heavily over the phone and relented to Galveston's request.

"Okay, but on one condition; I have men standing by to take him into custody for questioning. You can offer him whatever you want, but no mention of me, the Bureau, or any other connection. You can say that you'll work on a deal for him if he cooperates—that's it."

"Agreed," Galveston said, knowing he would end up offering this leverage to Placer. "We're going there tonight. We'll get him to spill the beans. I have a plan."

"Well, don't tell me about it. Just give me the location where you'll be, and I'll have men standing by. I don't want him to flee." May was noticeably uneasy about the arrangement, because now his job was on the line. "Oh, I almost forgot. I have another piece of information you'll be interested in," May started again. "Your friend Alex should be proud of this."

"What is it?"

"The San Diego P.D. picked up a group of men at a local hotel about an hour ago. They were tinted a strange blue. They found heavy armament, masks, electronics—the works. None of them would talk, but the agents that we sent over said they had managed to get some cell phone numbers from them. They are being interrogated now."

"Alex's subtle security. They must have tried to break into his computer system, not a smart move," Galveston laughed. "Another one of Murray's teams, I bet, looking for Dr. Sloan, and the same ones who probably tried to accost Roger and Jane."

"We have a number they were communicating to regularly, probably Murray, but none of them are talking. They're all using the same line about first seeing a lawyer."

Galveston thought for a second about how this may work in their favor before they saw Placer.

"David, do me a favor. Do you think your men can get a message sent that Dr. Sloan is dead, and the team got to him. Or that he tried to fight and they shot him? Something to that effect. Send it to that number that you have. It's got to get to Murray. I'm curious to see how much Placer is involved and if this pushes more cockroaches out of the woodwork."

"I think the agents can do that," May answered.

"As quickly as possible," Galveston responded.

"I'll make sure it happens. What do you hope to gain from that?" May asked.

"I think that a primary goal of everyone involved is to have Dr. Sloan out of the way. The having him dead part is a better lie for us. He would be the only remaining link in the chain to their plan; the only other one who knows what's going on."

"I see where you're going. We'll get it done within the hour. Just do me a favor and don't get yourselves in hot water. Having you guys on the job puts me on the line too, you know."

"Don't worry, David," Galveston told him confidently.

"Good luck, try not to get me fired."

"It looks like we're on stage," Galveston announced to me, putting his phone away. "May reluctantly gave us the go-ahead."

"Yippee," I said without emotion.

"You could show a little more excitement. Just wait until you hear this."

Galveston told me the news of Alex's incredible security coup and his ability to form a blue man group. It must have been a sight.

Galveston's plan to send a fake message to Murray was stellar. It showed how well he could think on his feet. The news of Dr. Sloan's death should spread like wildfire through everyone involved in this scheme. Dr. Sloan was the final connective link in the chain. They needed him out of the way, and the news would work in perfectly with our uninvited meeting with Placer. We needed to find out what Placer knew about Murray and Chase. They must have a plan in place when Dr. Sloan was out of the way.

Alex finally called and was able to locate Placer. It had been no easy task, and he had to do some interesting detective work.

"So, what did you find out, Alex?" Galveston asked.

"I called his office earlier in the day and managed to get through to his secretary. This part I know you'll like, Galveston. I posed as a reporter for Wall Street Week. His secretary said he would be in the office until six and probably at his home after that," Alex explained proudly.

"Ah, very good. You remembered Lesson 127—a fake reporter always gets the best information," Galveston said.

"Yeah, sure, I was thinking about that lesson," Alex said dismissively. "Placer lives in the affluent suburb of Spring Valley in northwest D.C."

Spring Valley is an area that houses embassies, the campus of American University, and many of Washington's elites. Galveston knew the area relatively well from his time spent in D.C. many years ago. The homes weren't available for those light in the pocketbook.

"Anything else?" Galveston questioned cautiously.

"Nope, that's about it. Good luck. Remember rule 232," Alex instructed.

"Rule 232? I don't have anything for that."

"That's my rule," Alex said. "It means, don't get your ass caught."

"I'll have to add that one in. Thanks, Alex. Good work. I'll talk to you soon. Stay near the phone," Galveston told him and hung up.

Galveston drove our rental car in classic D.C. style, honking his horn at the person in front of him at red lights when he saw the light turn yellow. We wouldn't need to even go through D.C. itself, instead taking the I-495 to MacArthur Blvd that hugged the Potomac. It took us over an hour and a half to finally reach the Spring Valley neighborhood.

Galveston came up with a simplified plan on how we would get in. Jane would get to exercise some of her acting muscle and distract the guard at the gated community, while Galveston, Elizabeth, and I gained entry, any way we could. Galveston convinced Elizabeth that she needed to be in on this one; we needed all the eyes we could get.

Placer's house was huge and surrounded by a large brick wall with trees that lined it on either side. The obstructions were helpful, but the security cameras were poised at every corner. Jane was going to have to do some really good acting and use all her womanly charms. It would be up to her to get us in.

The guard house stood at a large metal gate and the entrance to the enclave of spacious homes. Jane got in the driver's seat and buckled up. She moved the car slowly up the road while we stayed out of view on the sidewalk. Jane reached the turnoff in front of the gate, put the car in park, got out, and pushed the intercom.

"Security," a gruff voice answered.

Jane immediately changed personas from a strong, vibrant woman to a blithering mess.

"My name is Sally," she cried into the intercom, "I'm lost and from Kentucky. I can't find my way back to my hotel," she said in a southern drawl.

"What do you need, ma'am?" the voice replied in a harsh tone.

"I can't find my way. I'm almost out of gas, please," Jane pleaded, an act worthy of an Oscar.

About that time the guard must have seen who he was dealing with, because the gate swung open and the voice changed over the intercom.

"Just stay right there, let me see what I can do for you," he said, this time in a much more pleasant tone.

"Oh, thank you, sir, thank you," she stammered appreciatively. Jane gave us a wink and a devilish smile. She loved every minute of this, I figured.

A guard in a gray uniform appeared at the gate as it slowly opened. He walked to her confidently, and she went into acting overdrive.

"Oh, thank goodness. Thank you so much." Jane reached for the guards arm above the elbow and let the tears fly, money well spent in acting class.

We saw our opportunity and took it. The three of us crouched behind the car as Jane turned the guard's back toward us. We then quickly slid through the gate without being seen. We hugged the brick wall on the other side of the gate as Jane turned on the waterworks further, causing the guard to prop her up as we moved well out of sight.

Placer's incredibly massive house was lit up like a Christmas tree. Huge stone pillars lined the front, and the perimeter seemed to go on forever. Near the back of the home stood a bank of French doors in front of a pool. Luckily, one of the doors was open, and we let ourselves in unannounced. Just a little case of unlawful entry.

Galveston and I moved silently through the rear rooms of the house while Elizabeth kept an eye out from behind. The bottom level of the house seemed empty, so we decided to move deeper inside. We traversed the winding staircase that led to the second floor, and my heart raced. I figured there had to be a better way than this.

Galveston continued to move swiftly. We got to the top of the staircase where the hall led in either direction. Galveston stopped and listened. He heard a faint tapping at the end of hall to the right where a room was illuminated. We moved down the hall in that direction until we arrived at the door to the lit room. It was difficult to see in, but we noticed it wasn't a bedroom. Galveston motioned to me to get behind him and for Elizabeth to take a position on the other side of the door. She surveyed the hall behind us and listened intently for footsteps or voices. Galveston crouched low and peeked around the corner, giving himself a better vantage point of the room. He looked back at me and nodded his head— Placer was in the room. Galveston stood up and slowly walked into the room as I followed close behind. He motioned for Elizabeth to stay out of sight.

As I went around the corner behind Galveston, I noticed Placer sitting with his back was to us, typing away at a computer. A large, flat screen monitor stood in front of him and a large picture window displayed a view of the landscaped yard. Galveston moved behind him slowly and motioned for me to stop in my current position. He made a gun-like pose with his hand, put his finger out, and poked it into the back of the man.

"Freeze, Placer, don't move," Galveston said with authority.

Placer stiffened, and we heard an audible gasp as the blood rushed from his face. He quivered from the touch of what he thought was a gun. He didn't turn around, stopped typing, and simply looked straight ahead.

"What, what," he panted, trying to take air into his lungs.

"Just freeze, Placer, don't move, we have you covered," Galveston said again forcefully. He pulled his hand away slowly. "Now turn around slowly and keep your hands where I can see them."

Placer did as he was told until he was face-to-face with Galveston, who bent down to his eye level.

"Who are you?" he managed to ask, looking at Galveston and then at me.

"We'll ask the questions, Placer," Galveston told him.

Placer had turned even grayer now and was clearly having trouble with our intrusion, just as anyone would.

"Placer we know what you've been up to at Black Bear, and we're here to find out everything you know. And you're going to tell us."

"What? Who are you?" he attempted to ask again.

"Let's just say we're consultants for the Federal Government. We know all about your plans with the company, and we're here to find out what you know."

"This is illegal breaking and entering. How dare you come in here," Placer exclaimed, beginning to grow angry at our intrusion.

"Watch it, Placer. You're going to listen to what I have to say, and then you're going to answer all the questions we ask. Do you see that man over there?" Galveston asked, awaiting a response.

"Yes," Placer answered slowly.

"He practices the ancient art of Kilim. If you don't talk, he'll get you to talk. He can break a man's legs with just his hands. I would prefer not to resort to using him. Do you understand?" Galveston threatened, and then looked at me.

"Yes, okay. Please don't hurt me, I'll answer whatever you want," he pleaded.

The ancient art of Kilim? I had no clue what he was talking about, but I went along with it. Unbeknownst to me, a Kilim was a Persian or Turkish woven carpet. They are used across the Middle East as prayer rugs or in homes as a floor covering. If I had known that at the time I would have laughed hard. I could weave Placer a mean rug from what Galveston was saying. But I went along with the lie and tried to look menacing; which for me meant squinty eyes and a scowl. I ended up looking like I had gas, however.

Galveston continued to press Placer, who now eyed me with fear and disdain.

"We know about the battery you are producing at Ecomax and what you plan to do with it. You're going to go to jail for a long time, Placer. Why did you think you could get away with it and hurt so many people?" Galveston questioned.

Placer looked at him with open eyes and then did something none of us would have expected; he literally burst into tears.

"I know, we shouldn't have done it," he began to sob. "I can't take it anymore. I was desperate."

Placer began to burble loudly and put his head in his hands. "It was supposed to be simple. I don't know how it went this far," he continued.

Galveston moved back from him, shocked, as I was, at his reaction. Galveston took a few steps toward me as Placer continued to sob uncontrollably.

"That isn't quite the reaction I was expecting," he said to me.

"You still want me to break his legs?" I mocked, and Galveston gave me a look of disgust.

He moved back to Placer and began to question him again. We still needed some answers.

"Placer, take it easy," he said. "Why did you order the explosions and the deaths of three innocent men?"

Placer stopped sobbing and looked up, his eyes clearly red and swollen.

"Hold it, what?" he asked, wiping his nose.

"Those three men—Espinosa, Patelo, and Dr. Blout. Why did you have them killed? And why the explosions in Africa and South America?" Galveston asked more clearly.

"Patelo killed? I don't know what you're talking about, and I don't know about explosions or those other men."

"Don't play dumb with us," Galveston said. "We know you're involved in this."

"I'm not. I really don't know what you're talking about."

"Cochese, do your work," Galveston instructed me and stepped back from Placer.

"No, no," he exclaimed, beginning to sob again, "I swear I don't know who you're talking about. I've never heard of them in my life. I really don't know them, and I don't know anything about any explosions."

I shrugged my shoulders, and Galveston noticed my concern. I didn't think he knew what we were talking about.

"What about Murray? Are you going to say you don't know about him too?"

"Murray? Yeah, I know Murray. He was in charge of getting the operation set up in Brazil."

We were going nowhere with this. Galveston was getting frustrated at the lack of information, but we both began to believe him. What if he didn't know what we knew?

"I think you better start from the beginning, Placer. How and why did this all start?" Galveston questioned him.

Placer composed himself slightly and began to lay out what he knew. "Back six months ago, the company was beginning to falter. We had some bad investments, lost contracts, and lawsuits filed against us. We were heading for bankruptcy and fast. Then this came along. I wish I wouldn't have been so desperate, but at the time I was. I had the SEC breathing down my neck, and the investors and the Board of Directors wanted results. We were sinking. That's when I got wind of an opportunity to get the company some much needed profit and avoid insolvency. If the news broke about our accounting practices, we would have ended up like another Enron."

"But who gave you the battery then, the prototype?"

Placer wiped his eyes again and gave us the connection we were waiting to hear.

"Weston Chase gave it to us," he said flatly and without emotion. "We were doing security for Global Energy Enterprise, and he was an important investor in our company. He knew we were having serious problems."

Galveston and I looked at each other, and another bout of shock crossed our faces.

"He had the battery and wanted it developed, but couldn't, due to the fact that they were a non-profit company. That's when he enlisted our help. He arranged to give it to us. He stood to lose a lot of money if we went under. I figured he was just trying to recoup his investment. He even recommended Murray for the job of getting it started in Brazil, out of the eyes of our government."

"We know all about Murray," Galveston told him. "So you didn't arrange a break-in to steal the prototype?"

"A break-in? Heavens no. Chase said he had the prototype, and Murray transported the battery to Brazil for production using Chase's private plane under a foreign registration. I didn't ask how, and I didn't want to know. We called the project *Adamanthea*." Placer said, beginning to feel more comfortable, and probably relieved he could get all this off his chest.

"There are some other things you need to know, Placer."

Galveston began to relate the same story we had explained almost three times this day. Placer grew horrified at the news of the explosions and the murders of the three men. He truly was in the dark. It became evident to us and him that he was being played the patsy.

"I can't believe it," was all he could muster saying. "This could implicate all of Black Bear because of Murray's actions. He's still on the payroll of the company."

"I know," Galveston said. "Was there anyone else that is involved with this?"

Placer hesitated at the question. "Only one other person," he started, "Senator Edward Eastman, another one of Chase's contacts. He has been working on legislation for us to import the product with no import tax." Placer remembered how Chase had insisted the Senator needed to be involved in the operation.

Galveston saw the connections clearly now, as did I. Placer and Black Bear were being set up, and the Senator was in on it.

"I don't understand why Chase would do this," Placer told us.

"When the news of this goes public, everyone will be coming after you and Black Bear. They won't care how it started. It would be his word against yours, and he's eliminated every other link in the chain," Galveston responded.

"But what can I do?" Placer asked.

"If you cooperate, I can get you some leniency from the government. I've been given permission to offer that. It will be up to them as to how much. I can tell you that if you don't help us the Feds will go after you to the fullest extent of the law."

"I don't care now. I'll do anything to get them. What do you need me to do?"

"We need you to contact the Senator and get him to go to San Diego the day after tomorrow. Tell him that Ecomax is releasing the product there, and it's imperative that he be there. I don't care how you do it, just get him there. The best you can do now is cooperate, because the FBI is watching you as we speak."

"Whatever you need. I just want to make things right," Placer said, placing his head in his hands.

"Good, we'll be in touch. Federal agents will be outside your house for safety until we contact you. Don't speak to anyone until we tell you."

"I understand. I'll do what you say." Placer answered.

I followed Galveston out of the door, and Elizabeth trailed behind staying out of sight of Placer. She had heard every word and didn't need to get involved. We walked down the stairs and out the front door onto a circular driveway.

"How'd we do?" I asked Galveston.

"I think pretty well. We didn't resort to breaking his legs so I would deem it a success. I didn't realize how far in the dark he was. Chase has planned this well."

"I agree," Elizabeth added. "This goes far beyond what I could have imagined."

"Chase is setting Black Bear up. I can't believe we missed that. He must have hired Murray independently, and he must have an arrangement with the Senator," Galveston added.

The plan was ingenious, and we discussed it as we walked back to the guardhouse. From what we could infer from our information, Chase had hired Murray when Black Bear was working for Global Energy. He must have arranged the break-in to Dr. Sloan's lab and stolen the prototypes, then had Murray transport them to Brazil, making sure there was no trail that could lead back to them. That is why he eliminated Espinosa. Then, when they got it to Brazil, they had it reverse engineered.

We walked straight through the gate and gave the guard a wave. It was sort of a test. Galveston wanted to see if Placer was going to tell the guard that we had just broken into his home. The guard didn't move or say anything, and opened the gate for us. We walked down the sidewalk until Jane saw us and stopped the car.

"How did I do?" she asked as we settled into our seats.

"Fantastic. You were incredible!" I told her, and she beamed with pride.

"Where to?" she asked us.

Galveston thought for a moment. "Let's find a hotel. Head for central D.C., and tomorrow we'll get out of here. For now, let's get some sleep."

-Chapter 62-

"Excuse me, Senator?" the woman asked peering through the door to the large office. Eastman was working late into the night.

"Yes?" Senator Eastman replied gruffly.

"Your call, sir, line two." Eastman dismissed the aide with a wave of his hand and picked up the phone.

"I don't think I like the way things are going," he said loudly into the receiver.

"What do you mean, Senator?" asked the voice on the other end.

"I held up my end of the bargain, now where are my results?"

"Relax, Ed. Things are going according to plan. We have the prototype and the doctor is dead."

"Dead? Who said?"

"I found out from a reliable source," the man on the other end said.

"Does Placer know this?"

"No, of course not. Murray works for us, remember? He did what I told him to do."

"If things go bad, I don't want to be holding the bag," the Senator announced.

"That's why we have Placer, isn't it? When Ecomax completes the battery, then we can inform the Feds about Black Bear stealing the design from us," the man said, placating the Senator.

"And what about Murray. Is it time for him to leave us?" the Senator asked.

"Yes, I have my man working on that now. He'll be out of the way."

"Good. He's the only one that can link us to all of this."

"I know. He will be taken care of, don't worry. Just make a scene in Congress. We need the demand to be higher."

"I'm harping on it every day. It will get done, like shooting fish in a barrel."

"I hope so Senator and keep Placer quiet. I don't want him getting jittery."

"I agree. I'll keep him quiet."

"Good day, Senator."

"Uh-huh," replied Eastman. He hung up the phone and leaned back in his chair as an air of contentment crossed his face.

-Chapter 63-

Galveston called May from the front seat and filled him in on the latest turn of events. Placer was being set up. May was shocked at the news. At every turn there seemed to be a new wrinkle, but we were getting closer. We seemed to have the upper hand.

"So what is Chase trying to do?" I wondered.

"Well, we know he had Murray eliminate those men to stop any links. That much is clear. But why the Senator?" Galveston thought aloud. "Is it a money thing?"

The legislation the Senator introduced was useless and would never pass. But what if it was just a cover to a bigger piece of the puzzle? How would they get Black Bear implicated without exposing themselves?

Chase needed Black Bear to release the product and implicate themselves in the disappearance of Dr. Sloan and the prototypes. Chase already had tipped the FBI about the *Adamanthea* project. Now the Feds would move in for the kill.

I figured Eastman had alternate plans, probably a bigger piece of legislation. I believed he wasn't as interested in the money as he was in the glory of being the one who established the United States on a new energy course.

Black Bear had one prototype and Chase must have had the other. Black Bear probably had the more inferior prototype. Dr. Patelo likely had worked on both, and that was the reason for the secrecy and the new lab location. It was also why they killed him.

Chase needed both of the prototypes engineered by Dr. Patelo. The superior one went back to Chase in the U.S. for production, while the inferior battery went to Ecomax in Brazil. Lucky for us, Dr. Patelo threw a wrench in the works and bought us time, but it got him killed. Now Dr. Sloan's fake death would be the last piece Chase and Eastman would need to succeed.

It was intricate and complicated but amazingly simple. Chase's band of instigators used Black Bear to get their goal accomplished; the ability to produce their own battery while Black Bear took the fall. He was just waiting to put the battery on the market. Eastman would help him by introducing a piece of legislation that supported the sale of this battery in every way, and no one would be the wiser. But how were we going to stop them? That was the essential question.

We found a nice hotel in downtown D.C., just steps from the Capitol building. Galveston had Alex and Dr. Sloan return to San Diego from Mexico. They were going to be busy setting up a presentation on Dr. Sloan's technology, and we needed Placer, Eastman, and Chase there with them.

Chapter 64

Murray gathered his things into a bag and left his room at the downtown Chicago Hilton. He had done his job and done it well. He wasn't proud about it in the least, but he had no remorse for his actions.

Murray received the message of Dr. Sloan's death earlier in the day. It wasn't in the proper format the team had agreed on, but at this point it didn't matter, he was just glad it was done. The professor's death essentially terminated his contract. The money Murray made had been successfully transmitted to his account in the Cayman Islands, and he now sat on over two million in funds. It was an ample amount of money to comfortably live on in a far-flung paradise.

Murray walked down to the lobby, checked out with the attendant, and reached for an old daily newspaper. He had a few minutes to kill before his late flight to Los Angeles from Chicago O'Hare. His final destination would be Bora Bora, in the French Polynesian Islands. He decided he would stay there a few months until the havoc he wrought in the U.S. died down. After that time, Murray planned to move to a villa he had purchased in Italy. He figured possible extradition from that country would be difficult, if they could even find him. The teams he put together to perform his tasks had been ordered to disperse and leave the country individually by tomorrow, with no exceptions. Murray decided he was done with this business. His hands were sullied from so much clandestine work.

Murray reached in his bag and pulled out a small digital recorder and placed it on his lap. He then pulled out a pre-printed FedEx pack. He placed the recorder in a bubble wrap protective holder and slid it in the pack. The address on the package read, "Walter Monroe, Hanley, Grop, and Associates, LLC, Chicago, Illinois". He slid in a handwritten note beside the recorder, sealed it, and walked to the lobby desk.

"I would like this to go out tomorrow," he said to the hotel receptionist.

"Yes, sir. FedEx has a scheduled pickup in the morning."

"Good. Thank you."

He walked back to his seat, zipped up his bag, and headed for the elevators that would take him to the parking garage and his rental car. He looked tired and couldn't wait to sun himself on the beach the next day.

Murray traveled down to the lowest level and walked slowly to his car. It was late, about 11:00 P.M., and this level of the garage was deserted. He opened the trunk of the car and placed his bag in, closed it, and moved to the door with the keys of the car in his hand.

All of a sudden he heard a soft, muffled bang, followed by another. Murray immediately felt pain in his back. He dropped the keys and crumpled to the ground until he was on his side; his eyes level with the concrete floor of the garage. The pain emanated throughout his body, and he felt a warm trickle of blood going down his spine while his breathing became labored. He forced himself on his back and squinted at the lights overhead.

He made out the form of a man coming toward him slowly, his features dark against the light background. Murray noticed with horror that the man held a gun down at his side with a silencer attached. As the man's face grew closer, Murray recognized him, but from where? As his vision began to blur, he remembered where he had seen the man—at the bar the night he met Chase. It was Chase's bodyguard, Campbell, and he had just mortally wounded Murray in the back. He tried to form some words, but it was too late as the massive blood loss made speaking impossible. "This was how it's going to end," he thought. He should have expected this to happen. He momentarily flashed to what all those men he had callously cut down must have felt, and he had an instant of remorse before he was dead.

Campbell walked over and knelt down next to the body and felt for a pulse—nothing. The man was gone. He checked through his pockets and found what he was looking for, a ticket to get out of the parking garage. He picked up Murray and placed him in the trunk of the car, stuffing his body awkwardly into the cramped space. He used some clothes from Murray's bag to quickly wipe up the puddle of blood that had been under the body and drove the car slowly up the ramp to the exit of the hotel.

Chapter 65

We awoke the next morning with renewed energy, all thanks to a good night's sleep. We needed to get out of D.C. and back to San Diego as quickly as possible. Galveston had already talked to Alex who was traveling back to San Diego from Mexico with Dr. Sloan. Galveston quickly laid out the plan to Alex and enlisted him to come up with a presentation for Dr. Sloan's device. They had a day to get it done and the pressure was on. It needed to be fantastic and incredible. A tall order to be done in one day, but if anyone could do it, it was Alex.

Alex had told the professor about the demise of his friend, Dr. Richard Blout, on the drive from Mexico. He had taken the news hard, as any friend would, but it fueled his desire to do whatever it took to bring the perpetrators to justice. The two men were in relatively good spirits under the circumstances. Dr. Sloan was beginning to realize the repercussions of his device. If he would have known the problems it produced, he would have destroyed it in an instant. The world was not ready for such a revolutionary idea.

Galveston contacted Placer at his home in D.C. and informed him of the date and time to get the Senator to San Diego. It would be an easy task for Placer to convince the Senator once Eastman got the pictures of the two women who would be there to meet him. Luckily, Jane and Elizabeth didn't yet know about this part of the plan. I planned to leave it to Galveston to tell them of their role.

We arrived in San Diego at 2:00 P.M., and Galveston arranged a meeting of all our team members in a downtown San Diego hotel. We still didn't know who was after us and what they might do to find us.

"Now to the good stuff," Galveston told us, starting the impromptu meeting. "This is how we're going to bust these bastards."

Galveston began to work the room like an evangelical preacher hopped up on caffeine and the glory of the Lord. He continuously sipped on a 44-ounce Big Gulp and barked orders like a general, which made us sit at attention.

"We're going to get this bozo, Senator Eastman, here in San Diego. Jane and Elizabeth, you two are in charge of the Senator when he gets here. You're the contacts for him at the unveiling. I've informed Placer of your role in this. Elizabeth, I want you to set up a private jet for Eastman out of Reagan National in D.C. Dr. Sloan, I need the working prototype and a lavish display of its capabilities. It needs to be eye-popping, and whatever you need, we'll get you. Alex, contact the newspapers, TV, technology mags, anybody and everybody you can think of that would be interested in seeing the latest and greatest in new energy technology. Don't take 'no' for an answer. Any questions?"

Galveston finished and sipped the rest of his soda in one big gulp, breathless from the long oration. We all sat wide eyed after the deluge of information. We had our marching orders.

"Okay, everybody," Galveston clapped his hands together in front of him, "go get some sleep."

Everyone left until Galveston and I were alone in the room.

"Why do I always have to room with you?" I asked, pulling out my night bag.

"Hey, I'm just saving us money. You think I like hearing you snore every night. That's lesson 23."

"Now you're just making those silly rules up as you go," I chided him.

"No, that really is a rule. No snoring, it gives me a headache. Now get some sleep. We have a big day tomorrow."

Chapter 66

The next day started quickly. Galveston was up before me gathering phone numbers, names, and a new, little white lie for Placer to extend to the Senator. I was immediately put in charge of food patrol while various members of the team stuck their heads in to give progress reports and to ask questions. I managed to steal Jane away from her duties to help me locate sustenance for all of us. She gladly obliged.

"This is crazy," she told me as we walked to the hotel lobby.

"You're telling me. Did you ever think you'd be involved in something like this? I mean it wasn't exactly in your job description," I said back to her.

"I wouldn't be here if you weren't," she said grabbing my hand as we walked to the hotel restaurant. I melted at her touch. "She really digs me," I thought.

We had been through so much together, mostly in spirit. She always had the most positive attitude about everything going on. It made me like her even more, and it even made me want to tell her the word a new couple is scared to say. I pushed the thought back, it was too soon. How could I feel that "L word" this quickly? No, It was too soon. Or was it? She glowed beautifully in the heat lamps of the morning buffet table. To me she could be beautiful sitting under a pigeon coop, but I didn't plan to give her that analogy.

We gathered up some greasy morning fare; muffins, hash browns, eggs, something that looked like a sausage, and a pitcher of orange juice. I paid the attendant, placed all the food on a tray, and went back to the elevator to return upstairs.

"So what is the deal with Elizabeth and Galveston? Are they going to get back together?" she asked me on the ride up the elevator.

"I don't know. They are an interesting pair. I think I see why they broke up in the first place, but I also see why they are so well-suited to each other."

"They are both so focused on their jobs, unlike you," she said to me.

"Oh, thanks," I replied at the seemingly direct smack.

"I don't mean it like that. It's just, you always seem to have me in mind first, before the job. A girl likes that sort of thing."

"Well, it's good to know I'm on the right track," I responded. Jane gave a little laugh. She even did that cute. Oh, boy, did I have it bad.

The elevator doors opened, and we walked back to the room to find that Alex had made a hasty entrance and exit. He was busy in the next room helping Dr. Sloan troubleshoot his idea while supplying other members of the team with information.

Alex informed us that he had contacted all the members of the media he could. So far he had confirmation from two TV stations, three newspapers, two magazines, eight online websites—one of which agreed to stream the feed of the presentation live—and a pair of bloggers that he knew that called themselves, "The Tech Junkies". He sent emails to the Associated Press, Universal Press Syndicate, and even CNN. The message he sent all of them had been clear and succinct, but not overly specific.

> The Energy Freedom Foundation, a consortium of scientists and citizens, is releasing a new technology that will revolutionize energy storage and usage for all nations of the world. Playa Park Hotel, downtown San Diego 5:00 P.M. The Honorable Senator Edward Eastman will be in attendance for the event. Please confirm for your official press pass. Refreshments will be served.

I found it interesting that we even had press passes and would be serving snacks.

Elizabeth and Jane arranged a private jet for the Senator out of Reagan airport and a chauffeured limousine from San Diego Lindbergh Field to the hotel. Galveston had sealed the deal with the Senator when he emailed pictures of Jane and Elizabeth to Timothy Placer. Both women were dressed rather provocatively, and I noticed that Galveston must have taken them the night before. Placer sent the pictures to Eastman with the explanation that these were the women that would be his contact in San Diego for the unveiling of the Ecomax product.

Getting the two women to agree to pose for these pictures may have been the toughest operation for Galveston. They were not pleased with being used as objects to convince the horny Senator to take a visit. Galveston convinced them they were performing a noble cause. They held all the power over this Senator and could get this man to do anything they wanted. The women were intelligent and strong and could control the situation. Galveston performed like a professional photographer and fashion designer. He fabricated a tasteful and provoking picture that showed the woman from head to toe, wearing the rather seductive looking clothes the women had. The picture showed just enough leg and cleavage to send the man's head in a tailspin.

I was not particularly thrilled with some old fart ogling my girlfriend, but payback would be a bitch. Plus the women now seemed to delight in the fact that they would be pulling this man's strings.

In the email that Placer sent to the Senator, Elizabeth and Jane called themselves the League for Environmental Protectionism. It wouldn't have mattered if they called themselves the Society of Urinal Cakes, the Senator would be on our plane once he saw those pictures.

During the short time I had spent getting breakfast, Galveston had received an email from Morales in Brazil. Galveston had his extra insurance. Ecomax had a fully workable product just in case someone dared to investigate the validity of the device.

Chase must have known Ecomax had finished the product. The FBI had already been called to the fake release of the product in San Diego and the supposed implication of Black Bear. Everything was a go.

The pieces were coming together perfectly. Our puppets were following the movements of their strings. Eastman and Chase were fueled by their own level of corruption, greed, fear, and power, and we planned to expose each one of those faults.

Someone was going down tomorrow, and we all told ourselves that just one person would walk out in handcuffs.

We passed the day away preparing for the next day's events until I decided to invite Jane to the lobby bar for a nightcap. I had some love work to do.

-Chapter 67-

Jane and I went to the lobby bar and ordered a pair of drinks. I had a frosty beer from the tap while she chose the house chardonnay. We sipped slowly at our drinks and talked about the day's events. She looked beautiful in dim lights of the bar, and I couldn't help but stare at her lips as she talked.

We managed to change the subject off of the previous topic and began to discuss life goals. Jane had always wanted to be an actress. She had dreams of a spot in a theatrical play or Broadway show. She had performed in a few large scale productions in San Diego; *Annie*, *Fiddler on the Roof*, *A Christmas Carol*, even some Shakespearean productions. It was never enough to hold as a steady job, but she was living her dream.

I listened intently to her resume, and she had a pleasing and peaceful air about her. She had traveled the world; ridden rapids on the Snake River in Oregon, hiked to the top of Machu Picchu in Peru, and skied in the French Alps. She was versed in Spanish and French, which would have come in handy for us if I had known this sooner. She was an amazing, strong, and vibrant woman. What the hell was she doing here with me?

My mind wandered at the thought. Why would a woman like this want to be with a man like me? It sounded like she needed to be with a guy named Sven, who had big muscles and liked to parachute out of airplanes over the Grand Canyon while reading Tolstoy's *War and Peace*. I wasn't that type of guy. I got jittery before a shower because of the problems steam may cause to the toilet paper. Jane noticed my consternation.

"What's wrong?" she asked politely. "It seems like your mind is elsewhere."

"I'm sorry, Jane," I said, not wanting to tell her of my lack of self-esteem. "You were saying?"

"No. It's okay. What's on your mind?"

This is always a dangerous question from a woman to a man. Men don't usually have anything on their minds. We usually are thinking about some mundane thing that was unemotional and not important. If a woman really knew what we were thinking about they would probably not want to speak to us again. But this time was different. I badly wanted her to know what I was thinking, but I didn't want to appear vulnerable or wimpy.

"I don't want to say. It's silly, it's nothing," I stammered.

"No, really. I want to know," she answered sweetly.

I garnered my courage to tell her. It was best she realize what she was getting now rather than later.

"I'm," I tried to pose the thoughts in my head. "I'm not sure why you're with me." As the words came out, I knew it wasn't the way I wanted it said.

"What do you mean, Roger?" She played down her response. I figured she knew she was talking to a crazy person.

"It's just I can't understand why a woman like you, with all that you have done and experienced, would want to spend time and be with a man like me." That's better, I thought. That was a much clearer, wimpy statement.

Jane gave me with a confused look. Then with a shot of realization understood what I was talking about. She smiled and reached for my hand across the table.

"Let me tell you something, Roger," she started, holding my hand tighter. "Those first days I came to work with you, I was down and not feeling good about my life. Then I saw you. You had such a confidence about you, and you were nice to me. You probably don't remember, but you helped me that whole first day. You told me about the best places to get lunch, the best spot to get some quiet time, even the best route from my house. You did all this with Galveston barking at you and people running in and out of the office all day. Then I got to talk to you on those plane rides, and spend time with you more than I have spent with a man I've been dating for three months. In all that time you always made me feel like I could conquer the world. I've told you things I didn't tell my old boyfriend of four years. Plus, you are really handsome."

She flashed a wide smile, and I blushed like a schoolboy at the accolades. I was floored at the response and my lowered ego didn't know how to handle it. She reached her other hand under the table and touched my knee, which sent goose bumps down my leg.

"I've always looked for the wrong type of man. I don't want a man like me. I want a man like you. You're caring, trustworthy, and most importantly you're stable, in every way. I've never had that in a man. It's very hard to find. I know that you can challenge me, but I know that you can just be there. I don't care if I do anything like I've done before, because I know you'll be here and you'll support me."

I was amazed at her words and even began to well-up a little. Never had a woman as beautiful as this said such things to me. It was a breath of fresh air. Jane cared for me more than I had realized, and I had an enormous sense of relief. This intelligent woman knew exactly what she wanted, and I respected that.

"You're amazing, Jane. You know you'll be able to accomplish whatever you want," I told her.

She took her hand off mine, leaned over, and touched my cheek.

"Thank you, Roger," she said softly and tenderly kissed me on my lips.

The kiss sent electrical shocks through my body. This was my moment, I thought. This was when I would say those three tough words.

"Jane," I started, looking deep into her eyes. "I…"

"Last call!" Exclaimed the bartender as he rang a bell and switched on the overhead lights, illuminating the entire room.

"I, I guess we have to leave," I said dejectedly, giving the bartender a dirty look.

"I think you're right," Jane replied smiling, before she gave me a peck on my cheek.

I paid the tab for our two drinks and walked hand in hand to the elevator and back to her room.

"I'd ask you in, but I know Galveston wants us bright-eyed and bushy-tailed tomorrow," Jane told me.

"Yeah," I responded. "That would be best." No it wouldn't, I thought.

"Don't worry. I'll see you tomorrow," Jane said as we exchanged one last hug and kiss.

Just as I was backing out the door, Jane grabbed me by the arm.

"Maybe we could talk some more," she said. My heart leapt.

"Yeah, I think that would be okay," I responded excitedly. I followed Jane into her room and shut the door behind us.

A lot of finish work still needed to be done the next day, and as bad as we all wanted to rest, it would prove to be extremely difficult.

-Chapter 68-

Galveston was up early again the next morning, and this time I startled him as I walked in our room.

"And where have you been, young man," he said giving me one of his judging looks.

"No where, Dad, just putting up the car," I replied sarcastically.

"I'll bet you did," he smirked.

"Yeah, I have no idea what that means."

"You know, putting away the car," he said motioning with his hands in a circular fashion, trying to get me to say more.

"Yeah, that doesn't work," I replied again.

"Yeah, it really doesn't," he said, sort of broken. "So you were with Jane, huh?"

"No, I was out helping stray cats, yes, of course I was with Jane."

"You sly dog. How did that happen?" he asked.

"You know, I'm not sure. We had a couple of drinks and then we were tired. I didn't want to wake you. There's not much more to say than that. How about Elizabeth? I noticed she didn't arrive back to Jane's room."

"Same as you two, just too tired," he replied, following my lead. "You really like her, don't you?"

"Yes, I really do. I think I'm even falling in…" Galveston stopped me mid-sentence with a raised finger.

"I wouldn't say that," he told me.

"And why not?" I inquired.

"It's a little soon, don't you think? I'm just saying; when you say those words everything changes. Maybe just give it a little time before you drop that bomb and scare her off," he instructed me.

"Uh-huh," was all I could respond back.

But I wanted to say it, and I would have last night, but the timing wasn't right. What did he know anyway? I decided to keep my thoughts about my love life to myself. I knew I hadn't felt this way about someone in a long time, and I was tired of thinking I needed to play games. Once this was over I was going to tell her, but for now we had business to deal with.

My part for the day's events would be vital to its success. I was in charge of sequestering Placer and Eastman before the big unveiling. I had bought a nice blue outfit from a hip clothier that had the name Dave on one side and Eagle Maintenance on the other. I decided it would be better to be slightly incognito to allow better movement about the rooms. I set the outfit out on the bed, ready to get into character. I went over my duties, what to say, and how to act.

The bottom floor convention area of the hotel was open for our operation. Alex came into the room as we were finishing the final touches to our plan.

"Dr. Sloan is done, and it's impressive," he told us briefly. "It's going to be an eye-popper."

"Good," Galveston replied. "Go ahead and tell everyone we'll get breakfast across the street, and we'll work over any new information or concerns. I need to check on one more thing before we go."

Alex left to relay the message to the other group members while Galveston dialed his phone.

"David, do you have anything new for us. We're all ready here. Your colleagues are on their way, and they've been briefed."

"Excellent job," May said to Galveston.

"Do you have anything about Murray?" Galveston asked.

"Yeah, we can't find him anywhere. We know he's in Chicago. We were able to locate the hotel he was staying at, but he's not there. He checked out late at night a day ago. He never returned his rental car to O'Hare, and he was scheduled on a flight to L.A. under the name of Horace Guildman. He never made it. We have a bulletin out for the car, but nothing has come up yet."

"Where was he going from L.A.?"

"Tahiti and Bora Bora, that's what was scheduled. I think he's still in Chicago, though."

"He was trying to get out of the country. It looks like the bait about Dr. Sloan's death worked. I'm sure he informed Chase about the professor's demise," Galveston said.

"I agree. We'll continue to look for him. He's an important suspect in this case. That's all I got. Let me know how the operation goes. We'll apprehend Chase if we can get some credible information on him."

"Got ya, David. We'll do our best," Galveston replied before hanging up the phone. He then relayed the information to me.

We needed Murray in custody to stop this thing from going further and to help the case against Chase. He couldn't go on hiding forever.

Boy, were we wrong on that one.

-Chapter 69-

Alex, Dr. Sloan, Galveston, and I sat down for breakfast, minus Elizabeth and Jane. They had opted for some exercise instead, probably to look extra good for Eastman.

The twists and turns of this whole case, and the current operation, began to run us down, but now we were on the final stretch.

Alex and Dr. Sloan had already ordered and sat busily eating large stacks of pancakes with sides of eggs and bacon. We quickly ordered some food so we could join in on the gorge-fest.

"Save some for the rest of us, will ya?" Galveston said to Alex, smiling.

He grunted like a caveman and continued his feast.

"Dr. Sloan, could you explain, maybe in layman's terms, how your battery works? I mean, during this whole time, I don't think any of us really know how it works," I asked the professor as he neatly wiped egg from his face.

"Gladly, let me see," he stroked his chin. "Why don't I use my pancakes to demonstrate."

He cut his pancakes into a rectangular shape.

"Think of these as layers of metal, a ceramic material, and a lithium alloy, with a chemical compound called barium titanate between them. They're stacked one on top of the other. These layers are paper thin, and have a layer of cellulose material between each stack that acts as an insulator, minimizing voltage loss."

He took a piece of bacon and placed it between one of the pancake stacks. "There is a group of nanowires that run between these layers. A group at Stanford designed this technology for use in ultracapacitors. I reworked the same concept into my battery design. Think of a capacitor as a storage depot of energy. Now an ultracapacitor is able to store a tremendous amount of energy which increases the speed of conduction. All this is enclosed in a case and filled with a hydrochloric acid solution, very similar in viscosity to syrup." He poured syrup over his rectangular pancakes.

"It's then energized using high voltage which allows the ions to attach themselves onto the sheets. Now here's the part you gentlemen are familiar with," he placed his fork next to his pancakes. "There is an output circuit, and it can switch from direct current to alternating current. Instead of the current continuously flowing out, it can change and essentially trap the current. It can propagate back to the sheets, increasing their efficiency, allowing the maximum current to be used with little resistance. Think of it as a faucet that sucks the water back up that doesn't need to be used. This battery acts like any other, just more efficient with a larger amount of stored usable energy. That's about it."

He peeled the pancakes back and grabbed the piece of bacon while Alex nodded his head and smiled widely, chewing on more food.

"Brilliant," I said, pretending to fully understand his explanation.

"You know, Professor, we don't even have a name for your battery. What do you call it?" Galveston asked.

"You know, I haven't even thought of it before. Do you have any suggestions?"

"I have one. Electrical Amplitude Transistor," Alex suggested.

"Yeah, abbreviated EAT. It's not food you know," Galveston quipped. "It needs a name for what it looks like, something catchy and a little whimsical."

Everyone thought hard for a name.

"You like pancakes, right Dr. Sloan?" I asked him.

"Of course, I eat them every chance I can get," he responded.

"Well how about we call it *Flapjack*? I mean, you did just use your breakfast to explain it to us, and it does resemble a stack of pancakes, albeit rectangular pancakes," I said proudly.

"You know, I like it. I think it sums it up well without being wordy," the professor agreed.

"Well that settles it then, *Flapjack* it is," Galveston announced.

-Chapter 70-

Galveston and I spent the remainder of the day out of sight, as did Dr. Sloan. Alex had the enormous task of setting up Dr. Sloan's demonstration with the help of the hotel staff.

In the hall, Alex had managed to get all the things Dr. Sloan had asked for. There were three small cars parked side by side, two tables filled with lamps of various sizes, cellular phones, and a multitude of Christmas lights. Next to the table sat three computers with monitors, and at the very end sat a lone coffee pot on a small table. Wires connected all the items together to a rectangular box sitting in the middle of the various pieces.

Alex had made a crude sign that read, "Flapjack-Sponsored by the Energy Freedom Foundation". The time read 4:45 P.M. Our main guest was to arrive shortly. Placer had arrived about an hour earlier and been led to the room where he would do his work, while Elizabeth and Jane waited for the Senator to arrive in the hotel lobby.

Alex corralled the media into the hall as quickly as he could to keep the outside lobby relatively quiet. As he entered the convention hall, he closed the door behind him. My heart began to race as 4:50 hit my watch. I looked nervously toward the stairs from the main hotel lobby, anxiously awaiting Elizabeth and Jane to appear with Eastman, and as Placer informed us, a brown attaché bag that the Senator always kept by his side. Finally, I heard the footsteps I had been listening for, followed by a booming voice. The ladies walked beside Eastman who was already trying to impress them with his pseudo charms. He carried the bag at his side, just as we hoped.

I walked to the door and opened it slightly. Placer was pacing the room nervously, back and forth from one wall to another.

"He's here," I whispered to him as I stuck my head in the door.

Placer jumped at the sound of my voice but managed to compose himself to give me a nod of his head.

I closed the door slightly and retreated around the corner and to an adjacent room. I knocked and was let in by Special Agent Avery of the San Diego FBI field office. He was in charge of this portion of the operation. Two other agents were huddled around a group of monitors showing the room Placer was in. I could hear Placer breathing hard via the hidden microphones in the room.

"You can have a seat there," Agent Avery told me, pointing to a chair next to the other men.

"Thanks, I'm really nervous," I told him.

"As long as our boy does what he's told, we'll be alright," he said, motioning to Placer on the monitor.

Back in the hall, the ladies had led the Senator to the room. Luckily he had traveled alone, except for the brown attaché case he was carrying. This wasn't something he wanted an aide around for. The women had managed to get a few drinks in him before he came down, the reason for the delay.

"Senator, Mr. Placer is in this room. He's been waiting for you. We'll retrieve you when the presentation is ready and the media is set," Elizabeth told him.

"I'd rather stay with you ladies, but I guess its business first," Eastman said, trying to be charming while giving a slight pat to Jane's bottom.

"Don't worry, we'll be back," Jane assured him with a wink as she tried to hold down her lunch.

The Senator opened the door, went in, and Elizabeth closed the door behind him. I saw him enter on the video monitor and noticed he had a crass air about him. He even walked like a prick. I hoped he wouldn't just steamroll over Placer, but Placer surprised me immediately. I noticed his body language change from passivity to that of dominance. He perked up and stood taller with his hands on the back of a chair. It was at this moment that I figured he knew he had the upper hand in their meeting.

"I take it everything is in place?" Eastman immediately asked Placer.

"Of course. The device is ready," he lied with confidence.

"I'm a little confused why we're having the unveiling here in San Diego. I thought you were going to do this in Brazil?"

"Things change, Senator. The part we needed to finish the product was here, so I decided to save time and release it here. It's going to be produced in Brazil," Placer told him emphatically.

"Good, and no other problems?" he asked.

"None," Placer lied again, "except one."

"And what would that be?"

"It's come to my attention that you haven't been completely honest with me, Senator, about your role in all this," Placer stated, beginning to press him.

"What are you talking about, Tim?"

"I know you've been talking to Weston Chase," he said bluntly. Eastman didn't flinch.

"Chase? No, I haven't been talking with Chase. And if I had, what does that have to do with anything?" Eastman responded coolly.

"I've heard from Murray, Wallace Murray."

"What the hell are you talking about, Tim? I don't know any Wallace Murray." Eastman continued to stay calm and didn't let the name affect him.

"I know that Chase is setting me up, and I know you are too." I noticed on the monitor that Placer was becoming angry, but Eastman continued to hold his ground.

"I don't know what you're talking about, Tim. Setting you up for what, exactly?" he inquired.

"I know you're setting Black Bear up to fail, and you're going to turn us in to the Feds. Murray told me. Just be straight with me, and tell the truth for once in your life," Placer said emphatically.

"Look, Tim, you little jerk. I don't know what you're talking about, and you better watch your mouth, or I'll call the SEC myself about your little accounting practices," Eastman shot back.

But Placer didn't stop.

"Ed, I want in on this. Don't leave me hanging out to dry here. I'll offer more than what Chase is giving you. How about an offshore account with, let's say, eight million. Will that do it? I can make it worth your while." Placer had changed tactics, but the Senator continued to choose his words carefully.

"I'm not involved with Chase, and I haven't spoken to him." Eastman was guarding his golden ticket well and wouldn't reveal his connection.

"Sixteen million. Eight now and eight after we start getting orders. You can't beat that. It would be untraceable. I have it sitting in Brazil right now."

"You don't have access to that kind of money from Black Bear," Eastman countered.

"I do in my personal account. I'm going to make that back four times over after this thing breaks. I'll transfer eight million right after the presentation to your offshore account. Simple as that."

"And what do you want in return?" Eastman asked.

"I want you to get Chase off my back. I know you can get the Feds involved in his life. Just keep him away from us. You'll get your usual payment that we agreed to before. How much did we agree to again?" Placer asked, setting Eastman up nicely.

"You know what we agreed—ten percent of the profits," Eastman answered and unknowingly implicated himself. I watched him on the monitor, and I could sense the greed bubbling to the top. "So, if I get Chase out of the picture for whatever he's up to, and like I told you, I haven't spoke to him, then we'll agree on these amounts," Eastman announced, almost licking his chops.

He had no intention of stopping Chase. His payback from the operation was too great, but he could be eight million dollars richer in the process. His greed had just proven to be his downfall.

"Agreed, Senator, there will be eight million in your account after the presentation," Placer told him.

Agent Avery looked at me and nodded his head. "He just made a bad mistake," he announced to the other men who continued to monitor the conversation.

In one simple conversation the Senator had implicated himself. He was using his position to gain profit, and on top of that, he was breaking a host of other Federal laws. We were still missing an implication of Chase's involvement, however, and that's what we desperately needed. Placer had done an excellent job, but the Senator knew there was no reason to talk about Chase further. It was our hope that once he realized that this wasn't an Ecomax event, and that the press was there in droves, he would sing like a canary about Chase to the FBI. That was our hope, at least.

"I think that's all we're going to get," Special Agent Avery told me. "Get the ladies to take them in the convention hall."

I jumped at the instruction and went out into the hallway. I found Jane and Elizabeth sitting on chairs outside the room. I motioned for them to start phase two. The ladies knocked on the door and opened it, telling the men that they were ready for them to enter the presentation.

They led the men out of the room and walked them toward the front entrance of the large hall. Elizabeth stopped the men before they entered.

"I'm sorry, Senator, but there is a lot of media at this event. Do you need to use the bathroom first, maybe to freshen up?" she asked nicely, knowing the substance she had placed in the Senator's drink earlier would increase his urge to use the bathroom.

"How old do you think I am, honey? I don't need to use the john. I didn't drink that much," Eastman said smirking, but feeling that he did in fact need to urinate quickly.

"I insist, Senator. You have a few hairs out of place, and I want you to look as good as you usually do. Plus I don't want to be the reason you had to leave a function with the press unexpectedly," she said, batting her eyes at him.

"Alright, darlin'. If you insist." He clearly thought she was trying to get him alone.

"The bathroom is right over there, around the corner," she said pointing in its general direction. He disappointedly followed her instruction and hurried to the bathroom.

I managed to walk behind him unnoticed in my fashionable, blue repairman coveralls and entered the bathroom before Eastman arrived. I picked up a bucket filled with water I had left there earlier, put it down beside the urinal, and proceeded to tinker around with the chrome flushing mechanism. The Senator entered the bathroom and saw me standing in front of them.

"I'm sorry, sir," I began to say, "these are out of order. You'll have to use one of the stalls."

He only grunted a reply and proceeded to the nearest toilet stall. I peeked under the door as he closed it and saw that he had placed the brown attaché bag on the floor. Immediately I flushed both urinals, kicked over the bucket, and sent a torrent of water flowing over the floor and under the stall.

"Shit!" was all I heard from Eastman when the water splashed over the bag and his feet.

"I'm sorry, sir. This leak is getting worse. Just hold on a second. I'll clean that up for you."

I grabbed a bunch of paper towels and knocked on the stall door. He opened it up and looked at me with fury, as the water had splashed up his pant leg.

"I'm sorry about that. Here," I said handing him the towels, "and let me get your bag dried off." I reached for the attaché and pulled it out of the stall as he began dabbing at his pant leg.

"Get out and let me piss," he scowled at me.

"Yes, sir, sorry, just let me get this dried up," I tried to say to him. He only grunted again in return.

"I can't believe this," I said continuously, letting the sound hide what I was doing.

I quickly opened the case and peered inside as I dabbed at it with the towels. Inside were a bunch of papers and a blue binder. I scanned the papers quickly and found they were mostly messages and pending legislation, nothing of interest to us. I then pulled out the blue binder and looked at the first page. It read, "United States Energy Revitalization and Alternative Energy Act". "This seems promising," I thought. I pulled out the entire binder and stuffed it deep into the trashcan, underneath a pile of used paper towels. I closed the case and slid it under the door on top of a fresh pile of paper towels.

"Here you go, sir. Good as new," I announced. The door swung open, and Eastman grabbed the case and another wad of towels before he stormed out of the bathroom.

"You idiot," he said as he left, "your manager will hear about this."

I laughed at the statement. "If you only knew, you clod," I thought.

Back in the hallway, the Senator was still fuming, but once he caught sight of Elizabeth and Jane his demeanor changed back to charming.

"Some joker spilled water on me in there. Damn idiot," he announced to them.

"That's too bad," Jane lied. "You look great. Shall we go in?" she continued, stroking his ego.

Eastman nodded and went to the door, straightened his suit, and walked in. He would be even more surprised and angry at what was to happen inside.

When I saw that they had left the vicinity of the bathroom, I dug the blue binder out of the trash and walked back to the room where the FBI agents were stationed.

"I found something in the bathroom, Agent Avery," I said handing him the binder. "I don't know whose it is." I smiled as I said this. Avery smiled back.

"What a good, friendly maintenance worker you are! Thanks, I'll see if I can locate the rightful owner to this." He walked back in the room and placed it in front of the other agents who immediately opened it and began to pore over the contents. From the looks on their faces, I must have done well.

I excused myself and raced to the convention hall. I was supposed to stay out of sight, but I had to see this.

Chapter 71

Galveston, Alex, and Dr. Sloan had all been waiting in the convention hall, putting the finishing touches on the upcoming presentation while trying to keep the media from getting restless. The turnout was better than we could have imagined. Every major news source was present, for the most part. They had been intrigued by the message Alex had sent and wanted to see what the hubbub was about.

Dr. Sloan had already started a slide show on the benefits of his battery and was just nearing the last slide. Galveston saw the Senator come in the door with Elizabeth and Jane and motioned to Alex who then whispered to Dr. Sloan on the podium. Now the fun began.

"I'll now show you the battery's unlimited capabilities," he stated as he moved to the vast array of objects sitting on the tables. The three cars were first in line, and he walked to the first one. A wire protruded from its open hood and the engine was exposed.

"There are no batteries in these cars or in any other object you see before you," the professor announced.

From the car the wire was connected to a rectangular box sitting in the middle of all the other objects. All the other devices connected to it as well, and from there, on top of a small table, stood the *Flapjack*. It was about the size of a deck of playing cards, and a single wire connected the rectangular box to it.

"This is the *Flapjack*," he said pointing to the device, "and it will be the only power source."

He walked back to the first car, got in, and started it. It immediately roared to life. He went to the second and third car and did the same. The members in the audience sat glued at what they were watching. Alex followed and cut off the engines behind him. Carbon monoxide in a closed room was usually not a good thing.

"Now how many of you think the *Flapjack* can't do anymore?" Dr. Sloan asked the audience. The small crowd murmured while most raised their hands. There was a reason that car batteries were so huge, and to see this small device start them was amazing.

Dr. Sloan walked to the lamps sitting on the table and began to switch them on. As the electrical current flowed, the lamps came on one by one. He then began to switch on the cell phones. Each one came to life as he pushed the power button. Alex followed Dr. Sloan and held up each phone to show they were indeed on and there was no battery in them. It all had an air of a good magic trick. Dr. Sloan next flipped a switch on top of the table, and the Christmas lights illuminated the tables across the front of the room. Senator Eastman continued to stand at the back, confused at what he was witnessing. Next, Dr. Sloan clicked on each of the computers. Each one whirled up in succession, and their monitors flickered with the new onset of power. Finally, Dr. Sloan moved to the last table that had the coffee pot and switched it on. It began to percolate, sending fresh coffee into the pot—a whimsical end to an impressive display.

"No other sources of electrical energy are present. All this is being done by the *Flapjack*. If you stay for over an hour, you'll see that everything will still be on." He walked back to the coffee pot. "Now who would like a fresh cup of coffee?"

The crowd roared and clapped at the sight with many "oohs" and "ahhs" thrown in. Flashes went off one by one, and Dr. Sloan basked in the lights, smiling widely. Alex managed to scoot his way into the background to get his mug into the pictures.

"I invite all of you up to examine the *Flapjack*," Dr. Sloan told the crowd, "and I'll answer any questions."

It began to sink in to the Senator what he was really watching. He saw the hand painted sign Alex had made with the professor's name on it.

"What the hell is going on here?" he demanded angrily to Placer and the ladies.

Galveston noticed the Senator's dismay at the back of the room and grabbed the microphone at the front of the hall.

"Ladies and gentlemen, Senator Edward Eastman has graciously arrived to witness the release of this amazing device," Galveston said, pointing to the back of the room.

The press corps immediately turned to the Senator whose anger turned to smiles, as he had been trained when members of the press were present. The flashes grew intense toward the Senator who managed to wave at the cameras.

"I wouldn't try to go anywhere, Senator," Elizabeth said, stepping out of view from the cameras and blocked any escape back out through the door.

I had heard the ruckus and peeked in a side door. Galveston was just making his next play.

"Senator, why don't you come up and get a few pictures with the *Flapjack*."

Eastman looked very uncomfortable and managed a weak smile while he made his way through the press, even shaking hands as he went. The reporters followed him to the front, leaving the back of the room empty. I noticed the FBI agents in the room move to cover all the exit areas.

Eastman smiled for the cameras with none other than Dr. Sloan. Eastman's weak smile turned flat as he realized he was caught and his career was over. He looked like a scared rabbit, and for a moment looked like he would try to escape, until he noticed the various men standing by the exits. It was then that he knew he would be arrested by the FBI.

"I wouldn't think about leaving, Senator. I think you're done," Galveston yelled to him over the clamor of the crowd.

The Senator stumbled down the step to the nearest exit. The agent waiting at the door spoke to him and led him into the hall, followed by other agents. They whisked him out of the hotel through the service entrance and into an awaiting SUV. The Senator had been arrested.

Back in the ballroom, the scene had subsided. The press didn't have any idea of what had just taken place and stuck around to check out the *Flapjack* as it continued to keep everything working. Dr. Sloan fielded questions for over an hour as the *Flapjack* kept sending out an amazing torrent of power—and many of cups of coffee.

The FBI agents now had the Senator, but even with intense FBI interrogation and mounting evidence of his improprieties, Eastman still wouldn't implicate Chase. Eastman knew that if he fingered Chase his crimes would become that much worse. He would then be an accessory to an act of terrorism on foreign soil as well as murder. May was shocked at the news. He still didn't have the necessary evidence to get Chase—yet.

Chapter 72

Agent Avery joined us in the large convention hall a few hours later after he finished examining the binder from Eastman's bag and after the furor from the presentation had subsided.

"Excuse me, gentlemen, it's May on the phone," Avery said.

"Tell David I want more pay," Galveston yelled at him and laughed.

Agent Avery, with a serious look on his face, handed the phone to Galveston.

"Hello, David," Galveston said with noticeable fatigue in his voice.

"Galveston, Chase is on the run, and we need your help in finding him. He must have seen the online stream of the presentation," he started, "and I've just received something that is going to blow this thing apart."

Galveston noticed the tone in his voice and stood up.

"What've you got?" he asked.

"You guys need to get here, now," May told him urgently.

"To Chicago?" Galveston exclaimed. "Are you crazy, David? What have you been drinking?"

"I'm serious. Get to the airport. We have a government jet standing by. I'll tell you all about it when you get here. Actually, I'll show you. This is huge."

"I don't see why..." Galveston tried say to get out of it.

"Just get here, we're running out of time. I insist. You two need to be here to help us find him," May told him.

"Okay, David," Galveston relented, "we'll do it."

May gave him the instructions about where to meet Avery at the airport. Galveston then had the unscrupulous job of getting me to go along; an idea I was not fond of. Secretly I wanted to be there, but I wasn't going to tell him that. Finally, I agreed to go.

"I've got to tell Jane I'm leaving. I recommend you do the same with Elizabeth," I told him.

"Five minutes, no more," he chided me, and I agreed to his request.

I found Jane outside the hall sitting in a comfortable chair, relaxing. She looked lovely, and I explained the situation to her. Somehow she understood.

"I promise when I get back we'll do all the things we planned," I told her.

"You better," she joked back.

"Jane, I just want you to know that I..." and I stopped midsentence, chickening out again and became fearful of her reaction. "Have a good night, and I will see you tomorrow—I hope."

I gave her a hug and a kiss on her soft lips and turned around ready to meet Galveston. I just didn't think she felt the same way about me.

As I turned to walk down the hall, I suddenly felt a hand on my shoulder. I turned around and Jane kissed me passionately, pulling me close to her.

"I, I love you Roger, I do," she said welling up with emotion and squeezing me hard.

I pulled together my courage after hearing the words I longed to hear. "I love you too, Jane, so much, and I, I, just love you," the words flowed easily, and I felt a weight lift from my shoulders. In this short period of time I couldn't deny it further. I did love her, and I was no longer falling in love with her—I had truly fallen. I kissed her again and I could sense the emotion between us. I could do anything now.

Jane looked in my eyes, the tears beginning to show slowly at the corners.

"You better get going, you know how Galveston gets if you're late for anything."

"Yeah, I know. I'll see you soon," I said hugging her one more time. I turned and literally bounded down the hallway. Before I turned the corner, I gave her another wave and watched as she disappeared back into the hall.

-Chapter 73-

"What happened? Did you take some happy pills or something?" Galveston asked as we met.

"I took the happiest of pills," was all I said.

We made our way to Galveston's car and raced for the airport. A Gulfstream jet was waiting to fly us to Chicago.

May welcomed us to Chicago O'Hare—alone. He hurried us into a car, and we sped toward the northern outskirts of the city. Agents had already begun to cover Chase's mansion in the North Shore. May had managed to get a warrant to search the home and arrest Chase. It was all based on the new information he had obtained.

"So you still haven't told us what this new evidence is," Galveston inquired.

"You see that bag there," he said pointing to a black bag on the floorboard. "There's a packing envelope in it. Pull out the recorder and press play," he ordered.

Galveston did what he was told and pressed the play button. The sounds that came out shocked us, and I saw why May had waited. It had to be heard in person. On the recording were two voices, and what they talked about meshed perfectly with our complete theory. The voices were of Murray and Chase. On the recording they spelled out every portion of their plan. One conversation poured into the next, like a movie, and incriminated Chase at every turn.

"How did you get this?" I exclaimed.

"I received a call from the Chicago office that a package had been dropped off. It was under the care of a law firm that had explicit orders to deliver the package if Wallace Murray hadn't contacted them within a day of his safe journey out of the country. If he didn't, they were to deliver the package to the Chicago FBI office. There was even a timeline enclosed. After the proposed initial contact, Murray would contact them every six months. If at any time he didn't contact them, the firm was to deliver the package to the FBI."

We were shocked at this turn of events and the evidence that had been neatly placed in our laps. This was the evidence we had been hoping for.

"I've listened to most of it, and the most chilling part is when Chase gave the order for Murray to kill Dr. Blout. That one made my blood boil," May told us as he raced to Chase's house.

We still couldn't believe it. Murray was an evil, unscrupulous man, but he had made one last attempt at redemption. He was still a criminal and had done one good deed, but only to make sure that if he went down, everyone would. It was obvious that Chase must have had Murray eliminated because he was the last link in the chain.

When we finally arrived to Chase's mansion, May gave the order to go in, but the agents returned quickly, the house was empty. Chase had managed to escape since seeing the presentation and was probably trying to get out of the country.

We sat in May's car and tried to think through it rationally of where Chase could go; O'Hare or Midway? No, these were too obvious, and too easily tracked. I began to search back through our miles and miles of information and suddenly I remembered one of the messages Alex had acquired over a week ago. I pulled out my trusty notepad, now bulging from the wealth of information. It wasn't until a minute later that I found what I was looking for. Aircraft number *27982*, the jet Espinosa had transferred to in Mexico before going to Brazil, and the one Placer said Chase owned under a foreign registration. We hadn't realized this was Chase's plane number in the text messages Alex had hacked almost a full week ago. I relayed the information to Galveston and May, and they looked at each other as I spilled my theory.

"*27982*," I exclaimed. "It's Chase's personal plane. He used it in Mexico to transport Espinosa."

"I think you're on to something," Galveston told me proudly. "We need to contact the FAA. They will have to file a flight plan with that number to get out of the country. We just need to find out where they are starting the flight from."

May was already dialing the FBI office to get the information from the FAA. We bantered where we thought it would be until May finally received a call back.

"Gary International, the last of the three in the Chicago airport system. Do you think we have time?" he asked us.

"We should," Galveston said. "He'll have a tough time getting a crew together on such short notice. That should buy us some time."

Gary Airport sat south of the city, and we had a long way to drive. Luckily, the time of day allowed us quick access from the north part of Chicago to the south via interstate ninety. It took us about an hour to drive to the airport that sat across the border of Illinois in Indiana. The agents from the house followed us as May called the airport office and found out the plane was on the ground but had not yet asked for a clearance.

May picked up his speed until we were on the outskirts of the airport. He used his radio to direct the other agents to get into position, and they fanned out with their cars in front of the security gate to block any possible escape. We could see the plane sitting on the tarmac in the distance illuminated by beams of white light.

Men were moving around the plane, quickly loading boxes and bags into the cargo hold. We were too far away to notice any of the features of the men or if they were armed.

May parked the car behind a group of hangars and got out. We had the element of surprise and wanted to use it to the fullest. The agents rapidly put on their flak jackets with their FBI letters emblazoned on the back and readied their weapons, preparing for the assault.

May used his binoculars to pick out three armed men. He could tell they were carrying weapons from the way they held their coats as they walked. One man stood at the entrance to the plane scanning every direction, while the other two stood on either side of the plane's entrance. Everyone waited for May's go ahead.

When he was satisfied with the agents' positions and safety, he gave the order to go in, which sent us scurrying back into the car.

Agent May slammed the car into drive and screeched from behind the hangar followed by the other cars. The sudden acceleration threw me back in the back seat, and I struggled to hold myself upright as we followed the curves of the airport road. The men didn't see us until we were about a hundred yards away, and we were closing quickly. They reacted slowly, but I saw the men draw their guns from beneath their coats, raise them, and begin to fire—a visual that shocked me. I figured they would just give up, but as I heard the loud popping inside the car, I knew they meant business. I bent down low in the seat, as did Galveston, praying we wouldn't be hit by the random gunfire.

When May was about thirty yards away, he jammed the brakes and slammed the wheel to the left, causing us to be thrown hard to the right of the car. The car's tires squealed as he placed the vehicle pointing at the airplane. May jumped out, and the other agents in the following cars did the same. The gunmen continued to fire at the cars with no regard to the credentials of the men inside. They crouched low and tried to find some cover beneath the plane, but it offered little in the way of protection. May strategically placed himself behind the door in a crouched position and then stood up to let off a few rounds.

Galveston and I got out of the car and went to the back bumper, out of view of the gun battle. The man that stood at the door began to fire again and motioned for someone inside to come out. The gunman shielded the man from the gunfire as he flew down the steps of the airplane and disappeared behind it. The guard tried to follow him but was peppered with the accurate gunfire of the highly trained agents. He doubled over as a round pierced his thigh and back, and he fell to the ground in excruciating pain. May continued to survey the situation and motioned for the other agents to flank the aircraft from behind.

"This isn't what I came to do," I yelled at Galveston over the rapid gunfire.

"Me neither," Galveston replied, crouching as low as he could to the ground.

The agents now had the upper hand, but the other men continued to fire. We noticed a shape, crouched low, running to the nearby hangar. He turned his head slightly toward our direction, and we saw it was Chase.

"Come on," Galveston yelled at me, already getting up and moving backwards away from the car.

"What? Are you crazy?" I tried to yell back, but he was already out of earshot.

I watched as Galveston stayed low to the ground and shielded himself behind the other cars until he arrived at the side of the large hangar. Stupidly, I followed him.

I had no training for this sort of thing and did my best not to get shot. I lurched awkwardly across the ground, hearing the bullets ricochet off the metal of the cars. I heard a scream as I closed in on Galveston at the side of the building. The agents had just wounded another one of the gunmen. The last man, realizing he was outnumbered, out-trained, and outgunned, threw down his weapon and then threw up his hands. The agents swarmed on him quickly, pushing him into the ground as they cuffed him. The gunfire ceased and the air grew quiet as I ran toward Galveston, who was peering intently around the corner of the building.

I arrived at Galveston's location, breathless and unharmed, but before I could ask him what he was doing, he lunged forward and disappeared. I attempted to follow again, and as I rounded the corner, I watched as Galveston rammed an unsuspecting Chase with his body from behind as he stepped out from the front hangar door. Chase's legs lifted in the air before his body slammed into the ground. He groaned at the sudden, unexpected impact.

But Chase wasn't going to go without a fight. The larger man pushed himself up to a standing position and managed to move Galveston away. Chase was still weary from the unexpected blow, but he was able to turn and face Galveston. Chase charged and rammed him into the wall of the hanger.

I attempted to grab Chase from behind as he held Galveston against the wall, but the man threw an elbow that caught me in my jaw. I recoiled from the shot, and it sent me falling backward. I was shocked at the man's strength.

Chase continued to push Galveston into the wall, and it was then that I noticed him trying to reach for something from the waistband of his pants—it was a handgun.

I pushed myself up and ignored the pain in face. Chase had a hold of the gun now and drew it up as Galveston fought him to keep it down. I didn't know what to do. I instinctively grabbed some of the loose dirt from the ground and threw it at the two men. It had the intended effect and momentarily distracted Chase, but unfortunately it temporarily blinded Galveston in the process. I rushed toward the armed man and threw my shoulder into him, knocking him into the wall with Galveston.

We now struggled to free the gun from his grip. Even though Galveston couldn't clearly see, he was able to get a hand on the gun. He pushed the man's arm above his head, and I heard the rapid release of bullets above us as Galveston got his hand on the trigger and unloaded the magazine.

With dirt still covering his eyes, Galveston released his grip on the gun and unloaded with punches to the man's stomach. Chase doubled over in pain from the shots, and I assisted by jumping on the man's back to drive him to the ground.

Galveston immediately jammed his knee into Chase's back and secured his hands, causing him to groan again.

I tried to speak, but couldn't, and stood over the pair. I bent over with my hands on my knees and tried to catch my breath.

"We got him, Roger," Galveston turned and said wearily, while holding Chase steady, now semi-unconscious from the takedown.

"You sure did," I told him, breathing heavily, as I attempted to get my heart back in my chest.

Several agents finally found us after hearing the gunshots. Galveston extricated himself from Chase, and the agents took the man's hands and cuffed him. He never knew who hit him. Galveston got up and walked slowly toward me.

"I'm not sure I want to do that again, but it sure reminded me of old times," he said, out of breath and dusting himself off.

"Yeah, that's great, but I think I've had my fill," I responded with quick sarcasm.

The agents dragged Chase back to the runway side of the hangar. May and the other agents were leaning over two wounded men who were lucky to be alive, with the third lying face down, his hands cuffed behind his back. The agents could have just as easily mortally wounded them, but they wanted them for questioning. I marveled at the agents' professionalism and precision.

Campbell, Chase's personal bodyguard, lay bleeding on the ground from his leg and back. The agents would discover later that he was the one who had shot and killed Murray.

Galveston and I returned to the car and sat down on the seats with the doors open. We heard sirens in the distance of an approaching ambulance and local police racing to the scene.

May walked toward us as the wounded men were loaded into the ambulance.

"You guys okay?" he inquired.

"Fine, David, a little more excitement than we wanted, but we're okay nonetheless," Galveston responded.

"I'm sure glad I convinced you two to come. We couldn't have done it without you," he said, the adrenaline still pumping through his body. "Great work."

"I'll expect a promotion and some vacation time," I joked.

"You got it, Roger. You deserve it," he replied.

May left us to gather our senses as he coordinated the transport of the criminals. We watched as May escorted Chase to one of the awaiting vehicles. He held his head low and was scratched up from our struggle. He would never know that the two men that brought him down were sitting in a car about forty feet away, and he had only been a few steps away from escape. He put his head in his hands, but I could still tell he had an air of pompousness about him as he raised his head to scold an agent. He probably thought he was going to buy his way out of this scot-free, but having your bodyguards shoot at Federal agents was not a way to go about it. We pictured his reaction when he heard the tapes Murray had recorded without his knowledge, and soon his demeanor would change. No political or monetary force could help him now.

"You've come a long way, Roger. If it wasn't for you, I never would have been able to do this—not that I would do it again," Galveston said seriously, slapping me on the knee.

"You're not going to get all sappy on me, are you?" I jokingly replied.

"I might cry, and you may have to hold me."

"Yeah, that's never going to happen. How about Elizabeth? I bet she would."

"I don't know. Maybe I'll take her on a vacation. We'll see. You and Jane though, that looks good, huh?" Galveston asked.

"Yeah, I'm really fond of her, especially after all of this," I said, not telling him of our moment back at the hotel in San Diego.

"Do you want me to tell her you like her?" Galveston asked.

"Yeah, do that. Maybe pass her a note during gym class," I quipped and then paused, pasting a goofy grin on my face. "I haven't met anyone like her before."

"Alright, lover boy. Back to reality. Let's get May to get us out of here and back home before Alex pawns everything out of our office to buy more toys."

May drove us to O'Hare Airport and arranged an early departure back to San Diego. We said our farewells and left May to guide the Bureau in the mess of information we had for them. It was their baby now, and at this point we didn't care what they did.

I felt no ill feelings against May for dragging us into this. I'm sure in his wildest dreams he didn't imagine it would go this far. He was an upstanding man who would have pulled us out at the slightest request, but he knew he had Galveston to rely on, and he trusted him fully.

The *Flapjack's* future was uncertain and unwritten. The demonstration would create a buzz in the industry, but it was now up to Dr. Sloan to see where that would go.

We planned to help him at any turn. There were many proponents, but there would also be many forces against it. It was just too revolutionary for anyone to handle. People don't react well to radical changes in technology, and this was no exception. It could physically change the makeup of the world.

Dr. Sloan would have to do a lot of soul searching on the best plan for implementation of the battery, because his name would be the one to go down in the history books.

It was finally over, and I was looking forward to sleeping in my own bed without worries. I hadn't done the books on our finances, and I wondered if we would have anything to show for our work. Frankly, I didn't care. At least we would have peace of mind.

We boarded the plane to San Diego, and Galveston and I talked about everything except what we had just gone through the last few weeks. Our eyes grew heavy, and we both found a comfortable position and fell hard asleep in our seats. I was looking forward to a hot shower and to seeing Jane. But more than that, I was finally beginning to feel like a nice, normal person again—at least until the next case.

Author

Daniel Ganninger lives with his wife and two children in Central Texas and has a love of useless trivia and flying airplanes. He graduated from the University of Texas and when not writing works at his other profession in the medical field.

Join Galveston and Murphy in their next adventures:

Peeking Duck, Case File #2
Snow Cone, Case File #3
Coconut Water, Case File #4

For all the latest news, upcoming books, writer's blog, or to join the newsletter, please visit me at:

www.danielganninger.com

www.facebook.com/danielganninger

www.twitter.com/danielganninger

For some other enjoyable reading, visit my blog of useless facts and random knowledge at **www.knowledgestew.com**

Thank you so much for reading. I hope you had as much fun reading as I did writing the story. My goal is to provide an enjoyable escape and fun, and I hope that was accomplished.

CPSIA information can be obtained
at www.ICGtesting.com
Printed in the USA
LVHW011050041118
595901LV00019B/1774/P